DRAGON
SPRINGS
ROAD

Also by Janie Chang

Three Souls

DRAGON SPRINGS ROAD

JANIE CHANG

wm

WILLIAM MORROW

An Imprint of HarperCollins*Publishers*

DRAGON SPRINGS ROAD. Copyright © 2017 by Janie Chang. All rights reserved. Printed in the United States of America. No part of this book may be used or reproduced in any manner whatsoever without written permission except in the case of brief quotations embodied in critical articles and reviews. For information, address HarperCollins Publishers, 195 Broadway, New York, NY 10007.

HarperCollins books may be purchased for educational, business, or sales promotional use. For information, please email the Special Markets Department at SPsales@harpercollins.com.

FIRST EDITION

Designed by Diahann Sturge

Chinese Lattice Pattern © Elmery/Shutterstock, Inc.

Library of Congress Cataloging-in-Publication Data
Names: Chang, Janie.
Title: Dragon Springs Road : a novel / Janie Chang.
Description: First edition. | New York, NY : William Morrow, 2016.
Identifiers: LCCN 2016024337 (print) | LCCN 2016028609 (ebook) | ISBN 9780062388957 (pbk.) | ISBN 9780062388971 (e-book)
Subjects: LCSH: Abandoned children--China--Fiction. | Racially mixed people--Fiction. | GSAFD: Historical fiction
Classification: LCC PS3603.H35729 D83 2016 (print) | LCC PS3603.H35729 (ebook) | DDC 813/.6--dc23
LC record available at https://lccn.loc.gov/2016024337

ISBN 978-0-06-238895-7

17 18 19 20 21   RRD   10 9 8 7 6 5 4 3 2 1

For Geoffrey

DRAGON SPRINGS ROAD

CHAPTER 1

November 1908, Year of the Monkey

The morning my mother went away, she burned incense in front of the Fox altar.

The emperor Guangxu and the dowager empress had both died that week. My mother told me our new emperor was a little boy of almost three called Puyi. A child less than half my age now ruled China and she was praying for him. And for us.

My mother knelt, eyes shut, rocking back and forth with clasped hands. I couldn't hear the prayers she murmured and did my best to imitate her, but I couldn't help lifting my eyes to steal glances at the picture pasted on the brick wall, a colorful print of a woman dressed in flowing silks, her face sweetly bland, one hand lifted in blessing. A large red fox sat by her feet. A Fox spirit, pictured in her human and animal forms.

The altar was just a low table placed against the back wall of the kitchen. Its cracked wooden surface held an earthenware jar filled with sand. My mother had let me poke our last handful of incense sticks into the sand and even let me strike a match to light them. We had no food to offer that morning except a few withered plums.

The Fox gazed down at me with its painted smile.

After we prayed, my mother dressed me in my new winter tunic.

"Stay here, Jialing," she said, pushing the last knot button through its loop. "Be quiet and don't let anyone know you're here. Stay inside the Western Residence until Mama comes back."

But three days passed and she didn't come back.

WE LIVED BY ourselves, just the two of us, in the main house of the Western Residence. I usually slept with my mother in her bed, but I was just as used to spending nights in my playroom. It was out in the *erfang*, a single-story row of five connected rooms, each with a door that opened onto the veranda that wrapped around the front of the building, steps leading down to a paved courtyard. There were two *erfang* that faced each other across the courtyard, but the other was derelict, its roof fallen in.

Whenever Noble Uncle came to visit my mother, I had to leave the main house. She would send me to my playroom and fetch me the next morning after he left. Then our placid life would resume.

Sometimes Noble Uncle took her away for a day or two, but never for this long.

ON THE FIRST day of my mother's absence, I paged through the few books in my playroom, then wandered out to the courtyard to shake more plums from the fruit trees. I pulled off their desiccated flesh and put the pits in my pocket. Using the charred end of a stick from the kitchen stove I drew a checkers board on the paving stones and placed pits in the squares. Morning and afternoon I shook the trees, hoping more fruit would fall so that I could have more pieces for my game.

After two days, I began eating the plums despite their moldy taste.

But mostly, I watched and waited for my mother to return.

The smaller front courtyard had gates that opened out to Dragon Springs Road. Years ago my mother had pushed broken furniture against one corner of the courtyard's walls, tying wooden legs and chair backs together to steady the stack into a platform we could climb. From this perch we had spied on the world outside.

The honeysuckle that clambered across the top of the wall was bare of leaves, but the tangle of vines was still thick enough for concealment. Looking down to the left, I could see the front courtyard of the Central Residence, the home where Noble Uncle and his family lived. There was a door in the wall between the two front courtyards, but the only one who ever used it had been Noble Uncle.

To the right was the street. Standing on tiptoe I peered through the vines, hoping to see my mother's figure alight from a sedan chair or rickshaw, but all I saw were our neighbors, unwitting and uncaring of my presence.

Back at the Fox altar I knelt down to pray, rocking on my haunches, gaze fixed on the picture pasted to the wall. My nostrils prickled with the musty fragrance of incense. *Please, bring back my mama.* But the Fox woman looked into the distance, and the Fox merely smiled.

"Fox spirits are almost always female," my mother had said.

"They can appear in Fox shape or as beautiful women. They help those who befriend them. Some are especially sympathetic to unfortunate women."

Now I wondered at my mother's words. Did she pray to a Fox because she was an unfortunate woman?

That night I dreamed that I had wandered out to Dragon Springs Road all on my own, when a dreadful knowledge seized me that my mother had gone away never to return. Fear jolted me out of sleep and into the gray light of early morning. I was utterly alone. I cried and cried, but my forlorn wails went unheeded. Curling up under the quilt, I sobbed myself back to sleep.

The next morning, I lay on the pallet bed with all my clothes on, quilt pulled over my head, trying to keep warm. The plate on the floor taunted me with reminders of chicken and sticky rice steamed in lotus leaf packets, the scent of garlic and sesame oil still clinging to the leaves. My stomach ached, a harsh kneading that twisted my insides. I tried chewing on a lotus leaf, but when I tried to swallow, the tough fibers made me retch and I spat them out.

Finally, I went outside to get a drink from the well in the courtyard. I knelt beside its low stone wall and pushed aside the wooden lid. I tossed in my tin cup, heard it splash in the dark depths, and pulled on the rope, hand over hand as my mother had taught me. I took care not to lean too far over the stone rim, as she'd always cautioned, and replaced the lid. I didn't want to end up as the ghost of a drowned girl, dank hair hanging over my face, luring victims to share my fate.

It won't be long now, a voice behind me said. People are coming. I can hear them up the road. The voice was high pitched, the words pronounced precisely.

I swung around. An animal with tawny red fur yawned, showing a pink tongue and sharp white teeth. It looked like one of the stray dogs that sometimes came into Dragon Springs Road, but it was sleek, not mangy, with a plume of a tail. A fox. Its eyes shone amber yellow, dark centers with flecks of green in their depths. Its snout was long and elegant, its paws neat and stockinged in black. Then it vanished.

Startled, I dropped my cup and toppled over, my back against the well. Had I fallen asleep and dreamed the creature?

Then I heard voices. Unfamiliar voices. Voices shouting commands, voices shouting in reply.

I hurried through the bamboo grove to the front courtyard and climbed up the pile of furniture. Next door, the gates stood wide open. There was excited laughter and chatter from the street, and then a woman's voice called out in stern tones.

"Silence! Show respect for the spirits in our new home!"

The chatter ceased immediately.

"All the doors and windows are open, Old Mistress." A sturdy man in plain blue servant's garb came out from the main courtyard to face the entrance gate. "Any spirits who wanted to leave should be gone now."

"Does everyone have something to carry?" A male voice, deep and jovial. "We mustn't enter our new home empty-handed."

A man stepped over the threshold of the entrance gate. An exuberant smile lit his round face. His long queue gleamed with the same dark shine as his satin skullcap, and he carried a bundle of books under his arm.

The old woman by his side wore her white hair scraped severely into a bun, her forehead covered by a wide band of black silk. She carried a pair of scrolls and tottered in on tiny feet. Then two younger women stepped into the entrance courtyard. One had a rounded, smiling face and a rounded belly; she held a basket of fruit against her hip. The other was tall and pale, with pursed lips that gave her a dour expression; a panel of embroidered fabric hung over one thin arm.

A young man and a girl followed. The young man carried a small lacquerware box, the girl a covered basket. She was tall, nearly as tall as my mother, with hair dressed in two heavy braids looped with ribbons on either side of her head, glossy and thick. Her padded winter tunic of dark blue flannel just reached her ankles.

Then came a female servant holding a little boy by the hand. Two more female servants entered, gazing around and up, but they didn't see my face peering from behind the vines.

"Lao-er, where's our lucky orange tree?" The jovial voice belonged to the round-faced man. He stood at the threshold of the inner gate, ready to enter the main courtyard. "Go, go. Plant it!"

The servant who had first spoken pushed the entrance gate open wide and wheeled in a barrow. On the barrow were gardening tools and a small orange tree, its root ball bound inside a muddy burlap bag. The small procession crossed through the inner gate and into the main courtyard. More handbarrows and workers followed, loaded down with furniture and belongings.

My mother wasn't among those parading in and out.

Back in the courtyard, I shook one of the plum trees at the edge of the bamboo garden. Four aged fruits fell from its branches. I scooped what I could into my hands and ate it all, not caring about the grit that covered the plums. I spat out the pits and arranged them on my checkerboard.

A scraping noise sent me scuttling into the playroom, the sound of the gate between the two front courtyards opening. I waited, kneeling by the window. Through the carved latticework of the window shutters, I saw a figure enter the courtyard. It was the girl.

For a moment she vanished from sight as the path took her through the bamboo trees, then she appeared again, following the path through the rockery and under the garden arch. She took her time, pausing to look at a rock, a striped bamboo trunk, the carved stone of the arch. She gazed around the courtyard and the buildings that enclosed it, the two-level main house at the far end of the courtyard, the *erfang* where I was hiding, the derelict *erfang* opposite, the bamboo garden she had just come through. She climbed the steps to the veranda of the main house and peered through the carved lattice windows, into the rooms where my mother and I had lived. Then she walked back down the veranda steps and paused to look down at the plum pits lying on the makeshift checkerboard.

Show yourself to her, the voice said.

I blinked at the Fox who had appeared beside me. I reached my hand out to touch, to feel whether it was real. The creature gave me a small lick, a raspy warm sensation that gave me courage.

"Who are you?" I whispered.

Your mother burned incense to a Fox spirit, it said. Don't you remember?

My mother had been fond of telling stories about Fox spirits. "Are you a good spirit or an evil one?"

She gave a small bark of disdain. How can you tell whether anyone is truly good or evil? I've been a Fox for hundreds of years and from what I've seen it takes generations before consequences truly run their course.

This answer made no sense to me, but her next suggestion did. Go to that girl. She'll give you something to eat.

"My mother said not to let anyone know I was here," I said, but my words of protest were feeble. The hollowness in my stomach mattered more.

In response, the Fox nudged me toward the door.

CLOSER, THE GIRL'S eyes were the first thing I noticed. Her looks were unremarkable, smooth flat features on a plain face. But her eyes were large and deep-set, solemn and serene.

She spoke first. "The neighbors outside said they've heard crying for the last two nights since the Fong family moved away. They say it's the ghost of a concubine who committed suicide. Have you seen such a ghost?"

I shook my head. My mother had never mentioned any ghost.

"You were the one crying, weren't you?" she said. "I thought so. I knew there was someone here when I saw those plum pits. They were still damp."

"Have you seen my mother?" The question tumbled out, more important than food.

"Who's your mother?"

"Her name is Mama." What other name could she have? The girl looked at me, as if expecting more. "She went away with everyone else. But she's coming back."

"Why didn't you go away with her?" the girl asked.

I had asked myself this question for days and could only look away, unable to answer.

"What's your name?"

"Jialing."

"My family name is Yang," she said. "Yang Anjuin. What's your family name?"

"Zhu. I think." How could I have been uncertain of my own name? My mother had never made a family name seem important. She only ever called me Jialing. *My little Ling-ling,* she sometimes teased, like the sound of a bell.

"Let's go talk to my grandmother, Jialing."

Anjuin held her hand out and I took it. My fingers were cold and rather sticky, but Anjuin's grip was firm, and her eyes as she looked down were clear and kind. My wariness dissolved, and when she squeezed my hand, I squeezed back.

As we left, I heard a rustle in the bamboos. A small note of caution from Fox sounded in my mind, warning me not to mention anything about a Fox spirit to anyone.

And behave yourself, the voice added. Be good and make it easier for them to let you stay.

"You must call her Grandmother Yang," Anjuin whispered.

As soon as we entered the Central Residence, Anjuin sent a servant ahead to tell her grandmother. I followed Anjuin to the main house, where we entered a room on the ground floor. Members of the household were already gathered, all talking at once. I'd never seen so many people in one place before. I clung to Anjuin's hand.

"So she's the one the neighbors heard crying," said the young woman with the round belly. "There, you see, First Wife. There's no ghost. Our new home isn't haunted."

"She's an unlucky omen," the other woman replied. She seemed much older, or perhaps it was her thin figure and dour face, her look of discontent. When I glanced up timidly, she glared at me.

Anjuin led me to the far end of the room where an elderly woman rested on a daybed. The round-faced, jovial man stood beside her, but it was the old woman who commanded my attention. She beckoned, and Anjuin gave me a small push.

Grandmother Yang's face was gaunt, papery skin pulled tight over her cheekbones, fine wrinkles around her eyes. She had the same eyes as Anjuin, alert and deep-set.

Her trousers and tunic were of plain fabric, a row of black knot buttons the only ornamentation across her dove-gray bodice. There wasn't a hint of needlework on her wide cuffs. Then I noticed her tiny shoes, which dangled on feet that didn't quite touch the floor. They were red satin, lavishly embroidered.

The old woman looked me up and down. "Who is your family?"

She tapped her finger on the bed frame, waiting for my reply. I looked up pleadingly at Anjuin, who answered. "Her family name is Zhu. Her name is Jialing. She says she lived with her mother in the main house of the Western Residence. She's seven. The same age as our Kejuin."

"We bought this estate from a man called Fong, not Zhu." The old woman frowned and lifted my chin with one finger. She studied my face. "First Wife, give me your handkerchief."

The dour-faced woman hurried over from the doorway, a handkerchief held out in her thin fingers. Grandmother Yang dipped the cloth into a cup of tea on the tray beside her and wiped my face. She looked at me again, more closely.

"I thought so. *Zazhong.*"

There were gasps. First Wife hissed. It seemed as though the entire room crowded around me, turning me around to stare, to prod, and exclaim. I didn't know what *zazhong* meant. Only that suddenly my presence caused fascination. And disgust.

"It's been at least three days since the Fongs vacated this property," Grandmother Yang said. "We need to find where they went. First Son, see what you can learn."

"Of course, Mother," the man replied. "Dajuin and I can begin by calling on the neighbors. We need to introduce ourselves anyway."

Behind me, I heard First Wife say, "Send her to an orphanage. She was abandoned. Her mother was trying to get rid of the little mongrel."

All my misery exploded into rage, and I hurled myself at the woman. "My mother's coming back for me! She's coming back!"

Unbalanced, the woman staggered back on her tiny feet and fell onto the daybed with a cry.

"You worthless creature!" she cried, standing up. She slapped my face. "Daughter of a whore!"

The blow sent me to the floor, but I refused to make any noise. I glared at her, ready to launch myself again.

Grandmother Yang stood up. The room went silent. When she spoke, her tones were mild. "Anjuin, take the girl to the kitchen for some food. First Wife, be mindful of your dignity."

Orphanage. Zazhong. Whore. New words.

THE SERVANTS TALKED over my head, giving me curious glances, but all that mattered was the large bowl of warm soy milk that the cook, Mrs. Hao, had set down in front of me.

According to Mrs. Hao, Master Yang wanted to send me to an orphanage. Grandmother Yang, however, was intrigued by the mystery of my identity and inclined to keep me a bit longer. Lao-er, the gatekeeper, said Master Yang always deferred to his mother, so my fate was up to Grandmother Yang.

"Hey, girl," he said, pinching my cheek with large brown fingers. "What was your mother doing over in the Western Residence? Was she running a brothel?"

"She doesn't even know what you're talking about, Lao-er," said Mrs. Hao. "Get back to the front gate, would you? That rice shop is supposed to deliver three sacks today. Ah-Jien, aren't you supposed to be sweeping out the upstairs rooms?"

The other two obediently filed out of her domain. I finished the soy milk, and Mrs. Hao paused from stringing beans to hand me a steamed bun. It was warm, filled with minced pork and salted vegetables. I'd never tasted anything so delicious.

Finally I got up the courage to speak. "What's an orphanage?"

"It's a place for children without parents." A short reply, but not unfriendly.

"But I have a mother. My mother said she would come back."

She snorted.

"What's a whore?" And what did it mean if my mother was one?

"A woman who sleeps with men to earn money." She looked at me. "Were there a lot of men who came to visit your mother?"

"Noble Uncle was the only one who came to visit," I said, not sure of what she meant. I wiped my mouth on my sleeve. Perhaps she would give me another bun. "What's *zazhong*?"

Mrs. Hao paused. "It means someone who's half foreign. Your father is foreign."

Foreign was the metal box my mother used for storing her cosmetics, the lid printed with a garden scene. Foreign were the thin wafer biscuits she sometimes gave me when she returned from the outside world. I didn't know foreign could be a person, let alone a father.

"Has she eaten?" Anjuin's voice from the kitchen door. "Grandmother wants to see her again."

THIS TIME, I only had to face Grandmother Yang, Master Yang, and the eldest son, Dajuin. Anjuin stood behind me, a hand on my shoulder.

"There's an orphanage out by Yung An Cemetery," Master Yang said. "We can leave the girl there, Mother. Foreign missionaries treat children very well, I hear."

No, no. My fingers clenched. I had to stay here. Otherwise, how would my mother find me when she came back? I wanted to protest, but Fox's warning growled in my head and restrained me.

"What have you learned from the neighbors?" Grandmother Yang asked.

"No one knows," Dajuin replied. He and Anjuin shared a strong family resemblance. His face was broad and pleasant, his eyes alert. "The neighbors didn't even know Master Fong had sold the property until the day the family left. They kept to themselves more and more as they got poorer and poorer."

"What about the girl? Whose child is she?"

"The neighbors say Master Fong only had daughters, no sons," Master Yang said. "He had a younger brother, but the boy went away years ago to live with relatives in Manchuria." He paused. "There was talk of a woman who also lived here, but no mention of any girl child. Or any foreigner."

"I've been praying to the Buddha for guidance," Grandmother Yang said. "She may be *zazhong*, but she is a living creature. Come here, girl. I've been wanting a closer look at your tunic."

She pulled it over my head. I shivered in my thin undershirt and moved closer to Anjuin.

"Beautiful embroidery," Grandmother Yang said, under her breath. She turned my tunic inside out. "Very neat stitching. Exceptional work."

"It's silk, isn't it, Grandmother?" Anjuin said, rubbing the fabric between her fingers.

My mother had cut down one of her own jackets to sew me this winter tunic. It was silk crepe, green as her jade earrings and printed with bronze chrysanthemums. She had spent days embroidering a garland of chrysanthemum leaves on the cuffs and collar. Grandmother Yang picked apart the hem with small embroidery scissors.

"The tunic hangs strangely on her," she said. "By feel, it's lined with silk padding and should be very light. There's something in the hem weighing it down. Do you know what's in here, girl?"

I shook my head, watching as the old woman picked open several inches of hem. She put down the scissors and drew out a narrow sash of unbleached cotton. On one side was a string of characters stitched in black thread. Grandmother Yang handed it to Master Yang, who read the words out loud.

> *I entrust my daughter to your care. These coins should be enough to buy her many years of rice. May the Buddha bless your kindness and reward you in this life and the next.*

Basting stitches across the cloth, each a few inches apart from the other, made a series of pockets. Grandmother Yang slit open the sash along its seam. As her scissors ripped through each pocket, a coin fell on the daybed. Ten in all.

Dajuin examined the coins. "Real gold. English sovereigns."

Then Grandmother Yang sighed into the silence. "It doesn't look like the mother ever intends to come back for the girl."

In that moment, I finally understood. My mother had abandoned me. The realization slammed into my ribs, knocking the breath out of my body.

I tumbled through air as thick as ink, as bottomless as the well.

WHEN I STOPPED falling, I was back in the Western Residence. But it wasn't early winter. The fruit trees were in bloom, their branches a froth of pink and white. The main house and *erfang* houses looked well kept, newly whitewashed, the carved wooden panels on all the verandas varnished. The gray tiled roof of the second *erfang* was whole, not caved in, and the lattice windows on all the houses were fitted with clean white mulberry paper panes.

A woman's figure by the door of the main house made my heart jump, but it wasn't my mother. Her clothing was strange to my eyes, not the long tunic and trousers my mother wore, but a short jacket with loose sleeves and a softly pleated skirt of light silk that barely touched the ground. She floated toward me, a slender figure in autumn colors, swaying on tiny feet encased in gold satin. The shadow she cast was that of a Fox.

As she came closer, I saw that she was beautiful, her chin small and pointed, her forehead wide. Although her skin was as pale and unblemished as a newly opened lotus, she gave the impression of being much older. Her eyes gleamed amber, a dark glow with green lights in their depths.

"Where am I?" I said. "This isn't the Western Residence."

This is how it looked three hundred years ago, Fox replied, when I was a much younger Fox.

"Why did Mama leave me?" I cried. "Did I do something naughty?"

Whatever I'd done, if only someone would tell me, I would never do it again.

You didn't do anything wrong. You must believe she left you behind for a good reason. What matters is that you survive on your own in this world.

She sat on the stone bench at the edge of the rock garden and took both my hands in hers. Her hands were slim and neat, the fingers pointed, the nails long. Clusters of bright blue butterflies bobbed on gold wires above her elaborate hairstyle, ornaments of kingfisher feathers.

Your first duty is to please Grandmother Yang. Whether you stay or go is her decision. I can only do so much, so you must be obedient and help things along.

"Will Mama come back if I'm good?" I asked. "Will you help me find her?"

The courtyard spun around me; petals of plum blossom drifted up in a slow, dizzying swirl. I fell back into darkness and heard Fox's answer, so soft it might have been no more than the rustle of bamboo leaves.

Maybe when you're older.

WHEN I OPENED my eyes, it was Anjuin who held my hands. I lay on Grandmother Yang's daybed, propped up on pillows. The room was empty.

"Grandmother is walking around, looking at the property," Anjuin said. "All three courtyards. Everyone else has gone with her. How do you feel?"

She smiled, and a small kernel of hope planted itself in my heart.

Slowly, I sat up. "Will Grandmother Yang let me stay? I promise to be good."

"The message from your mother invoked the Buddha," she

said. "Grandmother has decided to take you in. She believes it will earn merit for her next life. You'll be her bond servant."

I could stay. I would not be sent to an orphanage. If Mama came back, I would still be here.

Looking around the room again, I climbed down from the bed to stand in front of a low dresser and the mirror propped above it. I knew what I looked like, of course. I'd looked into my mother's hand mirror often enough. Now I stood in front of Grandmother Yang's mirror, and Anjuin came behind me.

Her hair was thick and black, sleek as lacquer. My hair looked black, but out in the sunlight I knew it was wispy and dark brown. My eyes were a lighter shade than hers, and my eyelashes curled up while hers were beautifully straight and sparse. Beside her, my skin looked sickly, too pale. Her eyebrows were curved, each a perfect willow leaf, the exact shape my mother used to paint her brows. Mine were straight.

Was I really so different?

DURING THOSE FIRST weeks, Grandmother Yang kept me by her side. She told me about the Yang family in Ningpo, her conversation circling in slowly as she talked about her two other sons and their families, the Yang cousins, the in-laws.

"And what about your family?" she would ask suddenly, her eyes sharp, her words swooping down at me, her curiosity voracious as a raptor. "What do you remember?"

But all I did was repeat the words my mother had made me memorize, words to use should anyone ask what I was doing in the Western Residence, words of appeasement if she wasn't beside me to offer up explanations in her light voice, with her dimpled smile. It was what my mother had told me to say, and I did not deviate.

"My mother and I lived in the Western Residence as guests of the Fong family."

Eventually Grandmother Yang gave up prodding and so did everyone else.

Of course I remembered my mother. I remembered everything about our secluded life. I just didn't want to share it with Grandmother Yang or anyone else.

CHAPTER 2

My mother said we came to the Western Residence in a sedan chair. She rode here with me sleeping on her lap.

"Noble Uncle gave us a home," she often told me. "We must be grateful that he is so kind; otherwise, we wouldn't have a roof over our heads."

She didn't say how Noble Uncle was related to us, nor did I know enough to ask. At that age, without any knowledge of the wider world, I didn't even know what "uncle" meant exactly. I thought it was part of his name. Just as "Mama" was my mother's name. I knew that Noble Uncle lived in the next courtyard, the large Central Residence, with his wives and daughters. I'd never seen him face-to-face. He was the only person who ever came into the Western Residence.

The Central Residence next door was quiet, with only the occasional female voice calling out. If not for those soft voices and my mother's daily trips there to fetch our meals, I might have believed the place deserted.

Of far more interest was the world outside on Dragon Springs Road. Nearly every day my mother and I spied on the street, standing on our platform of old furniture. The conversation of neighbors, their servants' gossip, and the talk of street vendors made us feel a part of their lives even though we had to stay out of sight.

On windy days, the kite vendor made his rounds. He toted a shoulder pole, one end carrying a basket of kites painted with tiger faces, butterflies, and the figures of heroes. At the other end, a woven bamboo panel held paper pinwheels that spun so fast when the wind blew they were nothing but blurs of color. I longed for one of those pinwheels.

During the New Year, dragon dancers swirled their way into the street accompanied by gongs and drums, their acrobatics making cloth scales shimmer. There were weddings, red-painted sedan chairs hung with red curtains and brass bells, processions led by a column of musicians. There were funerals, the family all in white robes, hired mourners behind them wailing and crying, calling upon heaven to show favor to the departed.

SOMETIMES WHEN MY mother returned from next door with our supper, there would be a slip of paper on the tray. On those evenings, she would hurry me through supper. Then she would stoke up the stove, feeding it just enough coal to heat a kettle of water, which she poured into a large wooden basin. To this she added a few drops of orange blossom water. Fragrant steam rose up, and she would dip a towel in the basin and wash every part of her body.

Back in her bedroom, she would light the oil lamp and set it by her mirror, open the cedarwood box that held her jewelry and the foreign metal box that held her cosmetics. She applied white rice powder to her cheeks and a small dab of paste that reddened her lips to pomegranate. She could twist her smooth hair a dozen different ways, securing her locks with carved combs and hairpins. Sometimes she simply brushed it out so that it swept down to rest on the seat of her stool.

She owned three sets of gold earrings, one with gold filigree flowers, another with coral drops red as persimmons, and her favorites, green jade beads that dangled like clusters of grapes.

Then she would take me to the playroom in the *erfang* and put me to bed. I hardly ever stayed in bed, though. If I jumped out and stood by the window, I could hear the sound of her *liuqin* mandolin, its repetitive twanging as she tightened strings and tested the notes, the satisfied strumming when she was pleased with the tones. Then she would light the white paper lantern, which hung like a full moon beneath the veranda roof of the main house.

The creak of the door between the front courtyards of the Western and Central Residences would announce Noble Uncle's arrival. He never glanced in the direction of the *erfang,* but I ducked below the windowsill anyway. Then I would raise my head and peek out the window to watch him stroll up to the main house where my mother waited.

His voice carried over the stillness of the night air, frequently gruff and impatient. Then my mother's placating voice, sweet and high, eventually lilting into a song accompanied by her *liuqin.* I imagined her dexterous fingers on the four-stringed instrument, plucking out a cascade of notes. I would stumble back to the pallet bed and fall asleep to faraway music, "Plum Blossom Melodies," "Ambush from Ten Sides," or "Spring Snow," her favorite.

Sometimes my mother went away for a day or two, taking with her the *liuqin* carefully wrapped in a felt bag, extra strings for the instrument tucked in her tunic pocket. I didn't like her being away, but we had to do as Noble Uncle wanted because otherwise we wouldn't be allowed to live in the Western Residence anymore.

"Why must you go?" I remembered crying when I was younger. "Why can't I go too?"

"Noble Uncle wants me to play at a banquet," she said, pushing the hair off my face. "We must obey Noble Uncle or he will throw us out."

That was our fate should we ever displease Noble Uncle. I was vague on the exact consequences of becoming home-less, but I obeyed the fear in my mother's voice and stayed inside the Western Residence's courtyard, making not a single sound while she was gone. When my mother returned, she would have treats tied up in her scarf: sugared walnuts, dried sour plums or bright orange kumquats, sesame candies or thin wafer cookies. I became used to these brief absences. She always came back.

ONE EVENING THERE was no *liuqin* music or singing. All I could hear were loud words and weeping.

"I can barely afford to feed my own family!" Noble Uncle's voice slashed across the courtyard, filled with rage and something else. Anguish. "You think you can solve my problems with the pittance you earn playing that bit of wood? When I must sell the home of my ancestors!"

In the morning, my mother's eyes were red and swollen.

There was broken crockery and two empty jars of wine in the kitchen.

She returned from the Central Residence with our breakfast, two steamed buns.

"That's all, Jialing," she said. "The cook gave me these and then he left. Here, you can have both. I'm not hungry."

I gnawed on a bun and stood beside the mirror while she put up her hair. When she opened her cedarwood box, all the jeweled hairpins were gone. The partition that held her earrings was empty. Only the carved sandalwood combs remained. I looked around the room. The chair she used as a stand for her *liuqin* was pushed into a corner, and an unfamiliar shape rested on its seat. I ran over to take a look. It was the instrument, its willow wood neck broken.

MY MOTHER BEGAN going over to the Central Residence every day.

"The Fongs can't afford any servants right now, Ling-ling," she said. "If we're to stay, I must do more to earn our keep. I must do their cleaning and cooking."

We still ate by ourselves in the Western Residence. My mother put meals on the table for the Fongs, and afterward the Fong women would take the dirty dishes to their kitchen, where my mother would do the washing up.

"Those ladies have never carried a dirty plate until now," she said. "They embroider nicely, but they should prepare for worse."

What "worse" meant, I didn't know.

Once, I dared to creep through the door between courtyards while my mother cooked supper for the Fong women. I stole into the main reception hall, where the Fongs' ancestors stared out from stiff portraits, stern and disapproving. I peered through the windows of the main house and saw Noble Uncle's family. There were two women and five girls, the girls all older than me. The eldest of them looked directly at the window and caught me staring in, but she didn't say anything, just gazed back with an air of sad resignation.

THEN ONE DAY, the Central Residence wasn't quiet. We could hear men's voices.

"*Hei ho, hei ho,* lift! Again!"

"Jialing, see what's going on," my mother said.

I needed no further encouragement. I skipped through the bamboo garden to the front courtyard and climbed the heap of furniture.

On the other side of the wall, workmen were pushing handbarrows stacked high with the Fongs' belongings. One held a table inlaid with mother-of-pearl, which I knew came from the main hall where the ancestral portraits hung. Two men carried panels from a huge bed, which they transferred to an oxcart outside the front gate. More tables, chairs, cabinets, and storage chests. Vases, side tables, and an altar. A bundle of scrolls in a long basket.

Noble Uncle watched all this while another man, seated at a small table and chair, made notes on a list. I looked down on the seated man, his black skullcap, his queue oiled and shining. When the handbarrows had made their last trip, he ran one finger slowly down the list and, with his other hand, clicked away at an abacus.

Then he opened a small metal box and counted out several stacks of coins, silver and gold. Noble Uncle scooped the coins into a cloth bag. With a nod, the other man tucked abacus, box, and account book under his arm and went outside to a waiting sedan chair.

There was still quite a lot to see, so I stayed at the wall. Led by the sedan chair, the oxcart and handbarrows made their way slowly out of Dragon Springs Road. The neighbors were all outside their gates, watching the sad procession. Some even followed to get a closer look at the contents.

"I remember that inlaid table," an elderly man said, "from when Old Master Fong was alive. We used to have a pipe and a pot of tea together. It was part of his wife's dowry, carved by a very famous craftsman."

"Was that Ming the Pawnbroker in the sedan chair?" his companion asked.

"No, Old Ming died in the summer. Cholera. That's his second eldest. Just as venal."

THE NEXT MORNING, the smell of steamed bread woke me and I sat up. Mama was stuffing clothes into a canvas sack. When she saw me, she smiled and gestured to the table by the window.

"The soy milk vendor came around this morning. Drink while it's hot," she said. "And we have sweet bean paste buns."

The soy milk was slightly sweetened and there was a strange taste to it. I looked at her inquiringly.

"Juice of the poppy," she said. "So you can sleep a little more after breakfast. There's lots of food. You have a whole packet of sticky rice in lotus leaf, the kind you like with chicken and a salted duck egg in the middle. The last of the persimmons are on the platter. Now, remember what I said about the food?"

I nodded. "Not to eat it all at once."

Then we went to the Fox altar.

When we returned, my mother held out the emerald-green trousers and tunic. "Your new winter clothes are ready." She buttoned me into the tunic and stepped back to look at me.

"Remember what Mama said last night?" Her voice was light and careless, but it trembled slightly.

"Yes. You're going away with the Fongs for a little while." I was back at the table, my attention on the sweet bean paste inside the steamed bun, warm and flavored with honey. "And you'll come back in two days to get me, and we'll go join them. I must be very quiet and stay here. I won't leave the Western Residence."

When I finished the bun, she carried me back to bed. "It's still early, Ling-ling. Sleep some more. I must go now. It's only for two days."

She leaned over to tuck the quilt around me. I could smell the sandalwood combs in her hair. My belly warm and full with soy milk, my eyes drowsy, I watched her tighten the drawstring around the canvas sack. She wrapped the bag in a length of blue flowered cotton cloth. She carried it in her arms, holding it against her chest as though it were a child. Then with swaying, graceful steps, she left the room. She didn't look back.

I was sure she would return as usual.

CHAPTER 3

In my new life with the Yangs, I struggled out of bed each morning when daylight was just a pale shimmer on the horizon to draw water for Mrs. Hao's kitchen barrel. Fortunately, like the Western Residence, the Central Residence had its own well. As I trudged back and forth with the heavy wooden bucket, I would see Master Yang and his sons hurry to the family shrine where they burned incense to their ancestors. Dajuin, who was sixteen and treated as an adult, would then leave for work with Master Yang, while Kejuin, who was my age, would return to bed, carried in his amah's arms.

Shortly after Master Yang and Dajuin left for the factory, the household would come alive. Voices rang out: Mrs. Hao shouting at me to carry a kettle of hot water to Grandmother Yang, Lao-er, the gate-keeper, calling out to the night soil collector. After the quiet of the Western Residence, all this activity was a confusing bustle.

The other servants were paid wages, food, and lodgings, but I was a bond servant. The Yangs weren't obliged to do any more than provide a roof over my head and enough food to keep me from starving. Mrs. Hao often reminded me of this. Until I could buy my freedom, the Yangs owned me.

With scolding and slaps, Ah-Jien, the house servant, taught me what to do. Each morning, I replaced Grandmother Yang's chamber pot with a clean one, then ran to the outhouse to empty the used one before the night soil collector came in. I kept her rooms swept and dusted. Whenever her teapot grew cold, I ran to the kitchen to refill a kettle with hot water.

While Grandmother Yang took her daily naps, I would join Anjuin, who helped in the kitchen almost every day. Mrs. Hao instructed her on cooking, making preserves, and brewing medicinal infusions. This was part of Anjuin's training, for she was recently betrothed and the Yangs would lose face if she entered her husband's home unable to manage a kitchen or run a household.

ON MY FIRST night I had slept on a folding cot in the kitchen. When Anjuin heard me crying for my mother, she brought me to her room and I fell asleep pressed against her back, comforted by the soft regular sighs of her breathing. The next day, she had Lao-er set up the cot in her room.

"What will happen to me when you get married?" I asked.

I was seated in front of her dresser mirror, and she stood behind the chair, braiding my hair. It was the day after Grandmother Yang confirmed the news of Anjuin's betrothal, to the third son of a family named Chen, also from a merchant clan in Ningpo. The groom was several years younger, so the wedding

was to be held in eight years' time, when he was eighteen and
Anjuin twenty-one.

She paused to tie a ribbon to the end of my pigtail. "You might
be working for another family by then. You might even be married by then."

I shook my head. "Mrs. Hao says no one will ever marry me."

"I've an idea," Anjuin said. "When I get married, I'll ask
Grandmother to make you part of my dowry. You can come with
me as my bond servant."

Reassured, I nodded. I wanted to offer her something in
return, but all I had was my secret that the Western Residence was
home to a Fox spirit. But before I could open my mouth, a small,
wordless rebuke in my mind, like a tug on my pigtails, made me
pause. Then any compulsion to talk about Fox slipped away. Next
day the memory returned, of the desire to tell Anjuin about Fox,
of how it had wavered in my mind and then extinguished like a
weak candle flame. That was when I first became truly aware of
Fox's influence.

ALTHOUGH I WAS allowed to sleep in Anjuin's room, there was no
question that I would eat in the kitchen with the other servants.
Amah Wu, the nanny, was allowed at the family table only because she helped feed Kejuin. Lao-er leered at me, and Ah-Jien,
the house servant, openly despised me, but at least in Mrs. Hao's
domain I was safe from their slaps and pinches. Ah-Jien refused
to have me at the same table so Mrs. Hao ladled my meals into a
big bowl and sat me on a stool in the corner. I listened to them
gossip while I ate.

Their favorite topic was the Yang family. They pooled every
tidbit gleaned during the day to exchange over supper. On the
verge of prosperity, still careful with his money, Master Yang

had moved from Ningpo to the outskirts of Shanghai to build a cotton-weaving mill. His younger brothers were still in Ningpo, running the family's chain of dry goods stores. Master Yang bustled between Dragon Springs Road and his mill in the factory district of Chapei. He smiled frequently, and his every stride bristled with confidence.

"The poor depend on the rich and the rich depend on heaven," said Lao-er. "Let's hope the gods favor Master Yang and his mill or we'll all be begging on the streets."

"The Old Mistress doesn't trust his judgment," Mrs. Hao said. "He was so proud of the bargain he got with this estate he wouldn't listen to the Old Mistress's fortune-teller. The fortune-teller warned of hard times if the master came to Shanghai."

Mrs. Hao was a widow and slept in a room beside the kitchen. She held an unusually prominent position among the servants because she was a distant cousin to First Wife. Mrs. Hao generally had the last word.

First Wife was childless and spent most of her time embroidering a huge altar cloth. She was a woman of some education, tasked with tutoring Anjuin. She was moody and the lesson schedule erratic.

Master Yang's Second Wife had died many years ago. She had borne him two children, Dajuin and then Anjuin, before dying in childbirth.

Third Wife was lazy and amiable. Kejuin was her son. She spent her time gossiping with the house servants. Her round belly meant there would be another child soon to keep Amah Wu even busier. She was also the first to read the newspapers after Master Yang and Dajuin finished with them.

Anjuin's eldest brother, Dajuin, was sixteen years old, an adult in my eyes. Anjuin adored him and because he read the newspapers every day, she did too, struggling to learn new words with the help of a dictionary. Whenever he discussed the latest news with his father, she listened with great attention, but never joined in. In front of Master Yang, Dajuin said very little about the imperial government, but when he was with Anjuin, he was open about his contempt for the corrupt regime. Whenever she asked him about some article in the newspaper, he always took her questions seriously. I would see them through the window of his study, their heads close together, Dajuin explaining, Anjuin listening.

Dajuin paid no attention to me, just a nod of the head now and then to acknowledge my presence if we passed each other in the courtyard. This couldn't be said for Kejuin, who was my age, a much-indulged youngest son. Kejuin pulled at my pigtails and taunted me with cries of *zazhong, foreign devil, big nose*.

As a bond servant, I could buy my freedom eventually. Grandmother Yang was strict but fair, taking every care to smooth her entry into the next life through scrupulous honesty in this one. Master Yang had drawn up a contract and set a price. The gold coins from my mother were noted on the contract, partial payment for my bond.

I could talk to Anjuin and sometimes Mrs. Hao but turned tongue-tied in front of others. I'd never had to speak with anyone but my mother before. I replied to questions with a mumbled yes or no. If not for Anjuin's assurances that I was merely shy, the Yangs would've given up on me as dim-witted.

"She's pretty enough," I once overheard Grandmother Yang remark, "and obedient enough. But what a standoffish child she is."

"As though waiting for a slap even after you've said something kind to her," Third Wife agreed.

Not a slap. The other servants slapped me enough that I no longer cried out, for that only encouraged them to hit me again. What I waited for was betrayal. For if my own mother could abandon me, what could I count on from the Yangs? Even Anjuin.

GRANDMOTHER YANG TOOK a nap every day. During those few hours, I was free to do as I pleased. More often than not this meant slipping into the Western Residence to visit Fox. She wasn't always there, but when she was, we liked to stand side by side atop the stack of furniture in the front courtyard. When she was in her Fox shape, she would stand on hind legs, paws pressed against the top of the wall. I knew, however, that if anyone looked up, they would see only my face.

When I was outside the Western Residence, the list of questions I wanted to ask Fox were endless. When did we come to Dragon Springs Road? Where did we live before? Who was my father? How were we related to Noble Uncle? Sometimes she answered my queries, but more often she simply made me forget what I wanted to ask. In her presence, unwanted questions vanished like raindrops in a puddle.

"Why doesn't anyone ever come into the Western Residence except for me?"

Her muzzle wrinkled up in what looked like a smirk. This courtyard has been my home for three hundred years, she said. I see no reason to share it with others.

"But my mother and I lived here," I said, admiring her lovely paws, their velvetlike black fur.

Your mother made a Fox altar. She burned incense. She showed respect, so I let you stay. The paws blurred and became hands, dainty and smooth skinned, and then it was Fox in her human shape balanced delicately on the chair beside me.

"It wasn't a very grand altar," I said, thinking of the Buddhist temple I'd been to with Grandmother Yang. That had been my first outing from the estate. Grandmother Yang had made me burn incense in thanks to the Buddha and there she had made her vow to care for me as her act of benevolence. Our little altar was humble compared to ones that stood before the huge gilded statues.

Foxes don't need much of an altar. She wrinkled her nose at me in a Fox smile. A corner in a farmhouse, a box turned on its end, or even just a niche dug out from the side of a haystack. Our supplicants are the poor and disadvantaged. Some need to keep their prayers secret. Why burden them with the need to build costly temples?

"Tell me about the others who lived in the Western Residence, from before," I said.

There was a time, oh, at least three hundred years ago, when bandits threatened the area. The family who owned this land built a high wall to enclose their home. There was a son and a daughter. They were my good friends.

Her voice grew slower, dreamier. But it was a terrible time, when gangs of bandits roved the countryside. The family's tenant farmers would come inside the walls for safety and to help defend the property.

The walls protected houses and stables, vegetable gardens and chicken coops. Farmers would herd families and livestock through the huge gates. They camped in the middle of the enclosure, a wide strip of empty ground bordered by the landlord's houses and gardens, and hid from the lawlessness outside. Generations later, when the bandits were gone and Shanghai had spread so far inland that homes and shops sprouted in fields where mustard greens used to grow, the landlord's family fell into poverty. They had to sell off their houses and land. The gates were removed and the walls torn down, the empty stretch of ground where tenant farmers had camped paved over to become Dragon Springs Road.

I craned my neck to look at the tall brick piers that still guarded the entrance to Dragon Springs Road. Their bulk hinted at the size of the huge gates that once hung from massive hinges. Beyond them I could see Chung San Road, the donkey carts hurrying by, vendors toting their wares from shoulder poles, pedestrians ambling along.

In those days, if I didn't like the humans who lived here, I just ignored them, Fox continued. Or I would go away and live somewhere else for a while. The worst humans are the ones who harass you with prayers and offerings, always wanting you to make them wealthy.

"But isn't that what Foxes do?" I asked. "When they become friends with humans, they bring gold and treasure."

Such wealth, unless it's buried and unclaimed, always belongs to someone. I'm not the kind of Fox who steals, though it would be easy enough. Her eyes glowed green and her hips gave a twitch that would've made her tail slash back and forth had she been in her Fox shape.

"Why aren't you always here when I come?" I said. "Where do you go?"

Fox stepped down from the wall and held her arms up. She lifted me down to the ground. Out to where there are fields and trees. Into the hills. To the river. To the grasslands. The places where Foxes like to go.

ONCE BOUNDED BY the walls of the Western Residence, my world now expanded to the small realm that was Dragon Springs Road and just beyond. In this I was luckier than Anjuin. She was a daughter of the house, but I was only a servant. Thus I was the one who skipped behind Mrs. Hao, following the cook to market in the morning and returning some hours later, lugging a string bag of mushrooms or spinach leaves while Mrs. Hao carried a basket of turnips or a pail of live shrimp.

In the market square, most of the stalls were no more than wooden frames covered with straw matting to keep the sun off. The vegetable vendors sold only what they could tote on their shoulder poles, deep baskets the size of small barrels swinging from the ends, filled with bundles of miniature cabbages that seemed carved from pale jade or long purple eggplants. The fish-mongers sheltered their handbarrows beneath straw awnings, spreading silvery fish on beds of wet seaweed and splashing water into pails where river shrimp waved wispy feelers. Surrounding the market square were shops whose owners lived above. The rice merchant, a teahouse, the herbalist. The spice merchant who measured out bags of star anise and dried red chilies.

In the shade beside the basket vendor's stall, the blind sto-ryteller chanted his repertoire of tales. Although I could never stand beside him long enough to hear a complete story, after some months I was able to piece them together from the bits and snatches I overheard as I followed Mrs. Hao from stall to stall and shop to shop.

On these walks, the cook never failed to remind me of my debt to the Yangs. She recounted stories of other bond servants she had known, worked to exhaustion and an early death.

"How you're treated depends on the family," she said. "In kind homes, the matriarch will even find husbands for favored bond servants. But it's rare, very rare. Just count yourself fortunate that the Yangs are decent folk."

She left unspoken the certainty that I shouldn't count myself a favored bond servant. I was a tainted creature. I was *zazhong*. I walked unmolested in the marketplace only because I trailed in the shadow of her protection. Once a barrow pusher outside the rice shop leered at me and said something, words I didn't understand.

Mrs. Hao swung around to face him, her voice louder than I'd ever heard. "This little girl is bond servant to Old Mistress Yang. Are you implying my mistress runs a brothel?"

The shopkeeper rushed out and beat the barrow pusher about the head with a feather duster. "*Wah, wah,* you stupid ox. How dare you speak so rudely to my customers! Finish stacking those rice sacks and get on your way."

Even then I knew Mrs. Hao was only defending me to preserve the prestige of the Yangs. I never managed to get used to the gibes and stares, but I got better at pretending to ignore them. The outside world, daunting though it was, couldn't dampen my curiosity.

For one thing, it was my duty to tell Anjuin everything I'd seen. At night in our room, we exchanged news.

"Today the blind storyteller brought his daughter to the market," I might say, "and she played the *erhu* while he sang the story of the Butterfly Lovers."

Or "A vegetable seller lifted his shoulder pole without looking behind and knocked over the fishmonger's stall. There was fish everywhere! And so much shouting!"

I wondered how I could have been content, how my mother could have been content, to live enclosed within the Western Residence. On the other side of its walls, other people went about their lives, lives that in no way resembled ours. How could I have lived inside these four walls, obedient and unquestioning? How was it that I'd never thought of disobeying my mother and running out to Dragon Springs Road?

Had it been fear of Noble Uncle that kept me docile?

Or had it been Fox?

CHAPTER 4

January 1909, Year of the Rooster

Master Yang handed out red paper envelopes of New Year's money to all his wives and children, and then the servants. I took mine and tucked it into the bodice of my tunic, unwilling to open it until I was in the safety of my room.

"Goodness, child," Third Wife said, giving my cheek a pinch. "No one's going to take it away from you. It's the New Year. What a strange, suspicious little thing you are."

Out on Dragon Springs Road we clapped hands over ears to muffle the sharp percussive retorts of firecrackers that echoed up and down the street.

"The louder, the better," Lao-er cried, handing a long match to Kejuin. "Drives away evil spirits."

Kejuin lit another long string of firecrackers.

They dangled from the small gabled roof above the front gate, each string made up of hundreds of tiny red cardboard tubes tied together. Lighting one powder-filled tube set off the rest, small explosions of flames and noise that sent shreds of red paper blowing through the street.

"May the Year of the Rooster bring prosperity to your family," Master Yang said, bowing to our neighbor, Master Shen.

"A three-year-old sits on the Dragon Throne," Master Shen said. "The prince regent is twenty-five years old and takes advice from the new dowager empress, a power-hungry general, and a court full of eunuchs."

From his glum expression, the old man didn't seem to think the coming year held much hope for China. Then he forced a smile. "May the New Year bring great profits to your business, Master Yang."

"We work hard and hope the gods favor us," was Master Yang's modest reply.

Back inside the walls of his home, however, he proclaimed otherwise.

"This is the year!" he said, raising his wine cup to finish off their New Year's dinner. "The looms will operate at capacity, enough to supply our own stores and sell to department stores in Shanghai."

First Wife looked worried. "Husband, it's not wise to tempt evil spirits."

He waved his cup at her. "With all the noise from fireworks, there isn't a single spirit, good or evil, who can hear me. I tell you, our luck began with the purchase of this property. A real bargain. Those Fongs were in far more desperate straits than anyone suspected."

But First Wife was not convinced. She glared when I set down a plate of dried fruit between her and Third Wife.

"I'm sure that Western Residence is haunted," she said. "I get a queer feeling every time I think about going in there. Like a hand in my mind pushing me away. And you, *zazhong* girl. You're unlucky too."

THERE WAS ANOTHER courtyard on the estate, the Eastern Residence. Until the Yangs came, I hadn't realized it was also part of the property. It flanked the other side of the Central Residence, but unlike the Western Residence, which stood inside its own walls, only a garden path separated the Eastern Residence from the Central.

Shortly after the New Year, Master Yang hired carpenters to make repairs to the houses in the Eastern Residence and had a sturdy bamboo fence built along the garden path to separate the two homes.

"Should we rent out the Western Residence as well?" Grandmother Yang suggested. Master Yang was showing her the newspaper advertisements he had placed for the Eastern Residence.

There was the slightest wavering of air, the softest of breaths. I could almost see the suggestion skim above their heads like a dragonfly, hovering uncertainly.

"Those houses in the Western Residence are too run-down," Master Yang said, his voice dreamy. "It would cost a lot to repair them. Let's wait and see what happens with the Eastern Residence."

The idea darted away. Fox.

A SUCCESSION OF prospective tenants came to see the Eastern Residence, but none ever returned with an offer to rent. Months went by and the Eastern Residence remained empty.

"They look around and they're pleased. Then they chat with

the neighbors," Mrs. Hao said. "The Shens' gatekeeper is only too happy to talk about wailing ghosts and all the misfortunes that fell upon the previous owners."

"You would think that having a well in their own courtyard would matter more than gossipy rumors," Third Wife remarked.

Every one of the three courtyards had its own well of clear, cold water, but the haunted courtyard was proof to our neighbors that the gods always balanced the scales, advantage with adversity.

"Dajuin just paid for our ad to be translated for a foreign newspaper," Anjuin said. "The *North China Herald*. He told Father that foreigners don't believe in Chinese ghosts."

I had never seen a foreign person, even from a distance, and now entire families of foreigners might be moving in. I knew they had big noses and ghostly white skin like rice paper. Some had eyes as pale as the sky. They sounded frightening, but I couldn't wait for them to arrive.

When the Yangs saw that I looked nothing like a foreigner, they would realize I wasn't *zazhong* after all.

WITHIN A WEEK, the English advertisement brought a reply, and scarcely a week after that, shouting voices and the rumble of an oxcart brought us to the front gates.

In the uncertain light of early evening, the first impression I had of the foreign man was his size, a broad torso and long legs. He climbed down from the seat beside the oxcart driver, and I gasped at how tall he was compared to Dajuin. A rickshaw followed the cart. The canopy hid its passengers in shadow, but the dark skirt and button boots that were visible undoubtedly belonged to a foreign woman.

"The state of the roads outside Shanghai made for a slow journey," I heard the foreign man say to Dajuin. He spoke strangely accented Chinese. "It's a good thing we were able to push the cart over the worst of the ruts."

A low moan escaped from the rickshaw, and he hurried over to help the woman out of the rickshaw. I saw a thin figure step down, in a long dark coat that flared out from the waist. She leaned unsteadily against the wall and immediately vomited. Then a little girl jumped out of the rickshaw, white ruffled skirts flaring out below the hem of a blue coat. The dress reached only just to her ankles, and she wore leather shoes. Her father said something to Dajuin, who nodded in our direction, and the foreign man pointed us out to the little girl. The laborers who had followed the oxcart on foot began unloading furniture, and the man led his wife inside to their new home.

The girl came skipping toward us.

I clutched Anjuin's hand. If the girl hadn't been so small, I might've been terrified at her alarming appearance. Below a wide-brimmed hat, copper-colored curls hung to her shoulders. Her skin was not paper white but almost. Rust-colored flecks sprinkled her face, especially plentiful across her nose and cheeks. Most astonishing of all, her eyes were amber brown with glints of green and gold. Was she a type of foreign Fox spirit?

When she spoke, her Chinese was perfect, with none of the uncertain, wavering tones that made her father's speech awkward.

"My father asks if you could have someone bring hot water and tea for my mother."

Anjuin gestured to the girl to follow us, and she skipped alongside, chattering nonstop about their ride in from Shanghai, a guileless outpouring of words.

"You speak Chinese!" Anjuin managed to say when the girl finally paused.

"Yes, my amah was Chinese. My family name is Shea, and my name is Anna. What are your names?"

"I'm Yang Anjuin. This is Jialing, our bond servant. Where's your amah?"

"My mother didn't like her so we didn't bring her. How old are you? I'm eight."

"I'm thirteen," Anjuin said, "and Jialing is eight also."

Anna smiled at me and I smiled back. It didn't seem to matter to her that I was *zazhong*.

In the kitchen, Third Wife and Mrs. Hao were at the kitchen table cutting string beans into short, even lengths. They stared at Anna, amazed as the girl made her request in fluent Chinese. After some discussion, Mrs. Hao left for the Eastern Residence, a kettle of hot water in one hand, a basket holding cups and a paper twist of tea in the other. Anna followed, skipping along, still talking.

That night, there was shouting and weeping from the Eastern Residence. Voices bruised the air in a language I couldn't understand.

In Shanghai, foreigners were so common that only visitors from small towns or the truly unsophisticated gaped at their strange appearance. But we were west of Shanghai, in the External Roads area where foreigners were still a rare sight. Whenever Anna and her mother went out to Chung San Road to signal for a rickshaw, urchins followed them, laughing and pointing. Mrs. Shea pressed her lips tightly and twitched her long skirts away when the children came too close. Anna merely grinned and insulted them in fluent Chinese, but this only made some of them bolder and they would reach for her copper curls or tug at her dress.

After a while, Mrs. Shea no longer ventured out but instead made their only servant, a surly cook, go out to Chung San Road and bring a rickshaw into their courtyard. Then she and Anna would ride out with the canopy up to shelter them from inquisitive eyes.

Anna's father was a constable with the Shanghai Municipal Police.

"He's the most senior constable at the Gordon Road Station," Anna said. "He earns more than most constables because he passed the police force's Chinese exams. He says it's all thanks to practicing with me!"

Anna's father wanted to live closer to the police station, but their other reason for moving was that her mother wanted a house with a garden of her own, like the ones back in England. Constable Shea could afford this only by moving out of Shanghai's city limits. The Sheas were a small family for such a large home. The three foreigners and their cook occupied the entire Eastern Residence compound: a main house, two *erfang*, and a reception hall. A wealth of space, yet Anna said her mother was unhappy and complained they were now too far away from her friends.

Mrs. Shea borrowed Lao-er to dig a bed for rosebushes, but she didn't bother planting anything else in their courtyard garden. Nor did she seem to care about the roses once they were in the ground. She stayed indoors all day, behind latticed windows hung with flowered draperies, roses and ferns that didn't need her care.

It was during the afternoons, while Grandmother Yang napped and Mrs. Shea hid inside her house, that Anna and I became friends. Our friendship began when I showed her how to draw water from the well and helped her carry buckets to water the roses. Anna inspected each bloom with anxiety, frowning over every brown leaf and misshapen bud. The flower bed was a wide straight trench, incongruously rigid beside the pebbled path that curved through a miniature landscape of bamboo and mossy rocks.

"Look, flowers from home," she said one day. "My grand-mother sent them."

She held out three small brown envelopes printed with foreign words and drawings of strange flowers. She opened them to show me tiny seeds. "Mother says they'll die in this climate. But let's try. If they grow, what a nice surprise for her."

She used an old chopstick and poked a series of holes in the dirt beneath the roses. Into each one she placed a few seeds.

"Except for these," she said, scattering a thimbleful of seeds from the last packet. "Grandmother's letter said to sprinkle them anywhere you want them to grow. There. I've still got some left, just in case."

WITH ANNA'S ARRIVAL, my world expanded even more.

On school days a donkey cart came by in the morning and she climbed in to join a half-dozen other foreign girls whose laughing faces I glimpsed briefly through the opening in the canvas canopy. Kejuin went to school, always trailing behind his amah on their way out of Dragon Springs Road, but Anjuin wasn't allowed to attend school. How different life was for foreign girls.

Anna's self-assurance was the most foreign thing about her. She ran around with her socks falling down and hair ribbon half untied, her curiosity boundless and uninhibited. She thought nothing of chatting with the servants up and down Dragon Springs Road.

"Mummy doesn't like me playing with you because you're half Chinese," Anna said. "But she doesn't like me playing with Chinese girls either. And she didn't like the other English families around us when we lived in Shanghai."

There was usually an hour each afternoon when we could play together, after she came home from school and before Grandmother Yang woke from her nap. We never played in the Eastern Residence, for fear of disturbing Anna's mother. We played in the garden behind the main house of the Central Residence, where I could hear Grandmother Yang call for me.

Anna sometimes brought books and let me turn the pages. The color plates that illustrated the stories were so strange. Pictures of small humans with dragonfly wings, gnarled little men coming out of a mountain cave, a fox talking to a raven who sat in a tree. The most beautiful picture was of a girl with a fish tail instead of legs, seaweed and shells woven into her long yellow hair. Anna would read a line in English, then repeat it in Chinese. At times she mixed English and Chinese in a flowing stream that carried me along, confident of her meaning, if not the specific words.

In return, I told her the stories I knew, including the ones I'd heard from the blind storyteller in the marketplace. Anna was familiar with many of the tales and knew even more. Her Chinese amah had been a prodigious storyteller with a great fondness for gruesome folktales. Potbellied hungry ghosts, drowned girls, hanged ghosts with long black tongues, ghosts with ancient grievances seeking revenge. These now filled my imagination as Anna's hushed words warned of their existence.

I often sensed Fox listening to us from beneath a tangle of quince shrubs. At times she snorted. I could tell, however, that Fox liked Anna.

"What about foreign ghosts?" I asked Anna, shivering with pleasant anticipation.

Just like Chinese ghosts, there were foreign spirits who haunted their place of death. There were also monsters similar to *jiangshi,* except that instead of draining a human's *qi* life force, they drank the blood of their victims. She told me about men who turned into wolves when the moon was full.

"So you must be very careful," she said, "of anyone who goes away once a month."

"Did your amah tell you anything about Fox spirits?" I queried.

"Yes. She met one many years ago at her grandmother's home, when she was just a girl," Anna said. "She said the Fox often visited her grandmother. She appeared as a nice middle-aged woman, very friendly and talkative. I'd like to meet one."

"But you're English. Foreigners don't believe in Chinese spirits." I doubted Fox would show herself to Anna.

She shook her head. "I'm Irish. My father says we Irish can see the spirit world."

She's very amusing, Fox said, trotting beside me on the path back to the main house after Anna and I parted. *Such interesting stories. Talking animals with magical powers. Doors into magical worlds. And clever foxes of course.*

Despite my initial hopes, the foreigners didn't change how the Yangs thought of me. Although I looked nothing like the Sheas, I was still *zazhong*. Kejuin was convinced that Anna played with me only because of our shared foreign blood.

ALL TENANTS COME with their own problems, and the Sheas turned out to be more troublesome than the Yangs ever expected.

Constable Shea sometimes had to sleep at the barracks of the Gordon Road police station in Chapei. Our lives were quieter when he was away. When he was home, the sound of arguments frequently disturbed our evenings, and the Sheas' fights always ended with sobs.

If Constable Shea was home on a Sunday, the family took rickshaws to attend church, which Anna said was like a temple. They only had one deity, but Anna assured me he had a mother and many disciples who shared the work of attending to the prayers of all the foreigners.

Several times a week, Mrs. Shea would get into a rickshaw to go shopping in Shanghai. Invariably she returned in a foul mood. She berated their only servant in a mix of pidgin English and badly pronounced Chinese. The servant, also nominally the cook, soon let it be known that Mrs. Shea's shopping baskets contained more liquor than food.

Finally, Mrs. Shea shouted at her cook once too often. If Constable Shea had been home that day, he might have talked the cook out of leaving, but this time the long-suffering servant declared he could take no more. He left Dragon Springs Road, shouting insults against foreigners as he stormed away. It was nearly unheard of for servants to leave a foreign household, where wages were higher and mistresses less vigilant.

There followed a series of new servants, none of whom lasted more than a few weeks. When one of them departed, we knew Mrs. Shea's rage would erupt later in the evening. If Mr. Shea was home, her wrathful words were for him. If he wasn't, her anger was unleashed on Anna.

Anna would flinch when her mother called her home. Sometimes Mrs. Shea's voice seemed to sing with laughter, but there was always a note of despair in the gaiety. Other times, her cries were ugly, hoarse with recrimination. I didn't understand her words, but I understood their meaning.

After a night of loud arguments from the Sheas, Anna would be quiet and disconsolate.

"Mummy wants to go back to England," Anna said. "She doesn't want us to live in China anymore. She hates it here."

"Then why did she come?" I asked.

"She says it was because of me." Anna sniffled. "She said Father wrote her hundreds of letters asking her to bring me to Shanghai. He didn't want to leave the Shanghai Police Force and begged her to join him. So we could be a real family."

A real family. Were all foreign parents so quarrelsome?

It occurred to me that in the short time I'd known her, Anna's carefree brightness had dimmed. She rubbed absently at a spot above her elbow and then winced.

Then she jumped up. "Come and see something."

She took my hand and I followed her to the very back of the Central Residence, to the sturdy bamboo fence that stood between the Eastern and Central Residences.

"See, I've loosened these slats," she said. "Just slide them apart like this, and we can slip through and slide them back. I can visit you any time, without having to go in and out of the front gates."

She beamed, cheerful again. "No one else knows. It's our secret."

For once, I had something to give her in exchange. Something Fox had agreed I could do.

An unused garden shed leaned against the wall between the Central and Western Residences. The shed was an open-sided shack, just a sloping roof on posts that sheltered a jumble of cast-off tools, furniture, and broken pots. Creepers and climbing hydrangea had taken hold and a curtain of vines hung down from the roof, almost to the ground.

Soon after the Yangs moved in, Master Yang had locked the front gates of the Western Residence as well as the door between the two front courtyards. "Until we're ready to use this property, let's keep people out."

How brief your human lives and how short your memories, Fox had said, the first time she took me to the shed. It only took a generation for people to forget the door was here.

Now Anna followed me through the cascade of vines, between stacks of broken clay pots. The wooden door was nearly hidden behind a broken sedan chair. Although its planks were warped and its hinges rusty, the door opened quietly and we stepped through. Pushing past vines that covered the other side of the door, we stepped into the rear garden of the Western Residence.

Anna ran into the courtyard and spun around. "That's a *real* secret door! It's like going through the doorway into a magic world. Is this the haunted courtyard?"

"There aren't any ghosts here," I said. Unless you counted Fox, who would've been offended to be called a ghost.

"The Shens' cook told me this place is haunted," Anna said. "He says it's haunted by the ghost of a woman who couldn't give her husband sons. She grew so sad she killed herself."

I shook my head and repeated. "There aren't any ghosts."

Anna looked around the courtyard. "If there had been a sad concubine who died here, the courtyard would feel sad. But it doesn't. It feels safe."

I showed her the main house, my playroom in the undamaged *erfang,* and inside the door of the derelict *erfang,* where wisteria vines had crowded their way through the hole in the roof, clusters of pale purple blossoms dropping their fragrant petals on the floor.

In the kitchen, I showed her the Fox altar. Every so often I stole incense sticks from the Yangs' family shrine, and now I pushed one into the jar of sand and lit it. I knelt down and bowed my head.

To my surprise, so did Anna, her face solemn as she rocked back and forth on her knees. When she leaned forward, her dress pulled up at the back. As usual, her stockings were bunched down at her ankles. Not so usual were the welts on her calves, stripes of purple against her white skin. As if she could sense my eyes, she reached behind and flicked her dress down, never breaking the rhythm of her prayers.

"Why did you pray?" I asked when we got up. "You're not Chinese."

"My amah used to take me to the temple with her," she said. "She said heaven is a big place. Big enough for everyone's gods."

We spent the afternoon there. We pulled some furniture from my playroom onto the veranda of the *erfang* and played at having a tea party. We used small bowls from the kitchen as teacups, and she showed me how to drink the foreign way, little fingers sticking out.

"Next time, I'll bring some biscuits and we can have a real tea party," she said. "Mother won't notice if I take a few."

"I've got something for you," I said, suddenly remembering.

The folded page had been in my pocket all day. It was an illustrated story torn from one of Third Wife's old magazines. The simple inkbrush sketch showed an old man facing an open door. The door was set in a high wall, and behind the wall was an orchard filled with blossoming trees. The landscape beyond the orchard rose up to layers of cloud, the land of immortals.

Anjuin had read the story to me, and now I could tell it to Anna.

> There was a man named Zhang who lived in the small town of Pinghu, not far from Shanghai. At New Year's, when red lanterns hang outside every front gate, he would make his way through the alleys of poor neighborhoods. Whenever he heard laughter and the clattering of dishes, he would walk past. Whenever he heard crying and laments, he would throw a string of cash through the door and hurry away.

Even when he was so old that he had to walk with a stick, he continued this practice.

One New Year's, even though he was very ill, he made his usual rounds. He turned down an alley and was surprised to see the grand double gates of a mansion between ramshackle houses. The gates were painted cerulean blue and one of them stood wide open. He glanced inside, expecting to see a courtyard but instead there was an orchard in full bloom. A light breeze blew petals out to the alley, inviting him in. Zhang did not hesitate. He stepped across the threshold and entered the land of immortals. The doorway vanished, leaving only a few scattered white petals in the alley to prove that any such event had ever happened.

"He was such a good person that he was allowed to enter the land of immortals," I said. "It's a true story. That's why it's in the magazine."

"My father says Ireland is full of doors to the land of fairies," Anna said. "When you come back, you're still young, but everyone you know has grown old because fifty years have gone by."

"In China, when you enter the land of immortals, you never come back," I said.

In the hydrangea bushes below us, I sensed rather than saw Fox lift one eyelid. Why would anyone want to come back? She settled back to her nap.

Anna sat up. "Maybe your mother went away to the Chinese land of immortals. She'll come back for you one day."

She was steadfast in her conviction that my mother would return for me.

By August of that year the weather was relentlessly hot. I learned a new word, *drought*.

When I went to the market with Mrs. Hao, all the talk was about the food riots. They were so bad that in Shandong Province imperial troops had been forced to fire on rioters. Shanghai and its surrounding areas were spared the unrest that embroiled the rest of China, but even I could sense the tension on Dragon Springs Road. Neighbors stopped Dajuin and Master Yang to ask what the mood was like among the warehouse and factory laborers in Chapei.

What interested me more was that Grandmother Yang was preparing for the Magpie Festival. All the women of the household, even the servants, were going to sit in the courtyard to gaze at the heavens while Grandmother Yang recited the story of the Weaving Maid and the Cowherd. Mrs. Hao had made a vat of sweetened chrysanthemum tea for the occasion.

I already knew the story, of course. I had stayed up late the night before so that Fox could point out the patch of sky between constellations where the magpies of China would fly, their bodies forming a bridge across the river of stars so the exiled lovers could meet in the middle.

But you won't be able to see the bridge of birds, Fox remarked. Magpies are black. If it had been white egrets that responded to the Goddess's call, the bridge might be visible.

"You can see the bridge though, can't you?" I asked. "Your Fox eyes must be better than human eyes."

She yawned. Yes, and every year I think the Weaving Maid should've known better, even if she was only a minor deity.

It was still early morning when I accompanied Mrs. Hao to the market, but the heat was already oppressive, the air heavy with the threat of rain. With luck, it would rain during the day, leaving a clear sky at night.

Mrs. Hao argued with the vegetable sellers, who insisted their greens were fresh but had wilted because the day was so unusually hot. Vendors brewed chrysanthemum tea for those who wanted a cooling drink, and the noodle shop owner shredded cucumbers to garnish bowls of cold noodles mixed with spicy peanut sauce.

A small troupe of musicians was tuning up at the center of the square. The *dizi* player piped a few practice bars. Then the gongs crashed in, and the strings began singing an accompaniment. Festive notes swirled through the air, making me want to dance. I felt as though I'd known the tune all my life.

My delight in the music must've been obvious because Mrs. Hao actually smiled at me. "It's an old, old melody called 'Full of Joy.'"

That's exactly how it sounded. Full of joy.

It was so hot Mrs. Hao paid for us to ride back on a handbarrow so we wouldn't have to tote our heavy shopping baskets in the scorching sun. I'd always been amazed that a single man could push the long, single-wheeled barrow with so many people riding on it. The four other passengers, all servants returning to Dragon Springs Road, joked about the heat.

"*Wah, wah,* it's too hot," Mrs. Hao said, wiping her forehead. "If the Cowherd and Weaving Maid have any sense, they'll cool off in the River of Stars instead of walking across the bridge of birds."

Everyone laughed, including the barrow pusher.

"Let's hope the celestial river is cleaner than Soochow Creek," he said. "With all the filth those factories pour into the water, the skin peels off your legs if you stand in it too long."

When we returned, Anjuin was in the kitchen rinsing a basin of rice. I filled two pails with water from the well for washing the vegetables. The rain barrel by the kitchen door was almost empty, so I filled it again.

My duty done, I went to look for Anna.

CHAPTER 5

As soon as I slipped into the Western Residence and saw Anna, I knew something was wrong.

She sat on the steps, her face in her hands. She made no sound, but from the way her shoulders heaved, I knew she was crying. When she finally lifted her face, there were purple bruises on her pale, freckled skin. Dirt streaked her dress, and one ruffle was ripped. The frill around her neckline was stained with blood from a cut on her lower lip.

"Mummy was angry with me," Anna said, when I sat beside her. "She isn't well. My father will be back from the station soon. She'll be all right when she wakes up."

But I knew Mrs. Shea wouldn't be all right for long. She would get drunk again, blame her husband for her unhappy life, and spew her rage at

Anna. I'd seen the bruises on Anna's arms and legs before, but never on her face. And never blood.

"She'll be all right," Anna repeated in a dull voice. She wiped her eyes with the back of a dirty hand. "It's just that she's angry with me. I'm the reason she came to China and she hates it here."

Overhead, a faint rumble of thunder promised rain and relief from the heat. Then we heard Mrs. Shea shouting. She was out on Dragon Springs Road. Her tones were both pleading and angry as she called Anna's name.

Anna stood up, terror on her face. She was no longer the talkative and confident girl I'd first met.

"You can't go," I whispered. "Stay here where it's safe."

"She'll be angry with me for running away," Anna said. She sounded forlorn, helpless. "I should've stayed in the storeroom, but I was so frightened of the rats."

Outside on the street, her mother's cries sounded again, harsher. Anna looked dumbfounded. "She knows we're in here. She thinks we found a way to climb in."

A pause. Then more shouting.

"She's gone next door to get one of the Yangs," Anna said, now in a panic. "To unlock the gate so she can get me."

"Go through the secret door and run back to your house through the fence," I said. "You can pretend you were out on Chung San Road all this time."

"No, I can't." Anna's eyes were round with terror, and her breath came in shallow gasps. "She'll be even angrier if she thinks people have seen me with my face like this. Oh, I wish I were dead."

"Let's go," I said, standing up. "Back through the door."

As I ran toward the wall beside the main house, rain fell on my skin, a sudden downpour as though a bucket had emptied over me. The wind began to roar and the bamboos rustled as though in a frenzy. I turned to see whether Anna was following, and in that moment of distraction, I tripped. The side of my head slammed against stone paving and a lightning-sharp flash of pain shot through my skull.

Too shocked to cry out, I lay on the ground trying to regain my breath. Then slowly, I pushed myself up by the hands. I felt too dizzy to stand. Even turning my head to look for Anna made me nauseated, and my elbows collapsed under me.

"Fox, do something," I whispered, my head sinking back to the ground.

Beneath the rumble of thunder, faraway strains of music came to my ears. "Full of Joy." A light drew my gaze to the bamboo garden. A door was taking shape beneath the arch, a wooden door with brass studs. A door without handle or lock. A door whose edges glowed. Slowly, ever so slowly, it swung open. Rain was pelting down in the courtyard, but sunlight and a scent of peach blossom spilled out from the doorway.

Anna never even turned her head when I called her name.

She stepped over the threshold of the Door, and her bright curls shone even brighter under the sunlight of that other world. Her shoes sank into thick grass, and a drift of white petals fell on her from above. Slowly, the Door began closing.

Then I saw Fox.

Her entire body quivered with eagerness. She ran back and forth in front of the arch, whining. Then the Door shut, and a moment later it was gone. There was only the garden seat, the bamboos, and the lingering scent of peach blossom.

Fox lifted her nose to the rain and howled. A long, animal wail of sorrow that constricted my heart and compressed my breath. Her cry stirred in me such a torrent of nameless longing that I curled up and began to sob, hiding my face in my hands. When I finally sat up, Fox was gone.

I dragged myself over to the *erfang* and sat on floor of the veranda. For how long I sat there, I couldn't tell. Nor could I prevent my eyes from closing.

VOICES JOLTED ME awake. I heard Master Yang's voice in the bamboo garden. "I don't understand it, that gate should've been locked."

Mr. Shea said something in English, and then I heard Mrs. Shea's voice, angry and defensive.

"Apparently the girls play here even though it's supposed to be locked," Mr. Shea said, this time in Chinese. "My wife has heard them talking from inside these walls."

They saw me as soon as they came out of the bamboo garden. Anjuin was with them and she ran to me.

"That little foreign girl has gone missing," she said. "Have you seen her?"

I pointed at the arch and whispered to Anjuin, "She went through the Door. To the land of immortals, where it's safe."

She turned around and repeated my words.

"What door?" Mr. Shea asked. "Where is it safe?"

Mrs. Shea glared down, as if daring me to say what I knew. What could I do? She was an adult, a foreign adult.

"She ran away," I said, trying again. "She wanted to go someplace safe."

"Where did she run to?" Master Yang asked, but I could only stare helplessly at the arch.

Mrs. Shea said something in English, but Mr. Shea held up his hand. "If Anna has run away, then we need to search the neighborhood immediately."

EVERYONE DISMISSED MY outburst about a Door to the land of immortals as childish imagination, some game we had been playing.

A day later, Constable Shea came to see me again. This time he brought another foreigner with him, an older woman who introduced herself in perfect Chinese as Miss Morris, the headmistress of the Unity Mission School. Master Yang wasn't present, nor was Mrs. Shea. Anjuin and I sat together on a wooden bench in the reception hall, alone with the two foreigners.

I felt sad for Constable Shea. The circles under his eyes were almost purple, and his tall frame slumped in exhaustion. If only I could make him understand that Anna was safe and happy. He sat on a low stool that put him at eye level with me. The foreign woman took a seat on a chair beside him. She gave us an encouraging smile.

"Miss Morris is here because my Chinese isn't as good as hers," Constable Shea said to us, his tired voice gentle. "I want to be sure I understand what you say, Jialing. If the two of you were doing something naughty when Anna disappeared, I promise it doesn't matter. The most important thing is to find Anna."

I nodded but still couldn't speak.

"When Mister Shea first asked you about Anna," Miss Morris prompted, "you said she wanted to go someplace safe. What did she mean by that?"

They waited quietly while I stared at my feet. Anjuin gave me a prod and I looked up. "Anna was locked in the storeroom but she escaped. There was blood on her face and her dress was torn."

"Which storeroom? Who hurt her?" Constable Shea's hand curled into a trembling fist.

"The storeroom in your house," I said, defiant. "Her mother beat her and locked her in there. Anna was too scared to go back."

The foreign woman put a hand on Constable Shea's shoulder, but he shook it off and stood up, his lips set in a grim line. His face was no longer pale but flushed with anger as he strode out the door. The older woman hurried after him.

THE NEWSPAPERS PUBLISHED a photograph of Anna. Handbills in both English and Chinese appeared on the streets offering rewards for information. The police went into every house on Dragon Springs Road and questioned all the shopkeepers along Chung San Road. They even took the lids off wells and prodded their depths with a long pole.

The Shanghai Municipal Police came to the house and questioned all the adults. They put little faith in my testimony. I couldn't blame them. I was just a little girl, and my incoherent explanation made no sense. The newspapers played it up with speculations about a kidnapping gone wrong or gangs taking revenge on the Shanghai Municipal Police. The consensus seemed to be that Anna had wandered away from home and been abducted.

Each day, Third Wife read out loud from the newspapers the latest stories about the missing foreign girl. There was nothing about a Door to the land of immortals. But days passed, and the police came no closer to solving the mystery of her disappearance.

THEN THEY FOUND Anna's body at Yung An Cemetery.

A hired mourner at a funeral had ducked behind a tomb to relieve himself and gotten a fright. The police descended on the cemetery to search for clues.

After this, a steady stream of foreign women came to visit the Eastern Residence, offering their sympathies to Mrs. Shea. The newspapers quoted her as saying all she wanted to do was go home and put this nightmare behind her. The British Women's Club took up a collection and three months after Anna's disappearance, Mrs. Shea sailed back to England.

Stories about the investigation into Anna's death became less frequent as other crises of greater consequence took over the headlines.

Constable Shea stayed in Shanghai but moved away from Dragon Springs Road, leaving behind the rose-printed curtains. In the rubbish pile I found three envelopes of seeds and put them in my pocket. There were also some framed prints, but I kept just one. It was a picture I recognized from Anna's stories: a girl sitting on a rock, half human, half fish, gazing out at the sea. I tucked it in my clothes drawer.

Each time memories of Anna surfaced they carved a hollow in my chest, and bewilderment spun my thoughts. Hadn't I seen her go through the Door? Why had her body been at the cemetery?

I had so many questions for Fox, but I hadn't seen her since the day Anna vanished. My last memory of that incident was of Fox in front of the Door. Fox, her silhouette against a narrowing wedge of light. Fox, howling to the skies.

THEN ONE NIGHT I woke to the summons in my head and climbed out of my cot. I slipped out of Anjuin's room, my cloth shoes making no sound on wood or stone. In the back garden, I hurried to the garden shed. Moonlight pierced through the hanging foliage and guided my way to the secret door. It opened silently, as it always did.

In the Western Residence, Fox was in human shape, resting on the garden bench. She sat surrounded by a bright cloud of fireflies. They dipped and rose in a tentative bobbing dance, moving points of light that made the embroidery on her tunic sparkle as though spun from pearls. The night air was only just beginning to cool, and cicadas still droned in the trees, a monotonous hum punctuated by short clacks like the snap of dry wood.

"Where is Anna? I saw her go through the Door, but did she really?" I asked Fox. "Or is she dead? They found her body."

She really went through the Door, Fox said. Her spirit is there in the land of immortals. The body is only a shell. Why the gods chose to discard hers at Yung An Cemetery is not for me to guess.

"Then bring the Door back," I pleaded. "I want to go to the land of immortals too."

Fox shook her head. I don't control the Door. It's the gods who decide. She paused. Not everyone can see the Door, Jialing, but you did. Perhaps one day when you're ready, it will open for you.

"But what made Anna more ready than me?" I said. "Her father would've come home and seen what happened. He would've stopped her mother."

Anna wanted to go, Fox said. The gods only open the Door for those who are truly deserving, truly ready to leave this world. I think Anna felt she had lost her mother's love and so she lost hope in this world.

"But I'm the one who lost my mother," I said, "and the Door didn't stay open for me."

You still hope your mother left you behind for a good reason, Fox said. You still hope to find her. Anna thought she had lost her mother's love for all eternity.

I broke off a stem of hydrangea and jabbed it into the ground beside Fox. "I miss Anna. She was my only friend."

You have Anjuin. Fox looked at me, her elegant nostrils twitching. Then she sighed. Human feelings make life so difficult. It's so much easier not to love and even better not to trust.

"I wish I were a Fox," I said. "Then my life would be easier. Can you make me a Fox?"

Such a small person, such big ideas, she said.

And then the courtyard was empty but for the fireflies, flickering lights weaving through the shadowy green depths of the bamboo garden.

A moment later I was no longer in the courtyard. There were leaves overhead and I was looking out through a tangle of shrubs, two black paws stretched in front of me. Were those my feet?

Do you really want to know what it's like to be a Fox? Her voice echoed in my head, amused. And I settled inside this memory, seeing what Fox wanted to show me. I was myself and I was also Fox.

. . . I look out on fields frosted with dew, the sky hazy with moonlight dimmed by a wash of clouds. Overhead, the high-pitched chittering of bats as they swoop and dive in the air. I stand and stretch, and from the shrubbery come rustles of alarm, small creatures alert to my presence.

The ditch I follow meanders along the perimeters of fields. I come to a path, overgrown and invisible to human eyes, but I can see where the dirt is trampled from years of being trod by human feet. At the end of the path is a large bamboo grove, the edges of a cottage just visible. The cottage has been deserted for many decades, but the bamboo has flourished, surrounding the farm yard and growing right up to the cottage. Morning glory vines smother the straw roof, closed buds of white waiting to bloom with the sunrise.

There's nothing left of the people who lived here, no furniture or utensils, just some bricks blackened from cooking fires. Buried in one corner are rags wrapped around the small bones of a baby girl, abandoned when the family fled. From poverty or war, who's to know. Fox has been coming for years but has never seen her ghost. Such a tiny thing, no doubt her souls passed straight into the afterlife, but I offer a small prayer to the gods anyway.

Outside, a scrabbling sound and the beat of wings. An owl rises up from the fields, its hoot of triumph rising over despairing squeaks, a field mouse caged in its claws. The sky turns from charcoal gray to indigo, and then a lighter blue as sunrise paints the undersides of clouds. Birds call out, cautiously at first, then with more assurance.

I trot home, treading my way between brambles and undergrowth until I reach the back wall of the Western Residence, to the spot where fallen bricks leave a gap. No other foxes will come near while Fox's scent marks these shrubs. Inside, I enter the den beneath the veranda, behind the white hydrangea shrubs . . .

. . . and then I woke up in my cot, birdsong coming in through the window. From the other side of the room, Anjuin's quiet, regular breathing. I held up my hands and they were just hands, palms and fingers of soft skin, the nails thin and flat, useless for the hunt. I was no longer a Fox.

CHAPTER 6

February 1910, Year of the Dog

Dajuin placed another ad to find new tenants for the Eastern Residence. Because of Anna's mysterious death, Master Yang was afraid there would be no takers.

"From the outside looking in," Dajuin said to his father, "this property is bound to look ill-fated, even to foreigners. In time, though, people will forget. But it may take a while."

To the Yangs' relief, a tenant materialized almost immediately. Miss Morris, the woman who had helped Constable Shea question me, came to view the Eastern Residence. She climbed down from a donkey cart, followed by a dozen young women, three of them foreign.

"She said she knew it would be a suitable home because she'd already been here once before,"

Dajuin reported. "She's headmistress of that foreign mission school out by Yung An Cemetery. She's been looking for a bigger residence so all the teachers can live in one place."

A few days before the New Year, Miss Morris and the schoolteachers moved in. Everyone on Dragon Springs Road found excuses to be outside that day. They gawked at the foreign women and remarked on the Chinese schoolteachers, some dressed in Western skirts and jackets, some in the new-style short tunics worn over ankle-length skirts. Some even had curled hair.

By the afternoon, two donkey-cart drivers from Chung San Road had been hired to take the teachers to and from their school every day. The foreign headmistress, the servants reported, had bargained competently. All sides were pleased.

THE NEW YEAR dawned and I was nine years old. Not actually nine, but since no one knew my date of birth Grandmother Yang simply decided to consider me a year older every New Year. I was now old enough and trusted enough to tag along beside Anjuin on New Year's social calls to help carry baskets of small gifts. Flanked by First Wife and Third Wife, Grandmother Yang made her way along Dragon Springs Road, entering each home to pay respects to the womenfolk of the family.

It's a pleasant tradition, said Fox, appearing beside me. The families on this street have always been good neighbors. I'll come with you to see the Shens.

She wore servant's garb, a padded long winter tunic that fell to her knees and trousers that narrowed at the ankles. Instead of a single modest braid however, her hair was piled elaborately on top of her head, the loops and twists held secure with jeweled hairpins. We crossed the threshold into the Shens' courtyard. Fox glided along, silent and unnoticed, following as though part of Grandmother Yang's entourage.

Old Madame Shen and Grandmother Yang spent several minutes offering each other good wishes for the coming year. Fox made a circuit of the room, inspecting Madame Shen's trinkets, the carved lacquer fruit dish, the potted orchids. She picked up a porcelain clock and gave it a shake.

"Have you been to call on them?" Old Madame Shen asked.

"Not yet," said Grandmother Yang. "The foreign women only arrived a few days ago. I'll go pay my respects when they're more settled."

"Schoolteachers. They'll be modern and overeducated," Old Madame Shen remarked.

"Would you like to take a look at them?" Grandmother Yang said. "Some of the teachers are out on the street watching fireworks."

Led by the two elderly matrons, an inquisitive and giggling group of women emerged from the Shens' front gates to stare at the strangers.

The new tenants were gathered outside the front gate of the Eastern Residence, all young women, three foreigners, the rest Chinese. Like everyone else, they pointed up as sparks burst across the sky and covered their ears to shriek with delight when rockets exploded in deafening bangs. But there weren't any strings of red paper tubes hanging from the small gabled roof over the lintel of the Eastern Residence.

"Jialing, go see Lao-er," Grandmother Yang said, giving me a small push. "Tell him to give our new tenants a few strings of firecrackers to hang at the front gate. Lao-er can light them if their foreign religion forbids it."

"I'll go too," Anjuin said, and we ran across the road together, holding hands. Fox, once again in animal form, dashed ahead and vanished into the Western Residence.

MRS. HAO QUICKLY MADE friends with the schoolteachers' one and only servant. Maiyu was both housekeeper and washerwoman. The two women soon made a habit of sharing a half hour of gossip out by the front gate each day. I was as curious as anyone in Dragon Springs Road about the teachers who occupied the Eastern Residence and found myself sweeping the entrance area whenever the two women servants gathered there.

Maiyu admitted her work wasn't very taxing because the teachers had good habits. They kept their rooms tidy, washed their own clothes, and took turns making meals. Maiyu's main chores were to wash the bedclothes and keep the common areas clean.

"These foreign-educated women." Maiyu sighed. "Nothing is ever clean enough. You're not allowed to spit on the floors, and the floors must be swept every day. And the amount of water I have to boil! They want boiled water even for washing clothes."

"It's because they're unmarried," Mrs. Hao said. "Once they're busy with husbands and children and servants to manage, they won't be so picky."

"They won't find husbands now," Maiyu said. "Instead of finding husbands, they went to college. The old headmistress is at least fifty and even the youngest is at least twenty-two."

THE SCHOOLTEACHERS CAME and went as they pleased. They walked with confident strides, shoulders thrown back, in pairs and in groups, untroubled voices in a mix of Chinese and English that echoed down Dragon Springs Road. Anjuin frequently joined me at the front gate in the morning to watch the teachers board the hired donkey carts.

"How can they live unmarried, away from their families?" Anjuin said. She was fascinated by the schoolteachers, especially the Chinese ones. "Not even a brother or uncle to watch over them. Their families must be wealthy and very modern thinking."

Grandmother Yang finally went to call on Miss Morris. She had me collect six fresh eggs from the hens in the kitchen garden as a gift to the headmistress. She took Anjuin to the Eastern Residence with her. They returned with a square tin box of foreign biscuits, a gift from Miss Morris. Grandmother Yang had been very pleased with the foreign woman's manners.

"She's a woman of good family," she decared. "Nothing like our previous tenant. Well, Mrs. Shea was only the wife of a policeman."

She handed Kejuin a biscuit, which he downed in a single crunch. Then he reached into the tin for more. I stared at the box, so like the one my mother had used for her cosmetics. Kejuin mistook my interest in the box. He wolfed down another biscuit and grinned at me.

"MOST OF THEM aren't from wealthy families at all," Anjuin said that night from her bed. "I spoke to one of the teachers. They converted to the foreign religion, and the mission sent them to college in Hangchow. And two of the teachers got scholarships to go to college in America."

"Do you want be a teacher too?" I sensed a yearning in her voice.

A long silence. "There's no point. I am to be married."

No matter how much she might long for a different destiny, Anjuin's fate was unavoidable, as carefully stitched into her future as the threads First Wife pulled in and out of her heavy silk altar cloth.

FOX SOMETIMES VANISHED for weeks. There was no pattern to her comings and goings; they varied with the weather or simply by her whims. Once, when she returned from a particularly long journey, she had to take human form and comfort me. I sat on her lap and cried until my sobs turned into hiccups and then into giggles as we laughed together over my uncontrollable spasms.

"I thought you had gone away forever," I said between hiccups. "You were away for so long. You never tell me before you leave, either."

It's true, I lose track sometimes, she said, wiping my nose. I'll pay more attention to the passage of days from now on.

After that she always came to see me at night before setting off on her rambles, and I would know she was back when images from her travels took over my sleep. Invariably I forgot my own dreams almost as soon as my eyes opened, as though they'd been chased away by sunlight. But when Fox slid into my mind, the memories she shared of her travels stayed with me more vividly than the everyday routines of my small world. Because for a while I could be Fox, not an abandoned *zazhong* girl-child.

. . . there are watchtowers dotting the skyline, one on every peak of the mountain ridge across the plains. The towers are connected by a wall wide enough for three horses to walk abreast. Thousand-year-old ghosts are trapped in those walls. I hear them call out to their loved ones, who have been dead for almost as long as they. The undergrowth rustles and I am at the foot of the wall, out in the open chasing rabbits over an expanse of scrubby grass, my body twisting and leaping. I understand that Fox is not hunting because of hunger but for the sheer joy of speeding beneath the moon, running between copses of broadleaf trees. I stalk my prey, our shadows merging into the moon shadow of that long wall of stone that runs across the ridge for miles and miles, as far as the eye can see. . . .

. . . now I'm a thousand miles away from the wall, treading a mountain path shaded by the most ancient pines in China, their trunks gnarled and deformed by galls. Their tree spirits have departed. The decayed pine needles beneath my feet are soft and yielding. Their musty, resinous fragrance preserves the odor of other Creatures that have traveled this way. I sniff, detecting phoenix and tortoise, unicorn goat and poison-feather bird. But the scents are old, their details bleached away by age. There have been no other Creatures on this mountain for a hundred years. The pine trees on this mountain are so dense that what little sunlight finds its way in gets lost. I explore for days and the only creatures I meet are ordinary quails and ordinary monkeys. All ordinary . . .

It felt like a form of schooling, Fox sharing her travels with me. I sensed a purpose behind them as well as a searching, a need, but she wouldn't explain why she allowed me these experiences or why she made those journeys.

WHEN FOX WAS away, it was hard not to think about Anna for I daydreamed about her mysterious and wonderful fate. That Anna was safe and undoubtedly happy in the land of immortals did nothing to soften the aching in my chest every time I thought of her. I envied her, imagining what would be possible had I been able to follow her through the Door.

From the land of immortals, it would be possible to look down on China and see my mother. From the land of immortals, it would be possible to find a way to bring my mother through the Door to join me. I still dreamed of my mother even though I had trouble remembering her face now. Mostly I remembered feeling safe and loved.

After a while, I stopped waiting for the Door to reappear, waiting for it to let me in or Anna to come back out. The Western

Residence remained empty. Master Yang spoke no more of renting it out, for after Anna's disappearance, it was undoubtedly an unlucky place that no one would want.

ONE AFTERNOON WHEN I couldn't stop thinking of Anna, I wandered to the back of the Central Residence and pushed aside the bamboo slats in the fence, as we had done when she still lived there. It was a school day and the teachers were away. I peered inside each window at the Eastern Residence, curious to see how these young women lived. In every room, beds were neatly made, a clothes trunk at the foot of each. There was a desk in every room, and low bookcases lined the walls. The floors were immaculately clean.

Mrs. Shea's roses grew in the courtyard, well tended. The foreign ladies, Maiyu informed Mrs. Hao, had quite a passion for gardening. The ground beneath the roses was no longer bare and brown. There were flat purple and yellow flowers, their petals like velvet, and small pink blossoms with scalloped edges scented like cloves. Everywhere, as though scattered at random, tiny blue flowers with yellow centers. I gasped in delight. Anna's seeds had taken.

Then a hand grabbed my arm and wrenched me around. "What do you think you're doing?"

Maiyu glared down at me. I wanted to run, but her strong washerwoman's fingers gripped my shoulder, making me squirm with pain. "You know you're not supposed to be here. You're in big trouble now."

I nodded, frozen. Her eyes narrowed and then she smirked. "Make yourself useful and I won't tell anyone." She handed me a bucket. "Go to the well and fill the water barrels by the kitchen."

There were two huge water barrels, holding enough water to

wash clothes for a dozen women. I trudged back and forth for
what felt like hours, pulling and toting until my arms ached.
When the sun cast long shadows on the paving stones, I had to
speak up.

"I must go back," I said. "The Old Mistress will be awake now
and I have to wait on her."

Maiyu looked at the full water barrels and grinned. "Go. But
come back tomorrow little *zazhong*, or I'll tell Master Yang you
were sneaking around here."

FROM THEN ON, I did my share of chores each day as quickly as
possible then ran next door in the afternoon to do Maiyu's bidding. Once the water barrels were full, she made me mop floors
or clean the outhouse. She stood over me, making sure I worked
to her satisfaction. Soon the skin on my hands cracked from all
the rough work and water, making me wince each time I wrung
out the mop.

I didn't dare put a single foot wrong. I couldn't let the Yangs
know I'd been caught trespassing in their tenants' houses. Each
night I climbed into bed so tired I fell asleep before Anjuin and I
could talk, so tired I couldn't wake up to answer Fox's summons
to visit her in the Western Residence. Only in my dreams could I
visit with Fox.

I don't think you need to be so concerned, Fox said. We were in
what I now knew was the Western Residence as it had been three
hundred years ago. Maiyu is the one who's wrong to use you
this way.

Fox was a woman today, elegant and serene. The breeze lifted
her skirts and she strolled through the courtyard, a slim figure in
a drift of transparent silk, an ancient style of dress that goddesses

in paintings are depicted wearing. But a large straw hat perched on her head, wide-brimmed, wrapped in ribbons and tulle. I recognized it from one of Third Wife's foreign fashion journals.

"It was my fault," I said, miserable. "I shouldn't have looked in the windows. I shouldn't even have been in the Eastern Residence."

It's not as terrible a crime as you think, she said. You'll see.

"What are you going to do?" I said, suspicious. "Don't get me in more trouble."

I'm not the sort of common Fox who delights in mischief, she said, looking offended.

"What sort of Fox are you?" I asked. "I thought all Foxes were the same."

She yawned, showing her small white teeth and a bright pink tongue. Not at all. We're each of us different. Some humans are good at poetry, others at arithmetic. Some have no particular skills at all. It's the same with Foxes. We're individuals, each with our talents and likes and dislikes.

She patted me on the head, and before I could say anything, there was a flash of tawny fur, a rustle in the hydrangea shrubs, then silence.

IF I HADN'T been so tired, I would've heard Maiyu in the kitchen speaking with someone. I would've looked up in time to see her glare at me, her frown telling me to stay away. Instead I plodded to the kitchen door, head down, bucket sloshing.

"Who's this?" A friendly voice, perfect Chinese accents. "Why it's the Yangs' little maid."

I looked up to see the foreign headmistress.

"What are you doing, carrying water for us, little one?" she asked.

"She offered to help," Maiyu said. "Such a good child. You can go home now." Her tone betrayed anxiety.

For the first time I realized that perhaps she was as much in the wrong as I'd been, at least in the eyes of her mistress.

"How long have you been helping?" Miss Morris asked.

"Two months," I said.

"Just today," Maiyu said, at the same time.

"I see," said the foreign woman. "Thank you, my dear. I'm sure you have your own work to do. There's no need to help us here anymore."

I glanced up at Maiyu, but she shrugged without any sign of rancor.

THE NEXT DAY my worst fear came true. Miss Morris came to call on Grandmother Yang. Undoubtedly Maiyu had betrayed me and the foreign woman was here to complain. I busied myself sweeping out the rooms in Dajuin's *erfang*, wishing there was some place to hide. As I came out of the *erfang*, Mrs. Hao waved at me from the kitchen door.

"Take more hot water to the Old Mistress and the foreign lady," she hissed as I hurried over. "And when you get there, tell Ah-Jien to come back. And wipe your face before you go in."

I had to weave past most of the household to take Grandmother Yang the hot water kettle. First Wife, normally aloof, was in the chair beside Grandmother Yang, openly staring at the visitor. Beside her, Third Wife was barely holding back nervous giggles. Anjuin had an arm firmly around her half sister, a toddler who was gazing in fascination at the feather ornaments on Miss Morris's hat. I refilled the teapot and whispered to Ah-Jien that Mrs. Hao wanted her.

After Ah-Jien left, I crouched just outside the door, balanced on the balls of my feet.

"Is it true your foreign schools employ men to teach girls?" Grandmother Yang was saying.

"Yes, it's true in some schools," the headmistress replied. "At our girls' schools in China, however, all the teachers are women. At the boys' schools, all the teachers are men. We find this makes families more willing to send their children to us."

So far, it didn't seem as though Miss Morris had brought up my snooping around the Eastern Residence.

"I've heard there's a foreign hospital with women doctors," Grandmother Yang said.

"Yes, the Shanghai West Gate Women and Children's Hospital. All the doctors and nurses there are women. Both foreign and Chinese." She smiled, and despite her long nose and thin face, I thought she looked very kind.

There was murmuring at the notion of women as doctors.

"Honored Madame," the foreign woman said, "would you consider sending the girls in your household to our school? Our school prepares students for careers. Some go on to be governesses, even teachers and nurses. Others learn enough English to work in foreign households."

"My granddaughter won't need to work," Grandmother Yang said stiffly. "We arranged her marriage long ago."

Miss Morris inhaled the steam from her teacup and sighed, showing appreciation for the delicate vapors. "I do apologize. I didn't mean your granddaughter. I meant your orphan girl."

Grandmother Yang shook her head. "She's a bond servant and not worth educating."

"I would like to hire her from you," Miss Morris said. "Five days a week."

Was she hiring me to work for Maiyu? I almost crumpled to the floor in despair.

"Ah. For cleaning?" Grandmother Yang inquired, her expression alert.

"No. To attend the mission school. Until she graduates."

I lost my balance and sprawled to the ground.

CHAPTER 7

Even at that age, I knew my life was about to change.

I was only a child with no special skills, so Miss Morris didn't pay the Yangs very much for my time. But as Grandmother Yang pointed out, some cash was better than no income at all. More important, for the five days I attended school, the Yangs didn't have to feed me. The school provided breakfast, lunch, and an early supper. The school day ran much longer than at Anna's school, which finished in the early afternoon so that foreign children, unaccustomed to Shanghai's climate, could go home before the day grew too hot.

"You're earning your keep sooner than expected, Jialing," Grandmother Yang said, patting me on the head. "Make sure that foreign headmistress keeps her promise not to force their religion on you."

Anjuin was pleased for me. She also admitted to being envious.

"But Dajuin says he will show me how to do accounts," she said, "and he gave me his dictionary to help me read the newspaper. That's as much education as Grandmother thinks I need."

THE VERY NEXT morning I found myself in a donkey cart, seated between a half-dozen young women. Even though they pelted me with questions, their smiles were strained. Only one seemed genuinely friendly.

"How old are you?"

"Have you always lived with the Yangs?"

"Can you read or write at all?"

I replied in mumbles. Through the opening of the donkey cart's canvas cover I saw unfamiliar streets, glimpses of fields plowed in readiness for sowing, and a funeral procession entering a cemetery. The cart came to a halt outside a large open gate. One of the teachers, a sweet-faced young woman who told me to call her Teacher Lin, helped me off the cart and took my hand.

"I'll take you to Miss Morris," she said. "Our headmistress arrives earlier than anyone."

Teacher Lin led me through the front courtyard, where the smell of cooking oil and steamed rice indicated the school kitchen was nearby. She pointed out the classrooms to me, four long buildings arranged in a quadrangle around a large courtyard of hard-packed dirt, the playground. The main house at the far end was huge, five bays wide and two stories high, the library and teachers' offices. We entered through the center bay, a deep hall with a staircase. Upstairs, Teacher Lin knocked on a door.

"Come in," Miss Morris's voice called out.

Inside, a room that was utterly foreign. I stood on a strange, thick woven cloth. The windows were covered with curtains in a stiff, striped fabric and instead of being whitewashed, the walls were pale blue. The chairs were high-backed, and a long seat completely covered with padded fabric was pushed against one wall. Against the wall opposite stood a chest of drawers with brass handles. The pictures on the wall were very odd, their backgrounds dark and murky instead of white. I was so busy staring I didn't realize the teacher was no longer in the room and I was alone with the foreign headmistress.

Miss Morris opened one of the brass-handled drawers.

"Come over here, Jialing," she said, holding out what looked like a length of blue cloth.

Did she want me to sew for her? Sewing wasn't my best skill.

She held it against my shoulders and I realized it was a tunic. Then she pulled out a pair of dark blue trousers and a white blouse. "Try these on."

The tunic was warmly padded and came just below my knees. The clothes were new, so new the musty scent of indigo still clung to the cloth. These were the first new clothes I'd ever worn, not made over from other garments or hand-me-downs from Anjuin.

"Come," she said and held out her hand. "I will introduce you to your classmates."

When we entered the dining hall, every head turned. So many girls. They all stood up.

"Good morning, Headmistress," they chorused, and sat down again.

"Good morning, girls," she replied. "This is your new classmate, Zhu Jialing. Please make her welcome."

She guided me to where Teacher Lin sat at the head of a table. Without being told, all the girls shuffled along the bench to make room for me. An older girl deposited chopsticks and a bowl of boiled rice congee in front of me. The girl beside me poured a cup of soy milk and set it down by the bowl. I looked at the teacher.

"Eat while it's hot, Jialing."

The congee was delicious. It had been cooked in chicken broth and was full of chopped green vegetables, more like soup than porridge. Before I finished eating, Teacher Lin stood up and addressed the girl beside me.

"Classes begin in five minutes. Little Ning, take our new student with you to the classroom."

The girls stood up as the teachers left the dining room. There was silence again as they looked at me. I realized we all wore the same uniform and felt pride rush over me. For the first time, I felt as though I belonged. I smiled at Little Ning, but before I could say anything, she spoke.

"Listen carefully, little *zazhong*." She almost spit out the words. "Follow me to class like Teacher said. After that, don't come near me again. You stick with them."

She pointed at the corner, and my eyes followed.

There were three of them. One was like me, with dark brown hair and very pale skin. She was the youngest of the three. The tallest one had black hair, a broad forehead that jutted out over her eyes, and a square, mannish jaw. Most unusual looking of all was the girl with light brown hair whose skin was as golden as bamboo shoots. There was a sprinkling of freckles across her nose that made me think of Anna.

Zazhong.

Little Ning left me at the door of a classroom. I hesitated, then the youngest of the three girls, the one with pale skin, ran up and tugged me by the hand. She pulled me to a seat at the back of the room.

"Don't talk in class unless the teacher asks you a question," she whispered. "I'll introduce you to the others at recess." She flashed me a smile, but her friendliness wasn't enough to reassure me. I was still shaken by Little Ning's hostility.

THE THREE LIVED at the mission's orphanage next door to the school. They had been given foreign names. Mary, Leah, Grace. Names that felt strange on my tongue. A part of me wanted to shun their company, to show the rest of the girls that I wasn't like them, that I wasn't one of them. At the same time I recognized that if I didn't accept their friendship, I would have no one.

"*Zazhong* is an ugly word," said Mary, who was the oldest, the one with the square chin. She was fourteen, a year younger than Anjuin. "None of us are supposed to use it. The teachers say we are *hun xue*, mixed race."

The one who reminded me of Anna was Leah, who was eleven years old. The one named Grace was nine, my age.

At lunch, we sat by ourselves at the end of a table. The older students took turns serving meals, and our bowls held less rice, our soup fewer pieces of meat. At the playground, balls were snatched away from us, skipping ropes snaked out to trip us.

"Teacher Lin made a small speech once, telling our classmates to be kind to everyone, especially the more unfortunate," Grace said. "It only made things worse when the teachers' backs were turned."

"The teachers don't really like us either," Leah said. "You can tell because they try too hard to be nice. We make them uncomfortable. Both the foreign teachers and the Chinese ones. Miss Morris and Teacher Lin are the only ones who truly don't mind that we're *hun xue*."

Mary, the oldest, had no name before coming to the orphanage. She had been called "Girl" by the woman who raised her, a woman she had called Auntie, now dead.

Leah had been left at the orphanage door three years ago. Her mother was dead. That's all she would say. She showed no interest in any of our lessons except for English.

Grace wasn't an orphan. Her mother paid for her to attend the school and live at the orphanage. Her mother had been a prostitute, but now ran a food stall by the wharves on the Huangpu River. She came every month to pay school fees and visit Grace. Grace spoke of her mother without any embarrassment. Many of the orphans were daughters of prostitutes.

"You're so lucky," I said to Grace. To have a mother. To be wanted. What did it matter if her mother had worked in a brothel?

"You're lucky too," Mary said. "You may be a servant, but you live with a family. And your friend Anjuin sounds nice. They're not really unkind to you, are they?"

"And your mother is probably still alive," Grace added kindly. "When you're older, you can look for her."

She was only trying to be helpful.

CHAPTER 8

February 1911, Year of the Pig

At the start of the New Year, Master Yang and Dajuin returned from the barber, each carrying a brown paper package. Rather sheepishly, they handed the bundles to Grandmother Yang, who gazed at them both in shock. The men had cut off their queues, and the packages contained their pigtails, each neatly tied at the ends. Grandmother Yang wept at the sight of their shorn locks and wouldn't speak to them for the rest of the day.

The imperial government had decreed all men must cut their queues by the end of the year. They didn't want the rest of the world to regard China as backward. Influenced by the West, some men had cut off their hair even before the edict became official.

"I didn't do it because of the law or to be in fashion," Dajuin said. "With all the machinery at the mill, it's just safer to have short hair."

The household went outside to enjoy the fireworks. Grandmother Yang had made sure we all had something new to wear and mine was a winter jacket that Anjuin had outgrown, made "new" with knot buttons and fresh cuffs to replace the worn ones. Master Yang greeted neighbors and replied with good-natured retorts to jokes about his hair.

Fox joined the dragon dancers who were winding their way from house to house. Today she looked no more than fifteen; her face was painted white, her lips red as cherries, and there were bright ribbons woven into her pigtails. The turquoise blue satin of her trousers lifted as she ran, revealing brown leather button boots.

"May the Year of the Pig bring prosperity to your family," Master Yang said, bowing as he did every year to Master Shen, our elderly neighbor.

Master Shen looked out at the festivities with his usual gloomy expression. "Heaven has not been kind this year to our emperor."

Coming from Master Shen, that's almost treason, Fox whispered. She skipped past, a tambourine in her hand.

In a country as large as ours, calamities are routine. There was always an earthquake somewhere, a flood, or a famine. The past year, however, had brought more than the usual disasters, culminating with an epidemic of rheumatic plague in Manchuria. These were signs that the emperor had lost heaven's favor. But such opinions were best held close.

At supper, Master Yang gave his usual speech to the household.

"Dajuin has worked hard to find more customers for our cotton mill, and we will hire a new foreman. Our new tenants have been prompt with the rent. We can look forward to prosperity, if we're careful."

I was old enough now that I'd become sensitive to the ebb and flow of fortunes at the Yangs. I paid more attention to the tidbits I overheard from servants and the Yangs about the cotton mill. Everything revolved around its success. When things went well there, Master Yang was jovial and talkative. There was more meat at meals, and evening gatherings in Grandmother Yang's rooms were more convivial. When the mill had a bad month, Master Yang came home and went directly to his study, emerging only to eat supper.

Of late the factory's profits were barely sufficient to cover the monthly payments for Master Yang's bank loan. His brothers in Ningpo wrote anxious letters, letters that grew more accusing as the months went by.

First Wife fetched these letters from Master Yang's study while he was at the mill and brought them to Grandmother Yang, who read them carefully before First Wife put them back in Master Yang's desk. Then First Wife would seek out Mrs. Hao to bemoan her fate. Together the two women commiserated. They took no more notice of me than if I'd been a cobweb.

"Cousin Hao, where would I be without a kinswoman to confide in?" First Wife sighed. "My family had such hopes when they betrothed me to Master Yang. At this rate, he will ruin the Yang clan."

"Now, now, it's not that bad," Mrs. Hao would say in her most soothing voice. "His brothers just worry because they can't see for themselves what goes on at the mill. Young Master Dajuin is not yet twenty but he's clever. Master Yang can rely on his son for good advice."

"My husband can't even find a reliable foreman," First Wife said.

But everyone knew that her barren womb was the true cause of her discontent.

FIRST WIFE HAD retreated into solitude. She didn't bother tutoring Anjuin anymore. When this first happened, Anjuin had tried cajoling Grandmother Yang to let her attend school.

"The emperor has built public schools for girls as well as boys," Anjuin said. "There's a middle school for girls not far from the marketplace. I'd like to go."

"You know how to use the abacus," Grandmother Yang said. "You can read the newspaper. What more do you need to be a wife and mother? Anyway, when Third Wife has her next child, you'll be too busy helping with the baby to go to school."

Anjuin left the room, her straight back betraying nothing of the disappointment on her face. I knew what she wanted because she'd told me often enough while looking through my schoolbooks. To know the difference between science and superstition. To look up at the stars and understand there was more than what folk stories could teach, to look into a magnified drop of water and see what resided within that tiny liquid world. To learn the history of other nations and understand how they had become so strong and China so scornfully weak.

"Just to know, Jialing," she said. "I don't need to use that education for my livelihood, I realize that. But just to know."

When I came home from school, I washed up dishes in the kitchen as always and swept the brick floor. The difference now was that Anjuin kept me company in the kitchen. While I cleaned, I told her about my day at school. She listened to every detail and never seemed bored. She even listened to me recite the cleanliness rules.

Wash your hands after using the chamber pot or latrine. Diseases are passed along by dirty hands.

Kitchen floors must be swept and washed down every day. Spilled food attracts vermin.

When there is food or cut fruit in a dish, you should always cover it up. Flies spread disease.

Then together, we studied at the kitchen table. She sat beside me while I did my homework. She wrote out the same assignments, inscribing her answers conscientiously on paper retrieved from her father's study. At school I took care to note the correct answers on my own papers so that Anjuin could check her work.

"You'll be a very well-educated young woman," she said, turning the pages of my notebook. It was the weekend, a quiet afternoon. Kejuin had been ordered to accompany Grandmother Yang on her visit to the temple.

There was no envy at all in Anjuin's voice, but her words gave me pause. How could it be that I, a mere bond servant, could go to school but not her, a daughter of the house? That I was the one who sat in a classroom, being given a modern education? I was even learning English.

She was twice as clever as I could ever hope to be, as capable as her older brother, Dajuin. Master Yang often said so, joking that if she had been a boy, she and Dajuin would be running the mill and he could enjoy life while his sons made a profit.

How could I tell her there were days when I hated the privilege she yearned for?

Instead I picked up the water bucket and a bamboo ladle. "Let's go look at my flowers."

I had planted Anna's seeds in the garden behind the main house. Anjuin and I knelt down to peer at them.

"Look!" she said, pointing. "You can barely see them, but they're sprouting little leaves."

We ladled water as gently as we could over the seedlings. I wished I could've planted them in the Western Residence, but Anjuin was so interested in the foreign flowers I had felt obliged to plant them here. And I didn't want anyone to know about the secret door.

"I DON'T LIKE school very much," I said to Fox. Little Ning's contempt, the pinches and shoves, the hisses whenever I walked too close to a group of girls.

At home, Kejuin's schoolwork was getting harder, and it kept him too busy to bully me. Lao-er had long since lost interest in mocking me. Ah-Jien's slaps came my way less often now that I understood how to do my chores. It was easy enough to sidestep First Wife and her sour looks. But at school there was no avoiding my classmates.

"Get away! Think you're as good as us, do you?" I'd flinched the first time I heard this, even though Grace was with me and tucked her arm comfortingly in mine. Such insults were the least of a litany of small cruelties.

The first of these happened the day I won a small prize for reading out loud, and the teacher gave me a new pencil, red instead of the usual yellow. Returning to my desk I'd been speechless with delight, as much for the attention as for the prize.

"Eh, Jialing," said Little Ning, to my left. "Nice reading."

Pleased, I turned my head to smile in response. How could I breathe on this spark of friendship, bring it to a cautious flame? An ember of hope warmed my heart. Turning back to my desk, I saw my prize pencil was missing. I looked on the floor beside me, pushed back my chair to look under the desk, searching on the ground until snickers burst out all around. Little Ning's words had been a distraction while another girl stole my prize.

But I didn't tell Anjuin any of this. I avoided telling her how I was shunned by all except the other *hun xue* girls. The insults I endured jabbed at me, but they hurt again each time the memories surfaced. If they could hurt so much when contained in my mind, then surely giving voice to them would hurt even more.

Fox's tail switched from side to side. *You know that Anjuin would give anything to attend school.*

"If she did, no one would call her *zazhong*," I said. "No one would make her sit with other *zazhong*."

She ignored my sullen expression. *Grandmother Yang isn't obliged to keep you forever. What will you do when you've finished school?*

"Anjuin will get married, and I'll go live with her. I'll be her maid. It's what we decided years ago."

Fox leaped on the garden seat and cocked her head. *The only thing you can count on is that the gods make other plans. Go to school. You don't have teeth or claws, so you'll have to rely on your wits. Knowledge sharpens your wits.*

She was only saying what I already knew. I couldn't avoid school. Not when Miss Morris was paying the Yangs. Not when Anjuin depended on me to pass on my lessons to her.

CHAPTER 9

I n time I stopped gawking at the three tall American teachers who taught us English. We called them "the Miss Sons" because of their names: Miss Wilson, Miss Johnson, Miss Mason. They weren't married, nor did they seem to be in a hurry to find husbands. They praised my quickness in learning English and said my accent was very good, but I never felt totally comfortable in their presence. I felt, or perhaps I imagined, both pity and condemnation in their eyes.

Fox was bemused by the American school-teachers. We watched them from the stack of old furniture. A trio of peddlers had set up shop just inside the entrance of Dragon Springs Road. A barber, a letter writer, and a food vendor. The de-licious fragrance of green onion pancakes heating on a griddle filled the street. Some of the Chinese schoolteachers were outside, their gestures persuasive, trying to get one of the Miss Sons to try one.

I watch the foreign schoolteachers in the Eastern Residence, practicing their Chinese in those funny tones, Fox said. They're so earnest, so eager to improve China. Are we in such dire need of improvement? What does wise Young Master Dajuin say?

"He says our government is one big bundle of woe," I said. "They can't agree on how to do things. Something about factions."

I suppose I should read the newspapers, she said.

"I didn't know Foxes could read," I said.

Her shrewd eyes closed in mirth. Of course we can. Why do you suppose there are so many stories about Fox spirits marrying young scholars? I've been told my calligraphy is quite good.

Out on Dragon Springs Road, the hot onion pancakes were done and the vendor handed one over to Teacher Lin.

"Miss Mason doesn't like living here," I said, watching the foreign teacher shake her head at the onion pancake, "because she thinks it's dirty. She worries about clean water and boils everything."

At school we followed a myriad of rules about cleanliness. When we helped with the orphanage's toddlers, we set the children down on little seats placed over chamber pots instead of taking them out to the street, where we could simply hold them over the drains. We weren't allowed to spit indoors. Before the mission school, I'd never seen a faucet with running water. There was a large sign by the latrine sink to wash our hands with soap before meals and after using the latrine.

You don't need to worry about clean water here, Fox said. Your wells are fed by an underground spring. It's a gift from the first and most powerful Fox spirit who lived here.

I thought this over. "Then why isn't the road called 'Fox Springs Road'?"

In the beginning it *was* called "Fox Springs Road," she said. But the humans who lived here forgot about the Fox who gave them the spring. They decided "Fox" wasn't grand enough and renamed the street.

She sniffed. Dragons and phoenixes. It's always dragons and phoenixes, even though all they do is fly around looking superior. I've never met one who bothered doing anything useful. I believe one should always broaden one's horizons. Speaking of which, do you think I should learn English? Would it be useful?

I considered this. "Our teachers say English is important. I can teach you. They say my accent is very good."

At the mission school, the teachers taught in both Chinese and English. Kejuin sneered when he found out I was learning English. Proof, he said, that I belonged with foreigners. Anjuin said he was just jealous, but it was a worry. Would a foreign language make me even more of an outsider?

Put newspapers on the altar from now on, Fox said. English newspapers too, if you can get them. No more incense. It bothers my nose, actually. We Foxes have very sensitive noses.

In time, I also learned more about my new friends. Or at least, I learned more about Grace and Mary. Leah walked away if pressed.

Grace was open and talkative, the most confident of the three. But then, Grace had a mother and a future. Her father was British. He worked on a riverboat that carried goods up and down the Yangtze. He sent money each month on the condition that Grace went to school. Once she graduated, Grace would help her mother at the food stall. There were many such stalls on the river, all serving cheap meals to workmen and sailors.

"My father wants me to learn English," she said, "so that he can talk to us. My mother says if I can chat to foreign sailors, it will bring her more business and she won't have to sell me to a brothel."

She said "brothel" so casually, with none of the hushed and outraged tones that accompanied the word when pronounced by First Wife.

"Have you ever met your father?" I asked.

"Only a few times when I was small, so I don't remember him."

Sometimes when I climbed into the donkey cart to go home at the end of the day, I would see Grace just inside the school gates, peering up the street. Once, just once, when Teacher Lin forgot her books and we waited for her to get them, I saw a rickshaw pull up and Grace run up to meet it. A plump woman got off and knelt to enfold Grace in her embrace, then swung her onto the rickshaw. I watched the two of them as the rickshaw went past, their smiles mirrored in each other's faces, reflections of pure joy.

Unbidden, an image came to mind. My mother, kneeling down with arms outstretched, her face lit up with the same smile. She had loved me. Why had she abandoned me?

Grace's father hadn't abandoned her mother. He had acknowledged Grace as his daughter, had even given her mother money to leave the brothel and open a food stall. Did my foreign father know about me? Did he even know he had a child?

"What about you, Jialing?" Grace's voice broke into my thoughts. "How did Miss Morris pick you to come here?"

I told them about Maiyu, how she had made me work every afternoon until the skin on my hands cracked. How Miss Morris had seen me hauling water and negotiated with Grandmother Yang.

"So much hard work," I said. "And then I'd have to go back and do more cleaning at the Yangs'."

There was silence, and then Grace burst into laughter. "Oh, Jialing, you don't know how silly that sounds, your idea of hard work. Mary, show her your hands."

Mary held her hands out to me, skin covered in lumpy scars. Many of the orphans wore uniforms that were too large for them, clothing to grow into. I always thought Mary didn't bother rolling up her sleeves because she didn't mind them being too long. Now I realized she hid her hands on purpose.

"From my days at the silk factory," she said, with a grimace. "They made me dip my hands in hot water."

Until Mary was eight, she had lived with a woman she called Auntie. Auntie's husband was a gambler and opium sot. One day, he dragged Mary and Auntie to a silk thread factory in Chapei and bonded them to pay his debts.

The air in the factory stank; the smell came from the floor, which was puddled with the carcasses of silkworms rotting into slimy messes. Mary and the other children stood over vats of boiling water filled with silk cocoons.

"They told us children have more sensitive hands," she said, "so we can tell more quickly when a cocoon is ready to unwind. We had to plunge our hands into the water to test the cocoons."

If they hesitated, the foreman's bamboo cane whipped their calves, drawing blood. An open cut meant infection and possibly death.

After fourteen hours at the factory each day, they returned home to make supper for Auntie's husband and sleep a few scant hours before going to work again. Auntie had been pregnant when her husband bonded them. A few months into this punishing life, Auntie went into labor while at the factory. The foreman gave Mary permission to help but said they'd both have to make up for lost time the next day.

"Auntie gave birth behind the silk thread factory," she said. "It was a girl. She pushed the baby's face into the mud, and when it was dead, I put it in the garbage pit. Then she got up and we went back to work."

"Why didn't Auntie take the baby to an orphanage?" I asked, aghast.

Mary regarded me, mild astonishment on her face. "We couldn't afford more time away from work. Auntie said that we should pray for the baby to be reincarnated into a better life."

But the next day, Auntie collapsed and couldn't go to the factory. The neighbors shamed Auntie's husband into taking her to the foreign hospital nearby. He left his wife on the steps and hurried away. That was where Miss Morris found Mary, watching her only protector die. That was all Mary would say about her past.

It WAS MY turn to clean the blackboards and tidy the classroom. Teacher Lin and I had both finished lunch early and she was at her desk correcting papers. I swept the floor, unable to stop thinking about Mary's dead auntie.

"I've finished, Teacher Lin," I said. "Is there anything else you'd like me to do?"

"No, Jialing," she said. "But you seem worried today. What's troubling you?"

I hesitated, looking down at my cloth shoes. New, black, provided by the school. I didn't even know how to express my confusion. She took my hand, which was dusty with chalk.

"It's about Mary," I finally said. "Her auntie's husband made them work at a factory."

"Yes, I know."

"Why didn't her auntie refuse to work at the factory?" I asked.

She sighed. "For many reasons, Jialing, but the main one is that her husband was in debt and needed the bond money to pay off his creditors. Her auntie was raised to believe that women must always obey their husbands, even if they are selfish or unkind."

As Anjuin had been raised. Anjuin, whose main hope was that her future husband would be a kind and sensible man. Now I suspected that whatever her worries, she couldn't begin to imagine the cruelties my classmates had survived.

I had heard of sisters sold off so that fathers could fill their opium pipes one more time. Like Mary, some had worked in factories to pay family debts. Many had begged on the streets. Too many had seen parents and siblings die.

My days of sweeping, emptying chamber pots, and washing diapers were light work compared to what others had survived. If not for the mission, if not for the Yangs, I would've starved. Worse, I could've ended up in a factory.

I looked up from my shoes and saw Teacher Lin regarding me with a sad smile. "You may not need to worry about marriage at all. Perhaps that's not a bad thing, so long as you have a livelihood. Study hard and get into the mission's college for teachers."

EACH DAY, RIDING to and from school, I learned more about my teachers.

At first I just listened. I never dared speak unless spoken to. I could tell they were being careful, conscientious even, to discuss only topics they felt suitable for my young and inquisitive ears, so their conversation tended to the ordinary, never any gossip about my classmates or other teachers. They spoke English if there was anything they really wanted to keep secret, but as the years went by, they grew accustomed to my presence and I understood more of their English.

I learned that Miss Morris was an American heiress whose private money funded nearly all the school and orphanage's expenses. The school and orphanage were part of Unity Mission, the missionary arm of an American church. Miss Morris was headmistress, orphanage supervisor, and patron. There were a number of other girls like me, whose families she paid to let them attend school.

Teacher Lin hoped I would convert to the foreign religion when I was older, but it was the one thing I couldn't do. Wouldn't do. Even though it prevented me from attending the Mission's college for teachers.

Grandmother Yang had refused Miss Morris's offer at first. She didn't want me to attend the mission school. I was her good deed. By taking me in, she was earning merit for her next reincarnation. If she allowed foreigners to convert me to their religion, it might harm her prospects for the next life.

"We don't force religion on our students," Miss Morris had replied, very patiently. "If we did, families would never send us their children. We want the girls to get an education, to have a better future. It's up to them whether they convert."

"Well, then," Grandmother Yang had said after a long pause. "Then she can go. I don't mind you having a different god, Miss Morris. But I hear he doesn't allow his followers to worship other gods. How can a god have such a narrow heart?"

After Miss Morris left, Grandmother Yang beckoned to me. "Jialing, if they make you swallow the flesh and blood of their god, run back home right away."

The Yangs' goodwill mattered more to my survival than the mission school, so I obeyed. And true to her word, neither Miss Morris nor the teachers pressured me to adopt their religion. They urged me, along with all the girls whose families didn't want them to become Christians, to be open-minded and to convert once we truly felt we understood what it meant to love their god.

Every so often, Grandmother Yang would quiz me just to make sure I wasn't feeling tempted to throw in my lot with the Christian god.

"What's another god, more or less?" she'd say, shaking her head. "It hardly matters, there are so many already. I'm sure Miss Morris's temple would gain more followers if they weren't so stubborn on this point."

The only time I felt any real pressure was when Teacher Lin spoke to me before her wedding. Once she married, she would join her missionary husband in Soochow. I couldn't imagine a school day without her, without her kind words or the way she looked as me as though I was no different from any other.

"I know how hard it is for you and the others, Jialing," she said. "I hope you can forgive the girls who've been harsh to you. Some have lived terrible lives and seen much cruelty. All I ask is that when you're older, when you're no longer dependent on the Yangs, to think about putting your life in the hands of our Lord. Do it from the heart and your own free will."

I wanted so much to please her, this young woman with the earnest eyes and sweet voice. But all I could do was nod.

"Only from the heart, Jialing," she said. "I don't want you to be a rice Christian."

She saw my puzzled look. "There are poor folk who convert to Christianity because they want the church to feed them and find them work. In times of hunger, their numbers swell. In times of prosperity, they melt away and return to the gods they've always known."

"But I've seen many wealthy Chinese at church." Sometimes Miss Morris took the school's music class to sing at churches, where audiences included Chinese Christians. They didn't seem poor to me.

"That's more recent." Teacher Lin was silent for a moment. "When foreign missionaries first came to China, many resented them because it was foreigners who forced us to buy their opium, foreigners who occupied the Forbidden City, and foreigners who made our emperor open treaty ports. Good families wanted nothing to do with them. But now, students are returning from Europe and America filled with Western knowledge and the word of God. Perhaps it will be easier from now on."

There were many things about the foreign god I found difficult to understand. For one thing, I'd always believed every god had a special responsibility. Women who wanted sons prayed to the Goddess of Mercy at the Temple of the City God. Those who wanted a good reincarnation for loved ones prayed to the statue of the Buddha at Jing'an Temple on Bubbling Well Road. How could a single god find the time to answer the prayers of every single supplicant?

"But the girls who convert, they're no different afterwards," I said to Fox.

She was in her animal shape. We were sitting on the roof of the main house in the Western Residence, looking across a landscape from three hundred years ago. There was no Chung San Road, no shops, no other houses, just a few farm cottages scattered amid fields crisscrossed by irrigation ditches. A crescent moon glowed from behind a curtain of cloud, and an owl patrolled the countryside, its shadow moving swift and dark across the frosted ground.

"The girls who were nice before are still nice," I continued. "The ones who were mean are still mean when the teachers aren't around. And now Mary is converting because she wants to attend the mission college."

Ah. Is it from the heart? Does she truly believe?

I paused to consider. "I think she believes she will truly believe one day. She says she has no hope of a decent life if the mission doesn't help her."

What about you, Jialing? And suddenly Fox's eyes glowed green. In the distance, the owl swooped. It came up in a glide, hooting in triumph.

"Their god is mistaken," I said, confident. "How can there be no other gods or immortals or spirits? Here you are to prove them wrong. Fox, if you showed yourself to Teacher Lin or Miss Morris, they would see how wrong they are."

She shook her head. They wouldn't be able to see me because they truly believe in their own, exclusive god.

"Master Yang prays at the Buddhist temple because it pleases his mother," I said, "and at the start of each New Year, he hires Daoist priests to cleanse his home and factory of evil influences. Why doesn't he pray to Foxes?"

Perhaps he doesn't feel it's proper to pray to a Fox, she said. We're an odd sort of spirit, not deity, not demon. Not human, not fox. Perhaps that's why I like you, little *hun xue*. Neither one of us is fully one thing or another.

A bat dipped past us, so close I could see the outline of its ears. I could only see it so clearly because Fox was sharing her sharp vision with me.

Thousand of years ago, she said, Foxes were omens of good fortune. Since then we've have been called celestial beings, sorcerers, and demons. Some Foxes strive to attain enlightenment, to become true deities. Others enjoy the companionship of humans and remain common animal spirits.

"Most of the stories I've read are about Foxes who bewitch men."

Well, of course. She laughed, a sharp yipping sound. Since it's men who write the tales. If you believed only what the stories say, you'd think we do nothing but wreak mischief.

BY THIS TIME, my mother's face had grown indistinct in my memory. Recollections of our life in the Western Residence had settled into the depths of my mind like leaves drifting to the silt at the bottom of a pond. After a while, I could remember only a few meager details. A tiny shoe I used to play with. How my mother had loved the color green and that persimmons were her favorite fruit. I held on to an image of pale slim hands rubbing a cream made from powdered pearls into her skin. I could recall separate features, her small nose and the mole just beside her lower lip, eyebrows curved so perfectly above deep brown eyes, the span of her cheekbones, and the whiteness of her forehead. But no matter how hard I tried, I couldn't assemble them into a whole.

The emerald-green tunic had been too small for years, but I refused to part with it. It stayed at the bottom of a wooden box that served as my trunk. Once, when Third Wife unwrapped a bar of soap scented with orange blossom, I couldn't explain why I burst into tears.

I learned that if I didn't disturb those dark waters, I could almost convince myself that my life began on the day Anjuin found me. It was just easier to live that way until I had the means to search for my mother.

As for Anna, her freckles and smiles remained vivid in my memories. My little garden had bloomed with small, exotic flowers. Purple and yellow, fragrant and pink, a scatter of blue.

"You can collect the seeds later," Anjuin said, showing me the tiny pods. "Or take cuttings. I'm not familiar with these plants. But we can try to grow more."

When Anjuin and I stood hand in hand beside the small patch of ground, admiring Anna's flowers, those were my moments of perfect contentment. I forgot about my mother, about the bullies at school, about my uncertain future.

FOX ENJOYED SCHOOL even if I didn't.

From time to time in the playground, I would catch glimpses of a girl who always gave me a wink as she ran past. I saw her laughing in games of tag or chanting rhymes with her playmates as she skipped rope, pigtails flying. I didn't think anyone else saw the Fox shadow romping behind her. During classes, if I looked from the corner of my eye, I would see her at the back of the room, head bent industriously over a book, pink tongue thoughtfully licking the end of a yellow pencil.

She especially enjoyed it when the kitchen served our monthly Western-style meals, which we ate from plates using foreign cutlery so that we could learn foreign table manners. She giggled at the table, using her fork to stab at a soft mound of potatoes.

But afterward, no one could ever recall seeing such a girl.

I slipped away only occasionally now to visit Fox in the Western Residence, on nights when a full moon lit the pebbled paths and I could make my way there without a lamp. I would tiptoe out of the house and slip through the door under the garden shed. Anjuin never woke up, nor was I ever discovered coming or going, even by First Wife, who was a light sleeper. That was probably Fox's doing.

More often these days, we met while I was asleep. It was easier. She appeared frequently as a woman. She rarely wore ancient garb now and tried out clothing more familiar to my eyes. She was fond of a Manchu-style tunic in dark brown worn over black trousers, the sleeves embroidered with bands of yellow chrysanthemums.

Fox obviously studied the teachers next door because for several months she materialized in a long tunic over a fashionable paneled skirt. Sometimes she even appeared in foreign clothing, a white blouse with long puffy sleeves and lace around the collar, a plain dark skirt just long enough to hide the laces of her leather boots.

When she took over my dreams, we might walk through nearby fields or through memories of her travels. If she brought me to the Western Residence, we would chat and she would tell me what it was like to be a Fox.

There has been a Fox in residence in this spot for the past thousand years. I am but the latest.

"Why do you stay?" I asked. "You could live anywhere, see any place in China."

. . . and suddenly I'm stretched out in the den behind the white hydrangeas, looking out. We're still in the Western Residence and the purple wisteria is still in bloom, but there is a lived-in look about the courtyard. A pair of carved stools on the veranda, the sound of footfalls from the main house, the smell of roasting meat.

A young man and woman stroll into the courtyard. From their features I can tell they are brother and sister, the family resemblance is so strong. They're not handsome, but they're pleasing to look at, kindness and contentment in their smiles. From their clothing and Fox's nudges in my mind, I know I am seeing her earliest memories of the Western Residence, three hundred years ago.

I listen to the young man recite the classics. He's here at the family's seldom-used country estate to study for the imperial exams. He reads out loud the essays he's composed. He's talented but inattentive. His sister, who is more accomplished but ineligible for the imperial exams, tries to help him memorize the lessons, but verses and quotes slip out of his mind like minnows escaping a net.

Finally, Fox can't stand his bumbling efforts anymore. I'm still Fox but I'm also watching Fox as she comes out from the kitchen carrying an iron teapot. She wears the garb of a maidservant and enters the study. She bows slightly to the siblings, exchanges their cold tea for a fresh pot. The young man gazes after her, color rising in his cheeks.

"The new maid, Brother," the young woman says, laughing. "Don't let her distract you. The imperial examinations are why we're here."

But of course he falls under Fox's influence. With her help he studies more conscientiously, his mind guided to concentration. He remembers everything in his books. His infatuation with Fox is not surprising to me; it's an essential part of every story about relationships between Foxes and young men. The young man is besotted with Fox, oblivious to her true nature.

What's not expected is that Fox and his sister become close friends. The sister, wiser than her sibling, discerns Fox's true identity.

The young man returns from the imperial examinations, which he has passed with great distinction. He takes Fox into the family as his concubine, the best he can do, given the difference in their stations, but he treats her with all the honor due a Second Wife. He divides his time between his ancestral home, with his clan, and the country estate where Fox lives. His beloved but unmarried sister moves here to live with Fox. Fox's husband frequently brings his First Wife and their children when he visits. Many happy and harmonious years go by.

Then the inevitable happens. The First Wife grows jealous of

Fox. While the human woman's figure is shapeless as a sack from childbearing and the skin below her cheeks has sagged, Fox has not aged one bit in all this time.

When their husband is away, the First Wife comes to the Western Residence bringing with her a Daoist priest. The priest's spells force Fox back into her animal shape and he gives chase. He would have killed her, but the sister opens the secret door, which in those days was not secret but just a side door opening to the fields. Fox runs out and doesn't come back. Even after the jealous wife dies, Fox doesn't come back, no matter how much incense her husband burns to win her attention.

Decades pass, and there comes a time of great lawlessness. The clan retreats to their country estate and builds a high wall to enclose the entire property. Huge gates on brick piers protect the entrance to the strip of ground that is now Dragon Springs Road. Tenant farmers come inside to defend against the bandits.

A premonition of danger brings Fox back. Bandits are scaling the walls. Her now-elderly husband is wounded and his sons are outside getting slaughtered. Fox comes into the Western Residence just as her sister-in-law begs the gods to intervene.

The Door appears. It's the first time Fox has ever seen such a thing.

The sounds of battle, the clash of metal and screams of dying men fade away. There is music and the scent of peach blossom and a soft breeze that pushes away smoke from burning houses. Brother and sister drag themselves through. Fox runs to follow, but the Door closes too quickly and shuts in her face.

Fox lies on the paving stones. Rain like needles, sharp and cold, falls on her thick fur until she is soaked through, her delicate bones visible beneath the wet pelt. . . .

You've asked why I stay here. Fox's voice echoed in my mind as I rolled over on my cot. I stay because I know of no other place in China where a Door to the land of immortals still exists. I'm waiting for the Door to open again so I can rejoin the humans I love.

CHAPTER 10

February 1912, Year of the Rat

Our young emperor abdicated.

We heard the news at school. Our teachers didn't bother keeping order but talked excitedly among themselves. The Qing Dynasty was no more. General Yuan Shikai was to organize a new government, and in the interim, Dr. Sun Yat-sen would be our president. Our foreign teachers were jubilant.

"A Christian president for China!" exclaimed Miss Mason. She gave us a copy of the *Shanghai Daily News* to pass around. "You'll remember this day forever. I feel so privileged to be in China on the day it became a democracy."

At home that evening, Master Yang assembled the household, servants and all, in the formal reception hall. All the newspapers had printed the abdication decree, and his voice trembled as he read it out loud.

*The Whole Country is tending toward a republican form
of government. It is the Will of Heaven, and it is certain
that we couldn't reject the people's desire for the sake of
one family's honor and glory.*

*We, the Emperor, hand over sovereignty to the people.
We decide the form of government to be a constitutional
republic.*

*In this time of transition, in order to unite the South
and the North, We appoint Yuan Shikai to organize a provisional government, consulting the people's army regarding the union of the five peoples: Manchus, Han Chinese,
Mongolians, Mohammedans and Tibetans. These peoples
jointly constitute the great State of the Republic of China.*

*We now retire to a peaceful life and will enjoy the re-
spectful treatment of the nation.*

Weeping, Grandmother Yang retired to her room, followed by
First Wife.

Out on Dragon Springs Road, Dajuin and Master Yang joined
the neighbors who had collected outside to debate what this meant
for China. Even the women were out on the street, Old Mistress
Shen leaning on her cane and interrupting her husband.

Dajuin was thrilled, Master Yang skeptical and gloomy. I saw
Fox in human form weaving through the street, pausing at each
of the small gatherings. She shifted through different shapes: an
elderly man, a stout female servant, a curious child. No one would
remember her.

"China should be proud," Dajuin said. "This change of government has been a peaceful transfer of power."

"What, are you forgetting all that went on before?" old Master

Shen exclaimed. His goatee fairly wobbled with indignation. "The Taiping Rebellion, the Boxers, the Wuchang Uprising?"

"What I meant was that the handover from empire to republic was politically negotiated," Dajuin said, bowing to the elderly man. "It happened through legal means instead of civil war. There's much to celebrate. A man of great integrity leads as interim president until our new government can hold a formal election."

Dajuin and Kejuin went out to Chung San Road, where a joyous mob thronged the streets late into the night. Kejuin returned shouting, "*Sanmin zhuyi! Sanmin zhuyi!*" He was so excited he even grabbed my hands and swung me around before running up to Third Wife's rooms.

"What does it mean?" I asked Anjuin. "*Sanmin zhuyi?*"

"The Three People's Principles," she replied, pointing to an essay in the newspaper. "Nationalism, democracy, and livelihood."

The next day, Grandmother Yang called me to her room. I was no longer a bond servant. The new government had abolished the practice. I didn't have to buy back my contract anymore. Grandmother Yang's bargain with Miss Morris ended on the day of my graduation from the mission school, and the Yangs would carry no further responsibility for me.

In reality, I was still a bond servant in every other way. What else do you call a servant who is wholly dependent upon her employers?

MISS MASON'S JUBILATION WAS short lived. Dr. Sun Yat-sen lost the presidency. Without military backing, he couldn't hold on to power. To avert a potential civil war, he ceded leadership to the only man in China who could keep order. The powerful general

Yuan Shikai was sworn in as our provisional president until the new government could hold formal elections.

"This is terrible," Dajuin said, throwing down the newspaper. "Yuan is exactly the wrong sort of man. He cares nothing for democracy."

Uncertainty is bad for business, and for months, the cotton mill suffered. The household suffered with it, and I was glad to be at school all day, away from Grandmother Yang's irate impatience and First Wife's sharp tongue.

THE LIVELIEST PLACE in the Central Residence was the nursery, where Third Wife's new baby son slept and played. Third Wife was now mother to three children, two sons and a daughter. Anjuin spent as much time as she could there. Between Anjuin, Amah Wu, and the wet nurse, Third Wife hardly had to care for her own children.

"You'll make such a good wife and mother," Third Wife said to Anjuin.

Anjuin, who was holding the baby on her lap, looked up and smiled. "I'm lucky to have younger brothers and sisters to practice on."

"Oh dear," sighed Third Wife. "What will we do when you are married and gone? I supposed I'll have to be more diligent about the housekeeping. Unless First Wife comes out of her melancholy."

First Wife had become increasingly eccentric. She had come to the nursery only once to congratulate Third Wife on the birth of her son. Although it was her right as First Wife to run the household, she withdrew more and more from the family. She spent her waking hours embroidering obsessively on a huge altar cloth of heavy red silk but never seemed content with her work, for each time she completed a section of embroidery she would pick it apart to start over again until the heavy red silk was perforated with tiny needle holes. The embroidered figures she stitched were of little boys, each dressed differently, each in a different pose. One played with a ball, another chased a small dog, one napped under a tree.

"She's making a 'hundred boys altar cloth' for the temple," Anjuin replied when I first thought to ask.

Between the servants and Third Wife, it had been easy enough to learn First Wife's story.

First Wife was barren. Despite the herbal remedies and nourishing broths she consumed to balance her body's energies, all her efforts were futile. Because of this, Master Yang took a second wife, the woman who had been Dajuin and Anjuin's mother. After Second Wife died in childbirth, Master Yang married Third Wife, and the cheerful young woman had become pregnant almost immediately with Kejuin.

After Kejuin was born, First Wife began making weekly visits to the temple, where she burned incense and prayed with fanatical fervor. Master Yang had suggested she adopt one of their many nephews.

"My duty is to give you a son of my own body," she wept, when he made the suggestion. It was no shame for childless women to adopt a child from another branch of the clan, but she refused. This was the first sign that she wasn't behaving normally.

Then a nun at the temple gave her some advice. If First Wife embroidered an altar cloth with the images of one hundred baby boys and made an offering of the cloth, she would bear a son. First Wife began this needlework in Ningpo and was still working on it when the Yangs came to Dragon Springs Road. She picked apart what she stitched, working and reworking, as if afraid to complete the cloth.

First Wife's despair made her bad tempered. Only Mrs. Hao could soothe her. Without sons, First Wife's position meant little. Master Yang was too kind to put her aside, but she had less status than Third Wife, and even the servants were sometimes slow to do her bidding. I was one of the few she could bully. Whatever I did was less than adequate. First Wife's criticisms were loud and frequent, and never louder than when in front of Grandmother Yang.

"You dawdle too much, girl. By the time you bring the hot water, it's only lukewarm," was one of her frequent complaints. "This never happened when I waited on your mistress."

How First Wife, on her tiny bound feet, could've run any faster from the kitchen to Grandmother Yang's rooms was beyond me.

"She could've finished that altar cloth years ago," I said to Fox, "if she didn't pick out the stitches all the time."

Fox raised one perfect eyebrow. If she finished the cloth, she would have to produce a son.

MARY WAS LEAVING our school. Now eighteen, she stood with her classmates under a banner that read CONGRATULATIONS TO THE CLASS OF 1914. She had been accepted to the mission's training college. When she converted to Christianity two years ago and announced her intent to become a missionary, I'd been tempted to do so as well because our teachers had made such a fuss over her. Her elevated status after her baptism seemed to have faded the taint of being *hun xue*. After lunch and during her free hours, she and the other girls who were going on to college would study together in the library. Without abandoning us, she had managed to enter a different circle.

"Some of them convert out of gratitude," she said, of other orphans. "Some think they have to or else be forced to leave the orphanage."

Now, watching her say her farewells, I still couldn't be sure of Mary's sincerity. Was it for the sake of a livelihood? To remain within the safety of the missionary community? Yet knowing her, her sober nature, I couldn't imagine her taking up rice Christianity.

"Good-bye, Jialing," Mary said. "Study hard. Girls like us must keep as many doors open as possible. You may need college one day."

She said this even though she knew my test scores would never win me a place in college, let alone a scholarship. She gave Grace a quick hug, Leah a longer one. Then she joined the others on the donkey cart, and they rode off to the train station. The other girls' expressions were excited, hopeful; Mary's impassive.

FOX NEVER SPOKE of my mother even though she must've been watching us for all the years we lived here. Nor would she talk about the world beyond the Door where Anna had vanished. In Fox's presence, most of my questions melted out of my mind.

There's only so much you need to know for now, she would say.

I did try to overcome her influence. Once I wrote down several questions, thinking that if they were on paper, I could read them out to her the next time I went to the Western Residence. All that happened was that I forgot the list was in my pocket. After that, I gave up. Obviously there were questions she didn't want to answer and I couldn't prevail against her will.

She did answer some questions though. "Fox, how many human husbands have you had?"

Just the one, she said. She cleaned her muzzle with a neat black paw. The trouble is that some of the younger Fox spirits take human husbands for fun. They do it to test their skills and to make a little mischief. It gives us a bad reputation.

She finished grooming and sat up straight on her haunches,

head cocked slightly to one side. It was a familiar pose, one that signaled readiness to talk about herself. I settled down on the veranda steps. Just because we were only meeting in a dream didn't mean I shouldn't make myself comfortable.

Most humans believe there's no more to Foxes than tricks and seduction. When such humans burn incense and make offerings to Fox spirits, they want to flatter us into bringing them wealth.

The more educated humans, those who bother studying the ancient texts, know better. They know some Foxes aspire to become immortal *xian*. But as every human is different, so it is with Foxes. Not all retire to remote places to meditate, for not all are ascetic or intellectual. Most are content to live close to mortals, amusing themselves by dipping in and out of human society. The less scrupulous stir up trouble.

A very old Fox once told me Foxes used to be attendants to the goddess Queen Mother of the West, she said. But we've fallen down the hierarchy since then. The best hope for lesser Foxes who want the Door to the land of immortals to open for them is to live a virtuous life. We avoid crime and offer our help to the unfortunate: the poor who have been cheated, women who've been shunted aside, the disfigured and maimed, the ostracized.

"Am I one of those?" I asked, hoping to learn more. Did Fox have a plan for me? "Are you here to help me?"

But instead, I found myself in an unfamiliar landscape. I sighed in frustration. This was one of Fox's favorite ways of deflecting my questions. I could almost see her smirk.

. . . a lake gleams blue and purple, the water so clear that when I dip my muzzle in to drink it tastes of green leaves and the faint tang of minerals from faraway glaciers. Red maples edge the banks and I trot along the pebbled shores of the lake to where it cascades over a cliff, splitting into dozens of waterfalls. The falls create smaller lakes, each tinted a different color by accumulations of glacial silt. Blue, green, and violet, the colors so pure it's hard to believe they share the same water source. I look around for the dragons that used to nest here, but they have long since departed this region. All that's left are autumn leaves of gold and rust curved like dragon scales floating on the lakes . . .

When I woke up, moonlight glowed through the lattice windows. My hearing still retained some animal acuity, and I could hear the high-pitched squeaking of bats outside. Why did Fox have to be so evasive? Her tutelage lacked the thoroughness of my school lessons, and she offered up her knowledge at erratic intervals. I thumped my pillow in frustration.

CHAPTER 11

February 1916, Year of the Dragon

Master Shen's New Year greetings were subdued. Only three years after becoming president, President Yuan had declared himself emperor at the end of 1915. Our fledgling republic was no more.

Even during this festive time, talk swung away quickly from good wishes to gossip about Yuan—his nine wives and concubines, his thirty children, the forty-thousand-piece porcelain set he had ordered from the imperial kilns for his upcoming coronation. I hung around the front gate with the other servants, listening in on the conversations as neighbors strolled up and down the street.

Dajuin predicted the military governors Yuan had appointed to each province while president would now turn against him.

"Why? Because they've become used to ruling their provinces like feudal lords," he said, in reply to a neighbor's query. "Yuan has given them an excuse to break away from the central government and to do it in the name of patriotism."

Dajuin's predictions proved true. By the New Year, nine provinces had broken away, their military governors now effectively warlords.

"You, *zazhong* girl! Get over here!" A sharp voice cut through the air, and I hurried back into the main courtyard.

Of more direct consequence to my small world was Dajuin's wife. Her name was Yun Na, and the two had been married the previous summer. We servants had enjoyed a week of liberty while the Yangs were away at the wedding, held in their ancestral town of Ningpo. The highlight of the ceremonies was a lavish banquet that had lasted six hours, which the family talked about for days after they returned.

At first we thought Yun Na was shy. Anjuin and Third Wife went out of their way to make the newcomer feel welcome. All too soon we realized she wasn't interested in sharing any of the household work with the other women. Thus Anjuin and Third Wife continued managing the household. This really meant it was Anjuin who kept the accounts and showed them to Grandmother Yang, Anjuin who took note when anything needed repair, and Anjuin who planned the meals with Mrs. Hao.

Short and imperious, Yun Na was proving a difficult addition to the family. Her shrill words disturbed quiet afternoons and a perpetual scowl dragged down her round face. With plump lips and clear skin, she was pretty enough, but that frown hardly ever left her face.

"Young Master qualifies for divine transcendence," Lao-er said, shaking his head. "His bride is more trouble than three maiden aunts."

IN MARCH, YUAN Shikai stepped off the throne. He had misjudged the mood of the country as well as the support of his foreign allies. He never had a coronation. He died in June, whether of illness or poison, we would never know.

The fate of our country meant nothing to Yun Na; she was more concerned about her parents' first visit to her new home. Anxious to make a good impression, Yun Na stirred into action. Her work consisted of pointing out which corners were dusty and which surfaces needed polishing. Fortunately this burst of activity didn't last long because she was pregnant now and tired easily.

Now fifteen, I had been helping in the kitchen for years. I was slicing cucumber for a salad while Anjuin arranged candied fruit and lotus seeds on the bottom of a shallow bowl. Mrs. Hao was making up the sweet sticky rice mixture for the eight treasures pudding that would cover the fruit. Even Third Wife was in the kitchen, scoring pieces of squid so that they would curl up in neat tubes when cooked.

We all looked up when Yun Na came sweeping into the kitchen.

"You useless creature," she said, peering at my chopping board. "Remember, it's my parents who are the guests. Those slices should be paper thin, not thick as roof tiles."

"You're very knowledgeable about cuisine, Sister-in-Law," Anjuin said, going back to her work.

"Yes, yes," Yun Na replied. "Our kitchen at home has very high standards. It was something my mother insisted on when she trained me."

"Well, perhaps you'd like to prepare the eel to make sure it's to your parents' liking," Anjuin said. "Mrs. Hao has some right here in this bucket. They're still fresh and wriggling from the rice fields."

"I'm sure Mrs. Hao is perfectly competent to cook eels in the style she does best," said Yun Na, and she flounced out the kitchen door.

Mrs. Hao and Third Wife stifled their laughter, but the incident only reminded me how defenseless I would be once Anjuin married. I might join her husband's household, but how would his family treat me?

"Your Young Master Chen is a fortunate man," Third Wife said to Anjuin. "You're already so wise. At your age I was rather short on judgment. Your husband's family will love you."

"To be treated well is all I hope for," she said. "If my husband doesn't gamble or take opium, if his parents are reasonable people, what more could I expect?"

Third Wife sighed. "I'll miss you. We'll just have to make the most of our time together for the next six months."

Six months. So close.

As the date of Anjuin's wedding drew near, I worried about the promises we had made to each other. I knew I owed the Yangs much, but I longed to be free of my dependence on them. To be free of them all except Anjuin, even though the prospect of being a maid, even one in a house where Anjuin was mistress, didn't comfort me the way it had when we were children. I didn't know what a life outside Dragon Springs Road might be like, but between school and Fox, my horizons had stretched wider than I had ever imagined possible.

As for my childish hopes of finding my mother—how was I ever to accomplish that if my fate was tied to the Yangs? Now I understood it would take money because neither fate nor Fox were about to help me. Fox had known me for years and had never mentioned my mother.

My grades were passable, my English scores very good. I

wouldn't be able to attend missionary college since I didn't qualify for a scholarship. I needed a livelihood. At school, one of the teachers had passed around a newspaper article about the Shanghai Women's Commercial and Savings Bank. The bank's new general manager was a woman.

"Perhaps I could find work there as a bank teller," I whispered to Leah.

"I wouldn't count on any job that put you in front of customers," she replied in her blunt way. "They don't want our kind waiting on them."

As Fox instructed, I had been putting newspapers on her altar. This was much simpler than stealing incense from the Yang family shrine or food from the kitchen. My old playroom in the *erfang* was where Fox stacked the newspapers that I rescued from the kindling box or from Master Yang's study. There was a small stack of English newspapers I had collected from school.

I found Fox in the *erfang* one day, head cocked to one side, staring intently at the columns of English text in the *Shanghai Daily News*. She wore a creamy lace blouse with puffed sleeves and a long skirt. Her black, glossy hair was arranged in a pompadour, but when I looked more closely, the thick coil at the back was anchored with Chinese hairpins, dangling pendants of pearls and red coral.

Translate that for me, she said, pointing at a column on the page. I'm not yet fluent in this language.

> *Shanghai Municipal Police have concluded that two deaths at the Hotel Metropole were suicide. Henry Edward Wilkins and Dorothy "Dolly" Armstrong were found together in a room at the hotel on June 5, 1916. A medical examination determined they had swallowed opium.*

Wilkins was the nephew of shipping magnate Robert Edward Hayes, owner of the Star Sapphire Line. When Mr. Wilkins announced his intention to marry Miss Armstrong, whose mother is Chinese, Mr. Hayes refused to sanction the marriage and cut off his allowance.

Miss Armstrong was the daughter of the late Dr. Charles Armstrong and his wife, Bai Qin (Betty) Armstrong (née Lin).

"I've got nothing against Eurasians," said Mr. Hayes. "But Henry was my heir. I don't want mixed-race children inheriting the business after I'm gone. All Henry had to do was marry a white girl. He could've had his pick from all of Shanghai society."

I smoothed out the newsprint and set it down on the floor. I had seen the same story in a Chinese paper, *Xinwen Bao*, accompanied by an editorial deploring discrimination against Eurasians. Whatever a sympathetic editor might say, I knew that with my mixed blood and nonexistent dowry, it was impossible to hope that I would ever marry anyone respectable. Better not to marry at all.

"Fox, have you ever wanted another human husband?" I asked.

One was enough, she said, studying the front page of the week-old paper. I find it makes life too confusing.

"Confusing?"

We're pulled in too many directions as it is, she said. By our animal natures and by our desire to emulate humans. By our affection for mortal friends and our desire to become *xian*.

"Humans are so puny compared to what you are," I said, feeling envious, "why would any Fox ever want to become human? A Fox can do everything a human can do and more."

She looked up at me, amber eyes glowing. *My powers are minor compared to what some other Foxes can do.*

"You could make me rich. Foxes in stories often bring gold to poor young scholars."

Never. Her voice was severe. *That gold always belongs to someone. The gods would put a black mark against me for stealing and it would harm my chances of going through the Door. Only weak-willed Foxes steal. Unfortunately . . .*

"Yes, yes, I know." I sighed. "Unfortunately, it's stories about bad Foxes that people remember."

NOW THAT ANJUIN was to be married, she and Third Wife became more like sisters than stepmother and stepdaughter. Third Wife was full of advice.

"Just remember that we women must work quietly and patiently," she said to Anjuin. "We suggest, we placate, we flatter. We help those who oppose us believe they're the ones who've made wise choices."

Third Wife usually managed to get what she wanted. She exaggerated her girlish behavior to please Master Yang, who could always be jostled into a good mood by her little jokes.

"I won't mind how the Chens treat me," Anjuin said. "I just want children of my own. Sons or daughters, it doesn't matter."

"Young Mistress, one of the schoolteachers next door told me to give you this," Ah-Jien's voice came from the door. "They've been handing them out all over the neighborhood."

She held in her hand several copies of a leaflet.

HOW TO PROTECT YOUR FAMILY FROM CHOLERA

Cholera is carried by tainted food and water. Bathe and wash diapers away from sources of drinking water.

Drink only safe water. Safe water is water that has been heated to a boil for at least one minute. Store your safe water in a clean, covered container.

Wash your hands with soap and safe water before you prepare food or eat and before feeding your children. Wash your hands with soap and safe water after using the toilet, cleaning your child's bottom, or after taking care of someone with diarrhea.

Cook food well, eat it hot. Do not eat raw foods which you have not prepared yourself with clean hands and utensils.

It had been a horribly hot summer and now it was August, the peak of the sweltering season. There were reports of yet another cholera outbreak. Even though the other servants laughed at me, I used only boiled water to wash the dishes and refused to eat raw foods, even Mrs. Hao's pickled radishes, which I adored.

When Grandmother Yang saw the list, she shook her head. "Such a lot to remember. Do foreigners truly believe this? Do they teach you this at the mission school, Jialing?"

"Yes," I said. "They say that in America, they've followed these rules of cleanliness for twenty years and there have been only a few outbreaks, and not many people die anymore."

"These foreign ways may or may not help, but they certainly cannot hurt," Third Wife said, her voice soft and pleading. "Isn't it worth trying?"

"Please, Grandmother," Anjuin said. "The servants say the Shens' youngest grandson has diarrhea. It could be cholera."

"Let me think on it," the old woman said.

THAT NIGHT, I found myself sitting with Fox on the roof of the *erfang*.

Cicadas hummed in the courtyard below and the faint rustle of leaves teased with hope of breezes. Fox wore a loose gown of dark blue silk, her hair in a simple braid down her back.

I want you to see something, she said, her voice very quiet. She pointed a slim finger across the road, to the roof of the Shens' home.

I saw nothing, and then it appeared. A pale fog that gradually took shape.

There on the tiled roof, a woman dressed in white robes danced slowly along the ridgeline. Her hair and clothing were of a style centuries old. Long sleeves flowed in slow motion about her as she swayed gracefully to silent music. Her arms moved in the complicated patterns of an ancient dance, and her tiny shoes barely touched the curved gray tiles. Apparently unaware of our presence, she floated through the motions of her dance. When she reached the end of the peaked roof, the beautiful woman vanished.

"Is this a dream?" I asked Fox. "Who was that ghost?"

You're still in your bed, but what you just saw was real, she said. That ghost is one I haven't seen in a long time, and now she's appeared at the Shens'. She's doomed to foretell death, poor thing.

"Whose death?" I asked with a shudder.

Someone at the Shens'. Perhaps more than one. She fell silent. Jialing, I must take a long trip. It may take as long as six months. I must try again to find some other Foxes.

"What for? Why must you go away for so long?"

I have questions and it may take some time to find Foxes who can answer them.

"Why are they so hard to find?"

Goodness, she sighed. I'd forgotten how many questions

mortal children ask. I'm looking for some very special Foxes. They know far more than I do. They live in high mountains and lonely grasslands. They're very reclusive. They're old and wise, almost *xian*, nearly immortal.

"Nearly? Aren't Foxes immortal?"

We can't die from disease or starvation, but we can be killed, she said.

"What do you want to ask these special Foxes?" I asked, but before the words left my lips, I was back on my cot, the heavy cotton blanket kicked to one side.

There was an emptiness in one corner of my mind. Fox had gone.

EARLY NEXT MORNING, a woman's voice disturbed the household. Her cries rang out on Dragon Springs Road, frantic and filled with despair. When I ran out to the front gate, the other servants were already there.

The Shens' First Daughter-in-Law staggered along the road, clothing disheveled and hair unbound. Although sunrise tinted the whitewashed walls with golden light, she held an oil lamp in her hand, the flame burning high. She turned here and there with each step as if expecting to find someone beside her.

"Xiao Di, come back!" she called. "Can't you hear me, Xiao Di? It's your mother. Come back to your body. I've made you sweet rice cakes. Xiao Di!"

A servant trailed behind her, weeping helplessly.

"What is she doing?" I whispered to the other servants.

"Young Madame Shen is out searching for her son's souls," Ah-Jien said, civil to me for once. "He's very ill and they've gone wandering away in confusion. She has to find them and lead them back home to his body if she's to save his life."

But as the woman reached the end of the street, loud screams erupted from the Shens' estate. It was too late. Xiao Di's souls would never find their way home.

MISS MORRIS HALTED CLASSES that week. The schoolteachers went from house to house, nursing and caring for the fallen. By the end of the week, all that remained of the Shens was their youngest son. He had hurried home from university in Hangchow just in time to bury his family.

The Shens weren't the only neighbors to suffer tragedy. For weeks it seemed as though we witnessed a funeral procession every day. The Yangs remained blessedly unscathed. I burned incense at the Fox altar in thanks to the original Fox who had given us the spring. Just in case my prayers could reach her.

OLD MASTER SHEN'S funeral was the most elaborate I'd ever seen.

I had thought of him as just a gloomy old man but now we learned our elderly neighbor had once been an imperial scholar who had passed the civil service examinations with the highest of honors. Out of respect, Master Yang and Dajuin would walk in the procession. They didn't belong to the Shen family, but the Shens' youngest son accepted gratefully. He didn't have much family left to fill the procession.

Two dozen mourners hired from the beggars' guild led the procession. Their horns blared out woeful notes, and the deep, slow beat of drums set the pace. Master Yang and Dajuin followed young Master Shen behind the coffin. At the very end came other hired mourners. They carried boxes of incense sticks, offerings of food, and paper models of houses and furniture, all to burn at the grave.

It was the ninth day of the ninth month, an auspicious day for

Master Shen's burial. By now funerals were such a common sight that only neighbors bothered turning out to watch as the procession moved along Dragon Springs Road. That was why I noticed the stranger when he walked up to Mrs. Hao.

He wore a long blue student's gown and cloth shoes. His foreign hat, a wide-brimmed fedora, was a little too large for him and he kept pushing it off his forehead, an absentminded gesture. He was very handsome and Mrs. Hao was practically simpering as they talked. Then he walked away, out onto Chung San Road, his back as straight as if he were on parade.

"Was that man one of the Lins' tenants?" I asked Mrs. Hao when she returned.

"No, no. Just someone who came in from Chung San Road to watch the procession. He wanted to know whose funeral that was." She grinned at me. "Good looking, wasn't he? Not for the likes of you, of course."

I turned away before she could see my cheeks redden. Not in embarrassment that she had noticed me staring at the young man but because I was reliving the shame of a memory, the memory of a day when Teacher Ko took a group of us to visit St. John's University. The grounds of the private university were beautiful, its greenery and gardens meticulously tended, the buildings grander than anything I'd ever seen.

"Only the very best students and the very wealthy can attend because tuition is so expensive," Teacher Ko said. "This university is for men only, and professors teach all their classes in English."

We crossed paths with a group of students, some wearing Western clothes, some in long Chinese-style student gowns, all expensively dressed. One of them stared admiringly at Zhuhai, who at sixteen looked much older. She smiled back before looking down modestly.

Then one of them drawled, "Don't waste your sighs on those girls, my friends. They're just orphans from the mission school."

They strolled past, unaware that we were crimson with humiliation. What were we to these sons of rich fathers? To them we were daughters of beggars and prostitutes, born to women who gave us away to better feed a son, sold off by fathers desperate for another sticky brown pellet of opium.

In his long *changpao* gown, the scholarly young man had reminded me of that day, of those other young men. Whatever fate had in store for my classmates, mine would be worse. Grandmother Yang's obligations to me only lasted as long as Miss Morris's payments. I had to earn some money and find my mother. And somehow, I had to earn a living.

THE DAY AFTER Old Master Shen's funeral, Mrs. Hao and I moved the kitchen table to a spot where we could enjoy what little breeze flowed through the door. Mrs. Hao had a huge basket of taro root and put me to work peeling the tough skin while she prepared pork slices to steam with the taro. Third Wife sat beside the door, fanning herself. Anjuin joined us, sitting down with the weekend edition of *Xinwen Bao*, Dajuin's preferred newspaper. Master Yang subscribed to the more conservative *Shen Bao*.

She looked up from the paper. "Mah Juhou was murdered yesterday."

"Is he important?" Third Wife said, wiping her damp forehead. "Why do I know that name?"

"He was one of Shanghai's wealthiest businessmen," Anjuin said. "Wealthy and influential." She read the article out loud to us.

> *Yesterday afternoon, at four o'clock, prominent business-man Mah Juhou was shot down at No. 14 Rue Chapsal*

in the French Concession by an unknown assassin. Mah went to the house expecting a business meeting with executives of a mining company from Manchuria.

Mah, aged 55, was from one of Shanghai's oldest families. He was a supporter of the Nationalist Party and a personal friend of Dr. Sun Yat-sen.

Shanghai Municipal Police are following up rumors that the warlord General Zhang Zuolin was behind this murder.

"Is that the same General Zhang who is leader of the Fengtian clique?" Third Wife asked. "Isn't he the one who wants to bring back a Manchu emperor?"

Anjuin looked up. "Yes. And if he's behind this, it means the Nationalists will never agree to an alliance with the Fengtian clique, not while General Zhang is alive."

China had splintered into territories controlled by Yuan Shikai's former military governors. The governors were warlords now, forming alliances and cliques that balanced military strength to achieve some semblance of stability. All the while they plotted for ways to take over Peking because whichever clique controlled the capital city was the one foreign governments recognized as the official government of China. It was all very confusing.

Master Yang appeared at the kitchen door.

I nearly sliced through my hand in surprise, not only because of his sudden appearance but because the master of the house had no reason to come to the kitchen.

"First Daughter, your grandmother wishes to see you," he said. A somber expression clouded his usually cheerful face.

Third Wife hurried to follow Anjuin. I gazed imploringly at

Mrs. Hao, who shook her head. She too had seen the distress on Master Yang's face and wouldn't let me eavesdrop. We continued working in silence, waiting for Anjuin to return.

But when footsteps came to the kitchen door, they belonged to Yun Na, not Anjuin.

"You, girl, you bring the children their supper as usual," she said to me. "Mrs. Hao, Grandmother says to delay supper for the adults until everyone has come back from the temple."

"Temple?" Mrs. Hao said. "What's happened?"

"We're going to pray for Anjuin's betrothed," Yun Na said, with obvious relish. "He's dead. The entire Chen family's dead. The young man, his parents, brothers, and sisters. Cholera."

AS FAR AS Grandmother Yang was concerned, Anjuin was now a widow. Even though there hadn't been a wedding, the moment the marriage contract was signed, she belonged to the Chen family. The Yangs had merely been raising and training Anjuin on behalf of her in-laws.

"If her in-laws had survived the cholera," the old woman said, "I'd send Anjuin to live with them and care for them. As their daughter-in-law, it would be her duty."

"Well, we'd better hurry up and do some matchmaking for Anjuin," Third Wife said. "She's not getting any younger."

"There's no need," said Grandmother Yang. "She's a widow now. She can't remarry."

Anjuin walked out of the room.

THE CREAK OF the door intruded on my sleep. I turned over and saw that Anjuin's bed was empty. Outside, her footsteps pattered across the veranda's wooden floor. She was away a long time, longer than needed to go to the outhouse. The gray, uncertain light indicated early morning, so I got up.

Hesitant birdsong greeted me in the courtyard. It was just bright enough to see that one of the doors in Dajuin's *erfang* was slightly ajar. The nursery door. Looking in, I saw Amah Wu snoring on the bed she shared with Third Wife's youngest boy. Anjuin sat on a stool beside the other bed, looking down at her niece. One hand rested against the small dark head. Her face held all the calm of a mountain lake, but tears glimmered on her cheeks.

I remembered how carefully she had tended her younger siblings, how delighted she had been at the prospect of more children when Dajuin married Yun Na. How she doted on her little brother, Kejuin. How she had carried me to her bed when I was small, singing quietly until I stopped crying for my mother.

That evening, I gathered my courage. I waited until after supper, when I saw Dajuin enter his study. I hurried over, determined to speak my piece even though servants were never supposed to disturb Dajuin or Master Yang when they were in their studies.

"Please, Young Master," I said, my head just inside the door, "if you have time, there's something I'd like to say."

He looked up from his desk. "Of course, Jialing. What troubles you?" His voice was kind and calm, like Anjuin's. I relaxed. He would not berate me or report me to Grandmother Yang.

"It's not about me. It's about Anjuin. You're the only one who can speak up to the Old Mistress and the Master."

"What's wrong?"

"Anjuin's been crying, Young Master," I said. The words blurted out. "You know how much she loves children, how badly she wants children of her own. If the Old Mistress doesn't let her marry, she'll be unhappy for the rest of her life!"

He regarded me for a moment, his eyes deep-set and alert, his features a bolder version of Anjuin's. You couldn't mistake them for anything other than brother and sister.

"I'm glad you spoke up, Jialing. I'm glad you care enough about Anjuin to ask."

THIRD WIFE TOOK his side when Dajuin spoke to his father and grandmother. She offered to find a matchmaker. As usual, First Wife sided with Grandmother Yang. This put Master Yang uncomfortably in the middle.

"First Daughter is still a maiden," he said. "She deserves a husband and a family of her own, Mother."

"As far as I'm concerned she's a widow!" Grandmother Yang cried. "If she doesn't remain chaste, it will shame the family."

"Grandmother, how can you deny her a husband and children?" Dajuin said.

"If she married into a respectable family, how would that shame us?" Third Wife said in her most persuasive tones.

"Mother, I agree that an old-fashioned family might think as you do," Master Yang began.

"How can you say I'm old-fashioned? It's not as though I'm asking Anjuin to follow her husband to the grave." And with that, Grandmother Yang stormed out of the sitting room in a rage.

If only Fox were here to help change Grandmother Yang's mind. But I knew what Fox would say if she were here. If there wasn't the slightest inclination on Grandmother Yang's part, she had no way to coax it into action.

FOR THE FIRST time in his life, Master Yang disobeyed his mother. He had Third Wife send for a matchmaker and take charge. I contrived to be present at the meeting, pouring tea and fetching snacks.

The matchmaker looked Anjuin over, her glum expression dragging down her jowls even more. It was a short first meeting.

"The young lady's age calls for a larger dowry," she said. "Given Master Yang's status as a factory owner and head of a merchant clan, people will expect more. I'll ask around, but if you don't double the dowry, I can do very little."

"What about the gold coins my mother left with your family?" I asked Anjuin afterwards. It wasn't as though I would need them for my dowry. If Anjuin didn't marry, where would I go?

"That was how Father could afford such a big banquet for Da-juin's wedding," said Anjuin. "Your gold coins were spent to save face for our family."

She endured a series of unsuitable suggestions.

"The matchmaker found a wine merchant in Ningpo," she said, wrinkling her nose. "I would be Third Wife to a man who is fifty years old and with four children. He lives with a widowed mother and two unmarried sisters."

I shuddered. That was far too many women in one household with nothing better to do than find fault. Obedience to fathers before marriage, obedience to husbands and in-laws when married, and obedience to sons after husbands die. If a woman was fortunate, she might enter a family such as the Yangs where filial piety was stronger than obedience to sons. A woman could endure much if she could look forward to her turn as matriarch.

The wine merchant from Ningpo found a bride with better family connections and a larger dowry.

"I don't think Master Yang is trying very hard to find Anjuin a husband," I said to Mrs. Hao. "The matchmaker always says the dowry is too small and Anjuin's too old. Why doesn't Master Yang increase the dowry?"

"Perhaps Master Yang doesn't want to lose the one person who keeps the household running," the cook said. "If the matchmaker can't find a suitable husband, then the Young Mistress remains unmarried. As her grandmother wishes."

So Master Yang wasn't disobeying his mother after all.

CHAPTER 12

January 1917, Year of the Snake

Leah was not the best of students. Except for English, she never paid much attention to her classes. With her honey-colored skin and hair she was far more obviously *hun xue* than any of us. Even her eyes were a golden shade of brown. Her looks were so unusual that people shuddered when they saw her. The more superstitious stared and kept their distance. Few noticed how fine and smooth her skin was or that her wide tilted eyes and small chin gave her the look of a kitten. They were so busy noticing her differences they never seemed to realize that she was extraordinarily beautiful.

On the few occasions when Miss Morris and the teachers took our music class to perform at foreign churches, Leah's looks drew stares from foreigners. Especially the men. At such times, I thanked the gods for small mercies, that I was able to hide my mixed blood so long as I kept my head down.

From Leah I learned the art of smiling when you did not agree and smiling when you did. Her expression never varied, her smooth face never betrayed delight, resentment, or distress. She offered a bland and featureless surface that reflected whatever others wanted to see. It was a skill that served her well. Unlike Grace, whose lively expression gave away her every thought, Leah kept to herself without anyone thinking her aloof.

The year I was sixteen and Leah eighteen, her family found her. Or, rather, her aunt found her. Grace and I had just finished dusting the library shelves. Our lunchtime chores completed, we went to find Leah and saw her at the far end of the courtyard with Miss Morris and a strange woman who had her arm around Leah. Then Leah nodded rather stiffly and turned to walk in the other direction, toward the orphanage.

We caught up with her on the walkway between the school and orphanage buildings.

"Who was that woman?" I asked, panting a little.

"That was my aunt," she said. "She's taking me away with her."

Grace clasped her hands together. "How wonderful! You never mentioned an aunt."

"I hardly know her," Leah said, her voice dull. "She's come to claim me."

"You'll have a family," I said, puzzled at her lack of excitement. "It's like a fairy tale, your long-lost family."

"I must pack," she said, not responding to my comment.

Grace and I followed Leah to the orphanage dormitory where she put a few pieces of clothing in her pillowcase along with a few notebooks of English exercises.

Outside, Miss Morris and Leah's aunt waited beside the school gate. Leah's aunt was of medium height. It was winter and she wore a high-necked vest over her plain gown, the collar lined with squirrel fur. Her face was broad and attractive, her eyebrows carefully painted in. Modest gold hoops swung from her ears.

"Are you sure you wouldn't like to finish school, Leah?" asked Miss Morris in English. "You only have a few months left."

Leah shook her head. Her small, secret smile had returned. "I will go with my aunt, Headmistress."

"So fluent in English," Leah's aunt exclaimed. "When I finally learned where she'd been all these years, I never imagined she would be so well educated."

"You're always welcome if you want to return," Miss Morris said to Leah, ignoring the woman. Miss Morris, who was the soul of courtesy. "Good-bye, my dear." She held Leah's face between her hands for a moment.

We waved as the rickshaw puller jogged away, but despite her smile, Leah's face seemed forlorn. I glanced up at Miss Morris, who seemed sad, not at all pleased that Leah was going to live with her own family.

"We must write to Mary with this news," Grace murmured. Then she put a finger in her mouth and looked at me, embarrassed.

For a moment she had forgotten Mary was gone, dead from cholera. During the epidemic she and other teachers-in-training had helped at the mission clinic in Hangchow. Neither the foreign god nor the rules of cleanliness had been enough to protect our friend.

I WAS ONE of the best students when it came to speaking English, so Miss Morris often gave me the task of accompanying visitors who came to inspect the school. I would narrate a memorized introduction while taking them through the school and orphanage, finishing up in the front courtyard beside the donation box.

One day, three Englishwomen came to the school. Miss Morris greeted one of the ladies very warmly and joined us on the tour.

"How old are you, my dear?" one of the ladies asked, when we finished. She was the one Miss Morris treated like a friend.

"I am sixteen," I said, smiling. The lady put a small envelope into the donation box.

"The Chinese are so petite they look younger than their age, don't they?" the second lady remarked, as though I weren't there.

"What will you do after you graduate?" the first lady asked.

I hesitated, unsure of what to say. What aspirations did I have beyond surviving?

"She's just a little parrot," said the third. "Recites by rote with no idea of what she's saying."

"Not at all," Miss Morris said in her most pleasant voice. "Jialing has been very quick to learn English. She's just shy."

"Her mixed blood will become even more evident as she gets older," said the third lady. She examined me for a moment dismissively.

"She'll be hard-pressed to find a job or a husband," I heard her say, as they strolled out the gates. "Even a good Chinese Christian wouldn't want a half-Chinese wife, no matter how pretty."

I bit my lower lip. Somehow this matter-of-fact assessment of my future hurt more than the insults I'd learned to bear. From the way I was treated out on the streets, at the market square, and in shops, I knew what to expect when I grew older. When our teachers took us on outings, I'd seen how people treated Mary and Leah, who were older. I could expect contemptuous stares, people deliberately shoving me aside, spitting in my direction. Men making lewd suggestions.

I had no expectations when it came to marriage. I would have to earn my own living. As Fox had pointed out, I couldn't count on the Yangs forever. Especially now that Anjuin wouldn't be getting married. Furthermore, Fox had been gone for six months. I had no idea when she would return. She was very bad at keeping track of time. I couldn't count on her, either.

"Will that be all, Miss Morris?" I asked.

"Yes, dear. You did a lovely job as usual," she said. She noticed my hesitation. "Is there something you'd like to ask?"

"I'm worried about how I will earn a living," I said.

"Jialing, I'll do my best to help you find a job," Miss Morris said. "You know we do that for all our girls."

"I know, Miss Morris. But it will be difficult because I'm *za-zhong.*"

"Don't use that ugly word," she said. "Always say *hun xue,* mixed race. In English, say 'Eurasian.' To us you're always our dear Jialing, half Chinese, half European, the best of both worlds."

There was no point in telling her that even here, at her school, I was not immune to scorn. How would my life be any easier, away from the protection of the classroom and my teachers? I still had time before graduation. Could I find my mother before then?

"Please, Miss Morris," I said, not looking at her. "Is there work I could do for you to earn some money?"

"Do you need the money for anything in particular?" she asked. "Is it something I can help you with?"

How could I explain? Still looking down at my feet, I answered, "I just want some money of my own, Headmistress."

She gave my shoulder a pat. "Come to my office after lunch."

I EXPECTED VERY little, perhaps for Miss Morris to say that she would think on what work she might have for me. At the most, I'd hoped for some work cleaning the school, sweeping the grounds, or helping at the orphanage.

Instead she opened the door to the small workroom beside her office and sat me at the table there. She put a few sheets of manuscript in front of me. Each sheet of paper was divided in two columns, one neatly typed with lines of English, the other a Chinese translation.

"I've been working on these for years," she said. "It's a textbook for teaching Chinese to English-speaking adults. But unless other missionary teachers find it useful, there's no point in having them printed. So I must make copies to circulate to the other mission schools. Can you copy out the Chinese text and type the English?"

"Of course, Miss Morris," I said. "I can do this at lunch. But . . ."

She smiled at my eagerness. "But what?"

"Please, could you . . . could you not mention to anyone that you're paying me to do this?" I said in a low voice. "I don't want my classmates to know. They would be . . . envious."

EACH DAY I gobbled down my lunch and hurried to the workroom beside Miss Morris's office. I worked my way through the stack of pages, first typing the English side of a page, then copying out the Chinese characters in blue ink, using one of Miss Morris's fountain pens. At the end of the first week, when she handed me some coins, I couldn't believe it was possible to get paid for a task so simple and pleasurable.

For the first time in my life, I was earning some money. It wasn't very much, but there was something reassuring about the coins weighing down my pocket, tied up tightly in a handkerchief so they wouldn't jingle. Judging from the stack of papers on the table, I would have many, many more weeks of work.

"What will you do with the money?" Anjuin asked when I showed her the coins. She was the only one who knew. We were getting ready for bed and she was brushing her hair.

"There's something I've decided to do," I said, still hesitant to confide in her. "But don't laugh or scold me."

"Tell me."

"I want to find my mother."

She put down the hairbrush and turned to me. "How would you find her?"

No scoffing or ridicule, just interest and genuine concern. I pulled a newspaper from my school satchel and pointed at a narrow column of print. Small classified ads in search of missing people.

I was old enough now to realize that my foreign father must've been a brothel customer, that my mother had been Noble Uncle's mistress, and that Noble Uncle was the Master Fong who sold the estate to the Yangs. If I ever found her, I wanted my mother to tell me why she had left me behind. Had she been forced by Noble Uncle? Or had she abandoned me willingly, intending to come back once she was free of him? I wanted to know about my father, perhaps how to find him. Perhaps I could persuade her to contact him. In my daydreams, once he learned he had a daughter, he would look after me. The way Grace's father looked after them.

"Do you think an ad in the newspaper would be best?" I said. "Or do you think I should save up to hire a detective?"

"Let's ask Dajuin," she said. "He'll know what to do."

Approaching Dajuin was nearly as intimidating as asking a favor of Master Yang, but Anjuin had total confidence in her brother. The next evening, she pulled me into Dajuin's study. He studied me while Anjuin explained the situation, as though he were seeing me for the first time.

"A detective would be very expensive," he said, after a pause. "Why not start with newspapers and see whether we get any results?"

"We," as though it mattered to him. Perhaps because he could tell it mattered to Anjuin.

"But you must save enough to pay for many months of advertising," he said. "You can't count on your mother seeing the ad right away. Plus, you must advertise regularly to make sure enough people see it. Every week for six months, perhaps eight months. Can you afford that, Jialing?"

"I'll wait until I've earned enough," I said. "Thank you, Young Master. Thank you for your advice."

"LOOK AT THIS," Anjuin said, pointing at a small advertisement in the newspaper. We now read the classified to see how others wrote missing persons ads.

> *Wanted. Any intelligence concerning the abduction and murder of a foreign child, female, Anna Shea, last seen in the External Roads area, August 1909. Reward offered for information leading to the abductor. Write to R. Shea, Post Office Box 305, Shanghai Central Post Office, The Bund.*

After all these years, Anna's father was still living in Shanghai, still seeking justice for his daughter.

FIRST WIFE FINALLY completed her altar cloth and donated it to nearby Jing'an Temple, where it draped the table in front of the Goddess of Mercy. Now she awaited the miracle of pregnancy.

Master Yang had turned part of the front courtyard into a shop. It sold cloth from the mill, a suggestion from Anjuin. She wanted something more than just to run a small household.

"It won't be a very busy shop since we're not out on Chung San Road," Anjuin said to her father, "but it would cost us nothing to run, so it would be all profit."

Perhaps Master Yang conceded to his daughter out of guilt for letting her remain unmarried. Dajuin pasted signs on the wall that boasted FABRICS DIRECT FROM THE FACTORY, NO NEED TO GO IN TO SHANGHAI. Anjuin and Third Wife took turns working in the shop, at first under Grandmother Yang's sharp eyes, then on their own as Grandmother Yang realized Anjuin could more than manage.

When I wasn't at school or doing my chores for Grandmother Yang, I helped Anjuin and Third Wife at the store. Not that there was much to do, but it meant we could be on our own, a rare luxury. Without First Wife or Grandmother Yang around, we were less guarded, more easily moved to laughter by Third Wife's stories about her family.

"So in front of all the guests my father said to my eldest brother, 'Your son is a complete moron.'" Then Third Wife looked around the empty shop and lowered her voice. "And my brother replied, 'I'm sorry about my son, Papa. But it skips a generation, you know!'"

Anjuin looked shocked for a moment. Then we all dissolved into giggles, Anjuin laughing so hard she had to grasp my hand to hold herself upright.

A YEAR AFTER her first child was born, Yun Na had a second baby, this time a boy. As mother to a son, she lost no time asserting herself over Anjuin. She even snubbed Third Wife, whom she should've respected as a mother-in-law. Always difficult, now she was intolerable.

By July I had saved enough money to place some ads.

Anjuin and I took a handbarrow to Shanghai. We had let Grandmother Yang think we were just going to look at the shops along Nanking Road, and at first she had been reluctant to give permission.

"Ever since our government banned the opium trade, the streets are filled with gangsters," she said. "I've heard that warlords fund their armies by forcing their farmers to grow poppies, and the gangs are fighting for control of the Shanghai opium trade."

It had been Dajuin who calmed her. "I go to Shanghai every day to call on customers, Grandmother. It's safe. The Green Gang and the Red Gang don't care about schoolgirls. Only each other."

Anjuin and I shared a handbarrow with other passengers as far as the racecourse, then we walked the rest of the way to *Xinwen Bao* newspaper's office at the corner of Hankow and Nanking Roads. All the way there, I was conscious of the searching looks people gave me. I hung my head and held tight to Anjuin's hand.

The newspaper office was a scene of such chaos I wondered how they managed to print a newspaper at all. There was a great deal of shouting from a half-dozen men gathered around a desk at the far end of the room, all of them talking at once.

"Sun Yat-sen may be back from Japan, but the situation is too far gone. He can't stop General Zhang Zuolin from putting Puyi back on the Dragon Throne."

"I disagree. Zhang Zuolin may be the strongest of the warlords but he's insane if he thinks he can restore the old Manchu regime. The Qing Dynasty will never regain power!"

"He's got another agenda, just wait and see. That old fox has something to gain from all this."

I caught a glimpse of the man whose desk they surrounded. He ignored the uproar and continued writing, pausing only to glance at some notes before returning to his work, a quiet figure in pale gray. His very stillness gave him an air of authority.

Anjuin and I found signs that directed us up the staircase to the next floor, where a row of clerks sat behind a row of desks. PAYMENTS. DELIVERY INSTRUCTIONS. SUBSCRIPTIONS. ADVERTISEMENTS.

Anjuin prodded me over to the Advertisements desk. A middle-aged clerk with pockmarked cheeks looked up from his magazine and studied me. He turned and spat.

Anjuin took over. "How much for a classified advertisement?"

"Seventy-five cents per line. Ten words in a line," he said, his voice a grumble.

We knew this, but wanted to be sure. I pulled out the note from my tunic pocket and we quickly counted the words again.

Information wanted. The whereabouts of a woman named Zhu, who lived at the Fong residence on Dragon Springs Road, the External Roads area, around 1908.

"Twenty-five words," I said.

"Give it here." The clerk scanned my carefully penned sentences. "Three lines. And lucky for you, even after adding the reply box number, it's still three lines."

"The *Shun Bao* newspaper offices are just around the corner," Anjuin said. "They may be cheaper."

"The cost is based on circulation," the clerk said. "The bigger the circulation, the more people see your advertisement. At

Xinwen Bao we have a circulation of more than 90,000 every day. *Shun Bao* has more, so you'll pay more there. You can go to one of the smaller papers, but then you won't get the readership. We're a good middle ground."

"It's just that I need to place this advertisement every week for several months, or until I get a reply. Or give up." I couldn't decide.

"Well, if you promise to advertise at least five times I can give you a discount. Ten percent." He squinted at me and I nodded.

He began writing out my receipt then squinted at me again. "Can you afford more?"

"Why?" I asked.

"The woman you seek may not live in Shanghai anymore. You should probably advertise in other cities."

Dejected, I looked at Anjuin. I hadn't thought of that, but the clerk was right. What if my mother was living elsewhere in China?

"You can do it through this paper," he said. "We have reciprocal arrangements with all the big newspapers in other cities. Costs a little more and you get your ad in three other city newspapers. Can't hurt to try."

I counted over more coins from my cloth pouch, but it gave me new hope to think that if my mother was now in Hangchow or Soochow, she might see my little ad. Even if she couldn't afford to travel, surely she could afford a stamp to reply.

"Just do your best," said the clerk, encouragingly. "Advertise when you can."

After he finished writing up the order, Anjuin spoke up. "Is there always such a big commotion downstairs?"

He snorted. "The Royalist warlord Zhang Xun marched his army to Peking this morning and took over the Forbidden City. They put that child Puyi back on the throne. The Qing Dynasty is back in power and President Li is hiding at the French embassy."

In the end, the Manchu Restoration lasted only twelve days. The Republican government's forces defeated the Royalist army. Afterward, warlords recruited deserters from both sides. The warlord Zhang Zuolin did best. He now commanded the largest private army in China.

CHAPTER 13

January 1918, Year of the Horse

I worked away steadily in Miss Morris's office, adding to the stack of finished copies. Every so often, the old fountain pen she had given me would need a wipe and for this I used crumpled sheets of notepaper from her wastebasket. The letters were very dull, reports to the mission, never anything personal. One day the word *Eurasian* caught my eye, so I smoothed out the page.

Gentlemen,

In 1865, the Anglican Church closed its Diocesan Female Training School after only three years. The Church found that upon leaving school with some proficiency in English, almost all the Eurasian girls became mistresses to European men.

Today, the situation is not appreciably different.

I stress it is not lack of schooling that drives these girls into concubinage or brothels. It is lack of opportunity. ~~never~~ *Very rarely do our Eurasian girls find acceptance, let alone employment. They are bright and hardworking, but at best their mixed blood dooms them to menial work; at worst, they end up following their mothers' professions. The Mission must* ~~provide~~ *do more to help* ~~some employment for~~ *our Eurasian graduates.*

You may argue there are Eurasians who do well. Indeed there are entire communities of wealthy and middle-class Eurasians in Shanghai, Hong Kong, and other port cities. However, the girls in our care have no family and no such connections. There is no possibility of their being taken in by respectable Eurasian society. Therefore, I beg you to . . .

Concubinage and brothels. Factories. There had to be another way. I wondered where Fox was traveling. I wished I could wander as she did, undetected, unafraid, sometimes an animal, sometimes a human.

EACH MONTH I made the trip into Shanghai and the *Xinwen Bao* offices to see whether anyone had replied to my advertisement. Anjuin came with me sometimes, but mostly I walked there and back on my own, to save money. Each month, the clerk persuaded me to pay for another month of ads. But after nine months, I felt ready to give up. I had finished my work for Miss Morris, and my savings were nearly gone, all of it spent on finding my mother. I'd been foolish to hope that anyone would notice my little classified ads.

At the *Xinwen Bao* office I went up the now-familiar staircase. The clerk, now also familiar, urged me to try for one more month of advertising. His smile was sympathetic, and I felt so grateful for his kind manner that I agreed.

I trudged down the staircase, counting the few small coins in my cloth purse. I looked down just long enough that I didn't see the person running up the stairs until it was too late. I went sprawling down the steps.

"Are you hurt, miss?" A man's hand reached down to pull me up.

"Yes, I mean, no, I'm fine," I said, breathless. But I found it hard to stand. I winced and sat down on the bottom step, rubbing my ankle.

"I am so sorry," he said, looking helpless. It was the man I'd seen on my first visit to the newspaper, the one who had been writing quietly at his desk while his colleagues milled around shouting.

"I'll be fine in a minute, it's all right."

"Can you walk? Let's go to my desk," the man said. "Have some chrysanthemum tea. Give your ankle a bit more time to recover."

He sat me in a chair facing his own, rummaged in a bottom drawer, and pulled out a cup. Carefully he poured in some cold tea and handed it to me.

I looked around, emboldened by his kindness. "It's very quiet today. Almost no one here. Usually there's so much talking and shouting."

"It's a rare day of quiet for news," he said. "You commented 'usually.' Why do you usually come to this office?"

"I place a classified advertisement every month and come in to check for replies."

"Why are you advertising?" he asked, holding a box out. I took a biscuit.

"I'm looking for my mother. She left nearly ten years ago, though, so it's rather difficult. This will be my last advertisement."

"I see," he said, and his eyes studied my face closely for the first time. I waited for his expression to change to dislike, for him to realize I was *zazhong*.

"I should go now," I said. "You must be busy. Thank you for the tea."

"No, no. Stay. There's nothing going on, I'm not busy at all. Tell me your story. What makes you believe your mother is still in Shanghai?" His expression remained friendly.

"That's exactly what your clerk said. So he suggested advertising in other cities through your newspaper."

"Really? Tell me more." There was the slightest tightening in his voice.

"You have reciprocal relationships with other big newspapers. So I've paid your paper to advertise in other cities. Hangchow, Soochow, and Ningpo. "

"There's no such thing as reciprocal relationships for advertising," he said, pushing his chair away from the desk.

A small cry escaped me. The clerk had been so nice, so helpful, but he was like everyone else, always looking for a way to gain a bit more, even if it meant cheating a schoolgirl. A girl who was *zazhong*. I looked down at my hands and blinked tears from my eyes.

"Stay here," the man said, his face grim as he got up.

I heard his voice echoing down the stairwell, angry and loud, but not loud enough that I could make out his words.

When he returned, he sat down again, fingers drumming the tabletop.

"I told him to return the money or he'll be fired," he said.

"Do I have to go back upstairs to get my money?" I said. I didn't want to face the clerk again.

"No, I'll give it to you now. It's me he'll have to pay back." The man took a wallet out from his tunic pocket and counted out several bills. More than I had spent on ads. "Now tell me all about the search for your missing mother."

He listened with intense attention, leaning back on his chair. At the end of my short recitation, he brought the legs of his chair thudding down on the floor.

"Miss Zhu Jialing, I propose hiring a private investigator to follow your mother's trail after she left Dragon Springs Road. I'll take care of the cost."

"I don't mean to be rude, sir," I said cautiously, "but why do you want to help? You've given me back all my money. The newspaper doesn't owe me anything."

"Perhaps I'm hoping to earn a little merit with the gods." He gave me a wry smile. "I knew a young woman like you, once. *Hun xue*. I always wish I'd been able to help her in time."

In time for what? Something in his face kept me from asking more.

He stood up. "I'll get in touch if something turns up, Miss Zhu. Write down your name and an address where I can send you mail. My name is Liu. Liu Sanmu." He took a card from his desk and gave it to me.

On my way back I had so much to think about I barely noticed the long walk. I could hardly wait to share this turn of events with Anjuin. But when I got home, the household was in a state of turmoil.

First Wife had finally gone mad.

CHAPTER 14

"Some musicians came into Dragon Springs Road so we all went outside to listen," Anjuin said. "The musicians had a little boy who walked around holding out a basket for money. Just a toddler, a darling child."

First Wife ran over to the boy, crying out, "My son, my son!" She gathered him in her arms and began walking back to the house, the boy looking uncertainly over her shoulder at his mother.

The musicians had been amused until the boy's mother realized it wasn't a game. She dropped her flute and ran over. Master Yang took the boy away from First Wife. He gave the woman some money, which smoothed over the incident. But just as he guided her back to the front gate, First Wife saw another little boy in the crowd and tried to run to him, calling out that he was her son.

Master Yang and Dajuin dragged First Wife through the front gates. As soon as she was back inside the Central Residence, she became passive and docile. Grandmother Yang made a herbal infusion to calm First Wife's nerves. Master Yang gave her some account books to copy, just to keep her busy. First Wife was now working away quietly in her room, quite calm.

Dajuin's wife, however, wasn't appeased. She hurried her children away and shut them in her rooms. Then after supper, she confronted Master Yang.

"Send her away!" Yun Na demanded. "Send her to a Buddhist convent or back to Ningpo. She's mad. What if she steals away my boy?"

"She wouldn't take him very far, probably just to her own rooms," Grandmother Yang said, but her brow creased. There was no telling what a madwoman might do.

"We can't send her away," Master Yang said. "Her clan and ours are very close. It would insult them."

"Then lock her away!" the young woman cried.

Everyone knew the look on Yun Na's face. She was about to throw a tantrum.

Then Dajuin spoke up.

"Why not move her into the Western Residence? If we fix up a few of the rooms, she can live there on her own. We could hire a servant to care for her. I think we can afford that now."

Oh no. What would Fox do when she came back and found First Wife there?

IN ALL THE excitement, I had forgotten about the *Xinwen Bao* editor's offer to help find my mother. The next morning, after washing up the breakfast dishes, I showed Anjuin the business card.

"Liu Sanmu. Editor and board member," she read. "Goodness, he sounds important. Let's show Dajuin."

Dajuin was extremely impressed. "He must belong to the Liu family that owns *Xinwen Bao*. A very forward-thinking clan. They support the Nationalists."

"I still don't understand why he'd be willing to spend all that money to hire a detective for Jialing," Anjuin said. "He doesn't even know her."

"He probably doesn't think it's very expensive," Dajuin said. "The Liu family is one of the wealthiest south of the Yangtze River. For someone like Liu Sanmu, the cost of a detective is of no more consequence than the cost of a bowl of noodles is to us. We can't imagine how such people live."

"AN ENTIRE COURTYARD for me?" First Wife asked Master Yang. "Surely it's too much."

She turned and looked questioningly at Grandmother Yang. We stood inside the front courtyard of the Western Residence, the door between courtyards unlocked for the first time in years.

"It's your right as First Wife to have your own courtyard," the older woman said, giving her daughter-in-law's shoulder an encouraging pat. "Come see your rooms. We'll all go."

Its houses were old, but the Western Residence was at its most beautiful in late spring. Beneath the bamboos, wild bleeding heart had taken root and stands of feathery leaves with sprays of flowers the color of garnets bobbed in the breeze, brushing against my ankles as we walked along the path. In the courtyard, the fruit trees were shedding their blossoms and every small gust of wind blew a drift of white petals across the stone paving. Purple wisteria, which hadn't been pruned in years, draped the trellis and spanned the gap to climb onto the roof of the derelict *erfang,* spilling fragrant blooms across the roof tiles. It was still too early for daylilies, but their bright leaves sprang up like small green fountains against corners and walls.

Surrounding Fox's hydrangea, Anna's flowers grew in a wild, undisciplined mass. I had collected seeds from my little patch in the Central Residence and sown them here. Over the years they had multiplied with joyous abandon. I even knew their English names now. Miss Morris had told me. *Violas, clove pinks, forget-me-nots.*

After carpenters mended the windows and pasted new mulberry paper into the latticework frames, Anjuin and I had spent the better part of a week cleaning the lower floor of the house. Grandmother Yang sank into a chair in the sitting room, and I pushed open the window shutters. We watched Master Yang stroll with First Wife around the courtyard. When he pointed out the plum trees, the last to drop their blooms, she smiled and her face looked merely thin, not gaunt.

"She was seventeen and rather pretty when she first came to us," Grandmother Yang said.

Before disappointment dragged cruel lines down her cheeks and envy tightened her lips. Outside, the afternoon sun lent color to First Wife's face. I could almost imagine how she must have looked as a bride. From the wistful expression on Master Yang's face I could tell that like Grandmother Yang, he was remembering the bride of his youth.

But that night, First Wife wailed as though all the demons of hell were dragging her into the underworld.

Anjuin and I pulled on our shoes and ran for the Western Residence. When we reached First Wife's bedroom, Mrs. Hao was already there, an arm around First Wife, who was no longer screaming. She was sobbing in bed, rocking back and forth and clutching a pillow as though it were a child.

"They took away my son," she wept. "They took away my son!"

"I'll sleep in her room at night from now on," Mrs. Hao said, when Grandmother Yang arrived. "She's my kinswoman, after all."

Behind those soothing words I could tell Mrs. Hao was worried. If First Wife became troublesome, the Yangs might send her away. The cook might be expected to follow and look after her.

THE YANGS WERE unable to find anyone willing to take care of a madwoman in a haunted courtyard, so Anjuin and Third Wife went back and forth between the two residences. In the evenings, after I returned from school, I helped by taking First Wife her supper.

The situation was intolerable. Although Mrs. Hao stayed with her through the night, First Wife still woke up wailing for her phantom child. Whenever members of the household stepped out the front gate, any neighbors who happened to be strolling along Dragon Springs Road would saunter over purposefully.

"Is she well, your First Mistress?" they would ask. "We could tell she was in distress last night."

First Wife no longer seemed to notice the passage of time. It was easy convincing her that Master Yang was busy but would come see her soon. She would nod and smile, then return to her room. He did visit her regularly at first, but each time she made him uncomfortable with her eager face and the fuss she took over pouring his tea and lighting his pipe. Master Yang's visits grew less frequent.

"The master is very busy at the factory," we would say. "He sends greetings and will take supper with you another time."

When Mrs. Hao repeated this empty assurance one day, I glanced over at First Wife and saw silent tears trickling down her cheeks. She wasn't so oblivious after all, not all the time. She knew she had been put aside. When she pretended to believe our soothing lies, she was merely saving face for herself. And for everyone else.

I picked a small bunch of fragrant clove pinks and put them on her dressing table.

THE GOVERNMENT POSTAL service wasn't as reliable as the *minxin ju,* privately run letter agencies, so I had given Liu Sanmu the address of the agency out on Chung San Road that the Yangs used. Every day I dropped in to see whether he'd sent anything. To my surprise, a letter arrived within a few weeks. I gave the clerk at the *minxin ju* a few coppers to cover my share of delivery costs.

Dear Miss Zhu,

Yours has been a difficult case. It's been years since the Fongs departed Dragon Springs Road. You're not sure of your mother's name, and to complicate things even more, Master Fong had no sons. Rarely are women's names found in official documents unless they own land, so once Master Fong vanished from the records, there were no other names the investigator could use to cast a wider net.

However, he has located a woman who says she used to work for the Fongs. You can ask her what she knows. If you come to my office this Saturday, we can visit her together. I wouldn't want you to go into the Old City by yourself.

Liu Sanmu

"Would you like me to tell Dajuin?" Anjuin asked. "Do you want him to come with us?"

I shook my head. "We can just tell him what we find out."

All the way in to Shanghai, Anjuin and I didn't speak at all. There was only one topic on our minds, and I wasn't inclined to share it with the rest of the passengers on the handbarrow. We sat with our backs against the wheel frame, giving each other silent glances from time to time and listening to the conversation behind us from the other side of the barrow.

"I've been going to the Race Club without fail since they allowed Chinese to enter the grounds on race days," said one of the men, the eldest of the group.

"You must be an expert on horses, Master Fu."

"He's no expert!" another voice chortled. "Old Fu only goes to ogle rich men's mistresses!"

"Hah! Who doesn't enjoy looking at beautiful women? But you know I have a system for the horses. I cast their horoscopes."

The handbarrow stopped outside the racecourse, and we climbed off. It wouldn't take us long to walk to Hankow Road. Normally we would've paused at shop windows for a closer look at clothing or strange foreign wares, but today we were in a hurry. When we reached the corner, Anjuin pulled me back.

"Jialing, you realize your mother could be dead by now," she said.

"I know that," I said. "But at least I would know. I'm prepared."

What I wasn't prepared for was the man sitting by Liu Sanmu's desk.

"Mr. Shea!" I exclaimed.

It was Anna's father. Nearly nine years had passed since we'd seen him. He was slightly heavier, his face more lined, but his suit was well tailored and looked new. He stood up and gave us a slight bow.

"I never thought to see you girls again," he said, "then I realized the woman I was searching for had to be your mother, Jialing."

"Are you still with the Shanghai Police, Mr. Shea?" Anjuin asked.

"I left," he said. "I left the police force, but I stayed in Shanghai." His accent was nearly perfect now, only the slightest hint of foreign speech.

"Mr. Shea has built up one of the best private detective agencies in the city," Liu Sanmu said, motioning us to sit. "I frequently use his services. I'll let him tell you what he's done."

Shea had very little to go on since he didn't know my mother's real name, so he began by picking up Master Fong's trail. He sent an investigator out to the marketplace on Chung San Road, where rickshaw pullers, donkey cart drivers, and handbarrow pushers hung about waiting for work. One man, a rickshaw puller, remembered the day the Fongs left. He had taken Master Fong away from Dragon Springs Road, the Fong women following in a donkey cart. They had gone to a boardinghouse in the Old City, but the rickshaw puller no longer recalled which one.

"Shanghai is a huge place," Shea said, "but the lowest rents and cheapest opium are in the Old City."

Shea's man combed through the Old City, offering money for information. Soon Shea was reading notes every night from his investigator, interviews with people who claimed to have seen Master Fong and his women.

"We found a woman who actually mentioned Dragon Springs Road," Shea said. "A former servant of the Fongs called Ping Mei. She's been our only credible lead."

She gave Shea the name of the boardinghouse where the Fongs had lived after leaving Dragon Springs Road. When Shea's man went there, he learned that the owner of the boardinghouse had only taken over the business two years ago. A Master Fong and family were listed in the old records that came with the business, but of course the new owner knew nothing about guests from before his time.

"We're going to see the woman Ping Mei now," Liu Sanmu said, "to pay her for the information. You can ask her yourself what she knows, Miss Zhu."

If the woman really had worked for the Fongs, perhaps she had known my mother. Perhaps my mother had confided in her.

Anjuin and I shared a rickshaw. Mr. Shea led the way. His rickshaw puller ran in front of us, and Liu Sanmu's followed behind ours. The European-style buildings and wide avenues of the foreign concession stopped at the boundaries of the Old City, which foreigners called the Chinese City.

When the first Nationalist governor of Shanghai demolished the Old City walls, he had replaced the Ming Dynasty fortifications with a road that circled the area. Enclosed within the ring road were homes and stores pushed together in a maze of streets, Chinese territory that hadn't been taken over by foreign concessions.

The lanes narrowed as we rode deeper into the Old City. The entire area reeked of old cooking oil, sewage, and urine. An old woman squatted at the edge of the road, holding a toddler steady while the child defecated on the sidewalk. Through half-open gates I caught glimpses of squalid courtyards where small children ran about and women leaned over charcoal braziers to cook.

Shea's rickshaw stopped at one of these gates. Anjuin and I got out of our rickshaws and followed him into a small entrance courtyard. Bundles of straw were stacked against the walls, their golden stems aging to gray from damp and mold. Before I could continue through to the main courtyard, Anjuin gave me a nudge.

Mr. Shea had stopped beside a covered storage area and lifted up a tattered bamboo mat nailed over the entrance. In the dimness, I could make out shapes, all lying on the ground. The stench of unwashed bodies combined with the fetid sweet scent of opium wafted out from the makeshift room.

Four of the shapes muttered and turned away from the light. The fifth struggled up, then stood and came out to the doorway, half hidden in the shadows. The old woman patted her thin, gray plait.

"Mister Shea," she croaked, as she hobbled out with her stick. Her head tilted coyly at him. "Are you here to ask more questions? Was I right about that boardinghouse?"

"You were right," he replied, "and I brought your money. Now these young ladies have a few questions for you."

She came farther out into the courtyard and turned to face us. The left side of her grimy face was disfigured by patches of shiny skin, scars from a burn. Her cheeks were sunken, her lips fallen in over toothless gums. I winced and looked away.

"More questions," she said to Mr. Shea, leaning on her stick. "I thought you were trying to track down Master Fong, that rotten turtle egg. Well, if you want more information, it will cost you more money."

But Shea shook his head. "You tell these young women everything you know, right now. Or you don't get paid at all."

"And just who are these young ladies?" she asked. Her voice was hoarse, as though unable to clear her throat.

"My father bought the house on Dragon Springs Road from Master Fong," Anjuin said. "Who are you?"

"I'm called Ping Mei," she said, squinting at us. "I left the Fongs when they couldn't pay wages anymore."

"Did you know the people in the Western Residence?" I blurted out.

Ping Mei peered at me out of her good eye. "There was a woman. And a little girl."

Behind me, Liu Sanmu sighed in exasperation. "Tell us everything you know, old woman."

"And who are you?" she asked us, ignoring him. "You girls don't look like sisters."

"I'm that little girl," I said. "I'm looking for my mother. I don't care about the Fongs."

She stared at me. "Well, you grew up nicely. Did her family take you in?" She jerked a thumb at Anjuin.

"Yes, they did. Did you know my mother?"

She laughed, her face twisted in a horrible grimace of a smile that made me flinch away from her ruined features. "Take me back there. I'd like to see the old place again. I'll tell you everything I know when we get there."

Again, Shea shook his head. "Do you know what happened to the woman after the Fongs left Dragon Springs Road?"

"She died." Flatly and firmly.

All noise from the courtyard and the street outside faded; the calls from vendors, children crying—they all dwindled to silence. There was only the sound of my heart, a drumbeat of dismay. It seemed as though I was suspended for hours in that dull throbbing, but it couldn't have been more than a few seconds before Mr. Shea broke the silence.

"You said you didn't know what happened to the Fongs, only the name of that boardinghouse. Now you tell us the woman died."

"You didn't ask about a woman," she snapped at him. "You only mentioned the Fongs. I would've told you, for more money. But a daughter, that's something else. A daughter deserves to know."

My mother's name had been Zhu Yinglien, she said. Silver Lotus.

The name whispered in my mind.

"Your mother was widowed," Ping Mei said. "Master Fong brought her home to be his mistress."

Ping Mei left the Fongs and found work as housekeeper in a small inn. One day the owner of the inn brought home a new servant. It was my mother. Fong had sold her to be a bond servant. That was how Ping Mei learned the Fongs had left Dragon Springs Road and were living in a cheap boardinghouse in the Old City. Master Fong, the man my mother called "Noble Uncle," had been in so much debt that even after selling his home, he still owed money. So he had sold his womenfolk.

"How did she die?" Shea asked the question I couldn't bring myself to ask.

"There was a customer, a terrible, brutish man," Ping Mei said. "He drank and he had an eye for your mother. I heard screaming and things being knocked about in his room. He was on the ground strangling her. I tried to pull him off, but he threw me against the wall. Then he pushed my face into a charcoal brazier."

She spat out a gob of something brown.

The man knocked over another brazier while stumbling out, causing a fire that burned down most of the inn. Rescuers pulled Ping Mei and my mother out of the blaze, but my mother was already dead. The man ran away, and the innkeeper didn't bother reporting my mother's death as murder. It was less trouble to say she had been a casualty of the fire.

"So this was my reward for trying to help her." Ping Mei pointed at her scarred cheek.

She peered up at Shea. "I must go. I do cleaning for the brothel down the street. Give me my money."

Shea counted out some coins into her hand. Then Ping Mei turned to me. "Give me some money, enough for a rickshaw. I'll come out to Dragon Springs Road tomorrow and tell you more."

I could see that Anjuin didn't think we should have anything more to do with the woman, but if she was telling the truth, Ping Mei had tried to help my mother so I owed her that much. And I had more questions for her. She was the only connection I had to my past. I gave her a few coins, and she patted my hand when she took them from me. Then she hobbled out of the filthy courtyard and onto the street.

"I'm very sorry. You may have expected to learn that your mother had died," Shea said, "but it's still not easy to hear. I advise you not to have anything more to do with that woman."

"She'll just spend the money on opium," Liu said, on our way out. "She's swindling you."

Shea bid us farewell, and I watched him walk to his rickshaw. He paused to give a coin to a beggar, then hastened his step to avoid other beggars who were hobbling in his direction, hoping for a share in his largesse.

"I was hoping for a good human interest story, but those require a happy ending." Liu shrugged, but he smiled as he said it.

"Thank you, Mr. Liu," I said. "Thank you very much for your generous help. At least now I know my mother is dead."

But I would never know why she left me behind. Or my father's identity.

Anjuin and I were as silent on the trip home as we had been on the way in to Shanghai. When we were on Chung San Road and could see the brick piers that marked the entrance to Dragon Springs Road, Anjuin took my hand.

"Are you all right, Jialing?" she asked.

I shook my head. "My mother was free of Master Fong. She was working at an inn. Why didn't she come back to get me?"

THE DAY AFTER our visit to the Old City, Anjuin and I went to the Western Residence to deliver First Wife's lunch. We had just opened the door between the two courtyards when we heard Lao-er confronting an unwanted arrival.

"Get away from here," Lao-er's contemptuous voice rang out. "I'll report you to the beggars' guild."

A hoarse voice, just as contemptuous, replied. "I'm not a beggar. I'm here to see the young lady, Miss Zhu."

"Please, Anjuin," I begged. "Let her in just this once. I have to know more."

She relented with a sigh. "It's all right, Lao-er," she called. "I'll deal with the woman."

Ping Mei stepped inside, ignoring Lao-er's suspicious glare. She hadn't spent my coppers on opium; she really had spent the money on a ride out of Shanghai. She looked around as though satisfying herself that she was really back.

Anjuin pointed at the blanket roll slung over Ping Mei's shoulder. "Why did you bring your bedding? I hope you're not thinking of staying."

The woman chuckled. "Everything I own is in here. You think I'd leave it behind to be stolen?"

"Let's go into the Western Residence," Anjuin said, pushing open the door.

Anjuin and I took the trays to First Wife's rooms. When I returned to the courtyard, Ping Mei was resting on the steps of the *erfang,* the one where my playroom used to be. She sat with the blanket roll tucked under her like a cushion. I avoided looking at her, at the disfiguring scars and her toothless smile.

"I don't have any more money," I said. "So tell me the truth. Everything you remember about my mother."

"ALL I KNOW was from chatting with her a bit now and then. She kept very private about her past," Ping Mei said. "Other things I overheard from the Fongs."

Master Fong had met my mother while on a trip to sell off more of the Fong estates. His host had hired some women to sing and entertain during dinner. Master Fong took a fancy to my mother and purchased her from the brothel. He was so infatuated he even agreed to let her bring me along. He returned to Dragon Springs Road with my mother and a baby who wasn't his.

So the insults people flung at me were true. I was the daughter of a whore.

Master Fong's First Wife refused to let this new mistress live in the Central Residence with the rest of the family, so Master Fong put us in the Western Residence. A few months after we moved in, Master Fong and his younger brother had a violent argument.

"It was a blessing when their uncle in Manchuria wrote asking to adopt the boy," Ping Mei said. "The younger brother left Dragon Springs Road that week. One less mouth to feed."

"Do you know anything about my mother's family?" I said.

She shrugged. "Your mother had a good upbringing, I'm sure of it. You could tell by her manners. And she could read and write a little."

It was common enough for good families to fall into decline, to sell their daughters for a brief reprieve from complete destitution.

Anjuin emerged from the main house with a broom and began sweeping the veranda steps. I could see First Wife at the window, picking at her meal, looking out curiously from time to time. She was in a docile mood today and wouldn't come out without first being encouraged.

"Have the Yangs found a servant for the madwoman?" Ping Mei asked.

"How do you know?" I said, astonished.

"Gossip. The servants around this neighborhood like to talk." She coughed, a harsh, painful sound, and spat on the ground.

Anjuin finished sweeping and came to join us. "You can leave now," she said to Ping Mei. "There's nothing more for you here."

"Let me rest my feet a bit longer," Ping Mei said. She stretched out her legs and I saw her feet were bound. "It's noon. Is there something to eat?"

Anjuin gave me a long look. "All right, wait here."

Ping Mei continued to gaze around the courtyard. "When you were little," she said, "didn't you find your life strange, living here with no one but your mother?"

"I knew no other life, so I never wondered," I said. "How did you come to Dragon Springs Road?"

Her husband had been a soldier in the Qing Imperial Army. He went to Peking to defend the city during the Boxer Rebellion and never returned. She presumed he had been killed.

"But it's hard to say with soldiers," she said. "He might've found some other woman."

When her landlord threw her out, Ping Mei went to the marketplace. She heard the Fongs needed a housekeeper. It paid badly, but it was better than no pay at all.

"Then I left to work at the inn. But after this," she said, touching her mangled cheek, "even brothels were reluctant to have me clean their rooms. Put the customers off."

In a city hardened to the countless maimed and disfigured on its streets, her ravaged face elicited little sympathy. Ping Mei became the lowest kind of servant at the cheapest brothels in the Old City, scuttling around as invisibly as possible, mopping up when customers vomited or worse. She carried out chamber pots and washed soiled linens.

Anjuin returned and handed me two pork-and-vegetable *baozhi* and a small kettle of hot water. The look on her face told me she would not tolerate Ping Mei's presence for long. She went back into the main house with *baozhi* for herself and First Wife.

I took one *baozhi* and gave the other to Ping Mei, who took the stuffed bun without thanks. When I poured her a bowl of hot water, she merely nodded. She chewed slowly, all the while gazing around the courtyard.

She leaned back on the step and peered at me with her good eye. "Tell your mistress I'm willing to look after the madwoman."

"You? Live here?" I exclaimed. "They'd never agree. And I can't ask. I'm nobody."

"Your friend is a daughter of the house." She gave me a crafty look. "Get her to help you. How desperate are they to save face? To make sure the madwoman stops waking up the neighborhood at night? That she never escapes?"

"No," I said. "I have no obligation to do anything for you. You can leave now."

Besides, what would Fox say when she came back?

Ping Mei leaned back against the steps and shook her finger. "You owe me. My face is ruined because I tried to help your mother." Her rough voice softened, grew cajoling. "If I live here, I can tell you more about her, tell you what she was like."

Ping Mei unfolded her blanket, and I saw she had a clean tunic rolled up inside. She proceeded to wash up using the hot water and a rag.

It's all right, Fox said. She can stay.

If Fox hadn't returned, I wouldn't have dared go against Anjuin's wishes and approach Grandmother Yang.

The interview was a short one. In a clean tunic, Ping Mei made her case. She had been a servant for the Fongs and was now fallen on hard times. A poor woman, already so unlucky she hardly cared if she had to live in an unlucky home. Grandmother Yang agreed to try her out for a week. It also helped that Ping Mei asked for very little pay, only her food and a few coppers each week.

"After all, she used to work for the Fongs," Grandmother Yang said. "She must be somewhat reliable."

As far as the Yangs were concerned, Ping Mei had simply come back to her old employer's home to see whether the current owners needed a servant. Dajuin was the only one who knew how she had been found and my role in finding her; he had agreed not to say anything.

I couldn't believe that First Wife didn't protest Ping Mei moving in with her, that she was willing to ignore the woman's disfigured features and coarse voice.

But that night, First Wife was miraculously quiet.

"Was it you, Fox?" I asked, when she paid me a visit in my dreams.

Without Fox's influence, there was no way that Grandmother Yang would've allowed Ping Mei into the household. Nor would First Wife ever have agreed to someone like Ping Mei as her maid. Perhaps it was Fox who had given First Wife a night of quiet slumber.

It was midnight in the Western Residence. From the shelter of the *erfang*, Fox and I watched a light spring rain fall. Her fur was meticulously groomed as usual and she cocked her head at me with the same familiar insouciance.

Grandmother Yang was desperate. It's wasn't difficult giving things a nudge.

"I was so sure you would be unhappy to find First Wife living here. And now Ping Mei."

I don't understand everything, she said, but I believe this place attracts the broken. The influence of the first Fox spirit who lived here in ancient times is still strong. I acknowledged this when I made my home here, and I respect it.

I could hold back no longer. "Where have you been? It's been nearly two years, not six months!"

That's not so bad, she said, rubbing her ears with one neat paw. Sometimes I've been off by a decade.

I burst into tears. Almost immediately I felt an arm around my shoulders, and I buried my face against her shoulder. The soft cotton of her robes smelled like wild thyme. Fox's voice murmured to me, soothing as rainfall. Gradually my sobs abated into hiccups.

The skies cleared and we sat on the veranda railings side by side. The constellations were veiled by the thinnest of clouds and Fox pointed them out to me: the Winnowing Basket, the Oxherd, the Weaving Girl, and the Jade Well.

"Did you find other Foxes?" I said, remembering why she had gone away.

Yes. But not the sort I was looking for, she said. She sounded sad. My first destination wasn't far from Shanghai. I went to a town called Pinghu, where a man named Zhang walked through a Door and became an immortal.

She had visited Pinghu two hundred years ago when news of the incident was still fresh but had found no trace of a Door. This time she had gone to sniff out other Foxes, but all she found were ordinary foxes. She had enjoyed a brief period of wildness with them and continued on her way.

In Xian, a city that had been China's capital in ancient times, she saw a Fox. He was in the shape of an elderly scholar, on an early morning stroll beside the Big Goose Pagoda. The old man took one look at Fox and hurried away. Fox didn't follow.

In the city of Yangchow she found a female Fox living comfortably in the ruins of an abandoned house beside the home of a family called Wei. The women of the Wei family were Buddhist but had the good sense to respect Fox spirits. They made regular offerings of dried fruit and eggs at a Fox altar just behind the ruins of the house.

I learned from her, she said, that over the past several decades, most of our kind moved away from farms, away from river plains and cities, away from humans and their endless wars. This Fox stayed in Yangchow because she had become fond of the Weis' middle daughter.

The Yangchow Fox often took human form to visit her friend. The two would stroll around the courtyard chatting like the neighbors they had become. However, the Wei daughter had died recently and the Yangchow Fox would be leaving. Perhaps for Gansu Province in the west or Manchuria in the northeast. Perhaps the island of Taiwan, reputed to be a wild and uncivilized place with no native foxes.

"Two years," I said, "and you found just that one Fox?"

She shook her head. I found other Foxes. But they were the sort who wanted to remain Foxes. None of them were working to attain enlightenment. Perhaps by now all the Foxes who wanted to become human or *xian* have succeeded. Perhaps only the most ordinary Fox spirits like me remain.

"What does that mean for you?" I said.

It means there aren't any Foxes left who can offer guidance on how to become *xian* even if I possessed the right qualities, she sighed. There's no way I can enter the land of immortals now except through a Door.

"What about when Anna went through the Door?" I asked. "Why didn't the gods let you through then?"

There was a haunted look in her eyes, and then she looked away. She took my hand. The scent of wild thyme drifted in the air.

Let me show you the places where I traveled this time, she said.

. . . karst peaks loom through the morning drizzle, their sides rising up sheer and straight from the river valley, rank upon rank. I'm Fox in human form, a young woman disguised as a man. I'm lounging on a raft in the river, looking up at the peaks. I wear a rain cape made from layers of palm-tree leaves and a wide-brimmed hat of woven bamboo. A river dolphin swims near, unseen by the raft man. I trail a hand in the water and it nudges me, recognizing a kindred spirit. The raft man poles us toward a village where I will continue my journey. A rooster crows and I lick my lips . . .

. . . unnoticed, I follow behind the camels. We travel by night when it's cool. The concave slipface of the sand dune curves beside us, so huge a formation that it has been alongside the caravan for hours. There are no Foxes in the desert, but I've seen shy antelopes and tiny hopping jerboas. The leader of the caravan runs ahead to the low crest at the end of the dune and shouts in excitement. When we catch up, he is already running downhill, to a pagoda surrounded by guesthouses, a habitat of humans at the edge of an oasis, a blue crescent of water that captures the reflection of the silver crescent overhead. To have such trees and greenery amid an ocean of sand is so improbable Fox hopes to find other enchantments here. But the oasis is all there is . . .

I woke up, my mind filled with vast landscapes, visions of

China beyond my own constrained world, wilderness and beauty beyond imagining.

PING MEI HAD forced her way into our lives, but the strange woman was so discreet and looked after First Wife so attentively that after a while the household stopped worrying about her presence. If not for her occasional appearances in the kitchen, Ping Mei might've been invisible.

Once a week, she limped out to the shops on Chung San Road to buy tobacco and small treats for herself. I knew from the herbalist that she also bought a tincture of opium. Sometimes she hobbled into the kitchen to refill the tea canister or the oil jar. Mrs. Hao was openly curious, but Ping Mei said very little to her. She did, however, sometimes sit at the end of the kitchen table to help string beans or clean fish, as though hungry for companionship but reluctant to get drawn in too far.

"Have you spoken to any of the neighbors' servants?" I asked. "Do they remember you?"

She shook her head. "Hardly knew them back then anyway. And the old families are gone now, aren't they?"

It was true. The other houses up and down Dragon Springs Road no longer belonged to the same families who had lived there when the Yangs first arrived. Some had been auctioned off to pay debts, others had been sold by surviving family members after the cholera outbreak. The Shens' son had not wanted to keep his childhood home.

ON THE PRETEXT of looking in on First Wife, I visited the Western Residence every few days to talk to Ping Mei. Each time I hoped she would remember something else about my mother. I never stayed long, just enough to gauge whether she was in the mood to talk.

Anjuin didn't approve of Ping Mei. She thought I should stay away from the Western Residence.

"You're disappointed and angry that your mother left you behind," she said. "But she's dead now, and Ping Mei can't give you answers about your family or why your mother didn't come get you as soon as she was rid of Noble Uncle."

Yet I couldn't stay away even though I felt uneasy in the woman's presence. It was the way her one good eye looked at me with such intensity. Perhaps one eye had to do the work of two. I avoided looking directly at her face, the pitted, scarred features, the toothless gums.

Whenever I prodded her to tell me what she remembered, she would snort. "I've told you everything I know."

All the same, every so often she would drop a tidbit in my lap.

That when my mother first arrived at Dragon Springs Road, she had tried ingratiating herself with the Fong women. She embroidered pieces of satin as gifts to the daughters for making lotus slippers. The Fong girls had cried when Master Fong's First Wife threw the pieces of satin into the stove.

That when Master Fong took jewelry away from his eldest daughter to give my mother, she had sent it back when she learned who owned it.

That when my mother practiced on her *liuqin,* the notes carried over the wall and everyone would pause to listen, even Master Fong's resentful wives. They had no other music.

"They weren't bad, those women," Ping Mei said. "But they lived in despair. Master Fong had no thought for anything but his own pleasures."

Fox, who must have known all this, merely sat beneath the hydrangea shrubs and listened. I knew it was useless asking why she'd never told me anything about my mother, any of the incidents Ping Mei now recounted to me.

PING MEI CAME into the kitchen one day when Anjuin was there.

"She needs something to do," Ping Mei croaked. She was obviously addressing Anjuin, not me or Mrs. Hao. "First Wife can only read and sit for so long. It's not as though I have much to say to her."

"What do you suggest?" Anjuin said. "We don't dare ask her to embroider. That's where all this insanity began."

"Ask her to make shoes," Ping Mei replied promptly. "It's useful, and it will keep her busy. Just ask her to make plain black everyday cloth shoes for the family. No need for embroidery. What they don't need, you can sell at the shop."

"An excellent idea!" Mrs. Hao exclaimed, then glanced at Anjuin.

"I'll speak to my grandmother," Anjuin said. She gave Ping Mei a nod before leaving the kitchen.

I like a harmonious home, Fox said that night. We don't want Ping Mei to cause friction between you and Anjuin.

Life had been much easier since Fox's return. Who knew what dream world now filled First Wife's days, but she seemed content to drift disconnected from the rest of the Yang household. When Master Yang paid her a visit, she no longer fussed over him but smiled vaguely, as if he were a brother or cousin.

Fox seemed sadder after her long journey, but more settled as well. Sometimes we sat on the roof of the main house while First Wife and Ping Mei slept in the rooms below. Fox liked sitting on the roof, especially when she was in the mood for gossip.

The foreign teachers are starting to complain. They think Maiyu is stealing from them.

"More than usual?" I asked.

One way or another, all servants stole from their masters or found ways to profit from their employment. There was so little to go around and so many mouths to feed. Even the most honest man had to find ways to coax a little more advantage out of his situation. Take a commission from vendors. Get a better price for the master and keep the difference. Best of all, place a relative in a job and expand opportunities for the family.

Ah-Jien, the house servant, never bought needles, thread, or hairpins; she simply helped herself while cleaning rooms. Mrs. Hao bargained fiercely at the market for better prices and pocketed the savings. The rice store paid her so that she wouldn't go to another shop for the Yang's monthly rice purchase. Lao-er always hired his own nephews to help with garden cleanup every spring. The clerk at the newspaper who'd tried to cheat me was no more than a bit player in this ongoing endeavor.

Between Grandmother Yang and Anjuin, the Yang servants could only manage small liberties, the kind a wise employer was willing to overlook. Anjuin was extremely vigilant.

Maiyu steals tins of foreign food and sells them at the market before the teachers get back from school.

"They won't accuse her without proof," I said. "It's their way."

Master Yang's mill is doing very well, Fox continued. *Too well. He's had to increase the protection money he pays to the Green Gang.*

"Wasn't it the Red Gang?" I said. Every Shanghai business paid a "tax" to local gangs.

The Greens have a clever and ruthless leader, she said. They're in the ascendant now.

Before I could ask how she knew about gangs, I found myself down in the courtyard standing in front of the white hydrangeas. Fox pushed her muzzle into a patch of clove pinks growing beside the shrubs and sniffed. These foreign flowers smell very pretty. But they're all color, no structure. They don't really fit in a Chinese garden.

These courtyards where I had grown up were all I knew of gardens, and I thought Anna's flowers added a nice touch of color. I began to protest, but then . . .

. . . the skies are gray, as gray as the slate beneath my paws as I walk through a winter garden, brown earth covering peony roots, vines bare of leaves. A heavy frost whitens moss-covered stones and a light wind chills the air. There are low hillocks crowned by small pavilions. An arched bridge of stone spans the pond. The entire scene is austere and without color . . .

Look closer, Fox's voice whispers in my mind, and I look again.

. . . a low mist covers the pond. Tall rocks at the center of the pond rise above the mist, drawing the eye upward to take in a view of the tall pagoda that lies beyond the garden walls. Every path I wander offers its own view of the garden, careful compositions of trees and rocks that frame and conceal, obstruct and anticipate. There is no central highlight to the garden, no majestic water feature or bright concentrations of color. Enjoyment comes from wandering through a series of vistas, from noticing how bamboo shadows cast against a whitewashed wall create a scene or how latticework openings in a wall play a role in the illusion of shadow and light. The visitor is unaware and uncaring of the garden's boundaries, barely glimpsed through pine and bamboo, obscured so that the garden appears endless . . .

The best gardens are created through the art of deception, says Fox. Gardens should employ the art of the large in the small and the small in the large, providing for the real in the unreal and the unreal in the real.

CHAPTER 15

February 1919, Year of the Goat

I was eighteen now with only a few months before graduation from the mission school. Once my time at the school came to an end I could no longer count on the Yangs for support. Anjuin was in no position to help me. She was twenty-four and still unmarried.

She had convinced her father to buy a used sewing machine and earned a small income from her dressmaking business, which she ran from the small dry goods shop. She kept a few copies of foreign fashion magazines in the store, and although none of her customers were brave enough to wear Western styles, they liked Anjuin's small flourishes. A ruffle on the hem or artful pleats on a skirt panel made her customers feel daring and modern.

During his annual New Year's speech, Master

Yang said his prospects were looking up, and this time his assurances rang with unusual confidence. He had just signed a contract for a large order of heavy white twill to the company that supplied table linens for the Shanghai Club, the Astor Hotel, and a number of steamship companies.

"We've turned the corner," he declared and downed another cup of wine. "This will make our reputation."

From the other side of the table, Grandmother Yang gave him a worried look. Such talk tempted evil spirits.

"I'm a little stouter these days, eh?" he said, smiling at her. "People expect a successful businessman to look well fed and energetic."

Anjuin began ladling out the winter melon soup I'd just brought in, then paused. "Is someone banging at the door?"

"Unexpected visitors for the New Year," Master Yang cried. "Girl, tell Lao-er to open the gates. Invite them to share our supper!"

Lao-er was already on his way from the kitchen, his New Year's dinner interrupted, grumbling as he headed for the gate. But as I followed him, I thought the pounding sounded frenzied, not like the good-natured rappings of a drunken well-wisher.

Lao-er opened the gate, and I nearly collided with the man who burst in. "I'm Wu, foreman at the mill. I must see Master Yang immediately!"

Despite the cold evening air, he was damp with sweat. Through the open gate I saw a rickshaw puller leaning against the wall, hand on his side, panting as though he had run a long distance. Out on Dragon Springs Road, a knot of curious neighbors had gathered across the way, drawn by the frantic knocking. Lao-er had enough presence of mind to shut the gate against their inquisitive stares.

The foreman followed me, calling out as we ran for the dining hall.

"Master Yang, the mill is on fire! The mill is on fire! Master Yang!"

Master Yang came hurrying out of the dining hall, Dajuin by his side. Behind them, Grandmother Yang leaned against the open doorway, holding on as though unable to stand on her own.

THE RUMBLE OF thunder came closer, and I climbed out of bed to make sure the window shutters were latched. There were voices and footsteps. I pushed open the window to look out. It was nearly dawn, and in the dim light, Third Wife and Grandmother Yang stood at the center of the courtyard, facing the front gate. Wrapped in blankets, they were as still as boats becalmed on a lake. I sensed Anjuin beside me, and after a moment, she slipped out to join them. Yun Na came out of the *erfang* but remained on her veranda near the covered walkway.

More voices. Men's voices. The front gate slammed shut.

Then slowly, terribly slowly, figures appeared. Master Yang and Dajuin entered the courtyard, exhaustion evident in every step. The breeze carried with it smells of smoke, sweat, and fear.

"Go and get something to eat from Mrs. Hao," Master Yang said to Dajuin.

Dajuin shook his head. "I'd rather get some sleep, Father." Slowly he trudged up the steps of his *erfang*.

"Bring hot water for your husband's basin," Grandmother Yang called to Yun Na. "Then take all his clothes and wash them right away."

For once, Yun Na hastened to obey. It should've been my task to stir the ashes in the kitchen stove and get the kettle boiling, but I wanted to know what had become of the mill. I stayed by the window.

Master Yang trudged to the main house. He stumbled at the bottom step, too tired to lift his feet. The first drops of rain spit down, accompanied by thunder, louder this time. He sat down heavily and turned to look up at the sky.

"*Now* the rain comes," I heard him say. Then a low chuckle.

"Eldest Son?" Grandmother Yang's voice was impatient, frightened.

He stood up. "It's gone, Mother. The mill has burned down."

Workers in the district had formed a bucket line to the river. Master Yang, Dajuin, and Lao-er had joined in, but the flames went on to devour the factory. Filled with cotton, the mill and its warehouse burned to the ground. By the time the fire brigades arrived, the weaving machines were no better than scrap metal.

"The police came," Master Yang said. "They think it could be arson. Those foreign devils from the Shanghai Municipal Police actually asked me about insurance. As if I would set fire to my own factory to get insurance money."

Rain began falling, cold hard drops that bounced off the tiled roofs. Master Yang turned away from the sky to look at his mother and daughter.

He laughed, a hollow and choking sound. "I told them, there is no insurance."

Grandmother Yang staggered a little and clutched at Anjuin to regain her balance.

"I must write to my brothers," Master Yang said and entered the house. The three women stood in the rain, holding on to each other.

WE MAY AS well have draped white cloth across our gates, as families do when in mourning.

Through the peephole in the front gate I could see the curious clustered in twos and threes across the street. It was obvious they were gossiping about the Yangs, but none of them came by to rap on the door. Some passersby even crossed the street to avoid coming too close. A pall of ill fortune hung over the Yang household, and if any of it was leaking out, it was safer to stay away.

At noon Master Yang was still shut in his study. He came out briefly to send Dajuin to the telegraph office with a message for his brothers in Ningpo. Then he withdrew back into his study.

Yun Na didn't leave her room all morning. Mrs. Hao had me deliver broth to her room in the *erfang*. When I arrived, Grandmother Yang was sitting beside Yun Na's bed, looking exasperated. Dajuin's wife wept, rocking on the bed while holding tightly to her little daughter's hands.

"My poor daughter, what will become of us? How will we live? How can we afford your dowry?"

Grandmother Yang looked up when I entered, and I placed the bowl in her outstretched hands.

"Chicken broth with an infusion of Compassionate Sage mixture," I said, reciting what Mrs. Hao had made me memorize. "Sour jujube seed, golden thread rhizome, sweet flag rhizome, mimosa tree bark, red sage root, and *ling chih* mushroom powder. For hysteria."

"Can you drink this yourself or do I have to spoon-feed you?" Grandmother Yang asked Yun Na.

Yun Na struggled up. "I'm not hysterical," she said, grimacing at the pungent broth. "I'm angry. I'm angry and disappointed. We are in so much debt. We'll be working to pay off the bank for the rest of our lives."

Her eyes fell on me, and she pointed an accusing finger, nail chewed to the quick. "It's your fault, you . . . you cursed girl! They should've thrown you out on the streets! Your mother knew you were bad luck, that's why she abandoned you!"

"Eldest Granddaughter-in-Law." Grandmother Yang's voice was icy. In blaming the Yangs' decision to keep me, Yun Na was blaming Grandmother Yang.

The old woman turned to me. "Go back to your chores, now, Jialing."

But as I left, I felt her eyes piercing through my back. I could almost hear her mind working.

THE PLUM TREES in the Western Residence were always the first to leaf, spreading a haze of tender green over branches and twigs, so faint at first you would have thought it a trick of the light. Fox sat on the garden seat beneath their fragile shade, dressed in lilac hues. Behind her, the sun threw stippled green light through the bamboos. She patted the bench beside her.

So Yun Na has finally calmed down, she said.

"Mrs. Hao had to boil up some Compassionate Sage mixture," I sighed. "A relief to everyone. We were worried she would become hysterical."

Fox snorted. That one. I'd like to give her some of what Ping Mei gives First Wife.

I frowned at her. "What does Ping Mei give First Wife?"

Tincture of opium.

"But that means Ping Mei is turning her into an opium addict!"

Just a little at night, to help her sleep, Fox said. She puts it in First Wife's sweet red bean soup. I'm sure Grandmother Yang suspects but turns a blind eye. As for First Wife, it makes her sorrows easier to bear.

It was true. Insanity was an embarrassment and the Yangs wanted to save face. They didn't want First Wife going out or waking the neighborhood at night with her wailing. By giving her a courtyard of her own and a servant of her own, they were al-

ready treating her very well, for a barren wife who had been set
aside.

But you want to talk about something else, Fox said.

"You know about the fire at the mill. The Yangs are bankrupt.
I graduate soon and Miss Morris will stop paying the Yangs. They
won't keep me beyond that. Grandmother Yang wants to go back
to Ningpo and I know she won't take me. I need to earn a living."

Can the mission school give you work?

I shook my head. I knew how much effort Miss Morris put into
finding work for all of us, the obstacles she faced each day.

Fox cocked her head. With the right patron, it's possible to
live a good life for a while.

"What happens after 'for a while'?"

If a woman is frugal, she can put aside enough money to
buy a house or a small business after her patron sets her aside.
If a woman is clever and a credit to her patron, he will give her
money when they part.

"You have a story for me," I said, sighing.

I knew a young woman, once, Fox said, as if I hadn't spoken.
Her patron bought her from a brothel and her story would've
ended like so many others, but she was clever. She saved her
money against the day when she would lose his favor. She
kept only one maid and lived frugally. She made copies of the
jewelry he gave her and sold the real ones.

When her patron became infatuated with another woman,
he demanded the jewelry back, which she returned without a
murmur. Then she moved to another city, changed her name, and
called herself a widow. With her savings she bought an old house
and turned it into an inn. She became a respected innkeeper.
When she died, she left the estate to her faithful maid. The maid,
alas, got married and her husband squandered her inheritance.

"Have you no stories about happy marriages?" I asked.

Marriage isn't always a happy condition for women, Fox said. At least not the ones I've seen. Marriage doesn't guarantee happiness or a roof over your head. In your situation, a kind and wealthy benefactor would be a better solution.

"In my situation, I don't run into a lot of kind or wealthy men," I pointed out.

That newspaper editor seems nice. Her green pupils glowed brighter. Liu Sanmu. A nice name too.

"Women nowadays have more ways to earn a living than they did three hundred years ago, Fox," I said. "And anyway, Liu Sanmu and I are unlikely to meet again."

She stared into the bamboos, her eyes shining green, her brows drawn together as though in deep thought.

"What are you thinking?" I asked, after a few minutes of silence.

Oh. I was thinking that I still miss her, Fox said. The innkeeper. We were good friends.

"As good friends as you were with the sister of your scholar-husband?"

No. She was my first and dearest friend.

MASTER YANG RETURNED from Shanghai shortly after noon the following day, shoulders stooped and sagging, dejection seeping from every pore. He had been to see his bank manager, but that meeting couldn't possibly have been worse than the hour he spent with Grandmother Yang upon his return. The door to her room was shut, but paper-covered windows offer no privacy. We all heard her harsh words.

"We were doing badly this month, Mother," Master Yang sobbed. "It was either pay the insurance company or pay the gangsters."

"But afterwards, why didn't you renew the insurance?"

"I had to spend a lot of money to obtain that contract with the table linens company. I paid an introduction fee to a clerk just to get a meeting with his manager. Then more fees to the manager to arrange an appointment with the owner. It's the squeeze, Mother, always the squeeze."

There was silence from Grandmother Yang.

"I was going to renew the insurance next month," Master Yang said, "after getting paid for the first order of table linens."

Which he wouldn't be able to deliver, now that the mill was gone.

"Our clan can't afford to carry so much debt," Grandmother Yang said. "You will sell this property, Eldest Son. We are leaving Dragon Springs Road."

THE YANGS' PROSPECTS for selling Dragon Springs Road quickly were not good. No Chinese wanted to buy a place that had been so unlucky. As for foreigners, their countries were still embroiled in a war and until the fighting was over and the division of spoils clear, very few were willing to buy property outside the foreign concessions. Sooner or later, for the right price, the estate on Dragon Springs Road would sell. Just not quickly enough for Grandmother Yang.

She wanted the family away from this ill-omened home. They would leave immediately for Ningpo. She decided that Dajuin would stay behind to collect rent from the Eastern Residence and take care of selling the property. Anjuin would stay behind also, to run the little dry goods store and keep house for Dajuin.

Yun Na wasn't happy about leaving Dajuin, but she was with child again and Grandmother Yang wanted her in Ningpo, where she could supervise the pregnancy. Yun Na was in tears, not because she would miss Dragon Springs Road but because she didn't look forward to sharing a home with an entire clan's worth of Yang women. They would be returning to Ningpo with a madwoman and a mountain of debt. It would not be a joyous welcome. There were bad feelings among Master Yang's brothers over the weaving mill. Master Yang, the eldest brother, had lost face as well as the family fortune.

All the servants left to find work elsewhere. Only Mrs. Hao would be going to Ningpo with the Yangs, as cook and companion to First Wife.

At least Grandmother Yang didn't forbid me to live at Dragon Springs Road while the Yangs still owned it. As for Ping Mei, if Grandmother Yang suspected she might try to squat in the Western Residence, she never voiced any such concern. Perhaps Grandmother Yang had decided to leave that problem to the new owners.

"I don't need much," Ping Mei told me. "I'll go out and beg. I've done it before. I can pay the beggars' guild to let me work in this area. Until the property sells, I'll sleep here. That's a better life than any beggar can expect."

She took out a small brown bottle and took a sip.

"What is that?" I asked, although I already knew.

"Tincture of opium. For the pain in my throat." She grinned. "And my feet. And my chest."

ON THE DAY the Yangs left, I couldn't help but remember the day of their arrival ten years ago, Master Yang's cheerful voice calling out, the orange tree Lao-er wheeled in, the taste of the steamed bun from Anjuin.

In the front courtyard, I knelt in farewell to Grandmother Yang. It was a small enough gesture. I owed my life to her decision to keep me, even if Fox had nudged her toward it. In addition to my mother's note and the gold coins she had provided, there had to have been an inclination, an initial thought for Fox to build on to deepen the desire to follow through with an idea. Grandmother Yang's kindness had been real.

She patted me on the head. "You have a fine foreign education, Jialing. There's no need for you to worry about the future."

We both knew that wasn't true. But I didn't correct her. It allowed us both to save face.

NOW THAT THE rest of the Yang family was gone, Anjuin and I prepared the evening meal together when I came home from school. We talked freely with no fear of being overheard. If not for the uncertainty hanging over us all, it would've felt like a holiday.

The dining furniture was gone, so the three of us ate at the kitchen table. There was no servants' table, no ceremony.

Perhaps Dajuin had always been approachable, but I'd been intimidated by his status as the eldest son of the family and kept my distance. I found him less formal now and saw how affectionately he treated Anjuin, teasing her solemn features into a smile. He read out loud to us from the newspaper while we cleaned up.

Suddenly he seemed younger. I realized I'd only ever seen him bent under the weight of running the mill, correcting his father's missteps without appearing impatient, soothing Yun Na when she threatened the harmony of the household over some imagined slight.

"I've decided to look for work in Shanghai," he said. "I was thinking at one of the mills in Chapei, as an administrator or foreman."

"Why?" Anjuin asked, sitting back in surprise.

"There's not enough to go around in Ningpo," he said. "Since we've been in Shanghai, our uncles and cousins have been running the business by themselves and now they have to make room for Father and me. I'd rather strike out on my own even if it means working for strangers."

"Does Father know?"

Dajuin shook his head. "Let's not say anything unless I manage to find a job."

"If Father listened to him more, Dajuin would be less eager to find opportunities outside the family," Anjuin said to me later. It was as close as she would come to admitting that her father was incompetent. "I wish I could find work in Shanghai. I don't want to go back to Ningpo either."

But we all knew that was impossible. Anjuin's fate was to live out her days in the Yang household, allowed only to work at a Yang dry goods store.

By unspoken accord we never mentioned Ping Mei in front of Dajuin. As far as he knew, she had left with the other servants. Each day, the strange woman hobbled her way out to Chung San Road to beg and returned to the Western Residence before sundown. She came to the kitchen occasionally for a bit of oil or rice, and she always left a few coins in payment, evidence of a successful day on the streets. She never came when Dajuin was home. Sometimes she spent entire days in the Western Residence, sitting on the veranda with her pipe, sipping on weak tea and gazing about her with unfocused eyes.

"Why don't you go out to beg every day?" I asked her.

"Who knows how much longer I can enjoy this home?" she said, coughing into her sleeve. "It's not as though I enjoy begging. If I can afford what I need, why work any harder?"

I had seen her sidle into the herbalist's on Chung San Road to refill the small brown bottle she kept in her pocket. That was really all she wanted. She had grown even thinner, and when I offered her food, she nearly always refused. Ping Mei seemed content to live on hot water with a few tea leaves, bowls of boiled rice, and the occasional egg.

I wondered what she did for fuel until I noticed the lengths of wood heaped behind the kitchen stove, their ends carved with cloud patterns. She had salvaged railings and panels from the veranda of the unused *erfang* on the other side of the courtyard.

IN THE WEEKS before graduation I spent my lunch hours in the library poring over newspapers for job listings. I wrote application letters in careful brushstrokes if in Chinese or took my turn on the old school typewriter if the job was advertised in one of Shanghai's English-language papers.

Clerical or secretarial, tutoring or child care, I replied to them all. All this effort, even though I knew it was futile. There were just too many people in Shanghai, too many with more skills than I could offer. There were people willing to work for almost nothing. There were few enough ways a woman could earn a livelihood, and the decent work went first to young women whose family had *guanxi*, connections, women whose families could afford red envelopes of cash to ease an introduction. Families whose daughters weren't tainted with foreign blood.

The Shanghai Women's Commercial and Savings Bank advertised for a filing clerk. *A position suitable for the secondary school graduate. Must be tidy in dress and grooming, with clear handwriting.* It was the first bank founded by women, a fine place to begin a career, a place where I could use my English skills. I wanted this job very badly and was thrilled to receive a reply to my application.

"This is just a small bank, Miss Zhu," the manager said. Her hair was pulled back in a large bun, the only ornament on her black tunic a small pearl brooch. "We prefer girls with family connections, girls who can bring us more clients. I didn't notice you had graduated from a mission school. That was my mistake."

Her words were pleasant enough, but disdain clung to the corners of her lips. It was another, typically brief interview, the sort that was over as soon as I entered the door. I had let myself hope, a mistake.

Miss Morris did her best to help me.

"I met Mrs. Burns at a charity event," she said, handing me a name and address. "She wants a nanny who can also tutor her children, and I've persuaded her to meet with you. Here is your letter of reference."

ON THE DAY of the interview, Anjuin helped me dress. She plaited my hair into two neat braids and coiled them at the nape of my neck.

"Dajuin is going into Shanghai to meet someone who's interested in the property," she said. "I asked him to share a rickshaw with you, so you don't show up at this foreign woman's home all hot and dusty from walking the whole way. Just part of the way."

The rickshaw man grumbled at having to carry two adults but Dajuin pointed out that I was only a very light girl and would be getting off at the edge of the International Settlement. We were nearly there before I realized I'd said nothing to Dajuin during the ride, so caught up had I been in my own worries about the morning.

"Umm, so Anjuin says there's a potential buyer for the estate?"

"Yes," he said. "He has some questions and wanted to meet first. If he likes the answers, he'll come out to Dragon Springs Road with me for a look."

"Where are you meeting him?"

"At the offices of *Xinwen Bao* newspaper."

THE BURNS HOUSE made me gasp, each window as tall and wide as a man with arms outstretched. My nails dug small white crescents in the palm of my hand. A very superior young man opened the door. I realized that despite the impeccably white collar peeping above the high neck of his tunic, he was merely a servant.

Inside, sunshine flooded through clear glass panes. Each window was draped with enough fabric to sew an entire family's wardrobe. Vases filled with masses of flowers dazzled my eyes with their luxurious excess. It was so different from what I was used to, arrangements composed of a few well-chosen stems that invited stillness and contemplation.

The servant led me to a sitting room where a large foreign woman waited, a froth of mauve silk ruffles that overflowed a small chair. The man beside her was equally bulky, with a curly beard the color of chestnuts. His eyes traveled over me as Mrs. Burns opened the letter from Miss Morris.

"Well, my dear," he said, leaning down to brush his lips against her cheek. "I have some documents to read before going back to the office."

She nodded, barely glancing up at her husband as she read the letter. Then she asked rather curtly, "What you can teachee?"

"I can teach arithmetic and reading," I said, ignoring the insult of her pidgin English. "I have a lot of experience minding children. Also, if you need any secretarial help, Miss Morris says my penmanship is excellent."

She frowned, regarding me with a look I interpreted as doubt. "Well, at least your English is competent. I thought Miss Morris might've exaggerated."

I smiled, swallowing my anger. "Please, ma'am, how old are the children?"

"They are six and eight," she replied.

"For what they need right now, I believe my education is more than equal to the task." My words were confident, but I kept my voice soft and pleading.

She looked out the window. "My children spend too much time with their amah. They speak too much Chinese and have learned too many Chinese superstitions."

"Mrs. Burns," I said, as pleasantly as I could, "I would only speak English to them. As for superstitions, I've been raised by the mission school."

"Your English is excellent, but I only agreed to see you as a courtesy to Miss Morris. I want a nice English governess, not a half-breed Chinese."

I didn't allow the smile on my face to waver as I stood up, but my heart clenched, a fist of resentment. "I understand, ma'am. Do you know any other families who might need a governess? Or even just a nanny?"

"You people!" she said, crumpling up the letter. "Why do you always push for more? Always pushing, pushing. To give a job to a cousin or brother. As if I were obliged to support your entire family."

"There's no family to support, ma'am," I said. "I'm an orphan. Thank you for your time."

The same house servant took me back downstairs, but once outside the front door, he beckoned me to follow him.

"The master wants to see you," he said.

Around the side of the house, French doors looked out on a marble terrace. The servant knocked and opened one of the doors. Lined from floor to ceiling with bookshelves, the room was undoubtedly a study. A huge desk occupied one end of the room, a pair of armchairs the other. Mr. Burns rose from one of the armchairs. I looked around uncertainly. The house servant stood beside the door, so unobtrusive he was nearly invisible.

"Come closer, young lady. So did my wife hire you?" Mr. Burns asked. I could smell hair oil and the heavy sweet scent of foreign tobacco.

"No, sir."

"Didn't think she would, you being a half-breed," he said.

Suddenly he gripped me by the wrist and pulled me toward him. I lost my balance and fell against his chest. He chuckled, and I felt his hands pat my buttocks, travel down my thighs. Shock and embarrassment held me frozen.

"Good, good," he said, sounding satisfied. "Mrs. Burns goes to her garden club every Tuesday. Come by the house next Tuesday at noon and I'll pay you well."

I pushed him away with all my strength, and he fell back against the armchair with a grunt of pain. When I ran out the terrace door, the house servant made no attempt to stop me.

He called out in Chinese. "Why not earn money for yourself instead of some brothel? You think a *zazhong* girl like you can do better?"

Face burning, eyes stinging with tears, I hardly knew where I went once I ran out the Burnses' front gate. It wasn't this one incident that made me despair. It was all the rejected applications and unsuccessful interviews, the hopelessness of the road ahead. I had been better off illiterate, with no expectations of anything better than a factory or a brothel.

I wiped my eyes and began making my way west along Nanking Road. The faster I walked, the sooner I could get back home. I wanted nothing more than to lie on my cot and pull the covers over my head. But although I quickened my pace, the walk seemed longer than usual and I was tired and thirsty by the time I passed the shops on Chung San Road and finally came within view of the entrance to Dragon Springs Road.

Behind me, the rumble of an automobile.

"Jialing!" A man's voice called out.

It was Dajuin, waving from the passenger window of an automobile. Only the wealthy owned cars and none lived out here, so as soon as the car pulled to a stop, it was surrounded by street urchins, some actually daring to touch the shining dark-green panels.

"Get in, ride the rest of the way home with us," he said. Beside him in the driver's seat was a smiling Liu Sanmu.

I scrambled into the car, the disasters of the day receding with the thrill of being in an automobile for the first time, my skirt sliding across smooth leather seats. I couldn't believe how quickly we reached the entrance to Dragon Springs Road. As the car slowed down, the swarm of excited urchins caught up. Liu Sanmu obliged them by sounding the horn loudly and repeatedly. He got out of the car, laughing at the children, a different person from the serious editor I'd met at the newspaper offices.

The commotion brought Anjuin out from the shop. When Liu Sanmu greeted her with a friendly wave, she turned quite pink.

"Those children won't leave your car alone, Mr. Liu," Dajuin said, apologetically. "Let me open the gates of the Western Residence. It has a large entrance courtyard where you can park while looking at the property."

"Where is Ping Mei?" I whispered to Anjuin.

"Out begging, so they won't see her," she said. "And we may as well call it a day for the shop. Dajuin will want tea for Mr. Liu after he's seen the property."

She left me to take care of closing the shop. Then I gave the main hall a quick sweep before going to the kitchen. We arranged the tea tray and filled a platter with nuts and dried fruit, but as we carried the trays out of the kitchen, the automobile horn tooted from out on Dragon Springs Road. A few minutes later Dajuin came in to the main hall.

"Mr. Liu has left," he said. "He didn't need a close inspection of the houses, he only wanted an idea of how large a property we have."

Apparently the Lius, an old and established Shanghai family, were getting into the real estate business. In obedience to his grandfather's wishes, Liu Sanmu was acquiring land for development. If he bought the Yangs' home, he would tear down the old houses to build modern, Western-style villas.

"How sad," Anjuin said. "Three beautiful courtyard homes, each with its own well."

"Three old homes," Dajuin said, "each in need of expensive repairs. By the way, Jialing, it's thanks to you that Liu Sanmu noticed the ad."

"Me?" I said, looking up from my tea.

"Yes. Mr. Liu told me that when he glanced through the newspaper, the street name in our advertisement caught his attention. Then he remembered you. It made him curious and he decided to take a look at Dragon Springs Road even though it's farther out of Shanghai than he likes."

As soon as we had finished supper, I went to the Western Residence. Ping Mei was in the kitchen on a chair, her back against the wall, feet pointed at the charcoal brazier. Her lids were half closed, a sign that she had just taken some laudanum.

"Well. To what do I owe this visit?" she asked, but her tone wasn't unkind or sarcastic.

"To tell you it looks as though there might be a buyer for the estate," I said. "The automobile that was in the front courtyard earlier."

"I saw the car out on Chung San Road when it drove by," she said. "Well, I suppose I'd better make plans to leave."

Her voice was slightly slurred, and she didn't sound concerned. She sat up and peered at me. "What's worrying you, child?"

"Even with Miss Morris's help, I can't find work," I said, sitting on a kitchen stool. "The Englishwoman I went to see today didn't want me. She wanted a British governess for her children."

But Ping Mei had dozed off again.

Liu Sanmu would make a very suitable patron, a smug voice behind me said. You already know he's kind and wealthy. Now he's interested in buying this property.

"Fox, seduction isn't the only way to solve problems," I said, poking at the fire. "Anyway, to him I'm just a schoolgirl."

Turn around, Jialing.

I did, and it was unnerving. I had never seen Fox this way before. She wore a foreign dress, as she often did, but beneath the close-fitting velvet, her lithe form seemed more rounded, more voluptuous. What startled me most was the change in her face, the same and yet not the same. Her complexion glowed, her cheeks were flushed, and her lips, which were slightly parted, were moist and red, fuller than usual. She gazed down at me with shining eyes, the pupils wide and dark. Her hair, usually looped and twisted elaborately on her head, streamed down her back in a loose, shining ripple of ebony.

I wanted to reach out and stroke her hair. I wanted something I couldn't describe. In that moment, I knew how it would feel to have a man like Liu Sanmu under my spell. A surge of confidence swelled through my bones, a rush of triumph so warm and strong

I nearly fell off the stool. Then the moment passed and the heat drained away.

I agree there are other ways to approach problems, Fox said, but I can't help turning to my particular Fox talent when it's all I have to offer.

She gave her head a toss and once again her hair was coiled on top of her head. The brilliance that had streamed from her only a moment ago faded.

"What particular Fox talent?" I asked, the last of the heat tingling at my fingertips.

To influence. A small tug here, a slight prod there, touches so delicate the mortal mind never suspects, she said. Subtle influences last longer. Over time, they wear grooves into the mind that make the emotions real. Given the right subject, such feelings can even become real.

"No, Fox. I won't be some man's mistress." I pushed away the memory of heat coursing through my bones, of Fox's red lips.

Your foreign education has given you unrealistic expectations, she said. There's no shame in doing what's necessary to survive.

"There are women schoolteachers and nurses now," I said, "even doctors. There's a bank for women, run by women. I could be a clerk or a secretary. I could tutor small children. China is changing."

It's not changing fast enough for the likes of you, Fox said. You're the daughter of a prostitute and an unknown white man. You have no lineage, no family.

"Other orphans have careers," I snapped. "Mary attended the mission college for teachers."

If Mary had finished college, who would've hired her?

"Why can't you understand, Fox?" I cried. "I don't want to end up like my mother. Leave me alone!"

I ran out of the Western Residence.

THAT NIGHT, I dreamed on my own, wandering through a world of hazy colors and indistinct faces. There were voices and images, but nothing meaningful, nothing that stayed in my mind when I woke up.

After washing up the breakfast dishes, I hurried back to the Western Residence. From the kitchen, Ping Mei's voice drifted out, humming a vaguely familiar melody. Whatever the tune, it was made unrecognizable by her raspy voice. I knelt beside the veranda in front of the *erfang* and parted the hydrangea shrubs.

Then I sat on the garden bench and calmed my thoughts, but I couldn't feel her presence. An emptiness in one corner of my mind. I didn't know whether to worry or feel relieved.

Fox's den was empty. She was gone.

CHAPTER 16

Days passed into weeks and to the Yangs' disappointment, there was nothing more from Liu Sanmu.

"He's a wealthy man," Dajuin said. "This isn't as urgent for him as it is for us. He's busy with other matters."

"This is why," Anjuin said, holding out the newspaper, a copy of *Xinwen Bao*. She pointed at the editorial, written by Liu Sanmu. "He's in Peking, covering the student riots."

> *May 4, 1919. Peking. Thousands of students obstructed the streets of Peking to protest the Paris peace talks. Already there is talk of protests spreading across China as citizens gather in anger, and there is much to be angry about.*

China joined in the Great War on the side of the Allies. In exchange for sending noncombatants to Europe, the Allies promised to return to China territories held by Germany, most notably Shandong Province, the birthplace of Confucius.

More than 140,000 volunteers of the Chinese Labour Corps went to Europe. They dug trenches for the Allies, carried corpses off battlefields, unloaded cargo from trucks, trains, and ships. They built roads and repaired vehicles. Many lost their lives. We still don't know how many have returned now that the war is over.

What we do know is that the Allies have betrayed us by handing over Shandong Province to Japan. We have been betrayed by our foreign Allies, perhaps by our own government.

Dajuin put down the paper and sighed. "I don't suppose he'll be back in Shanghai any time soon."

I prayed the student protests in Peking would keep Liu Sanmu there for much, much longer and delay purchase of the estate. It would give me more time to find work.

There was more disappointment in store for the Yangs that day. A large house within walking distance of the mission school had come vacant and Miss Morris had decided to take it. There would be no more rent from the Eastern Residence. I couldn't blame Miss Morris. Dragon Springs Road, once a quiet neighborly enclave, had become a street of empty properties, some in the process of being torn down. There would be more noise and more dust soon. Instead of the quiet the teachers valued so much, there would be the shouts of workmen and the crash of sledgehammers.

"We're terribly sorry to leave our home of so many years,"

Miss Morris said to Dajuin, "but you can't predict when the property will sell and we can't risk having to move unexpectedly. We will leave at the end of this week."

Once more, a procession of oxcarts and handbarrows left Dragon Springs Road. Maiyu rode away on a handbarrow, her short legs dangling over the side, arms firmly wrapped around a canvas sack. She looked small and lost, not at all the terrifying washerwoman of my childhood.

"Good-bye, my dear," Miss Morris said, giving me a kiss on the cheek. "I will keep trying to find you a position."

She knew I was walking into Shanghai every day to find work. I delivered carefully written application letters to clerks whose smirking indifference told me my letters would be tossed in the wastebasket. Some didn't even wait for me to turn my back before crumpling up the paper.

"It's all right, miss," I said. "I know how difficult it is. I don't expect anything. Please, take these."

I pressed three small envelopes into her hand, the English words carefully printed on each in blue ink. *Violas, clove pinks, forget-me-nots.* Seeds I had gathered from Anna's flowers.

DAJUIN RETURNED FROM the post office, bringing letters from the Yangs in Ningpo. Master Yang never wrote more than a brief page of questions and instructions, never any mention of how the clan had been treating his family since their return.

For that, we could count on Yun Na. Rambling and filled with mistakes, her letters complained about being snubbed by the clan. Dajuin leaned on the counter of the shop and read the latest one out loud while Anjuin and I dusted the bolts of fabric on the shelves.

Husband, sell the property on Dragon Springs Road quickly and return to Ningpo. The only kind words I hear in this house are from your grandmother. Your relatives constantly remind me of the mill's failure: that they had to make room for us in the family home, that our children are badly behaved, that the Yang family fortunes will never recover from this setback. I swear, if the breakfast congee overcooks, it's somehow our fault.

Anjuin leaned back in her chair and sighed. "I don't look forward to Ningpo. It's a terrible thing to say, but I hope the property doesn't sell too quickly."

"It will now," Dajuin said. "Now that the war has ended, Shanghai's foreigners are more optimistic. The city will grow and it can only spread westward, out here to the External Roads. Every other property on this street has been sold. We'll be next."

"I suppose there's one good thing about losing our old neighbors," Anjuin said. "The new ones don't know any stories about ghosts and suicidal concubines. They can't frighten off buyers."

The cheerful blare of a horn made us jump to our feet. Dajuin hurried to the open gate.

"It's Mr. Liu," he called to us over his shoulder. "I'll go unlock the Western Residence."

When they came in, I saw that Liu Sanmu was carrying a white cardboard box tied with red string. Dajuin continued through to the main courtyard, but Liu Sanmu ducked into the shop and put the box on the counter. He gave me a wink, then hurried to catch up with Dajuin.

Anjuin opened the box, revealing six éclairs, each on a white paper doily.

"Let's hope Mr. Liu is serious," I said, "especially now that the teachers have left."

"Yes," she repeated. "Let's hope so."

Her eyes lingered, watching Dajuin and Liu Sanmu walk way. Anjuin was twenty-four, and while no one could call her pretty, her skin was pale and unblemished, her eyes clear and intelligent. I thought it was unfair that others didn't realize how attractive she was, with her demeanor of quiet self-assurance.

I put down the éclair. "I'm not hungry. My stomach is churning."

She looked at me with her deep calm eyes. "It's because Mr. Liu might buy the property. And then you'll have nowhere to live."

A quiet shuffling at the door of the shop, and we both turned to see Ping Mei, leaning on her stick, her ravaged features twisted in the grimace that we now knew was her smile. She jingled some coins in her hand and put them on the counter.

"For a bit of salt and rice," she said. "I was going to the kitchen to get it for myself, but there's an automobile in the Western Residence so I thought I'd check with you first."

"Yes, it belongs to someone who wants to buy the property," Anjuin said. "You'd better get out to Chung San Road before they see you."

"I'll bring you some salt and rice later, when you come back," I called to Ping Mei, as she shuffled away.

Anjuin flipped open the lid of the sewing machine and beckoned me to sit down. I was learning how to use it, sewing row after row, practicing to keep the stitches straight. But I'd set the tension too tight and the thread was bunching up. Only Anjuin seemed able to work the fickle machine.

"Why don't you come to Ningpo with us anyway?" she said, watching me slice a tangle of threads away from the needle.

"Once you get there, it will be harder for Grandmother to turn you away."

"You know your grandmother is finished with me," I said. "After the mill burned down, even she believes I'm part of the bad luck that came with this estate."

But Anjuin didn't reply. She was staring at the entrance of the shop. Just outside was a man, tall and broad shouldered, dressed in a Western-style suit of gray flannel, a fedora on his head. He was gazing around the front courtyard, his back to us. When he finally came inside the shop, I saw that he was even more handsome than Liu Sanmu. His face was tanned, his eyes alert and observant. The stranger's glance fell on me, then moved on to Anjuin.

"I'm looking for Yang Dajuin," he said, addressing her.

"He's inside, sir," she said. "Is he expecting you?"

The man held out a newspaper clipping. "I'm here to look at the property."

"I'll go get him." And she left me alone with the stranger, who ignored me.

The man stepped outside again. He walked around and looked through the moon gate at the main courtyard. He ran his hands over the whitewashed brick walls and pulled at a stray honeysuckle vine that had crept over the top of the wall. It seemed to me he was looking at everything very carefully, the sign of a serious buyer.

Dajuin came out, followed by Liu Sanmu, Anjuin right behind.

"I'm Yang Dajuin," Dajuin said, with a slight bow.

"My name is Wan Baoyuan," the stranger said. "I'm here to look at the property."

"Ah, well, ah, I'm afraid Mr. Liu here wants to make an offer," Dajuin said.

"An offer is not the same as a sale." Wan Baoyuan's voice was quiet, but it was the voice of a man used to taking command. "Is the property sold or isn't it?"

"I expect to have the funds in place soon," Liu Sanmu said with a smile.

Wan Baoyuan turned to Dajuin. "Mr. Yang, let me satisfy my curiosity by looking at the property. If it doesn't appeal to me, then that's the end of the matter. If it does and I'm willing to offer more than Mr. Liu, then you're in a better position, aren't you?"

Both Wan Baoyuan's expression and voice betrayed impatience, as though explaining something to a dim-witted schoolboy. Dajuin looked uncomfortable. Then Liu Sanmu laughed.

"Give Mr. Wan a tour," he said. "Let's all three of us go. I wouldn't mind another look myself."

"Of course," Dajuin said, sounding relieved. "Let's start with the Eastern Residence."

After all this time, suddenly there were two potential buyers. I watched them leave, my hands gripping the edge of the countertop. How soon would it be before I'd have to fend for myself? Outside the shop window, Ping Mei's figure limped out of Dragon Springs Road. Her timing was uncanny; she always managed to be away from the Western Residence whenever her presence would've raised questions.

That could be me in a few weeks, I thought. *Perhaps Ping Mei can teach me how to beg.*

Anjuin spent the next half hour tidying up an already tidy shop while I took the broom to the paving stones and swept furiously. Then I heard voices and the creaking sound of rusty hinges. Dajuin was opening the gate to the Western Residence. I couldn't catch their words, but the men's voices were lively and friendly, any earlier tension now absent.

There was a look about Wan Baoyuan, a look I'd come to recognize as confident arrogance. He was a man accustomed to getting his way. A faint memory stirred, something else about him, something I couldn't place. I put away the thought.

Then from the Western Residence came the rumble of Liu Sanmu's automobile starting up, the creaking of gates, and the sound of tires on stone driving away. Dajuin came into the shop, looking relieved.

"We've come to an arrangement," he said. "Mr. Wan did make a better offer, but it will take him a few weeks to get the money to Shanghai. The agreement is that if Mr. Wan doesn't get the money here by the first week of June, Liu Sanmu will buy this place at his original price."

"So we wait a bit longer, get more money," Anjuin said. "And if it doesn't work out, we still have the original offer. Didn't this upset Liu Sanmu?"

"The Liu family is one of the wealthiest in Shanghai," Dajuin said. "He doesn't really mind one way or the other. There are many other properties he could buy. In fact, Liu and Wan are quite friendly now."

"How on earth did Mr. Liu manage that?" Anjuin said.

It seemed that Wan Baoyuan was from Harbin. Ever the journalist, Liu Sanmu had asked Wan for his views on the situation in Manchuria. By the end of half an hour, the two were chatting quite amicably.

I could imagine it, Liu strolling through the courtyard, discussing news and politics with Wan Baoyuan. He would be at his most pleasant, his attention sincere, his questions well informed. He had charm enough to warm someone as stern as Wan Baoyuan.

Or as reserved as Anjuin.

WAN BAOYUAN CAME to Dragon Springs Road the next day driving a car that looked just like the one Liu Sanmu owned. I opened the front gate, and he gave me a brief nod. Two men followed him, carrying notebooks and a tripod.

"I've taken the liberty of bringing surveyors to measure the property," Wan Baoyuan said to Dajuin. "And please open the gate to the Western Residence again for the car. There are children climbing all over it."

"Of course," Dajuin said. "I'll walk around with your surveyors in case they have questions. Please come in to the main hall and have some tea. Jialing, tell Anjuin Mr. Wan is here."

Poor Anjuin. She would have to make small talk with this unsociable man. But when I carried the tea tray to the reception hall, Wan Baoyuan was almost animated. He had taken off his fedora and appeared quite relaxed.

"It's a historic problem," he was saying. "At the beginning, China's railways were financed by loans from Britain, Japan, and different European countries. It meant we were obliged to purchase machinery and equipment from those countries."

"So that's why the railway tracks are all different sizes?" Anjuin asked. "That seems very wasteful."

I didn't know how Anjuin managed to look so interested.

IT TURNED OUT that the car Wan Baoyuan was driving belonged to Liu Sanmu, who had loaned it to Wan. Liu Sanmu owned another car. A spare automobile. I couldn't imagine such wealth.

"Well, I suppose one of us will have to be home at all times," Anjuin said, "to open the gate to the Western Residence for that car."

"No need," Dajuin said. "I've given Mr. Wan a key to the Western Residence. More convenient for him when he brings surveyors and architects to take a look at the property."

SOMETIMES LIU SANMU would arrive in the car with Wan Baoyuan. I couldn't imagine how two men so different could've grown so friendly. When Liu Sanmu learned that Wan Baoyuan hadn't been to Shanghai in more than ten years, he'd insisted on showing him the sights: the shopping streets and nightlife, theaters, sports clubs, dog racing at the Canidrome.

Liu Sanmu included Dajuin in these invitations. Who would've thought such a man would consider Dajuin, a mere cloth merchant's son, worth his attention? Dajuin felt uncomfortable at the thought of such entertainments and always turned down the invitations.

"He seems so friendly," Anjuin said. "He likes you."

"Mr. Liu is a journalist," Dajuin said. "He's interested in my views of what's going on in the factories, what the workers have to say, because the situation with students and workers is getting explosive. He's friendly with Mr. Wan for the same reason, information. With General Zhang ruling Manchuria, every newspaper wants more insights on the situation."

I RECEIVED A note from Miss Morris. She had promised to keep trying to find me a position, but I never believed she would be successful. Yet here was hope.

> *My dear Jialing,*
>
> *There may be an opportunity for you. Mrs. James Ellis requires a governess for her two children. She is a very kind woman and you'll find her sympathetic to your situation. She is at home Wednesday morning.*
>
> *Enclosed is a reference letter for your interview.*
>
> *My very best wishes for your success,*
> *Jane Morris*

The Ellis villa was in one of the lanes behind the rue Joffre. It wasn't as grand as the Burnses' home, nor was the lawn as immaculate, but the overgrown hedges and cheerful yellow daylilies in the front yard seemed friendlier. A croquet set lay abandoned on the grass, and a large calico cat dozed on the front steps.

A young man in blue servant's garb opened the door. He smiled when he bowed, and I couldn't detect any contempt in his expression. I followed him along a wood-paneled hallway, my shoes sinking into thick carpet.

The woman who stood up from her chair to greet me wore a friendly smile. She spoke English with a soft accent.

"Miss Zhu? I am Suzanne Ellis. Miss Morris tells me you are good with children. Please sit."

I sank into the chair opposite hers and held out the reference letter. She scanned it quickly and then asked me to read from the *Shanghai Daily News*. She listened for a few minutes then stopped me. I folded the newspaper in my lap.

"Your accent is very good," she said, this time in perfect Chinese. "American English. Like your teachers at the mission school. Tell me about yourself. How many years did you spend at the mission school? Which subjects did you like the most?"

Her questions were straightforward, and there was nothing condescending in her manner. Slowly, I loosened my grip on the newspaper.

"Here are the books my children are reading," she said, pointing at some books on the side table. "Or rather, trying to read."

I looked through the small collection. *Just So Stories*. *The Blue Fairy Book*. *The Wonderful Wizard of Oz*.

"Who has been teaching them?" I asked.

She laughed. "I have. But I'm too fond a mother and not strict enough. Also, these days I have no time. My husband has a new job, and we must entertain more. Come upstairs."

The room she showed me contained a small desk, a bookcase, and a bed covered with a quilted bedspread. Pale yellow walls and curtains printed with fat yellow roses made the room cheerful and welcoming. Mrs. Ellis pulled back the drapes and beckoned me to look down. In the garden below, two children, a boy and a girl played a lopsided game of shuttlecock, the younger boy always missing. Their amah sat comfortably on a wicker chair, mending clothes.

"I'm afraid this is rather a small room," she said, "but the bathroom is just across the hall and you would only have to share it with the children."

"It's a wonderful room," I said, hardly daring to hope.

"I have no more questions, Miss Zhu," she said. "I would like to hire you. The children and I are going on a holiday to visit Mr. Ellis's cousins in Singapore. We'll come home at the end of June. Would you be ready to start on the first of July? Would that be all right?"

"Oh, it would be all right. Very all right!" I said. Had I ever felt such joy, such relief? A room of my own. A bathroom across the hall. Wages.

"Is there anything else you'd like to know?" she said, her smile even wider.

"Please, ma'am," I said, "how is it that you speak Chinese so well?"

"I was born in Shanghai," she said. "My parents are from France. But I have never lived there. Shanghai is my home."

Outside, I barely noticed the jostling of pedestrians and street vendors as I made my way home. Crossing a street, I was nearly run down by an automobile and grinned happily in response to the driver's curses. A beggar girl tugged at my skirt, and I gave her a copper.

My livelihood was secure. I had a place to live after the Yangs left Dragon Springs Road.

When Fox came back, she would see how wrong she had been. If she came back.

IT WAS A lucky day, a day of good omens. I returned to Dragon Springs Road to find Anjuin in a state of delight, but she insisted that I tell her my good news first.

"Your clothes," she exclaimed, squeezing my hands. "We must sew you some new ones. You must make a good impression."

"Never mind my clothes," I said. "What's your news?"

"Dajuin has a meeting with the International Cotton Manufacturing Company," she said. "Liu Sanmu knows Mr. Ching, the only Chinese director on the board. And you'll never guess—Mr. Liu is personally introducing Dajuin to Mr. Ching."

One of Dajuin's biggest obstacles in looking for work had been his refusal to make use of the Yang family's contacts, in case his father found out. Without *guanxi*, connections, it was hard to open doors. If Liu Sanmu was putting his weight behind Dajuin, it would be very difficult for the director to refuse.

"This is so sudden," I said. "Mr. Liu must've come by just after I went in to town."

"Yes. He turned up in his automobile and told Dajuin to get ready," Anjuin said. "Then they left for the meeting."

"Why is he being so helpful?" I wondered out loud.

"I think Mr. Liu is kind. And impulsive," Anjuin said. "Think of how he helped you search for your mother. Oh, and Dajuin invited Liu Sanmu to supper. And he agreed! Thank goodness you're back in time to help."

Anjuin had already been to the market. There were fresh vegetables in a basin and a gray mullet flapped in a bucket of water. She
would make a fish soup, simple and wholesome. I chopped cabbage as finely as I could and cut strips of bamboo into matchstick-
sized pieces. These would go in the soup.

She hummed as she prepared the meal. A salad of shredded
radish and carrot tossed in a light dressing of vinegar and sesame,
tofu with a spicy sauce, and pig's trotters stewed in a dark soy
marinade. I minced up the last of the ham, which Anjuin would
steam in a mixture of egg and mushroom. She even made a small
eight treasures sticky rice dessert.

"We'll have to serve Mr. Liu on the kitchen table," I said, pulling bowls out of the cupboard. "It's too bad the dining table went
to Ningpo with the rest of your furniture."

"He isn't a snob," she said, eyes shining. She arranged plain
wooden chopsticks beside the porcelain soup spoons. "As long as
the rice is cooked and the soup is hot, it's good enough."

Her smile peeped out, just barely, but her happiness revealed
itself in the glow of her skin, her animated gestures. But she knew,
just had to know, that Liu Sanmu was out of her reach. A tightness
formed in my chest every time I saw that small, unconscious smile
touch her lips. Poor Anjuin.

IT WAS A small celebration dinner, but a very lively one. Liu Sanmu
had brought two bottles of foreign wine, which we drank from
soup bowls, all we had to hold the wine.

"Is all foreign liquor like this?" Anjuin asked. The liquid was
pale and frothed when poured.

"It's called champagne," Liu Sanmu said. "From France.
Foreigners drink it on special occasions, especially when congratulations are in order. A toast to Miss Zhu and her career as a

governess. A toast to Dajuin, the new senior clerk at International Cotton Manufacturing Company."

"Nothing to do with me," Dajuin said. "How can I ever thank you, Mr. Liu?"

"If there's anyone you should thank, it's my wife," Liu Sanmu replied. "My connection to Mr. Ching is through her; he's one of her maternal uncles."

I said very little during the meal. I couldn't think of anything to add to the boisterous conversation, especially when it turned to politics. The discussion grew louder as the champagne emptied, mostly into Liu Sanmu's bowl.

"I read your piece on Mah Juhou's unsolved murder," Dajuin said. "Isn't it dangerous to criticize the police so openly?"

"I want to shame the Shanghai Municipal Police," Liu Sanmu said. "It's been nearly three years and they haven't come up with a single plausible suspect. My family and the Mah clan are close. In fact, Mah Juhou was my Fourth Uncle's dearest friend."

Anjuin's face was flushed from the wine. And maybe something else. She listened with attention, getting up only when it was time to take the eight treasures rice pudding out of the steamer. We lifted up the bowl by its muslin wrapping and turned it over carefully in a shallow bowl. Anjuin ladled a fragrant osmanthus flower syrup over the sticky dessert and carried it to the table.

But the discussion had become so heated the men barely noticed when Anjuin placed generous portions of the dessert in front of them.

"When they gave our Shandong Province to Japan," Liu Sanmu said, "the Allies were telling the world what they thought of China. One yellow race is the same as another to them."

"Do you really think there will be more unrest, Mr. Liu?" Dajuin said. "You hinted as much in one of your editorials about the May 4 student protests."

We read *Xinwen Bao* every day now, always on the lookout for Liu Sanmu's articles. Dajuin pronounced them impressive. Liu wrote at least two pieces each day for *Xinwen Bao,* a news item and an editorial. He might have belonged to a wealthy family, but Liu Sanmu wasn't dabbling.

"Students are organizing protests right now in every major city, Shanghai included," Liu Sanmu replied. "I'm looking into rumors that our government signed secret deals with other nations before the peace talks, while the war was still going on. If it's true, then China's position was already compromised. I'm going to ask Wan Baoyuan what he knows."

"Why would Mr. Wan know?" Dajuin asked.

"He used to be an officer in General Zhang Zuolin's army," Liu Sanmu said. "Zhang's Fengtian clique has as much power in Peking as the Anhui clique, so perhaps Wan can drop me some names to investigate."

"How do you know this about Mr. Wan?" Dajuin asked, his expression rapt.

"A journalist friend in Peking did some snooping for me," Liu Sanmu said with a large grin. "I thought it would be prudent to know more about my rival for this property. I'm seeing Mr. Wan tomorrow at the Race Club. He says he hasn't been to Shanghai in ten years and wants to bet on the horses. Why don't we all go?"

He included me in his smile.

Anjuin looked uncertain. According to Grandmother Yang, women of good family did not go to the races. It was fine for foreign women to gamble and socialize at the racecourse, but no

Chinese woman of good reputation could be seen there among gangsters and their mistresses. Yet it would be rude to refuse Liu Sanmu's invitation.

"Your brother can be your chaperone," Liu Sanmu said in a solemn tone. "And I promise not to tell your father."

Amid laughter, Anjuin and I cleared the kitchen table. Dajuin and Liu Sanmu continued their conversation while we washed up. Every so often Anjuin glanced over with a fond smile and I knew it wasn't all for her brother. We served tea, then excused ourselves. As we went to our room, the men's voices drifted out on the night air, fragments of troubled words, musings on our troubled country.

Although we had the house to ourselves now and could've used as many of the rooms as we liked, Anjuin and I kept to our old ways. My cot was still pushed up against the far end of her room, and we still used this time to talk over the day's events.

"A good day," she said. "You have a job, Dajuin has a job. To-morrow, we can worry about what Father says."

"But you, Anjuin," I said. "I want something good to happen for you."

"If Dajuin stays in Shanghai, I'll live with him and Yun Na and their children," she said. "He's agreed. Then you and I can visit together on your days off. Your good fortune is also mine."

In the dim lamp light, her serene smile shone.

"What do you think of Mr. Liu?" I asked in my most inno-cent voice. "He is so well informed. Are all journalists like that, I wonder?"

"He seems to think of every incident as part of a conspiracy," she said, "but I suppose that comes from being a journalist."

"Do you like him, Anjuin?" It was the most I dared ask.

"I've never met anyone like him before," she said, simply. "I admire him very much. It's enough just to know him."

"He's from a great family. His marriage was no doubt an arranged one," I said. "He probably only tolerates his wife. He could take a second wife. Or a third wife. Or a concubine."

Her smile was crooked. "I've always thought of marriage as a woman's duty. But I've realized I can't bear the thought of sharing someone I love with another woman, even a First Wife. There's duty and then there's your heart."

It was terribly unfair. Anjuin deserved so much more than to live with her brother and a demanding sister-in-law. She would end up running the household and minding the children, no better than an unpaid servant. Liu Sanmu was a wealthy man who could easily afford more wives. If only he could see her as more than just Dajuin's sister.

Then for a moment, I imagined Liu Sanmu seeing me as more than just a schoolgirl. I pushed the thought out of my mind. If only Fox hadn't shown me what it could be like.

IT WAS ANJUIN'S first ride in an automobile, and she sat quietly looking out the window. I'd long since given up all pretense of dignity and craned my neck in all directions. From the front seat, Liu Sanmu pointed out different landmarks. How little I'd seen of the wealthier areas of Shanghai. We passed Jessfield Park, the biggest park in Shanghai. I knew there were gardens, a conservatory, and playgrounds inside. There was even a zoo. I peered at the gate hoping the zoo was visible from the street but caught only a glimpse of large trees and flower beds.

"We can't go in. The park is for foreigners only," Dajuin said, seeing my interest.

"Chinese can enter if we apply in writing," Liu Sanmu said. "Only those from the very best and wealthiest of Chinese families ever gain admission. But plenty of Chinese have been inside, because if you're an amah or servant, you can follow your foreign master right in."

The bitter edge to his voice was barely noticeable.

OUTSIDE THE RACE Club, we paused to watch worshippers bow before the stone figure of a deity whose robes were blackened by incense smoke.

"This little shrine outside the Race Club stables is the busiest in all of Shanghai," Liu Sanmu said. "Even foreign gamblers have been known to light incense before an important race."

If foreigners were ready to worship a Chinese god for the sake of winning a bet, no wonder the missionaries were having a hard time converting Chinese.

Horse racing was Shanghai's passion. Inside the Race Club, cries and cheers in Chinese and an assortment of languages assaulted my ears. A confetti storm of torn betting slips and loud curses followed each race. Every nationality and every class of person was there, from the most venerable citizens to the worst of small-time gangsters. Elderly, staid gentlemen with goatees and glasses studied the racing sheets as if they contained lines of Tang poetry. Women with dangling jewelry and bright red lips hung on the arms of older men, coaxing for money to place bets.

Anjuin gave me a nudge. Across the aisle was a group of young women, all modestly dressed. They were giggling and looking around nervously. Girls of good family, out on an adventure.

"The Shanghai Race Club was meant for foreigners," said Liu Sanmu, leading us up the stairs. "But then they realized how much more money they could make by allowing Chinese to bet. Only the best Chinese families can join the club itself, but anyone can come in to place bets on race days."

"Well, Mr. Yang," said a voice from behind, "since anyone can bet, will you wager on the horses today?"

It took me a second to recognize Wan Baoyuan. Instead of a suit and tie, he was in traditional Chinese garb, a long gray *changshan* gown and black trousers. With his military bearing, he managed to make even a *changshan* look like a uniform. Traditional cloth shoes replaced his usual leather Oxfords, but he still wore his fedora.

"Our family doesn't gamble," Dajuin said, after exchanging greetings. "It's exciting enough just to be here, watching the races."

Wan Baoyuan frowned. "You can't experience the excitement of a race unless you bet. Even a small wager makes a difference. Come. I insist."

They went down the stairs to the betting windows, Dajuin's reluctance evident to everyone but Wan Baoyuan.

Just then an expensively dressed group of foreigners made their way from the grandstand toward the exit. A young couple in the lead walked down the steps like royalty. I stared at them.

"The newlywed McBains, back from England," Liu Sanmu said, seeing my eyes follow the small procession. "Young George McBain's mother is Chinese. The British Country Club struck McBain Senior off its membership list when he married her. But the McBains don't care. They're so wealthy, no one can afford to ignore them."

It was all right to be *hun xue* then, as long as there was money. Enough money not to care what others thought.

When they finally returned, Wan Baoyuan held up a bottle and Dajuin handed us glasses.

"Champagne," Wan Baoyuan said, pouring, "financed by our winnings from the last race."

I drank eagerly from the cool glass, taking large gulps. Wan Baoyuan refilled my glass, but Anjuin gave me a poke with her elbow and I sipped more slowly. On the track below, jockeys and horses lined up for the next race.

Another group of racegoers, less elegant than the McBain entourage, crowded their way down the staircase toward the exit.

"Wan Baoyuan, what a surprise!" A stocky man in a rumpled suit emerged from the group.

"Shih, how are you?" Wan Baoyuan shook his hand, a smile on his face. The first genuine smile I'd ever seen brighten his features. "Come meet my friends. Mr. Liu Sanmu and Mr. Yang Dajuin. This is Shih Yaopu. We were young army recruits together."

Shih bowed to Liu Sanmu and Dajuin. "Delighted, delighted," he said. "Please, take a card. My company, Nanyang Shipping. Please, please, go ahead and watch the track. Don't miss the next race on my account."

The crowd roared as the horses left the gate. Shih turned back to Wan Baoyuan. "Wan, are you on leave from the army or have you moved to Shanghai?"

"I'm no longer with the army. I'm here on business. How long have you been in Shanghai now? Four years?"

"Nearly six, can you believe it? How lucky to run into you this time. I saw you, oh, three years ago heading into the Shanghai North Railway Station, but by the time I caught up, I'd lost you in that crowd."

Was it my imagination or did Wan's smile become strained?

"Come to the Hotel Shanghai this evening, Shih," he said. "It's on the corner of Broadway and Nanzing Roads. Let's catch up."

Shih tipped his hat to us and hurried to follow his friends, now almost at the street-level exit. Wan Baoyuan's eyes followed the husky figure, a strange look on his face.

Why would Wan Boayuan tell us this was his first visit to Shanghai in more than ten years when his friend Mr. Shih said he'd been here just a few years ago?

Light-headed from the champagne, I sat down. Another race started, and Dajuin and Liu Sanmu passed a pair of binoculars between them. Anjuin stood beside Liu Sanmu, feigning interest in the horses. Wan Baoyuan peered down at the racing form in his hand, then looked up to survey the track. He pushed his hat farther back on his head, an absentminded gesture.

That same faint memory stirred again, and I realized where I'd seen Wan Baoyuan before. On Dragon Springs Road, the day of Master Shen's funeral. He was the young man who had spoken to Mrs. Hao. The same handsome features, the same absentminded adjustment to his hat. Now that he was in Chinese clothing, I recognized him. The memory had been niggling at the edges of my mind, and now I was sure. Exuberance bubbled up, frothy as champagne.

"You must have lost track of time, Mr. Wan," I said, "because I saw you too when you were in Shanghai a few years ago."

"Really? Where was that?" he said, his voice quiet.

I prattled on. "At Dragon Springs Road. You were watching Master Shen's funeral procession."

"What a coincidence."

There was nothing unpleasant about his tone, but it made me think of a wire pulled tight, ready to snap. I groaned silently. I had never dared speak to him before, and with my first words I had somehow managed to offend him. I hoped Anjuin hadn't overheard. She would scold me for being too forward. For getting drunk.

Wan reached over to tap Liu Sanmu on the shoulder.

"There's a pleasant café across the road," he said. "Shall we treat the young ladies to some ice cream?"

Liu Sanmu and Wan Baoyuan talked about their travels while we ate ice cream. *Xinwen Bao* sent Liu Sanmu all over China, and before that, he had lived in America during his university years. Wan Baoyuan had attended military college in Japan and now traveled frequently throughout China on business.

When Anjuin asked him about Harbin, Wan Baoyuan recited statistics: population and nationalities, distances and sources of commerce. Liu Sanmu's descriptions of Harbin, however, painted pictures in my mind.

"Winters are cold there, unbelievably cold for us Shanghai natives," Liu Sanmu said. "But without that cold, you'd never see how Harbin's lakes become smooth expanses of ice or the way trees hang heavy with clusters of frost that sparkle in the clear air. There's ice skating in the parks, even at night, because it's so bright from moonlight reflecting on all that snow. Those foreigners love ice skating."

I liked the sound of Harbin, exotic and not Chinese at all, with even more European residents than Shanghai. I wanted to see the Russian cathedral at the center of the city, its spires and domes built of wood, the entire edifice standing without a single iron nail. I wanted to stand at the edge of the city and gaze out at endless horizons beyond the river. Harbin sounded wonderful.

Liu Sanmu had captivated me with his descriptions. No, not just me. Even if no one else noticed, I could see how Anjuin's clear-eyed gaze softened in his presence and how her cheeks glowed.

That night I lay in my cot, reliving the excitement of the day.

Shrieks of delight from the women behind us when their horse won. The middle-aged foreigner in a plaid suit whose face had crumpled like the slips of paper clutched in his fist. The wealthy McBains gliding out, an entourage in their wake. Mr. Shih's outstretched hand as he greeted Wan Baoyuan, a large gold ring on one knuckle. Wan Baoyuan's expression as his friend hurried away. Had it been regret or unease?

I wondered whether Fox had ever been to Harbin. What if she never came back? But she had to. She was waiting for the Door to open.

When sleep finally came, I dreamed of streets where foreigners strolled in and out of shops and restaurants, the white smoke of their breaths lit by streetlamps, the echo of conversations in so many languages that one could well believe this was Russia or France and not China.

CHAPTER 17

Dajuin wrote to his father as soon as he started his new job at International Cotton Manufacturing. Master Yang's reply was filled with sorrowful accusations, disappointment that Dajuin had chosen to leave the family business.

"He's not that unhappy," Anjuin said to her brother, studying the letter. "I would say under all that disappointment he's pleased you've made Liu Sanmu's acquaintance. A valuable association."

Yun Na's letter left no doubt as to her feelings.

Husband, such wonderful news, but now you must find a home in a nice part of Shanghai. Of course it must be convenient to your place of work, but we should think of our children and their education. The

best schools are within Shanghai's international conces-
sions.

I will come as soon as you've found something suit-
able. Your grandmother can't keep me in Ningpo if you
have a job and a home ready for us in Shanghai. I would
rather have my baby there, at the foreign women's hospi-
tal. Tell Anjuin she's welcome to live with us, especially
since none of the servants are willing to come with me to
Shanghai.

After breakfast, Dajuin went out to the city to find a place to
rent. He took Anjuin with him. When I'd washed and put away all
the breakfast dishes, I scraped some leftovers into a bowl and went
to the Western Residence.

Anjuin had insisted I choose some fabric from the shop to sew
myself some new clothes before starting my job as a governess.
With her help, I'd managed to make the temperamental sewing
machine behave long enough to stitch some plain but perfectly
decent clothes. To our surprise, Ping Mei had offered to embroider for me. Rather dubious, Anjuin gave her a small swatch of
fabric, some thread, and an embroidery hoop.

"First, show us a sample of your work," she said.

The very next morning, as soon as Dajuin left, Ping Mei came
over and handed Anjuin the piece of fabric. Then she hobbled out
to beg.

Ping Mei's work was astonishing. A perfect lotus bud seemed
to grow out from the fabric, the petals shading from cream to
pink so naturally it looked like brushwork instead of needlework.
It was better than anything I'd seen from First Wife. I imagined
such embroidery on the cuffs of tunics, on the borders of bodices.
Peony, plum, chrysanthemum.

"But if she embroiders, she won't have time to beg," I said to Anjuin.

"If we give her food in exchange for the work, Ping Mei won't need to beg," she pointed out.

Ping Mei was in the *erfang*, in the shelter of the veranda, squinting at an embroidery hoop. She looked up when I came in to the courtyard, waved one hand in greeting, and bent again over her sewing. I was sure her embroidery could sell for much more than a bowl or two of vegetables and tofu, but she didn't seem to care.

On my way to the kitchen, I stood by the hydrangea shrub as I always did these days, but I couldn't sense Fox. Where could she be? Had I offended her so much that she wouldn't come back? What if she did come back after we had all gone? How could she know I'd found a job and that I would be living with the Ellis family? I'd have to leave a note on the altar and hope for the best. Hope she would come and find me.

I realized Ping Mei was watching and thought how I must look, staring into a shrub that wasn't even blooming. I hurried on to the kitchen and put away the bowl of leftovers. I hauled a bucket of water and splashed the flowers growing around the hydrangeas. Although I had sown seeds from Anna's flowers in all three court-yards, they grew best in the Western Residence courtyard. The violas nodded their yellow-and-purple heads at me, and the clove pinks bloomed incessantly. And everywhere, forget-me-nots had seeded themselves.

There was no need to speak to Ping Mei on my way out. She had dozed off, head nodding over the embroidery. I crept up silently to look at her work. She had created a border of yellow chrysanthemums, the green leaves so real I could almost smell the slightly bitter odor of crushed petals.

OUR FORMER NEIGHBORS on Dragon Springs Road had sold their property and moved away. The old houses around us now stood empty, front gates padlocked. The Shen estate was a construction site. Courtyards filled with rubble as workers tore off roof tiles and knocked down walls. There was a constant parade of laborers and oxcarts carrying out debris. Dust hung suspended in the air, even indoors.

The little dry goods shop in the front courtyard was no longer open for business, but the temperamental sewing machine was still there. After seeing Ping Mei's progress, I knew I'd have to hurry with my own sewing or she would be done with the skirt border before I'd finished the actual skirt. With a deep sigh I went to the shop and lifted the cover off the sewing machine.

Half an hour later, I was picking at a clump of thread caught under the needle, swearing out loud. It was with relief that I heard a rapping at the front gate. I opened the door to Liu Sanmu, who was wearing a simple dark blue *changshan* gown and carrying a satchel. He looked like a university student. A well-dressed university student.

"Is Dajuin here?" he asked.

"No, he and Anjuin have gone in to Shanghai to find a place to rent," I said. "Let me open the gate for your car."

"No need, I came by rickshaw in case demonstrators block the roads," he said. "Well, I was hoping Dajuin could guide me through the factory district in Chapei. I'd like to interview some of the workers there."

"They should be back very soon," I said, hoping to keep him there as long as possible, to give Anjuin the opportunity to see him again. "Will you wait in the reception hall? I'll bring you tea."

When I brought the teapot and cups to the reception hall, he was settled into a chair with his newspaper. It felt daring to be alone with a man.

He tapped the page with one finger. "Do you ever get that feeling when a memory refuses to come to mind? Elusive. Like a goldfish that keeps slipping out of your fingers. The name of the victim in this article sounds familiar."

I leaned over to read.

> *Homicide. Chinese male, identified as Shih Yaopu, a manager at Nanyang Shipping. Shih was found murdered in the alley behind the Starlight Gentleman's Club on Pakhoi Road. The Shanghai Municipal Police are asking for witnesses who might have seen anything suspicious on Tuesday night.*

I frowned. "The man who came up to Mr. Wan at the Race Club was a Mr. Shih. Could it be a coincidence? A different Shih?"

"That's it," he said, folding the newspaper. "And he worked for a shipping company. Shih gave me his business card. I should look for it when I get back to the office. Well, if this is Wan Baoyuan's friend, it's a sad coincidence. What do you remember about Mr. Shih?"

Mostly I remembered how my head had lolled against the leather seat of the automobile, the clumsiness of my limbs, my thoughts muddled from too much champagne. A voice like a wire pulled tight.

"Just one odd thing," I said. "Mr. Shih mentioned he'd seen Mr. Wan in Shanghai a few years ago, but Mr. Wan told you he hadn't been here in at least ten."

"He's really lost track of time. There's a big difference between a few years and ten."

"There was something else," I said. "Never mind. It's not important."

"Tell me anyway." His smile was friendly, his voice coaxing. This was how he persuaded people to give up their secrets to him, to write the stories he needed for his newspaper.

"I saw Mr. Wan in Shanghai before this too," I said. "When I mentioned it, he got rather irate. I shouldn't have said anything. But I did see him. Right here in Dragon Springs Road three years ago."

"You seem very sure it was three years ago."

"Only because it was the day of Old Master Shen's funeral," I said. "Nineteen sixteen, the ninth day of the ninth month. The Shens' fortune-teller picked the date to make sure the day of the burial was an auspicious one. It was easy to remember."

He sat up very suddenly, startling me so much I almost dropped my teacup. He opened the newspaper again to the page about Mr. Shih's murder, his expression intent.

"The ninth day of the ninth month. Nineteen sixteen. A date to remember indeed," Liu finally said, his voice soft. "Why didn't you recognize Wan Baoyuan before?"

"He always wore Western suits," I said, "and the man I saw was dressed like a student, in a long gown. It was only when I saw him at the Race Club in Chinese clothing that I remembered where I'd seen him before. And now he's come back to Dragon Springs Road to buy the property. Isn't that a coincidence?"

Liu Sanmu put the newspaper down on the table. He got up and paced outside in the courtyard for a few minutes.

"Have you mentioned to anyone else that you saw Wan Baoyuan at Dragon Springs Road three years ago?" There was an urgent tone to his voice as he stepped back inside the door.

I shook my head.

"Don't mention it to anyone, Jialing," he said, coming back inside the shop. "And don't tell Wan Baoyuan that you told me. It's very important. Promise me. Tell no one, not even Anjuin."

I nodded, startled by his intensity.

"I can't wait for Dajuin any longer, but please tell him I will come by tomorrow." He slung his satchel over his shoulder and left.

SHANGHAI'S STUDENTS AND workers held a general strike the next day.

"It will begin in the factories in Chapei. I need to meet some of their leaders," Liu Sanmu said. "Dajuin, will you come with me?"

He had come by rickshaw and was dressed very plainly again, a cotton scholar's gown and a long tunic vest, the pockets bulging with pencils. He carried a canvas satchel slung over one shoulder and his face glowed with excitement. With thousands of students flooding in to the city center, campuses in Shanghai had closed.

"There are banners strung across buildings blaming the government for losing Shandong Province to Japan," he said. "Businesses are boycotting Japanese goods. Let's go."

Liu Sanmu and Dajuin left for the walk across to Chapei. Anjuin's gaze followed them as they turned on to Chung San Road. She sighed. Then she gave a wry smile when she realized I'd been watching her.

A FEW HOURS later, Dajuin came back alone. Liu Sanmu had met some student leaders in Chapei and was following them around as they roused the workers.

Anjuin looked anxious. "I should go to the market and buy more food in case the strike spreads and they close the shops here too."

"I'll go with you," Dajuin said. "Things could get chaotic."

A scattering of clouds and a light wind foretold showers. Already I could see heavier clouds pushing their way across the sky. Any moment now, there would be the patter of rain on roof tiles.

I ladled some leftover soup into a bowl for Ping Mei, payment for her embroidery. It was best to take it over to the Western Residence before the rain started.

Ping Mei was on the veranda of the *erfang,* perched on a rickety wooden chair, a length of fabric spread across her knees. Pale yellow chrysanthemums grew on stalks of jade-green leaves. It was a wide piece of fabric, a panel that matched the skirt border she had just finished. It would contrast beautifully against the ink-blue of my new jacket.

"It's very quiet today," she remarked. "Nothing out on the street."

"It's the strike," I said. "The factories have shut down. Even the construction workers across the road are nowhere to be seen. Anjuin just left for the market to see whether any shops are open. Dajuin went with her, in case of trouble."

"Bring the soup inside." She folded the cloth onto the chair and hobbled into the *erfang.*

My former playroom still looked much the same, pallet bed on the floor, a low table and chair in the corner. I spotted my old enamel jug on the windowsill. A lopsided cupboard, missing its doors, was the only addition to the room. On its one shelf Ping Mei kept a neatly folded quilt made from scraps of fabric. I had seen her working on it. The space underneath the shelf was stuffed with rolls of cloth, old rags, and sacks.

Ping Mei gave the soup an appreciative sniff, then sat on the chair and began slurping it down. It was a hot day, despite the light breeze, and the humid air clung to my skin. I went outside to walk around the courtyard. The day would cool off once it rained.

A familiar sound made me pause, the creaking of the front gate of the Western Residence. There was the noise of an automobile engine. Was it Liu Sanmu? The front gate creaked shut, and a minute later, to my disappointment, Wan Baoyuan appeared on the path through the bamboo garden. He was wearing a suit and tie as usual, and there was a jaunty air about him.

"Mr. Wan, what a surprise," I said, a little too loudly, to warn Ping Mei to stay hidden. "How did you get in?"

"Dajuin lent me a key so I could park the car here, away from those street urchins," he said. "Is Dajuin home? No one answered when I knocked at the Central Residence."

"He's at the market with Anjuin," I said. "There's no one home."

"There's no one home," he repeated. His gaze swept over the main house and then to the bamboo garden. "How long do you think they'll be?"

"Perhaps an hour. Can I serve you some tea?" I asked, anxious to get him out of the courtyard. "Please, let's go to the reception hall in the Central Residence."

"There's no need," he said. "I only came by to give Dajuin some good news. As soon as the strike is over and the banks are open again, this property will be mine."

"Congratulations," I said, still uneasy.

He wandered over to the derelict *erfang* across the courtyard and pushed open one of its doors. Dust drifted down on him, but he just chuckled. I would never have believed Wan Baoyuan could be so cheerful. He strolled to the main house and peered into its windows. He went inside and came out a few minutes later, still smiling.

Yet when his smile turned in my direction, I shivered.

"Let me share something else with you, Miss Zhu," he said, walking toward the *erfang*. He was closer now, beside the bamboo garden. "I lived here when I was a boy. This estate was once my home."

"You lived here?" This made no sense.

"Yes, the Yangs bought this property from the Fong family, did you know?" Another wide smile. "I was born a Fong."

He grinned, a boy who had just played a trick. "An uncle on our mother's side wrote to us. He had no sons and wanted to adopt me. Since my Eldest Brother had squandered our inheritance there wasn't any point in staying here. So I went to live with my uncle in Harbin."

He was Noble Uncle's younger brother.

"Why didn't you say anything about this before?" I asked.

"If Dajuin realized how much this property meant to me, he might've raised the price," he said, still smiling. "When our uncle adopted me, I took his family name, Wan. But this is my ancestral home. I had to get it back. And now I have."

He did a slow turn, arms outstretched, and suddenly something fell into place.

"It *was* you on the day of Old Master Shen's funeral," I blurted out. "You came to see your old home."

"I wanted to know whether my brother was still here," he said. "That's when I learned he was gone, the estate sold."

I still didn't understand. "But why did you say you hadn't been to Shanghai for ten years?"

"Does anyone else know that you saw me?" The question was so casual, so matter of fact, but I found myself trembling. Not trusting my voice, I shook my head.

"Those were complicated times, Miss Zhu," he said. "I had business in Shanghai. Business no one could know about."

Although a smile remained fixed on his face, I had the urge to flee, away from the bamboo garden, away from Dragon Springs Road.

"Your friend, Mr. Shih," I said. "He saw you too."

His smile turned regretful. "Yes, unfortunately he saw me too."

And Mr. Shih was dead. Murdered in an alley behind a Shanghai nightclub.

With a small cry, I ran toward the *erfang*. All I could think of was to hide inside my playroom, shut the door between me and this man until Dajuin and Anjuin came home. Get Ping Mei to help me push the cupboard against the door.

But I wasn't fast enough. I barely made it up the steps. He caught me by one arm, and in one quick move, pinned me to the veranda floor. Before I could even cry out, he straddled me across the hips and held my arms down. I screamed for help, but there was no one but Ping Mei and what could she do?

"Such an unexpected opportunity," he murmured, almost tenderly. He put his hands around my throat. "There's no one home. The street is empty. No one can hear you. And no one will see you when I take your body out in the car."

His hands tightened, the courtyard spun. Light drained from the world. Then there was a loud crack, the sound of wood, and suddenly the choke hold was gone.

"Leave her be." A raspy voice and Wan Baoyuan's weight shifted, fell away from my body. My eyes refused to focus, but I could breathe again.

"I know you." His voice was a little unsteady. "You used to live here."

He had recognized Ping Mei, their former servant.

My vision cleared to see Wan Baoyuan on the floor beside me, rubbing the back of his head. He was staring at Ping Mei as though I wasn't there. Ping Mei held a wooden chair by one of its legs. She looked very small and frail. She could hardly lift the chair. She had barely injured him.

His eyes never left her face as he stood up and yanked the chair out of her hands. It clattered to the ground and broke, the flimsy seat separating from the wooden legs. Then he grabbed her by the shoulders and scrutinized her intently. She didn't resist.

"You lived *here*," he repeated. "In the Western Residence."

He flung her against the door frame of the playroom and she staggered, but remained upright. She didn't make a sound until she saw me looking at her, the bewilderment that must've been plain in my eyes. Then she whimpered, a sharp keening sound, and covered her face with her hands. A face I couldn't bear to look at. A face I never bothered to study, seeing only the scars, the disfigurement, the fallen cheeks.

"You said you were one of the house servants," I whispered.

A snort of laughter from Wan Baoyuan. "My brother's whore. To think I once fancied you. Look at you now."

"Did you live here in the Western Residence?" I whispered. The courtyard rotated in a slow and stomach-churning spin. The air turned heavy and viscous, harder to breathe. Only the force of my cry wrenched me up to my knees.

"Are you my mother? Ping Mei, are you my mother?"

"Your mother?" Wan Baoyuan stared at me, then looked again at Ping Mei, who had taken her hands away from her face. Her eyes were on me now, pleading. My mother's eyes.

The first rumblings of thunder rolled across the sky, and rain began falling on roof tiles, a harsh relentless drumming. This courtyard was the whole world, and the only living persons in it were Wan Baoyuan, me, and Ping Mei. Ping Mei. My mother.

Suddenly, he dealt her a blow that knocked her to the ground.

"Where's my worthless brother now?" he said. His voice was very quiet and made the hairs on my neck stand up. She sat up, blood running down her chin.

"Your worthless brother sold his wives and daughters to pay off his debts so that he could have his honor back," she spat. "His honor. Then he was going to throw himself in the river. But he was so incompetent, who knows if he actually managed it."

He kicked her in the ribs, and my scream was as loud as hers. Her head banged against the door frame, and then she lay still, arms clutching her side. I lurched a few steps toward her, but Wan Baoyuan covered the distance between us in a single stride. He grasped my arm with one hand and turned my face to his with the other. My struggles were futile.

"So you're the little *zazhong* daughter!" he muttered as if to himself. "When the Yangs said you attended the mission school, I thought you came from the orphanage. Yes, I can see her features in you now. Why didn't I notice before?"

For the same reason I hadn't noticed Ping Mei's features. I'd never paid attention, never bothered getting past my disgust. A look came over Wan Baoyuan's face, a look that was unmistakable. Desire. And something else, something cruel and bestial.

"No," I screamed. "Let me go!"

I tried to twist away, but he was stronger. He pushed me down and pinned me to the wooden floorboards. I screamed and kicked, but his weight crushed down on my hips.

"My brother forgot about everything, everyone except her," he said, undoing his belt. "His duty, his family. He was completely infatuated. It was as though he'd been bewitched by a Fox. I wanted to kill her as much as I wanted to get into her bed."

Fox, where are you? I cried in my mind.

There was another crash of thunder, but I thought I heard another, sharper sound, the squeal of the front gate. I screamed again, and he struck me across the face.

"Scream all you want, I enjoy the sound." He pulled off his necktie and looped it around my wrists. He tied my hands to a balustrade and leaned over me.

"Your mother ruined our family. I may as well enjoy you before I kill you," he said.

I screamed again, turned my face away from him. Then the sound of footsteps hurrying, the crunch of gravel, and Wan Baoyuan's weight lifted. I was still pinned beneath him, but he had straightened up to his knees.

"Leave her alone, Wan," Liu Sanmu's voice. "She's no threat."

"Threat? I've never thought of this little *zazhong* as a threat," Wan Baoyuan said. "This is nothing to do with you, Liu. Walk away and forget about it. Little Jialing here is willing to forget."

"He wants to kill me!" I managed to choke out the words.

"Get away from her, Wan. Now."

Wan Baoyuan stood up and nonchalantly buckled his belt. "You're overreacting, Liu."

Then, faster than I could've believed possible, he leaped from the veranda and threw himself at Liu Sanmu. They rolled on the ground and struggled, but it was no contest. Wan had been in the army. He was trained to fight, to kill. He pinned Liu Sanmu to the ground as he had done with me, then held him down by the throat. Liu's eyes began to close.

I struggled, but my hands were tied to the balustrade.

Then a small figure hobbled forward, holding a wooden club. No, a chair leg. Ping Mei struck down with all her strength, again and again, until Wan Baoyuan's head was bloody. Trails of scarlet stained puddles of rain.

Stop, said a familiar voice. That's enough, Yinglien.

My eyes closed in relief. The bonds at my wrists loosened and I sat up. Liu Sanmu was still on the ground, gasping, starting to move. Wan lay beside him, quite still. A perfectly ordinary-looking young woman in a perfectly ordinary cotton jacket and skirt looked down at me. Her hair was plaited, a single long pigtail down her back. Her golden-brown eyes glowed green.

The courtyard was silent except for the steady beat of rain. It flicked away at leaves and stems. It strummed insistently on roof tiles. Rain shuttered out the rest of the world. My heart beat in time to the rain. I crouched on the steps, my face lifted to the cold drops.

THEN THERE WAS no rain. I was in the Western Residence and it was springtime. The sky was a clear blue, shaken clean of clouds. There were only three of us.

Me. Fox. And my mother.

They sat on wicker chairs, side by side under the veranda, meek as children caught telling tales. They knew each other. Fox had known my mother all these years but never said anything. Not even when my mother reappeared as Ping Mei. Despite the soothing air of Fox's dream courtyard, my heartbeat was as frantic as a moth beating its wings against a window. And I was angry.

Take all the time you need, Fox said. Time does not go by in the real world while you're in here.

In Fox's world, Ping Mei's face was no longer scarred and deformed, but had I passed her in the street I never would've recognized this worn-out woman as the mother who had been so playful, so loving. Aged by suffering, she looked decades older than her years.

"Why did you leave me?" The question I'd wanted to ask for years.

"Noble Uncle was going to sell us to brothels," she said. "Even his own daughters. And you. I didn't want you growing up like that."

"Why didn't you come back?" I said, starting to cry. "What

if the Yangs had sold me to a brothel or bonded me to a factory? They could've sent me to an orphanage."

"Fox promised to look after you," my mother said, "and she did."

She didn't come to my side to try and comfort me. I would've shrunk away if she had.

"I was going to come back, Ling-ling, truly I was. But then this happened." She pointed at her face. "I was so ugly and you were so little. I didn't want to frighten you."

"Why didn't you tell me she was my mother?" I swung around to face Fox.

"Because I asked her not to," Ping Mei said. My mother. I couldn't call her "Mother," not yet. Not when I still thought of her as Ping Mei.

"And where have you been, Fox?" I demanded. "It's been weeks."

You know me. I get wanderlust. She patted her hair, looking nonchalant. Then she sighed. You were right, Jialing, what you said before I went away. It's your life, your decisions. You're not a child anymore. I should let you make your own decisions.

"Then tell me everything," I said. "No more lies from either of you."

THE MAN WE called Noble Uncle first saw my mother at a banquet in Hankow where she and two other singsong girls had been hired to play music and entertain guests.

"I had no illusions about him," my mother said, "even though he was infatuated enough to buy us both. I knew he'd sell us off the moment his infatuation faded."

She set up an altar at the back of the kitchen to appeal to any

Fox spirits who might be in the area. Pleased by my mother's gesture of respect, Fox decided to make an appearance and in doing so, became entangled in our lives.

It was Fox who made sure Noble Uncle's passion for my mother remained as fervent as the day he first met her, Fox who nudged his attention gently elsewhere to overlook my presence, Fox who made sure a precocious child was content to live a docile life within the walls of the Western Residence. Fox who made sure I didn't think to question our strange existence.

But in the end, even Fox wasn't strong enough to overcome the mountain of debt facing Noble Uncle. He had sunk into such a state of despair the only thoughts he could hold in his mind were schemes for paying off his creditors.

"He was in debt to the wrong sort of people and terrified for his life," my mother said. "He would've sold his firstborn son, if he'd had one."

On that last day, she had stuffed her clothing into a sack, then wrapped the sack in a flowered cloth and carried it like a child. Sunk in despair, and with a nudge from Fox, Noble Uncle never noticed the ruse, and the other women didn't give her away. They had resented my mother when she'd first arrived, but now they resented Noble Uncle more.

By the time he discovered my mother's deception, it was too late. They were in Shanghai, living in a cheap boardinghouse. A few days later, the Fong women were taken away, weeping and protesting. My mother he kept until last. He sobbed his farewells even as he took money from the madam who bought her. She had gone to a brothel, not an inn.

"When I thought you were Ping Mei," I said, "which of your stories was true?"

"I'd been at the brothel less than a week when a drunken customer wanted more than he'd paid for," she said. "When I refused, he held my face over a brazier until I fainted from the pain. And he did start a fire."

After that, she was put to work as a cleaner, a scarf tied over her face to hide her scarred features. Over the years, she lost her sweet lilting voice and could no longer entertain from behind a screen, singing and playing the *liuqin* to earn a bit of extra cash.

"I have lumps growing inside," she said, pointing a finger at her throat. "The doctor who came to the brothel every month said he could cure me, but I never had enough money. He was a fraud, anyway."

"How did you end up in a brothel in the first place?" I said. "What about my father?"

She sighed. "I was a widow. A childless widow. My husband killed himself."

Even though she sold all her jewelry so that her husband could pay his debts, her mother-in-law blamed her when he committed suicide. My mother returned to her own family, but they didn't want her either. She was the widow of a suicide, a bad luck token. They sold her to a brothel in the treaty port of Hankow.

There she gained a regular customer, a British soldier. The brothel owner could see the man had become fond of my mother, so when she fell pregnant, my mother was allowed to have the baby. The soldier offered to buy us both. He was still negotiating with the brothel owner when he fell ill and died of typhoid fever.

"When you were born, he gave me the gold coins," she said. "He told me to hide them, keep them for you, in case of need."

"What was his name?" I asked.

She hesitated and said carefully, "Toh-mahse. He was delighted with you, Jialing. He truly was. He didn't even mind that you were only a girl."

Thomas. Whether this was a first or last name, I would never know.

A year later, she met Master Fong. My mother hadn't liked him very much, but she had no say in the matter. He was infatuated with her and paid the brothel owner an exorbitant amount for the both of us.

"I told myself at least it got you out of the brothel," she said. "I thought you could work for the Fongs when you were older. But as soon as we arrived at Dragon Springs Road, I knew that would never happen. Fong had no idea how to earn or save. His money was nearly gone. I felt sick. Cheated."

"What about that story about your husband being a soldier in the imperial army?" I asked.

"That story belonged to the real Ping Mei," she said. "She was the only servant who bothered speaking to me. She left a year before Master Fong sold the estate."

"When Mr. Shea found you," I said, "why didn't you say who you really were?"

"I didn't know who was looking for me," she said. "It seemed safer."

Her eyes filled with tears. "Then when I met you, I was so ashamed of what I'd become. When I learned you were attending the mission school, I made up my mind to say nothing. You were an educated girl, you had a future. You didn't need to be burdened with a mother like me. It was enough for me to live here, close to you."

There were still questions. Hundreds of questions. But for now I only had one more, even though I couldn't bear to speak his name.

"Why did Wan Baoyuan say he once fancied you? What happened between you?"

"I wanted the Fong women to like me," my mother said, "I tried to befriend them. It was a mistake going over to visit the Central Residence because Wan Baoyuan saw me there. He couldn't have been more than fourteen or fifteen. I thought nothing of it."

Fox cleared her throat. It was my mistake. I tried to get the Fongs to like your mother. The women were so set against her there wasn't even the smallest inclination I could influence. But in his adolescent way, Wan Baoyuan already desired her, and the small nudge I gave pushed him over the edge. He fought with his brother over her. That was one of the reasons Master Fong was so quick to give up his younger brother to their uncle in Manchuria.

They sat together in silence, watching me.

She had left me behind for a good reason. Of all the unhappy roads before her, my mother had chosen one that allowed me the possibility of a decent future. How many unwanted girls were abandoned every day in Shanghai, let alone China? She had left me in Fox's care.

Yet I couldn't help feeling angry with her. And with Fox. For keeping all this from me.

"You don't need to acknowledge me as your mother," my mother said, as though she could hear my thoughts. "No one needs to know. You're angry with me, but if you can manage to believe I've always had your best interests at heart, it's enough."

Enough for her, but I didn't know if that would be enough for me. I couldn't summon up love, didn't know whether I could ever smooth away the prickles of resentment at the edges of my heart, didn't know if I could find forgiveness.

There was, however, duty. There was always duty. Duty to one's parents.

"I can't stay in this dream world," I said. "There's a dead body in the courtyard."

LIU SANMU SAT up and staggered to the edge of the bamboo garden. He knelt by the still figure and turned it over. I could see blood matting the skull, dripping onto the paving stones, a red shine on the wet surface.

He looked up at me. "Jialing, I think he's dead."

Suddenly the horror of what might have happened overwhelmed me and a cry swelled up, waiting only for my lungs to gather enough breath to expel it. Before that could happen, Liu Sanmu was kneeling beside me. He held me in his arms, and the scream died into moans muffled against his chest, followed by heaving sobs. He held me tightly for a few more minutes.

"Jialing, stop crying." He held me by the shoulders and looked into my face. "Don't worry, Jialing. I won't let you come to harm. You killed him to save me."

If he had ever noticed Ping Mei, the memory was now bleached from his mind. It was the one thing I'd asked of Fox. As far as Liu Sanmu knew, I was the only person who could've killed Wan Baoyuan.

"You're the one who saved me," I said. "You came just in time. Dajuin and Anjuin are both out."

"I wanted to ask Dajuin about going to Chapei again tomorrow," he said. "I was at the other gate when I heard you scream. I just hope the rickshaw driver was too far up the road by then to hear. We can't let anyone know about this, Jialing. We must get Wan's body away from here before anyone comes home."

"But surely the police will realize it was an accident," I said, struggling upright. "I was defending you. With your family's reputation, the police will believe us."

"Listen to me carefully, Jialing," he said. "We cannot let this go to the police. Unless we can make this look like a random murder, we're both in danger."

"But he was trying to kill us," I said. "And I'm sure he killed that poor Mr. Shih. How can we be the ones in danger now that Wan Baoyuan is dead?"

"Wan Baoyuan was mixed up with some very dangerous people," he said, "and some very dangerous politics. You don't want your name in any newspaper stories, Jialing."

"But I'm not involved in anything political. I don't understand."

"For now, you don't need to," he said gently. "You just need to keep quiet and help me get rid of this body. First we need to carry it to the car. Can you get a blanket, something big to wrap around it?"

I avoided looking at Wan Baoyuan's body, limp and still, his fine suit sodden with rain. Shivering, I ran into the *erfang*.

Use that quilt, Fox said, pointing. She was kneeling by the pallet bed where Ping Mei lay. My mother. It hadn't been a dream.

I yanked the folded quilt from the cupboard and ran out again. We lifted Wan Baoyuan's body onto the blanket.

"We need to wrap his head," Liu Sanmu said, "or he'll bleed through."

The embroidered skirt panel lay on the steps. With strangely cooperative fingers I removed the embroidery hoop and gave Liu Sanmu the fabric. He wrapped it several times around the head, but even then I fancied I could see through the delicate embroidery to a pale face and closed eyes. Then we rolled the body over and over in the blanket.

Liu Sanmu lifted the roll by one end and I lifted it by the other. Together we carried it to the front courtyard. Is there anything in the world so heavy as a corpse?

He opened the back door of the Pierce-Arrow, and together, we heaved the body inside. It lay on the floor of the car, the quilt a ludicrously colorful shroud. Liu Sanmu opened the door on the other side and tugged the corpse farther in. His coolness unnerved me almost as much as handling Wan Baoyuan's body.

"Say nothing about this," he said, holding me by the shoulders. "Wan Baoyuan never came here today. I'll explain everything later. I promise. This must be our secret, Jialing. Do you understand?"

I didn't, but I nodded. All I wanted was for him to drive away, take that horrible cargo with him. I opened the gate. The street outside was empty, rivulets of rain washing down the paving stones. The automobile pulled out onto Dragon Springs Road, and its dark shape vanished in the downpour. I shut the gates, my hands numb with cold, barely noticing the rain.

Then I stumbled through the courtyard and went into the kitchen. I picked up a twig broom. I swept water from the stones of the courtyard and into the bamboo garden, sluicing rain and blood into soil and moss until the puddles ran clear. I swept the same paving stones, over and over and over, until Fox came out and took the broom from my hands.

She led me into the *erfang* where I slumped with my back against the wall. Fox dabbed my face dry with a cloth. My mother was sitting up on the pallet bed.

"You're soaking wet," my mother said. "You must get changed into dry clothes. My poor Ling-ling."

That was a very filial thing to do, Fox said, letting Liu Sanmu think you were responsible for that horrible man's death instead of your mother.

"I didn't want her dragged into a police investigation," I said.

But it was a lie. I hadn't asked Fox to erase Ping Mei from Liu Sanmu's mind out of filial piety. I didn't want anyone to know she was my mother.

Wan Baoyuan, his lifeless body, the rolled-up quilt. I wouldn't think about it.

WHEN ANJUIN RETURNED, I was huddled on my cot running a fever. I slept for two days. While she put cold cloths on my forehead, she told me that Dajuin was confused and angry. Wan Baoyuan had vanished. There hadn't been a note or explanation, no money had been transferred to the Yangs' bank account.

"Was he toying with us?" Anjuin said. "He seemed so eager to buy the property. I hope Liu Sanmu is still interested. He hasn't been in touch either."

Recovered, I read the newspaper every day. There were editorials in support of the strikes, condemnation of Western nations, and criticism of our own government for being unprepared at the peace conference. The police were struggling to stay in control of the city. They had arrested so many protesters that one of the city's administrative buildings was being used as a temporary prison.

There was nothing about the body of a man dressed in expensive gray flannels, his skull beaten in. By a wooden chair leg long since burned in the kitchen stove.

Then Shanghai returned to normal. Students went back to classes and factory workers back to their jobs. Now every noise out on Dragon Springs Road made me tremble. The shouts of laborers across the street, the rumble of handbarrows, and the sound of tools tapping on wood.

And finally, there was news of Wan Baoyuan's death. The papers provided only the sketchiest information. Wan's body had been caught against a barge ferrying construction materials across the Huangpu River. Workers on the barge had found him, a body that had been floating in the water for days. At first they had thought it was the corpse of a pauper, someone whose family was too poor to pay for a proper burial, but there was no shroud wrapped around his body, not even a rope to prevent the indignity of splayed limbs. Then there was the suit, which made it clear he had not been one of the nameless poor. The unidentified corpse went to the morgue, another of Shanghai's many anonymous murder victims.

His body might have been consigned to an unmarked grave but for the manager of the Shanghai Hotel, who had grown concerned about Wan's unpaid bills. He reported Wan Baoyuan missing. His description led police to look through the morgue.

There was no mention of head wounds or a quilt. Or a length of fabric embroidered with orange chrysanthemums.

A single police detective came to Dragon Springs Road to speak with Dajuin. In Wan Baoyuan's hotel room they had found papers dealing with the Yang property. Dajuin was genuine in his confusion. There was no reason why he would want Wan Baoyuan dead. He had every reason for wanting him alive. The police detective agreed.

"Surely Liu Sanmu has seen the terrible news," Anjuin said. By now the investigation into Wan Baoyuan's murder had moved to the back pages of the newspaper. "I don't understand why he hasn't come to see us. At least to let us know whether or not he's still planning to buy the property."

"I'll call on him and find out," Dajuin said.

WITH FOX AT her side, my mother hobbled out onto Chung San Road each day to beg. Perhaps Fox had always been at her side, only I hadn't been allowed to see. It made me feel better to know she wasn't out on the streets alone, that Fox was with her.

I had grown accustomed to thinking of her as Ping Mei the servant, the disfigured beggar woman. Someone I could dismiss, someone who had been of interest only for what she could tell me about my mother. To my relief, she didn't expect me to treat her as a mother. Nor did she ever press me to spend more time with her.

For a decade, I had blamed her for abandoning me, blamed her for my foreign blood. I had believed her dead. Over the years my memories of her had become encrusted with a prickly shell of resentment. Yet I had also longed for her. I had wanted the sweet-faced woman whose laughter tinkled like wind chimes, the loving and playful companion who had made each day feel safe yet full of adventure.

But that mother was gone. The woman in front of me had suffered more sorrow than I'd ever seen, survived more cruelty than I could bear to imagine. She was drained of the liveliness that once suffused her being. She was content simply to exist.

Each time I saw her now, I searched for the clues I should've noticed. The mole on the side of her mouth, the once-shapely brows pulled taut by her scars. The tune she hummed unawares in her scratchy voice, "Spring Snow." Why hadn't I recognized the notes of her favorite melody, even in that hoarse rendition? And then there was the embroidery. Why had I not recognized my mother's skill in the tiny, perfect stitches, so smooth that every leaf seemed to unfurl from the fabric?

What I did recognize was that as mother and daughter, we were strangers. The woman who sat before me had missed a decade of my life, and I hers.

"As Ping Mei, you were so diffident," I said. "Taciturn."

"I didn't dare talk too much," said my mother, "because there was so much I wanted to ask you. It would've seemed overly curious."

"Did you always know my mother's whereabouts?" I asked Fox, who sat up and stretched, a long, luxurious elongation of limbs from nose tip to tail that nearly flattened her against the floorboards of the veranda.

I knew she was somewhere in Shanghai, she said, but that was all.

"Fox's powers are not unlimited," my mother said. "I made her promise to expend them all protecting you."

Yet my mother had been the one who had faced more danger, who had suffered more by losing Fox's protection. The hard shell of resentment softened ever so slightly.

"What binds a Fox to a promise?" I asked.

Only friendship, she said, yawning to show sharp white teeth and a pink tongue. No magic. Just ordinary friendship.

That night I dreamed I was in the Western Residence. It was my own dream, not one of Fox's. She had not come to see me in my sleep since her return. The ground beneath the bamboo was carpeted in flowers. *Violas, clove pinks, forget-me-nots.* Anna was there, under the bamboo, her features indistinct in the mottled green light.

Brightness like dawn lit the garden arch and then the Door opened. Anna walked through the arch, copper ringlets shining. The Door remained open, and I could see her wandering through the orchard, away from me. Then Fox was at the Door, whining as she ran back and forth while the Door closed, very slowly. I lost sight of Anna.

I woke up, my heart pounding, my thoughts confused.

Fox, running back and forth in front of the Door. A Door that closed on her slowly, very slowly.

"How LONELY IT will be once you're gone, Jialing," Anjuin said. She smiled, but it didn't reach her eyes.

I couldn't tell whether it was because I'd be leaving or because the reality was dawning on her that she would be living in a household where her sister-in-law was mistress. Yun Na and the children were arriving in a week's time, and they were all moving to a rented apartment in Shanghai. Thankfully, by then I would be living with the Ellis family.

Time couldn't pass quickly enough. I longed for the Ellis home, a place where I could hide myself in a different world, their world. Once I had some money I could move my mother somewhere, someplace inexpensive, but at least I could put a roof over her head. Then there would be no further reason to come back to Dragon Springs Road.

Liu Sanmu hadn't contacted me, but what I read from the newspapers was comfort enough. The investigation into Wan Baoyuan's death had faded away. I didn't need to know more, to be reminded of more. I wanted to distance myself from Dragon Springs Road, forget the horror of blood trickling into puddles, blood staining the moss between flagstones.

ANJUIN HAD GONE to the market for some white radishes to make my favorite pickles. It was my last afternoon at Dragon Springs Road. I would be going to work for Mrs. Ellis the next day. In the Western Residence, my mother and Fox were putting the finishing touches on my new skirt. I'd given up on the sewing machine.

They sat together like a pair of maiden aunts, Fox in the shape of a middle-aged woman, talking quietly while they sewed. There was something strangely peaceful about this sight.

"The Yangs are hoping Liu Sanmu will keep his promise to buy this property," I said. "He's coming to see Dajuin one of these evenings. What will you do? Where can you go?"

Fox shrugged. The Door is here. I'm staying. Your mother and I will be fine.

"You won't need to beg," I told my mother. "Once I've been paid, I'll bring you money for food. I'll find you a place to live."

"Don't worry," she said. "Fox will look after me."

"You're my mother," I said, "and I'm responsible for you. But I don't want you interfering with my life anymore. Either of you."

Both my words and voice came out more sharply than I'd intended, but my life had been a leaf, blown around a courtyard at the behest of others. My mother, then Fox. The Yangs, Anjuin. Even Miss Morris. They had made decisions on my behalf. It had been necessary, I knew that. I had been a helpless child.

From now on, however, the decisions ruling my life had to be my own. At the Ellis house my new life would begin, in the small bedroom with yellow roses on the curtains. I was leaving Dragon Springs Road behind.

And a sodden body, blood trickling onto moss.

CHAPTER 18

The next day, Anjuin walked me out to Chung San Road.

"You've got the address for Dajuin's new home?" she asked.

"Right here in my pocket. I'll come see you on my first day off," I said, swinging my modest bag of belongings onto the rickshaw seat. I climbed on and reached down to hold her hand for a moment. Anjuin was smiling, happy for me. Then the rickshaw puller set off. I looked back and waved, a twinge of guilt pricking my heart. Had I been too quick to get into the rickshaw? Should I have said a longer good-bye? But I would see her soon.

She had no idea, she would never know, how badly I wanted to get away from Dragon Springs Road and why.

The External Roads area was still partly farmland,

blocks of small shops and tired-looking houses spaced here and there between fields of cabbage and mustard greens. Women in wide straw hats bent low to weed between the rows, some with babies strapped to their chests. Then the buildings grew denser and became cleaner, more modern, built in the Western style.

On my first visit to the Ellises' I had been so nervous I hardly remembered what the neighborhood looked like. Now I would live here. Automobiles shared the road with carriages and handbarrows, and then the rickshaw entered a street lined with tall plane trees. I caught glimpses of grand mansions behind wrought-iron gates and smaller villas enclosed by low brick walls.

The gatekeeper was expecting me, and when I walked up the gravel path, the same young manservant who had greeted me last time hurried from the house to carry my bag.

"Mrs. Ellis is entertaining guests for lunch," he said. "I've been told to show you to your room. She'll come up to see you when the ladies are gone."

On the lawn, the croquet set had been put away. The flower beds were newly weeded, the hedges trimmed. Under a canvas canopy a dozen foreign women sat around a long table draped in white linen. Wide-brimmed hats framed their pale faces, and servants stood behind chairs plying palm-leaf fans.

Mrs. Ellis looked up and saw me. She smiled and gave me a small wave. The woman beside her looked up and smiled. It was Miss Morris. Beside her, another face I knew but didn't welcome, Mrs. Burns. I dropped them a curtsy in the foreign style and continued up the path. Today, not even the sight of Mrs. Burns could ruin my happiness.

It took only a few minutes to put away my clothing in the chest of drawers. I placed my notebooks and pencils on the desk. Then I went to the bathroom and splashed water on my face. The bathroom was a marvel of white tiles and porcelain, white towels neatly draped on a rack. Tentatively, I pulled the chain hanging from the tank above the toilet and jumped back, laughing as water splashed in the bowl.

Back in my room, I looked out the window to the small grassy playground below. I couldn't wait to meet the Ellis children. A light knock made me turn to the door.

Mrs. Ellis entered, Miss Morris behind her.

"Miss Morris," I cried, rushing to take her hands.

"Please, sit down, Jialing," Mrs. Ellis said, indicating the chair by the desk. "Miss Morris, perhaps we could sit on the bed?"

It was all strangely awkward. Something tightened at the base of my neck. Mrs. Ellis looked away for a moment, then cleared her throat.

"I understand you've met Mrs. Burns. You applied for a position there."

"Yes, but she found me . . . unsuitable," I replied. A small tendril of dread curled in the pit of my stomach.

"I can't hire you, Jialing," she said. "It would upset Mrs. Burns. She's very disappointed that I'd hired a governess of . . . mixed blood."

Tears filled my eyes. I couldn't speak. How could this be happening?

"I'm so sorry, my dear," Mrs. Ellis said. "Do try and understand. My husband works for Mr. Burns. I can't afford to offend his wife. Please, take this money." She pushed a small bag of coins into my hands.

She stood up. "I must get back to my guests. I am so, so sorry."

Miss Morris reached her hand out to me, but I flinched. Without a word, I pulled open the drawers and put my clothing back into my bag.

"If there's anything I can do to help you, my dear, I will," Miss Morris said.

But we both knew there was nothing she could do. Not anymore.

IT WAS A long walk back to Dragon Springs Road, and the strap of my bag hung heavy on my shoulders. I cursed Mrs. Burns and her lecherous husband. I cursed my tainted blood. I even cursed Mrs. Ellis even though I understood her reasons.

Reluctant to face Anjuin's helpless sympathy, I took my time. For a while I stood outside the gates of Jessfield Park, watching foreign families promenade in and out. They were so privileged and so heedless of their privilege. When I finally trudged along Chung San Road, it was late afternoon. The fields of cabbage and mustard greens were empty now, the farm women gone home to cook supper for their families. Stores were closing, and the street echoed with good-natured shouts between shopkeepers as they locked their doors.

For the next few nights I would have a roof over my head, but what would I do afterward, when Dajuin and Anjuin moved to their new home in Shanghai? Anjuin had said it was quite small, just an apartment with two rooms. I could squat at Dragon Springs Road with my mother and Fox, but for how long? If Liu Sanmu bought the property, the houses would come down. And how would I live? Go begging? Work in a factory? I shuddered, remembering Mary's auntie.

A car tooted its horn behind me and I jumped.

"Miss Zhu," a man's voice called. "Can I give you a ride home?"

An automobile pulled over to the curb, and Liu Sanmu pushed the passenger-side door open. A different car. Not the Pierce-Arrow.

"Climb in. I'm on my way to Dragon Springs Road to see Dajuin about the property," he said. "I should've come by sooner, but it seemed better to stay away until we knew what the police had found. Are you all right? You saw the newspapers?"

"Yes, I did. Thank you, Mr. Liu," I said, pulling the door shut. "Thank you for taking care of everything."

Such polite words. As though concealing murder was a trivial topic.

"We may as well talk here." He turned off the ignition. "I owe you a more complete explanation of why we can't involve the police."

I stared straight ahead. I wished he would stop. I didn't want to talk about Wan Baoyuan.

"When you told me you saw Wan Baoyuan three years ago," he said, "it was the date that caught my attention. That, and how he first claimed he hadn't been to Shanghai in a decade."

"Yes, I saw him on the day of Master Shen's funeral," I said, looking out the window. What would I do now? Could Miss Morris really help me find another position?

"That was also the day of Mah Juhou's murder," he said. "You may not remember but there were rumors that the warlord General Zhang Zuolin was behind the assassination. Wan Baoyuan used to be on the general's staff. I'd been interested in him since knowing that."

"So you suspected Wan Baoyuan might know something about Mah Juhou's death," I said.

"I only suspected. I still only suspected when you told me he'd been in Shanghai the day of Mah's murder," he said. "But when Wan tried to kill you, I knew he had been involved. He might even have been the assassin."

"Well, he's dead now, so it's all over, isn't it?"

"Jialing, you must understand," he said patiently. "The war-lord's people are very dangerous. They don't want any loose ends leading back to the general. That's why Mr. Shih was killed. He knew Wan Baoyuan was in Shanghai the day of the murder. He was a loose end. *You're* still a loose end. You can't say anything to anyone."

"Of course not," I said. "Do you think I want Anjuin to know I killed a man?"

"There's more to worry about than your friends," he said. "Let's hope Wan was cleaning up loose ends on his own and didn't tell anyone about you. Let's hope his accomplices never heard of you."

"So it might not be all over." Despair washed over me.

"I won't let anything happen to you," he said, sitting back. "You did a brave thing. You saved my life. General Zhang is an enemy of the Nationalist Party, no matter what he says in public. Our family is behind the Nationalists. Before Mah Juhou was killed, he and my uncle were making plans to bring Dr. Sun Yat-sen back into power."

He turned the key and started the car again. "What I don't understand is why Wan Baoyuan went to Dragon Springs Road three years ago. Why he would want the property. How that fits into the conspiracy."

"It wasn't to do with any conspiracy, it was family," I said, star-ing ahead listlessly. "He came to Dragon Springs Road to see his childhood home. He used to live here. His real family name was Fong. Wan is the name of the uncle who adopted him."

"Incredible," Liu Sanmu said, shaking his head. "He gave in to sentimentality." He glanced at me. "Is there anything I can do for you? Anything you need before you start your new job?"

I thought of the little bedroom in the Ellis house, the curtains printed with fat yellow roses, the view from the window. There was nothing Mrs. Ellis could do for me, nothing Miss Morris could do to salvage the situation. A door had slammed shut on my future. My education didn't matter because I was *zazhong*, illegitimate, and the daughter of a prostitute. I was eighteen and my life was over.

We turned into Dragon Springs Road, and the car pulled over by the front gate of the Central Residence. I was tired, so tired. Leaning my head against the car window, I closed my eyes.

"The job is gone," I said. "I have nothing."

Fox, help me.

THE COURTYARD OF the Western Residence spread out below me. I sat on a small wicker chair across a table from Fox and my mother. We were on the second-story veranda of the main house, a structure so rickety in the real world we never dared put a single foot on its unsteady floorboards. The plum trees below were in full bloom. It had just rained and the gray flagstones were flecked with damp white petals. My mother looked no different than usual in her beggar's rags. Fox wore a high-necked vest over a long green silk gown.

Are you sure? Fox asked.

"I have nothing to lose, Fox," I said. "I have no more ideas, and I've run out of time. He's a kind man. I like him well enough."

Fox cleared her throat. If you don't live here on Dragon Springs Road, it will be harder to manage.

"Fox, you've said this is your particular talent," I said. "You're the one who suggested this in the first place. Now you're saying you can't help me do it?"

She sat up very straight and lifted her chin. I can, but my powers are limited by distance.

"Come away from Dragon Springs Road then. You can both come live with me, wherever I go."

I'm not leaving the Door. And your mother needs to stay here with me. She sounded agitated.

"Fox, it's all right," my mother said. "Don't worry about me. I don't need your help."

I'm just a second-rate Fox spirit. Fox addressed my mother with great dignity. My powers are mediocre. I had very little talent to begin with, and I had to cultivate it for hundreds of years to achieve what I have today. But it's still not enough to look after both of you. I'm sorry.

What had it taken for Fox to admit that her powers, which I had always assumed she wielded according to her whims, were only just adequate?

"It's all right, Fox," my mother repeated. "It's enough for what Jialing needs. Perhaps you could visit Jialing every week to sustain your influence. Would that work?"

"Please, Fox," I begged. "I've run out of choices."

HEAT FLARED OUT from the center of my being, and the cold glass of the car window warmed against my cheek. Confidence and exhilaration surged through my veins, sensations far stronger than what Fox had let me feel that one time, years ago.

I raised my head to look at Liu Sanmu, and he was staring at me, eyes wide. He looked bewildered, then his expression softened and he was gazing at me in wonder. I knew how he saw me, eyes shining, red lips parted, skin glowing so petal smooth he could barely keep his hands from reaching out to stroke my face.

I knew his desire. I understood it. I understood everything about it. It was intoxicating.

And it wasn't real.

"You don't have nothing, Jialing," he said, his voice husky with longing. "Come with me."

He turned the car around, and we drove back into Shanghai.

It wasn't what I wanted. But what else was I to do?

CHAPTER 19

For the first two weeks I lived in the suite of a quiet hotel at the edge of the International Settlement. The drapes in the sitting room pulled back to reveal French doors opening onto a small private garden. It wasn't much more than a bit of lawn edged with flower beds, but it was private, enclosed by tall hedges, with a wrought-iron gate that allowed us to come and go without walking through the lobby. There was a dining room at the hotel, but we took meals in our room.

"I've rented a house for you," Sanmu said. "It's small but nicely furnished. It'll be ready next week. If you don't like it, you can move somewhere else after a year."

"It will be perfect," I said, sitting up against the pillows. "Everything you've chosen for me has been just perfect."

The dressing table held his latest gift, a set of silver-backed brushes and mirror. Three new dresses hung in the wardrobe, enough to see me through until the dressmaker returned with the clothes I had ordered. Everything was paid for on Sanmu's account.

My first visit to a dressmaker had been an awkward experience. Although I was on Sanmu's arm, I didn't feel as though I had any right to be in the shop, its glass cases of beaded trims and lace. The shopgirls who helped me try on dresses were so discreetly stylish it made me realize the new clothes Anjuin and I had sewn were old-fashioned, more suited to women twice our age. The owner ushered me into a private room where she brought in dress after dress. One fit well enough that I wore it out of the shop, a long tunic with fashionable wide sleeves and a skirt that fell to my ankles. We exchanged my plain cloth shoes for a pair of leather pumps.

"You've bought me too many clothes already." I climbed out of bed and opened the wardrobe. He came to stand behind me.

"I want you to look scandalously beautiful when I introduce you to my friends," he said. "Just show my card at any store and have them send the bill to my accountant there. I want you in a new dress every time we go out. But when we're alone, you can be a schoolgirl for me."

He slipped his hands around my waist and then over my breasts. His breathing quickened and I turned around for him to kiss me. Although he had been dressing to leave for work at *Xinwen Bao*, he now pulled me back into bed. This intimacy had been the part I had dreaded the most about becoming his mistress, to have Sanmu possess my body, to submit and yield to his pleasure.

Yet in many ways it had proven one of the easier charades in my new role.

Everything I knew about the act of love had been gleaned from classmates and the other servants. Some girls at the orphanage were rescued from brothels and had seen much. Away from the Yangs' hearing, the servants didn't hold back from making lewd jokes. Once in Shanghai, I had looked down an alley to see a man press himself with hurried and brutal urgency against a woman. The woman looked back at me with blank, opium-dilated eyes. She was a "pheasant," the lowest form of prostitute.

There was nothing brutal or hurried about Liu Sanmu's love-making. On our first night he had removed my simple cotton clothing with as much care as if it had been fine silk. He had spared me the embarrassment of nakedness by turning out all the lights, leaving the drapes open just enough to allow in a sliver of twilight. His movements had been gentle, his hands lingering over my breasts and thighs. His body moved slowly against mine until desire overcame him.

Afterward he had kissed me over and over, saying my name with every breath. And to my relief, I had felt nothing. I had felt no pleasure nor had I been moved to surrender. I knew his passion wasn't real. I knew I was only doing this to survive.

WHEN I LEFT the hotel to visit Anjuin, I wore my old clothes. I wanted to look the same. I climbed the stairs to the fifth-floor apartment where Dajuin's family now lived. It was an old building, with a shared toilet compartment on each floor. The inevitable odors of cooking oil and garlic drifted up the stairwell, along with the cries of children.

I paused before knocking, but there was no way around this visit. Liu Sanmu had told Dajuin about us the day they closed the property purchase.

"Dajuin was relieved," Sanmu said, "pleased even, that I would be taking care of you."

It didn't matter to me what Dajuin thought. It was Anjuin. That wasn't how I'd wanted her to learn about the situation. I wished there had been time to write to her first, a chance to explain what had happened at the Ellises'. That I had no choice.

She opened the door, pushing a strand of hair off her damp forehead. Looking behind her, I saw only two rooms. It was a tiny place. Yun Na shouted from the inside room.

"It's Jialing," Anjuin called back in reply. Was it sorrow or anger in her gaze?

"Jialing! Welcome, welcome! How is Mr. Liu?" A pregnant Yun Na bustled her way to the door. Her fawning tones confirmed they all knew I was now Sanmu's mistress.

"He is well," I said cautiously. "I was hoping Anjuin could come for a walk with me. Just a short one, I know you must be very busy getting settled in to your new home."

"Of course, of course," she said, beaming. "Take as long as you like. Old friends must have their time together."

Anjuin and I were silent all the way down the stairs.

"We can walk to Quinsan Park," she said. "It's just a public square with some greenery, but it's close by."

The silence between us was as wide and muddy as the Huangpu River and I couldn't think of a way to get across. It seemed best to be direct.

"Mrs. Ellis didn't hire me after all," I said as we approached the park. It seemed best to start with that. "Then Liu Sanmu asked me to be his mistress, and it seemed like my only option."

More silence. I couldn't read her, couldn't tell what she was feeling.

"I know you care about him, Anjuin. But you said yourself you wouldn't be able to stand sharing him with other wives."

"Your decisions are your own," she said, her voice as cool as polished stone. "But why couldn't you have talked to me first? We could've found another way."

"We've had years to find other ways, Anjuin," I said, grasping her hand. "I'm illegitimate and *zazhong*. My education counts for nothing. What could you have done? What could Dajuin have done? Look at where you're living now. Do you think there would've been room for me?"

"You showed no consideration for my feelings," she said, pulling her hand away.

The gesture was like a knife wound. It ripped open the distress of the past weeks, everything I had tried to keep at bay. Wan Baoyuan's death. My mother. The room with yellow roses on the wall.

"Your feelings?" I said. "Your feelings won't keep a roof over my head or food in my belly. Would you rather I took my clothes off for strangers in a brothel? Die of overwork in some factory?"

Her stricken face told me she knew the truth of my words and was already regretting hers. In that moment I should've apologized. I should've told her she meant more to me than a hundred Liu Sanmus, that she was the sister of my heart. But I didn't. Anger and disappointment wouldn't allow me to acknowledge my love, to reach out and mend the hurt on both sides.

"You're jealous, Anjuin," I said. "Jealous because Liu Sanmu chose me over you."

It was a childish, hurtful retort. And of course, completely untrue. Her expression crumpled, then hardened. Without a word, she walked away.

AT THE WESTERN Residence, I heard female voices as I walked through the bamboo garden. Fox was with my mother, the two of them seated on the veranda of the main house, a small platter of cakes between them. Today Fox was human, in a Western-style suit of brown wool, a cascade of creamy silk ruffles down her front.

I've dressed in your honor, Fox said. Like a foreigner. But here you are looking like a schoolgirl.

"I've been to see Anjuin," I said. "We argued. She's upset that I'm now Liu Sanmu's mistress. Why, when she knew she never had a chance with Liu Sanmu?"

"Give her time to get used to the idea," my mother said. "Feelings are rarely rational." Then she coughed, a harsh rasping that made me wince.

"I don't want to talk about it," I said. "Anyway, that's not why I'm here. You can probably stay here safely through the fall and winter, but after that, you must leave Dragon Springs Road. They'll be tearing down these houses in the New Year."

Sanmu told me that the Liu family's fortune-teller had picked a lucky day in the third week of the New Year to begin construction. The Yang houses would go the way of the old Shen estate and other properties on Dragon Springs Road, the old courtyard homes replaced with modern, Western-style villas.

The rocks placed so carefully as garden features in our neighbors' homes are gone, Fox sighed, standing up. The bamboo and azaleas that softened the corners of courtyards are gone. Those new villas are as sharp edged as the bricks used to build them.

There would be no more slow-paced evenings strolling up and down Dragon Springs Road, the twilight exchange of greetings and gossip, casual invitations to dine. The farmland behind us would turn into more streets and more buildings. There would be no more ponds and rice fields where children hunted for tadpoles, no more open skies where swallows swooped on insects.

I've kept humans from intruding on the Western Residence for hundreds of years, Fox said. I can do it for a bit longer.

But I could tell she was worried.

"I can't make Fox leave," I said to my mother, "but why can't you come live with me? Once these houses are torn down, where will you go?"

"My presence at your home would raise too many questions." My mother touched her ruined cheek. "Let's leave things the way they are for now."

"Sanmu is completely infatuated," I said. "He'll do whatever I ask."

You must never believe that, Fox said sternly. He's still the same person. His infatuation for you hasn't changed his character. If he were the jealous type, he would still be jealous. If he were miserly, he still wouldn't buy you expensive gifts.

"You must try and save some money," my mother said. "It could be another lifetime before the Door opens for Fox, or it could be tomorrow. If she goes through, what will you do without her help? Would Liu Sanmu still love you?"

THE HOUSE SANMU rented for me was in the French Concession, a Western-style villa on a street called Yuyang Lane. It was guarded by whitewashed walls, a set of heavy metal gates, and an unsmiling gatekeeper called Old Tan. The long gravel path to the house curved beneath magnolia trees and edged past flower beds bordered with low boxwood hedges. In Shanghai's warm climate, ivy flourished and clambered over the garden's brick walls, taking root in every crack.

Sanmu said it was just a small house, but to me it was enormous, more than enough for one person. At the back was a greenhouse filled with ferns and orchids. On the second floor I had a sitting room and bedroom with an adjoining bathroom. My bedroom windows faced the back garden, and the sitting room windows opened to look down on the front garden. There was also a spare room that Sanmu said could be my library.

My library. My house. My garden.

I had more servants than I needed. There was a gardener who came every day and never entered the house. The gatekeeper, Old Tan, nodded to me and hardly ever spoke. And there was Little Ko.

"You needn't hire anyone else, Young Mistress," she declared when I first met her. Feet planted wide, her sturdy figure reminded me of Third Wife. "Just pay me a little more and I'll do the work of three."

She was housekeeper, cook, and lady's maid. She didn't have to cook very often. Most days we ate simple meals of vegetables and tofu or reheated food that Little Ko purchased from the many small restaurants around the area. On the occasions when Sanmu came for dinner, he only wanted plain cooking, and this I could manage on my own.

Then there were the nights Sanmu took me out. Shanghai's streets were as busy at night as during the day. Light spilled out from restaurant doorways and shop windows; automobile headlamps swung their beams in arcs as they turned the corner. Muted strains of music from a dozen night clubs reverberated along the sidewalk, one melody suddenly blaring out in dominance as a door opened, then quieting down again as it shut.

At restaurants, Sanmu always asked for a table in a quiet corner so that we could avoid the many curious stares directed our way. A member of the Liu family and his Eurasian mistress. Invariably, we would be interrupted by one of his friends or a business acquaintance, stopping at our table for a few words, like courtiers paying their respects.

"You must know everyone in this city," I said. He had recently hired a driver, a White Russian, and now Sanmu sat in the back of the car with me whenever we went out, his arm always around me, his kisses deep and hungry.

"I don't, but it seems everyone wants a closer look at you," he said. "In fact my Fourth Uncle wants to meet you. He's coming for supper tomorrow evening, but don't worry. He's like me. Simple home cooking is fine. No meat."

I caught my breath. "But why? Surely he disapproves of me."

"Not at all. He's had mistresses of his own."

"Were any of his mistresses *hun xue*?"

Pause. "He knows you're special to me, Jialing."

THE NEXT DAY Little Ko and I cleaned all the rooms downstairs. Then we cleaned the upstairs rooms in case Fourth Uncle wanted to see the entire house. Then I started cleaning all over again.

"Eh, Young Mistress," she said, "I'd worry more about the food and drink. Menfolk don't notice cobwebs even if they're hanging over their heads. It's the women who look into corners hoping to find fault."

"All right," I said. "Just make sure we have both rice and noodles ready."

"There's nothing for you to do," she said. "Take off your apron. I'll finish up in the kitchen and then I'll draw you a bath."

Just then we heard the front gate buzzer, Old Tan warning

us that he had let in a visitor. A woman walked up the garden path. Her face was hidden by the light veil of her hat, but she was dressed very elegantly in Western clothing, a long belted dress and high-heeled shoes. Little Ko hurried to answer the door. I tore off my apron and stuffed it under a seat cushion. Although I had met many of Sanmu's friends at restaurants and clubs, he hadn't invited any of them yet to Yuyang Lane, and I hadn't met anyone I wanted to invite.

I heard Little Ko open the front door, and a moment later my visitor entered the drawing room. She lifted back the veil from her face.

It was Leah. I threw my arms around her.

"You look so grown up. And so beautiful," I cried. "How did you know where to find me?"

Her freckles were gone, and without them, her skin glowed with the warm luster of ivory. Her eyebrows had been darkened with pencil, and this emphasized the lightness of her eyes. Her coral red lips were perfectly drawn.

"You're the latest gossip," she said, pulling off her gloves. "A *hun xue* mistress comes to the Liu family, and she's for Liu Sanmu, who has never before taken up with an outside woman. A few questions and I found out where you lived."

"But what about you?" I said. "Grace and I always wondered because you didn't seem very happy when your aunt took you away."

"That wasn't my aunt, that was Madam Fu," she said. "She runs the brothel where my mother worked. My mother was an opium user and she ran up more debts than she could ever pay off from her earnings. It was her idea to send me to the mission school to learn English."

Foreign men were willing to pay a good price for girls who could talk to them in their own language, and Madam Fu agreed readily to a plan that would increase Leah's value. They left her on the orphanage steps. When Madam Fu came to get Leah years later, the coolness I'd observed in Miss Morris's behavior had been suspicion. But once Leah vouched for her "aunt" there was nothing the headmistress could do to stop her from leaving.

After three months of training and grooming, Madam Fu sold Leah to the highest bidder. Leah's patron was British, a manager with the Shanghai Land Investment Company. He had a wife in England who refused to come to Shanghai, a situation that didn't seem to bother Mr. Stephenson.

"He's nice enough," she said. "In his forties, consumed with making money. All he really wants is a warm bed and someone to have a drink with him when he gets home in the evenings. His routines are unvarying. He's generous enough and fond enough."

"What about your mother?" I asked.

Her lips tightened. "She died last year, still an opium sot, still asking me for money. But what could I do? She was my mother. Now you, you've landed on your feet, Jialing. The Liu family! Tell me everything."

It was the happiest afternoon I'd spent since leaving Dragon Springs Road. It was only when Little Ko came in and cleared her throat that I realized how much time had gone by.

"Just reminding you, Mistress. I'm going to draw your bath. You have visitors tonight."

"Oh no." I sighed. "I'd forgotten. Sanmu's uncle is coming tonight."

Leah clapped her hands. "You're almost part of the family."

"Don't make fun of me," I said.

She smiled. "Shanghai society is not as judgmental as a mission school."

A mistress could be as respected as a second wife or as reviled as a cheap prostitute. Family members had been known to criticize a jealous wife for being rude to a modest and well-behaved mistress. Some mistresses were women from good families fallen on hard times, their sophistication prized by men flush with new wealth but wanting in refinement. It all depended on name and money, upbringing and social circles. A thousand different influences came into play, and much depended on the quality of the woman in question.

"If you gave Liu Sanmu a son," Leah said, on her way out the door, "he would provide for you even after he tired of you."

I didn't want any children. Not by Sanmu, not by anyone. Why bear a child who would only blame me, as I had blamed my mother, for the shame of tainted blood? If I wanted to secure my future, it was far more practical to save money of my own, against the day Fox disappeared through the Door. For on that day, Sanmu would surely tire of me.

AT FIRST GLANCE Sanmu's Fourth Uncle seemed elderly because he carried a cane and wore a traditional scholar's gown and round skullcap. Closer, he proved merely middle-aged, ascetically lean and spare. He ate very little, although he praised the radish pickles, Mrs. Hao's recipe.

Apart from an initial greeting and the compliment about the pickles, Fourth Uncle didn't speak to me at all during the meal. He and Sanmu talked about the influx of White Russians who had escaped to Shanghai since the Bolshevik Revolution.

"My driver is Russian," Sanmu said. "Claims he was an officer in the czar's army before this, but that's what they all say. They're all aristocrats or officers."

"We should be more concerned about the Bolshevik influence," Fourth Uncle said. "Some of our students have gone to

Russia. They'll come back preaching socialism. It will be worse than the warlords if socialism takes root in China."

Suddenly he swiveled around to face me. I nearly dropped my chopsticks. "What about you, Miss Zhu? What interest do you have in our nation's politics?"

Sanmu gave me an encouraging smile. He had warned me about this.

"It's so complicated," I said. "I don't know enough to have a qualified opinion."

Fourth Uncle grunted. "I'm glad to hear you say that. Women should stay away from politics. What are your interests? Fashion? Gambling?"

"I like gardens," I said, thinking of Fox and the landscapes she had shown me. "The art of the large in the small, providing for the real in the unreal and the unreal in the real."

"Ah." Fourth Uncle's expression softened. "Sanmu, you must take her to Changchow someday to see our kinsman's home. Judge Liu has the most magnificent garden. A lake with two islands, beautiful rhododendrons."

"I will, Uncle. Are you ready for tea?"

This was the signal to leave them alone. Little Ko brought in the tea and I excused myself. Upstairs in my room I gave a sigh of relief and changed into a nightgown. Fourth Uncle's visit had not been as much of an ordeal as I'd feared. Suddenly tired, I sank into bed and turned out the light.

I woke to moonlight seeping through the drapes. I heard voices, Sanmu and his uncle. I got out of bed and went into the sitting room, where the windows overlooked the front garden. The night air was so still I could hear the crunch of gravel as they stepped onto the path. Under the magnolia tree, Fourth Uncle paused. There was a tiny momentary flare in the darkness as he lit a cigarette.

"She's very young, Sanmu," he said. "Not the sort I imagined you'd care for. Still, I suppose it's a good idea to keep her close. Is she discreet? Can she keep secrets?"

"She'll keep quiet, Uncle. Jialing is very sensible for her age, not a spoiled rich girl."

When Sanmu came to bed, I pretended to be asleep, but a small seed of doubt had buried itself in my chest. Why was it a good idea to keep me close? What had he told Fourth Uncle about me?

Did this mean I couldn't trust Sanmu, even though he was under Fox's influence?

SANMU ASKED ME to get a new dining set, something more suited to intimate meals. I had no idea how to go about doing this, but Leah did. She always seemed to know exactly what to do. She was comfortable in her role as mistress to a wealthy man and took me under her wing; we went out frequently, and after a while, I learned to behave as she did in shops and restaurants. I gained confidence and felt less like an apologetic, awkward schoolgirl.

She took me to a furniture gallery where the store manager greeted her effusively. She chose a round table in rosewood and ordered chairs made to match, then asked for something called a sideboard in the same style. I sat by the clerk's desk while he confirmed the order. Although the bill was being sent to Sanmu's accountant, I insisted on a copy for myself. I had begun doing that at every store. I wanted to know how much a mistress cost.

Reflected in the large mirror behind the clerk's desk, Leah was strolling around the store. I admired how she gave the impression of being gracefully posed even when leaning over to inspect a lacquered tabletop. Then I saw the store manager hand her an envelope. She looked inside the envelope, nodded, and tucked it in her purse.

At the next store, she selected four sets of porcelain for me, Chinese and Western, two sets for everyday use and two for entertaining. The cost was staggering, but she assured me it was absolutely necessary. Again, while I sat with the clerk, she accepted an envelope from the store's manager.

"Are you shocked at me?" she asked, as we came out of the store. She had seen me staring.

I shook my head. I didn't begrudge her making extra money.

"Good. We're not schoolgirls anymore, Jialing," she said. "There are many ways to earn money without getting it directly from your patron."

A few months before New Year's, Leah always sold part of her wardrobe to pawnshops. The poorer classes rented clothes and jewelry when they wanted to look well-to-do for special occasions. The shops never did so well as during the New Year when it was important to appear affluent.

"Pawnbrokers pay well for stylish clothes," she said, "because they know they can rent them out for a good price. But commissions from shops and pawning my clothes? That's small change compared what I make for using my influence with Mr. Stephenson."

There was a seemingly endless list of people in Shanghai, both foreign and Chinese, who wanted to do business with her patron's company. For this they were willing to pay for any small advantage. For this, they sent their women to beseech Leah.

"It's so ridiculous, Jialing," she said, pressing a napkin to her perfect red lips. She had taken me to a café on Avenue Joffre. "These men's wives, concubines, mistresses, they bring me gifts. Gifts of money and jewelry, which I don't even ask for half the time. They just assume I'm there to be bribed."

The requests varied. Would Mr. Stephenson take a second look at a proposal, view some property, agree to speak with a certain firm? Sometimes they asked Stephenson to accept a dinner invitation, other times they begged an invitation to one of his company's events. It could be something as small as an introduction to her patron in a public place, perhaps at the dining room of the Astor Hotel or in passing at the Shanghai Race Club.

"But can you fulfill those promises?" I asked.

"They're not promises," she assured me. "I never promise; I only say that I'll try. And I only accept if I feel there's a reasonable chance of success. I did learn something about morals from our school."

"What does Mr. Stephenson say? Does he know?"

"He's lived in Shanghai for a decade," she said. "I'm sure he knows. But the point of all this, Jialing, is that your Mr. Liu belongs to one of the oldest and wealthiest families in Shanghai. Think of how well you would do."

By now I had met more of Sanmu's friends, had even taken tea with some of their mistresses and concubines. The women were never openly rude to me, but neither did they seem interested in becoming friends. Their talk was all about clothes, gossip, and parties. It made me wonder whether they even read the newspaper.

At the Yangs', there had always been talk of politics and the general mood of the country, for all this affected business. At the mission school our teachers had encouraged us to read the news. They said we were living during an important time in China's history, so we should be aware of events.

"I've met some of Sanmu's friends," I said, feeling dubious. "I really don't think they want his help or mine."

"I can send someone your way," she said. "I know someone whose husband could use an introduction to Liu Sanmu. Word will get around."

"Leah, I'm not sure," I said. "If Liu Sanmu finds out . . ."

"You're being cautious until you know him better," she said approvingly. Then she leaned back and lit another cigarette. "You'll find the money isn't the best part. I get a lot of pleasure watching those society women pretend they don't mind that I'm *zazhong.*"

WITH SANMU AT the newspaper all day, I had no lack of free time. He split his hours between Yuyang Lane and his own home. Between family gatherings, the newspaper, and business for the Liu Family Property Development Company, it was never certain which days he would come. Sometimes he was away for days.

Fox found it very irritating to make the trip out to Yuyang Lane only to find me alone.

I can only do so much from afar you know, she said, walking around my room. You must get him here at least once a week. It's much easier if you're together.

Today she was a schoolgirl, wearing a school uniform, her hair in two pigtails tied with black ribbon. She picked up a porcelain fox, an English figurine. It was one of the few trinkets I had bought for myself. I displayed it on a small tabletop pedestal. She put it back, looking pleased.

"Stay until the evening; he will be here," I said. "His driver stopped by with a note to say we are going to a party tonight."

But when Sanmu came home, Fox did her work too well and we never made it to the party.

"I DON'T KNOW what it is," he had whispered, his lips traveling down my neck. "Even when we're together, I feel as though I will never truly understand how I feel about you. You bewilder me."

Then he had sworn his love with every kiss and every caress, made passionate promises to always take care of me. He even wept after our lovemaking. I felt like such a fraud.

Not a single breath of air stirred the light fabric at the windows. Moonlight flooded the garden with a cold radiance that silvered every leaf and glittered the gravel path. Shanghai was exciting, but it was too dense, too clamorous. Even though my little house was sheltered behind brick walls, I always sensed an undercurrent of noise, the hum of traffic from busy Avenue Joffre a few blocks away. I missed the quiet of evenings at Dragon Springs Road, when you could hear the rustle of vines as the air cooled and breezes lifted, when a restful silence descended, encouraging nocturnal creatures to venture out.

I turned away from the window to look at Sanmu's sleeping form, the sheets twisted about him, his hair still damp.

Sanmu came from wealth, but it hadn't spoiled him. He took his work at the newspaper seriously. I couldn't have asked for a better patron, but there was a hollow where I wanted my heart to be. I didn't want his love. I wanted someone whose feelings for me were real. If that was even possible.

Yet my mother had tolerated years with Noble Uncle, a weak and self-serving man. How had she endured someone like that fawning over her?

She had endured it because of me.

CHAPTER 20

February 1920, Year of the Monkey

Leah and I had a wonderful day. Dressed in plain cotton tunics and padded jackets, our faces bare of cosmetics, we crossed the Garden Bridge at the end of the Bund, where Soochow Creek flows into the Huangpu River. We passed alleys whose entrances were decorated with name plates, wooden signs carved with the names of the prostitutes who lived in the alley. Then we turned downhill to the wharves.

"There," Leah said, pointing to a narrow lane, "this one. Next to the Shanghai and Hongkew Wharf. That's how you remember where to find it. There isn't really a street name to look for."

Grace let out a squeal when she saw us, slapped down a bowl of noodles in front of a customer, and ran out to greet us. She was thinner, but the smile never left her face and she didn't stop talking.

"Consider these New Year's gifts," Leah said, when Grace protested over the boxes of foreign biscuits we gave her. "We're a few weeks late, but we've both been so busy."

I glanced around. The murky yellow waters of the Huangpu River were only a short walk away from the end of the lane. Factories poured their filth into the river, the poor sent their dead out to sea in its currents, and the breeze lifted odors from the water that did nothing to freshen the air. There wasn't any sign or a name above the food stall Grace's mother ran. It was just a wooden counter separating the cooking area from four small tables arranged out in the open. Grace's mother waved at us, then went back to ladling noodles into large bowls.

When Grace put one of the steaming bowls in front of me, I hesitated.

"Don't worry," she said. "I still remember the rules of cleanliness. It wasn't easy convincing my mother, but we follow the rules. It's good for business; no one's ever been sick from eating at our stall."

Leah was already digging into her bowl, and after I inhaled the pungent fragrance of spicy fish and tofu sauce, I wasted no time. It tasted better than anything from the fine restaurants I'd been to in recent weeks. Grace wouldn't take our money, so Leah gave her an unopened pack of foreign cigarettes, worth several bowls of noodles. Grace took them back to her mother, who tucked it in her apron. Then her mother took a moment to smooth Grace's hair back from her face.

That small gesture, more than anything, told me that Grace was happy.

"How's your father?" Leah asked, lighting yet another cigarette. We spoke English, for privacy.

"Mother says he's coming by more often now that I'm here," Grace replied. "I translate for them and we chat."

Her father was first mate on a riverboat. Whenever the boat docked at the Shanghai and Hongkew Wharf, he came to see Grace and her mother. He told Grace he was the youngest son of a British lord, and that he was in China because he couldn't pay his gambling debts in England.

"Oh, Grace," Leah exclaimed. "Do you really believe he's an aristocrat?"

"It makes him happy when he thinks I believe it," she said quietly.

Leah put her hand on Grace's. "Of course you must believe it. He's your father."

Grace gave a cheerful shrug. "He's a drunkard, but a happy one. How's your Mr. Stephenson?"

Mr. Stephenson had promised his English wife that he would never be unfaithful to her with any European or Chinese woman. Leah had read one of Mrs. Stephenson's letters.

"And as far as he's concerned," Leah said, "he's kept his promise because I'm not a European woman or even a Chinese woman of good family. I'm no more than a clever pet. That's all. Thank goodness Peng makes me feel like a human being."

"Who is Peng?" I asked.

"My lover," she said. Both she and Grace laughed at my shocked expression.

All too soon, we had to go. Grace walked with us as far as the Garden Bridge and there we said our farewells.

"Next time, my house," I promised.

I took a rickshaw back to Yuyang Lane, a pleasurable ride as I daydreamed of how I would entertain Leah and Grace in my own home. When I arrived home, Sanmu's car was there, his driver polishing an already gleaming hood. Sanmu had been at his most ardent the night before and promised to spend more time at Yuyang Lane, but I hadn't expected him back until the evening, after he had submitted his articles for the day to *Xinwen Bao's* printers.

Little Ko took my coat and whispered, "The master has been here for an hour. He's been drinking. He's in the greenhouse."

Sanmu paced between pots of delicate ferns and wicker furniture. In his dark clothes, his anxiety was so palpable he made me think of a cornered beast. One hand was clenched, and the other held a crystal tumbler. A whiskey bottle stood on the table. Without a word, he pointed at the envelope on the table beside the bottle.

First I examined the envelope, which was addressed to Sanmu, care of the newspaper. It was company stationery, the return address printed with the name and address of the Anshan Rail Inspection Services Company in Harbin, Manchuria. The postmark, however, was that of the government Postal Office in Shanghai.

"Read the letter," he said. His grim expression did nothing to reassure me.

Dear Mr. Liu:

Wan Baoyuan was my cousin. He wrote to me while he was in Shanghai and spoke highly of you, so I've taken the liberty of making contact. I'm staying in Shanghai for several weeks. I've wanted to come since learning of his death, but first I had to deal with various legal matters on behalf of his estate.

My cousin's death is still a mystery. While I am here, I plan to reopen the investigation. I'd like to meet you and learn more about his final days.

*Please write to me care of the Hotel Shanghai, on the
corner of Broadway and Nanzing Roads. I hope you can
spare the time for a meeting.*

> Wan Taiyong
> *Engineer, Anshan Rail Inspection Services*

Sanmu continued pacing. "If I were his family, I would reopen the case too. The police were so overwhelmed during the strikes they made only a very minimal investigation. They lumped it in with all the other crimes related to looting and assault."

The images I had worked so hard to submerge came to the surface with a rush. *A trail of scarlet trickling into a puddle.* A small moan escaped me and I staggered back.

He pulled me into his arms, where I stood, shivering. "Hush, my sweet. Nothing will come of this. I won't let anything happen to you."

Later that night, I climbed out of bed to get a drink of water. There was no point in pretending either of us could sleep. The bathroom light reflected in Sanmu's open eyes. When I returned to bed, he took me in his arms again.

"What does Fourth Uncle know about me?" I asked.

There wouldn't be a better time to ask. It had only been a day since Fox strengthened Sanmu's feelings for me, and she had done this with a heavy hand. Even the distress of hearing from Wan Taiyong had not lessened Sanmu's ardor. He might not answer my questions, but he wouldn't get angry, either.

I wished I hadn't asked, because it turned out Fourth Uncle knew everything.

At first, Sanmu had been interested in Wan Baoyuan simply because he wanted to know more about the situation in Manchuria. Then as Wan's association with the warlord emerged, Sanmu had stayed close to learn more about General Zhang. But it wasn't until I mentioned seeing Wan at Old Master Shen's funeral that Sanmu began to suspect something more sinister. That was when he confided in Fourth Uncle.

It was Fourth Uncle's contacts in the Nationalist Party who had investigated Wan Baoyuan, Fourth Uncle who confirmed Sanmu's hunch that Wan Baoyuan had been involved somehow in Mah Juhou's murder. It was Fourth Uncle who had helped Sanmu on that terrible day, Fourth Uncle who used his connections to dispose of Wan Baoyuan's body.

What kind of people did Fourth Uncle know who could handle a corpse without asking questions? If I'd known Sanmu would use others to get rid of Wan's body, I would've persuaded him to let me help, gone with him in the car, kept it to ourselves. But I suspected he would've told his Fourth Uncle anyway. Fourth Uncle was a strong supporter of the Nationalist party and now I knew he was also involved with some unsavory people. But what about Sanmu?

In all this, Sanmu had told his uncle one lie: that he had been the one who killed Wan Baoyuan in self-defense.

"There was a chance my uncle would refuse to help if he knew it was you, Jialing," he said "But I'm his nephew. I'm family."

"Will you tell Fourth Uncle about this?" I asked. "About the cousin?"

"You know I must," he said. "This Wan Taiyong could be part of the conspiracy."

Now I knew why Fourth Uncle had asked whether I could be trusted to keep quiet. Fourth Uncle wasn't just afraid I would put Sanmu in danger. He was afraid I would put him in danger too.

WORKERS WERE DEMOLISHING the Eastern Residence and taking it away in pieces. Fragments of the courtyard and its houses lay in a pile of rubble, a midden of carved railings and roof tiles, broken bricks and lattice window frames. Wilted rose shrubs lay on a stack of paving stones.

A memory of Anna pouring water from a bucket, the roses more receptive to her attention than her mother had been.

I picked my way along Dragon Springs Road, avoiding carts and laborers. In another week the Central Residence would be in ruins, and a few weeks after that, workmen would start on the Western Residence. I had to persuade my mother and Fox to leave.

It was late February, but it was still as cold as midwinter. As I stepped inside the courtyard, the brown ivy vines covering the walls changed to a tender green, and wilted peony shrubs sprouted heavy buds. The shouts of workmen faded, replaced by birdsong. My mother and Fox were together on the garden bench, throwing millet seeds on the ground for a flock of fan-tailed warblers.

Fox was in human shape, elegantly attired as always. My mother was bundled up in layers of padded jackets and trousers, a pair of thick woolen socks on her small feet. They were a picture of contentment. It reminded me of the days when Anjuin and I sat together at the kitchen table, leafing through my schoolbooks. Before I even spoke, Fox looked up, her gaze green gold and troubled, already sensing my unease.

Fox's features grew more vulpine as she and my mother listened to my story. A soft growl sounded in her throat.

"Sanmu has invited this Wan Taiyong to call on us this weekend," I said. "He feels we're better off to be friendly and learn what we can of his plans. We must find out whether Wan Taiyong is here on his own or at the behest of his cousin's fellow conspirators. He could be one of them."

My mother said nothing, just smiled at me and continued tossing seeds at the birds. Her eyes were vacant. There was something wrong about this. I looked questioningly at Fox.

Abruptly, Fox's dream courtyard vanished, and I was back in the real world. The hydrangeas were brown and brittle, the paving stones littered with dry leaves, and I was alone on the bench. Fox sat in front of me, the white tip of her tail twitching, dark amber eyes gleaming. There was something accusing in her expression.

Come with me, she said, there's something you should see. And she trotted up the stairs to the main house.

My mother lay on the bed, her breathing uneven. She looked unconscious, and on the table beside her were teacups and a large brown bottle. There was a sweet, cloying fragrance in the room.

I took the pipe out of her hands once she fell asleep, Fox said.

"Why is she taking opium?" I said.

Your mother is very ill. She's in a lot of pain.

"But this is so sudden. I came to see you less than a week ago."

Not trusting my mother to feed herself properly, I had brought food: dried scallops to flavor her soups, pastries filled with sweet red bean paste. Today I'd brought warm clothing and paper twists of herb mixtures to soften her cough.

She was already ill when she came back to Dragon Springs Road two years ago. Fox's tail switched from side to side. I can't cure her illness, but I can help her mind ignore the pain. My powers are limited, Jialing. Your mother insisted I use them all on you, to keep Liu Sanmu infatuated with you.

I sat on the edge of the bed. It was still hard calling her "Mother" to her face. I saw nothing in her of the mother I had longed for, either in looks or temperament. Or were my memories false because they were dim recollections, the yearnings of a lonely child?

What had made me think our reunion would immediately wash away all the years between us? I had spent a decade wavering between longing and anger, wondering why she had abandoned me. All the while she had spent those years barely surviving, no strength left at the end of each day to think of anything but how to get through the next.

It was enough for her now that I was willing to spend a little time with her every week, if only out of duty. I knew she hoped these fragments of time would eventually pave the distance between us. She had never asked for more than I was willing to extend. It pleased her to know I had a home, food, clothes, and a generous patron. It was what she understood of survival.

"I'm taking her to a hospital," I said.

Don't. She doesn't want that. Fox stood on her hind legs and put her paws on my knee. She doesn't have long and she wants to live out her days here, in this courtyard where she was happy with you, when you were a child. Where she's happy now.

When I'd asked Fox to use her influence on Liu Sanmu, I had thought it would give me a measure of control over my life. But since leaving Dragon Springs Road, it was as if sluice gates had opened. I was as helpless as a twig carried by the outflow, washed out of the calm pool that was the Western Residence and into the rapids of the wider world.

I had found my mother but lost Anjuin. Liu Sanmu had saved me then put me in danger. I had come to Fourth Uncle's attention but would never overcome his mistrust of one who was not of his blood. Nor could I control what Wan Taiyong might or might not learn about his cousin's murder.

There was only one thing I could control. I took a deep breath.

"Let her live out her days here, then, without pain. Use your powers on her, not me."

Fox leaped onto the bed. Are you sure? This Wan Taiyong could be dangerous. You're safer if Liu Sanmu adores you, if he's willing to do anything to keep you from harm.

I buried my face in her warm fur. "Go ahead, Fox. I have at least another week before your influence on Sanmu wears off. Perhaps longer."

It's possible I gave him too hard a nudge last time, she conceded, and we both laughed, Fox's body shaking from her small yips of mirth.

"I feel so old, Fox," I said, wiping my eyes, "as if a dozen lifetimes separate me from the girl I was so many months ago. And I don't just mean because I've become Sanmu's mistress."

She pushed her head against my hand, and for the first time in almost a year, I was Fox.

. . . it's night. The streets of the town are built along canals, and I cross an arched stone bridge. I pause for a moment at the crown of the bridge. The surface of each stone step is crosshatched with chisel marks to offer better footing on wet days. Carved at the edge of one step are the outlines of a horse, *mah,* and another of a fish, *yu.* Fox first visited the town when this bridge was built. In the guise of an idle urchin, she had watched two illiterate stonemasons carve these symbols so that even now, three hundred years later, observant pedestrians could know that a man named Mah and another called Yu had built this elegant little bridge.

The banks of the canal are planted with willow trees and their branches scratch my back as I hurry beneath them. I break into a run when I see the lake. Water hyacinths grow on its surface in such dense clumps they've formed floating islands that give rest to water birds and shelter to fish. I follow a track up the hill to an overgrown clearing that overlooks the lake. Humans have forgotten the family buried here, but Fox has not forgotten her old friends. Below, both moon and pagoda are reflected in the still waters of the lake that give the town its name. I drop my offering on a gravestone, the sprig of osmanthus blossom I've carried in my mouth all this time. Then I lie down to enjoy the view . . .

My eyes opened. Both Fox and I were curled on the floor beside the bed. My mother was still in a drugged sleep, but her breathing sounded easier. I smiled at Fox, who put a paw on my knee.

Did you like that? she asked. Running under the moon, unseen and unencumbered?

"That was the best part of my childhood," I said, "when you shared your ramblings with me. Sometimes it was all that made my life bearable."

Come back when you know more about this Wan Taiyong, she said. There may be something else I can do.

SANMU HAD INVITED Wan Taiyong to the house on Yuyang Lane. This made the meeting more informal. When I got ready that morning, Sanmu had me put on a modest Chinese gown of pale green silk. When the front gate buzzer sounded, Old Tan's warning that he had let a visitor into the property, Sanmu visibly squared his shoulders. He gave me a reassuring smile, his features seemingly untroubled, the slight clench to his jaw barely discernible. Then we both turned to the window to watch our guest approach the house.

I had been prepared for a man of menacing appearance, middle-aged and humorless, perhaps with a family resemblance so strong that I would think it was Wan Baoyuan's ghost walking up the gravel path.

What I hadn't been prepared for was how young he was. He looked like a university student.

Wan Taiyong was slimmer and taller than his cousin had been.

His mouth was generous, his nose well shaped with a high bridge. There was nothing military about him in posture or manner. He looked about the garden as he strolled up, leisurely, at ease in his well-cut camel hair coat. His movements were unhurried, and this distinguished him from Wan Baoyuan, whose mannerisms had simmered with barely concealed impatience.

When he shook hands with Sanmu, his smile was open, unreserved.

When his eyes settled on me, there was no contempt or dislike, only mild curiosity. His smile never dimmed.

When he spoke, Wan Taiyong's voice was eager, not at all as though he expected his words to be obeyed as commands. When he leaned forward to pick up his tea from the table, a wisp of hair fell across his forehead, making him look even more boyish and unguarded.

He couldn't have been much older than Anjuin.

I caught myself staring at him and hastened to make use of my new fan, a semicircle of finely carved ivory ribs. The fluttering of a fan was a good way to hide trembling hands. The shopkeeper who sold me the fan had claimed it was looted from the Forbidden City during the Boxer Rebellion. I doubted the dowager empress had held this very fan, but I'd bought it anyway.

"In addition to solving my cousin's murder, I'm hoping the detective I've hired can find Baoyuan's older brother," Taiyong said. "It's my duty to let him know of Baoyuan's death."

"How very odd," Sanmu said. "He never mentioned a brother."

"Baoyuan was adopted," Wan Taiyong said. "He was a distant cousin, and my uncle had no sons. Later, when my parents died, my uncle took me in. So Baoyuan and I lived in the same household for several years. He told me about his brother in Shanghai."

He paused. "Baoyuan's original name was Fong. The property on Dragon Springs Road was his ancestral home. That's why Baoyuan wanted to buy it."

Liu Sanmu straightened up in his seat. His feigned astonishment was utterly convincing. "But why didn't Wan Baoyuan say he once lived there?"

Wan Taiyong looked apologetic. "He was afraid he'd be in a weaker bargaining position if the seller knew of his attachment to the estate."

There was a pause, then Sanmu cleared his throat. "May I ask which detective agency you've hired? I may know it."

"The agency came highly recommended," Taiyong said. "The owner's name is Robert Shea, formerly of the Shanghai Municipal Police. His Chinese is surprisingly good. Unlike the other detectives I interviewed, he made no bold claims."

I wanted to choke. Shea's tenacity was well known.

"Shea's reputation is sterling, he's the best in Shanghai," Sanmu said, his manner sincere. "If he can't solve your mysteries, no one can."

The conversation drifted on, from the situation in Manchuria to Dr. Sun Yat-sen's return to Shanghai and whether it signaled a resurgence of the Nationalist Party. Either Wan Taiyong was very good at deception or he was truly as candid as he seemed. It was almost noon by the time he stood up to leave.

"I wonder if I could see the property on Dragon Springs Road sometime before I leave Shanghai," Wan Taiyong said. "I'm curious to see where my cousin spent his early years."

"You're welcome to see it any time," Sanmu said. "The Western Residence is the only one of the homes still standing. The other two courtyards have been knocked down. I would take you myself, but between the newspaper and family business, my time is not my own anymore. But Jialing can go with you tomorrow if you like."

He gave me a look. Behind my fan, I gulped.

"I'd be happy to," I said, trying my best to sound hospitable.

"I DON'T WANT to take him to Dragon Springs Road," I said, after Sanmu had seen Wan Taiyong out the front gate. "Why didn't you offer to take him yourself some other day?"

He kissed me on the forehead. "It'll be fine. Look at you, as innocent as a schoolgirl in that dress. He'll never suspect. I must go now."

I helped him into his coat. I knew he was going to make his report to Fourth Uncle.

Upstairs on my letter tray, there was a letter from Yun Na in her childish writing.

> *Dear Jialing,*
>
> *Next month we will move into the new apartment owned by Mr. Liu's family. How can we thank you for this kindness? The rent is so reasonable and the extra space so necessary now that we have the new baby.*
>
> *Truly, old friends are the best, but could I have expected any less of someone we raised like a sister? I hope you will come visit us in our new home, and perhaps one day we can visit you in your house. Anjuin is too polite to ask, but you know me . . .*

Self-centered though she was, even Yun Na had to know I had asked Sanmu to offer Dajuin a better apartment at a good price for Anjuin's sake, not anyone else's. I crumpled the note into the wastebasket.

I opened my cosmetics box and lifted the top tray. All the money I had managed to save so far was inside, more money than

I had ever held before in my hands, but in my new life, hardly enough for a new pair of shoes. I should've put more effort into saving money against a time when my life would have to change. Wan Taiyong was proof that surely as thunder follows lightning, my life was going to change again. In what way, I didn't know. But it wouldn't hurt to have more cash in hand.

From drawers and wardrobe shelves I collected items whose absence I didn't think Sanmu would notice. Scarves and gloves, shoes, an embroidered jacket. A few of my older dresses, some small pieces of jewelry. These all fit in a carpetbag. I slipped the paper with the address of the pawnshop Leah recommended into my pocket.

On my way out, Old Tan stared at the bag, but he waved for a rickshaw and said nothing. At the pawnshop, my imported accessories fetched more than I'd hoped, especially the shoes.

"They're Italian and like new," I pointed out to the pawnbroker. "Even a foreigner would buy these."

He'd grunted and said, "It's more likely they'll appeal to a taxi dancer," but he paid my asking price without grumbling. Which meant I'd set it too low.

"CAN I USE your den?" I asked Fox. "I need a place to hide some money."

The Western Residence was the only safe place that came to mind. I would add to the cache of silver coins with each visit. I knew Fox would look after my little coin bag if she and my mother had to leave for any reason.

My mother was much improved and didn't question why she was feeling better. Fox and I had agreed it would be best if she forgot all about her illness, forgot that Fox's powers couldn't extend to protect both of us. Her body was wasting away, her thoughts were confused, and she spent most of my visit dozing in the kitchen, which Fox kept well heated. With Fox's help and tincture of opium, however, she was out of pain.

She moves in and out of sleep, Fox said, but she's so dazed from the opium it's hard to know how much she remembers. The main thing is to keep her comfortable and warm.

Fox was proud of her scavenging. She went to the Eastern Residence at night to take wood from the demolished buildings. The kitchen in the Western Residence was too small to store all the wood, so she had used the veranda of the main house to stack lengths of wooden railings and posts. She had collected enough wood to last the winter, but I didn't know whether my mother would live that long.

"Thank you for looking after my mother, Fox," I said.

She's my friend, Fox replied, and she'll be gone soon. I've lost many human friends, some who mattered more than others.

I had to ask. "Is my mother one of those who matters more?"

Of course. Or I wouldn't have promised to take care of you. Fox laid her chin down on her paws, as if suddenly weary. I've outlived too many mortal friends.

I'd often envied Fox her powers. I'd never thought of how it must be for her to watch friends age and die.

My mother stirred from her sleep and looked up. She beamed at me. "Ling-ling. It's been such a long time," she said, although I'd been there just the day before. "What a beautiful coat. You're such a grand lady now."

"I've brought some sweet date soup for you," I said. "It's heating right now."

We need more wood, said Fox and she hurried out.

"Fox has been a very good friend to you," I said to my mother.

She blinked at me, then sat up on the bed. Standing up, she steadied herself then hobbled over to my side and took the wooden spoon from my hands. Her eyes were unfocused.

"She's been a good friend to you as well, Ling-ling" she said, stirring the soup. Then she paused to peer up at me again. "What a beautiful daughter I have."

"It's because I have a beautiful mother." I took off my white jade bracelet, one of the first gifts Sanmu had given me, and slid it onto her thin arm. She admired it and continued stirring.

IT WAS NEARLY ten o'clock before Sanmu came back to Yuyang Lane, tense and silent. I followed him upstairs to the bedroom.

"We still don't know whether Wan Taiyong took part in the conspiracy." He whispered as though there might be eavesdroppers. "Or whether he knew his cousin was an assassin."

"Wan Taiyong seems very open and sincere."

"The best conspirators are good at acting," he replied, kissing me behind the ear. He moved one hand along my shoulder down to my hip. "When you're with him in the Western Residence, see what you can learn. Ask him about his childhood. When people share childhood memories, it often leads to sharing other confidences."

I turned around in his arms. "No, Sanmu. I'm no good at this sort of thing. You go with him tomorrow."

But his only reply was to pull my hips against his.

In the morning, Sanmu was gone. He had been to the greenhouse. There was a stem of orchids on the pillow beside me, creamy flowers with a citrus scent. This tender gesture touched me more than anything he'd done for me so far. He knew today would be a distressing time for me.

But he couldn't begin to guess how distressing. Fear of being alone with Wan Taiyong, fear of learning he was a danger to us. One after the other, anxieties crashed against me in waves.

WAN TAIYONG HAD hired a large bicycle rickshaw for the day. As we pulled into Dragon Springs Road, I glimpsed my mother walking along the street, an old wool scarf tied around her head. Fox, dressed just as poorly, held her by the elbow. They were a pair of vagrants, ignored by all, practically invisible. Fox gave me a wink as I climbed down from the rickshaw. I gave a silent sigh of relief as they meandered away, glad my mother was well enough to leave the Western Residence. With Fox's small enchantments, Wan Taiyong wouldn't notice the signs of habitation in the courtyard.

Where the Eastern Residence had been there was nothing now but bare land, the foundations for three modern villas dug out on the ground. In the Central Residence, workers swarmed in and out, the air loud with curses and shouts, the noise of tools striking earth and wood, the crash of falling roof tiles.

Inside the Western Residence, all was dormant, waiting for warmer spring days. I avoided looking at the stones at the edge of the bamboo garden. Was it my imagination or was the moss still dark with blood?

"I prefer this to the new houses they're building," Taiyong said, looking around. "Baoyuan talked a lot about this estate. He said the Western Residence was the oldest of the three courtyard homes."

He wandered in to the main house, opened the lattice shutters in the downstairs bedroom where First Wife had slept, then carefully closed them again. He came out of the main house and crossed over to the derelict *erfang*.

"The roof has fallen in on that *erfang*," I called. "Be careful of tiles coming down on your head."

A moment later, he came out again, a grin on his face. He cleared the steps from the veranda with a single jump, landing with both feet on the paving. "My parents' house had a veranda too. I can't count the number of times I skinned my knees leaping off the steps."

He sat beside me on the garden bench. "In Harbin, we build courtyard homes with a high wall on the north side to block the coldest winds. I love the open plains, but when I come back from inspecting repair stations and railway tracks, I want to come home to a courtyard. Not a Western-style villa but this, a small, sheltered world of my own."

That was exactly how I felt about this courtyard. It was a sanctuary.

He leaned back, looking contented. That look stirred something warm in me, something I tried to push away.

Had Wan Taiyong known anything about his cousin's role as an assassin? I had been observing him as closely as I dared. When he spoke, his words were unhurried, his eyes clear and guileless. Was he truly as open as he seemed?

"Were you very close to your cousin?" My first cautious probe.

"Now I wish we'd been closer," he said. "My uncle died just a few years after he took me in, and Baoyuan took care of everything. Even though we were distant cousins, he was the elder and took on the duty."

Wan Baoyuan had believed in duty. Duty to his commanding officer and duty to his family. He'd made sure Wan Taiyong went to boarding school, attended college, and found a job.

"He used to come to my school every month and take me out for a meal," he said. "Out of duty, not affection. I knew that. But I was grateful. I had no one else."

His slightly crooked smile gave away the pain that still accompanied the memory. Losing his parents, losing his uncle. His only guardian Wan Baoyuan, a humorless young army officer. It wasn't hard to imagine Taiyong as a child, lonely and orphaned. Again, I pushed away that feeling.

"Baoyuan was a successful officer," he continued, "chosen to lead many important battles. He was very talented, one of the youngest majors in the Fengtian army. The military was his life. When he resigned to work for a mining company, I could hardly believe it. In fact, I couldn't believe General Zhang accepted his resignation."

Sanmu had speculated that Wan's career change had been to conceal his role as an assassin.

"After he left the military, did he miss the camaraderie of fellow officers?" I asked. "Did he still socialize with them? Invite them home?"

"I wouldn't know," Taiyong said. "He used to take me with him to dinner parties, introduce me to people he said would be important to my future. Then it all stopped. He became withdrawn. Perhaps he was disappointed I decided not to join the army."

He sounded genuinely sad. If he spoke the truth, then Wan Baoyuan had kept his distance and it was likely Wan Taiyong didn't know anything about his cousin's secret life. It may have been too soon for relief, but something loosened in my chest and I almost sighed out loud.

"What about you?" he asked. "All I know is that you grew up in the Yang household."

"I'm an orphan. The Yang family took me in because their grandmother wanted to earn merit in heaven. I became their bond servant," I said. "Then an American lady paid for me to attend a mission school."

"The mission schools offer a good education," he said.

"Alas, my grades weren't good enough to go on to college," I said. "I'd hoped to earn a living as a governess or nanny, but there isn't a single family in Shanghai, Chinese or European, that's willing to hire me. So here I am, mistress to Liu Sanmu."

The words came out with a bitterness that surprised me, for I thought I had accepted my fate. I tried to make light of my remarks. "In Shanghai, mistress can be quite a respectable career. I'm luckier than most. Liu Sanmu is kind and generous."

His wry smile reflected my own, and I thought I detected sympathy in his eyes.

Wan Taiyong insisted on taking me to lunch at the Astor Hotel.

Inside the hotel, I paused to scan the busy lobby, where a mix of wealthy Chinese and foreigners gathered, creatures of privilege. A number of the women, both Chinese and foreign, drew back their skirts as I passed. Some turned deliberately to avoid me, others stared.

Lifting my chin and squaring my shoulders, I made my way across the huge expanse of lobby toward the dining room. For a moment I thought I saw a familiar swaying walk. From behind, the woman looked like Leah. Her male companion was Chinese. Not Mr. Stephenson. The couple disappeared down a corridor in the direction of the private dining rooms.

A woman I recognized as the mistress of one of Sanmu's friends stared at us. Wan Taiyong was certainly a very handsome new face worth staring at, but I was also sure she was wondering whether I was having an affair. Let her wonder.

At lunch I looked at the menu, at my plate of fish croquettes, at the view of the riverfront, at anything but Taiyong's face, his eyes, the lock of hair that fell over his forehead. I said very little and listened to him talk about Harbin.

It was a city more European than Shanghai. More than twenty

years ago, Russian companies had sent engineers and construction workers there to build a rail system from China to Russia. Many had stayed.

"Some brought wives. Many more married Chinese women or took Chinese mistresses," he said. "Some have lived there more than a generation. You would not look out of place in Harbin, Miss Zhu."

"Perhaps, but nothing changes the fact that both Chinese and Europeans see *hun xue* as a betrayal of race," I said, a little stiffly. "Both sides see us as examples of moral degeneration. Those are not my opinions, Mr. Wan. You can read them in newspaper editorials."

"Forgive me. I can't begin to guess at the difficulties you've faced growing up, orphaned and *hun xue*."

It wouldn't do to create awkwardness. Not when Sanmu wanted me to spend more time with him. Not when I wanted to see him again. I smiled.

"Tell me more about Harbin," I said. "How does it compare to Shanghai?"

"All cities seem much the same to me," he said. "Except in winter. And then Harbin is transformed, as if by an enchantment. Everything is covered in snow, snow so clean it glows blue."

"Parks with frozen lakes," I said, unable to help myself.

"Yes. The lakes are beautiful in winter." He smiled, a slow lazy smile.

Winter arrives suddenly in Harbin. By October the nights are freezing cold, but the air is dry and skies are clear. Street vendors sell bags of roasted chestnuts, chunks of sausage on skewers, big rounds of hot, Russian-style bread. At night the winter moon hangs high in the sky and after the first freeze, lakes in city parks turn into ice rinks where courting couples hold fur-mittened hands to skate in circles together while boys race each other across the frozen expanse.

"There's nothing as glorious as ice skating," Taiyong said. "The cold air rushing past, the smoothness of the ice beneath your skates, so fast and quiet it's like flying. But did you know that blades don't touch ice? Friction creates a thin layer of water between ice and blade, so you're actually gliding on a film of water."

"I can't even imagine it," I said, resisting the urge to reach over and push the hair off his forehead. Instead I pushed away the picture in my head, of the two of us dressed in warm furs, the moon casting its platinum light on the ice, our shadows gliding ahead of us, chasing each other down the gleaming path.

What would happen to Wan Taiyong if Fourth Uncle and his associates decided he was a danger to them? I couldn't let that happen. I had to convince them of what I believed. That Taiyong knew nothing.

IN THE MORNING, I took a rickshaw along the Bund toward the Quai de France in the French Concession. This visit was something Sanmu had suggested.

I got out at the rue Fokien. Narrow stairs led to a hallway of small offices, the half-light doors of each painted with names in English and Chinese on the frosted glass. I opened the one for ROBERT SHEA INVESTIGATIONS.

Inside, two clerks looked up, one Chinese, the other European. The Chinese one, in a suit too large for his slight frame, stood up and gave me a small bow. He rapped on the door to his right before opening it.

"Miss Zhu." Shea stood up from behind the desk to greet me. "I was delighted to get your note."

"Please, call me Jialing," I said, settling in the chair opposite his desk. "I'm here to ask you a favor, Mr. Shea."

"Of course," he said. "I hope nothing troublesome has happened."

He looked solid and muscled, but his seamed face attested to too many late nights, too much drink. Too much grief and guilt. Shea was still searching for Anna's abductors. According to Sanmu, Shea could've been a very wealthy man, but he spent too much time and money following up every rumor, every report and sighting. He traveled to other cities if necessary and paid well for information. Whether it came from a swindler or someone who sincerely believed they had seen Anna so many years ago, he almost always paid.

"No. Nothing untoward," I said. "It's just that . . . I met a man the other day. A Mr. Wan Taiyong from Harbin. He said he hired you to find Master Fong, the one whose family lived at Dragon Springs Road. Please don't mention you already searched for Master Fong when you were looking for my mother."

"My clients are guaranteed confidentiality," he said. "He wouldn't know of our dealings any more than you would've known he was my client if he hadn't told you."

There was the slightest hint of rebuke in his voice, as if to a child who should've known better. Shea was known for his absolute incorruptibility, his dedication and persistence. There had been cases where he carried on searching for abducted children even when the parents could no longer afford his services.

"Do you need to know why?" I asked.

He shook his head. "Your reasons don't matter. Professional confidentiality holds."

It would do no good to probe further, to ask about his investigation into Wan Baoyuan's death. It was clear that Shea was unyielding in his discretion. Although I was sure he knew of my situation, I felt I owed him what honesty I could afford.

"Perhaps you know that I now live with Mr. Liu Sanmu," I said.

"Yes. You've found a generous patron." His smile was a little sad as I stood up to leave. "If you ever need help, please come see me, Jialing. You were Anna's dearest friend during her short time on this earth. I hope you always remember her."

"Of course I remember, Mr. Shea," I said. I held my hand out to him.

His hands were calloused but gentle. "You had such an imagination. You wanted me to believe Anna had walked through a door to the land of immortals. Not a day goes by without me wishing I could believe that story."

Anna had been gone eleven years. What words of comfort could I offer to a man who lived each waking hour tormented by the mystery of her final hours, by the constant grief that must grind against his heart every day?

"It's a story I still believe, Mr. Shea," I said softly.

Riding back home, a hundred memories of Anna cascaded over me. The way her hair ribbon was always untying itself from her curls, the freckles that spangled her eager face, her scraped knees, and the glints of green in her amber-brown eyes. Anna reading to me from a storybook open to a picture of a girl looking out to the sea, half fish, half human.

Then the bright edges of the Door, the scent of grass and orchards, and Anna in her torn white dress stepping over the threshold. And then Fox, whining as she ran back and forth in front of the Door. A Door that was closing very slowly, its opening wide enough for a child to pass through. Or a Fox.

I gasped and held on to the side of the rickshaw. Fox could've gone through the Door all those years ago. But she didn't.

"Fox promised to look after you," my mother had said.

Because of her promise to my mother, Fox hadn't dashed through the door.

Oh, Fox.

CHAPTER 21

Dear Sanmu,

I'm completely certain Wan Taiyong doesn't know anything about his cousin, nor is he part of any conspiracy. They were not close and his work for the railway inspection company meant he was away from Harbin much of the time.

I also went to see Mr. Shea, on the pretext you suggested. He is as discreet as ever, and we will not learn anything from him and in fact would arouse his suspicions if we prodded.

When are you coming home?

Jialing

Sanmu sent his driver back with a reply. He wouldn't be coming to Yuyang Lane for at least two days. His note was folded around a pair of tickets for an afternoon performance at the opera, the day after next.

> *I want you to attend this performance. I'm sure you will enjoy it. Take a friend if you like.*

What friend could I invite except Leah?

She came by on the afternoon of the opera.

"Can we go where your maid won't overhear us?" she whispered while Little Ko took away her coat and hat.

"Come upstairs and help me decide what to wear," I said. "Little Ko, please set out some cold drinks in the greenhouse, we'll be down shortly and then we'll be heading out to the opera."

"I saw you at the Astor Hotel the other day," Leah said as soon as I shut my bedroom door. "Who was that beautiful man with you? He was too young to have been Liu Sanmu."

"It's . . . a friend of Sanmu's from Manchuria," I said. "Was that Peng with you at the hotel?"

Leah tried to sound offhand, but her face glowed when I mentioned her lover's name. Her smile lit her eyes, suffused her entire being.

"He wants me to leave Stephenson," she said, "but I'm not willing. Peng can't support me. He's a gambler. Both of us are better off if I stay with Stephenson."

"But you love him, don't you?" I said. She was in love, real love. The kind of love I longed to feel, longed to have someone feel for me. Not an infatuation that depended upon a Fox's enchantments.

"Jialing, I'm not blind," she said. "Peng would never marry a *hun xue* girl. He wouldn't even take me into his home as a concubine. I'll be his mistress for a few years until the novelty wears off. I'm hoping he'll see that and stop trying to make me leave Stephenson."

"How can you live this way?" I said. "How can you love him all the while expecting it to end?"

"You forget I'm practically a third-generation prostitute." Her rueful smile made her look older. "I don't believe in happy endings. It's enough to feel life so intensely. Happiness that makes your heart twist in pain, Jialing, the exquisite pain of knowing such happiness will end."

I thought about Wan Taiyong, about all that was forbidden to me. It was small comfort that Leah, so cynical and self-contained, had been unable to resist her gambler any more than I'd been able to withstand the tidal pull of my feelings for Wan Taiyong.

"Tell me what to wear," I said, opening the wardrobe doors. "I'm glad you can come with me. Sanmu was quite insistent about this opera."

It was the first time the famous singer Cheng Yanqiu was performing in Shanghai. Even those who knew nothing about Peking opera were going to his performances.

"I'm glad you invited me," Leah said. "Peng has tickets for tomorrow night's performance, but of course I can't go. I must be home to pour drinks for Mr. Stephenson."

We rode to the opera in an automobile, vehicle and driver on loan from Peng. Leah had insisted it was too cold to ride in an open rickshaw. A lone figure on the street made me lean toward the window.

It was Anjuin. Even from a distance, I could tell it was her. In her dark, old-fashioned tunic she looked like a servant, not the daughter of a respectable merchant family. With a start I realized Anjuin looked as she always had. I was the one who had become used to fine clothes and expensive shoes. She stopped at a shop window and lifted a small child to look at the display. Her niece, Dajuin and Yun Na's eldest. Anjuin's expression was soft and fond, smiling as she talked to the little girl. I wanted to jump out of the car, buy for them whatever had caught their eye. But the car weaved its way along the street and I soon lost sight of them.

"WELL, IT WILL be interesting to see how he compares to Mei Lan-fang," said the man seated beside us. "I'll never forget that performance of 'The Dream in the Garden.' Cheng has a lot to live up to."

"You really can't compare them," the woman beside him said. "They are two completely different styles. Cheng's interpretation of female roles is more wistful, more tragic. We're lucky to be seeing him at this stage of developing his distinct style."

They spoke loudly over the noise of the audience below. The woman glanced over at us and her expression froze.

When Cheng Yanqiu came onstage, the noise died down. This was a sign of great respect, especially from an afternoon crowd who regarded the stage as background entertainment for the real business of gossiping. Face painted and dressed in blue satin, Cheng Yanqiu sang the first aria, his arms and body moving in stylized gestures that conveyed the feelings behind the heroine's words. She had dreamed of a handsome youth and, upon waking, suffered intense sorrow that it had only been a dream.

The audience was in raptures. Had Cheng Yanqiu been a dis-appointment, the unruly crowd would've shouted him down or thrown peanut shells at the stage.

All through the performance I had the sensation of being watched, but perhaps it was because I was with Leah. Dressed in a tunic of gold silk and black trousers, her honey-streaked tresses made her stand out.

During the intermission, we stood up to stretch. From our box seats we could look down on the ground floor, where theater attendants circulated through the audience selling packets of peanuts and pouring hot water for tea. The couple beside us left and didn't come back.

The houselights dimmed to begin the second act. That was when I saw the woman across from us, in a box seat close to the stage. There was no one else in the box with her. She was beautiful, well dressed. And she was staring at me, with a look on her face that pushed at the edges of a memory.

I sat down and leaned back into the shadows. Giving Leah's hand a small tug, I said in a low voice, "Leah, who is that woman across from us, all by herself in that box? Pretend you're not staring."

She appeared to scan the audience below, and then eased back into her seat. "She's in the Liu family box," she said. "Those wealthy clans never attend afternoon performances. My guess is that one of the Liu women wanted to get a look at you. In fact, I'm willing to bet that's your Sanmu's wife."

SANMU NEVER SPOKE of his wife in my presence. If I'd thought of her at all, it was as some faceless well-dressed matron, a dutiful woman married to Sanmu because of an arrangement between their families. The woman at the opera was not matronly. She was younger than Sanmu, with delicate features and an intelligent expression.

I had never been curious enough about his wife to try and catch a glimpse of her, but evidently she had wanted to know more about me. The shadowy memory came into focus. I remembered where I had seen such an expression before. On the day I crept into the Central Residence, I had peered through the window at Noble Uncle's family. One of his daughters had looked back at me. Sanmu's wife reminded me of that girl, her features dull with resignation and despair.

WHEN I ARRIVED back home, Sanmu's car was there. So was Fourth Uncle's bicycle rickshaw. Sanmu's uncle was one of the wealthiest men in Shanghai, but he only ever wore a dark-colored *changshan* gown and cloth shoes. He usually traveled by rickshaw, albeit a bicycle rickshaw and driver belonging to the Liu family. If sedan chairs had still been practical in Shanghai, I was sure Fourth Uncle would've preferred being carried behind curtained panels, a relic of feudal times.

"They're in the greenhouse," Little Ko said, "arguing very loudly. It must be politics."

I sighed. There was no avoiding the courtesies. "I'll take the tea tray to them, Little Ko." I followed the voices to the back of the house.

"It's wrongheaded of Dr. Sun Yat-sen to even consider taking help from the Soviets. We'll have Communists infiltrating our party." That was Sanmu.

"If another Western nation had helped us finance a campaign to bring down the warlords, Sun wouldn't have had to turn to the Soviets," Fourth Uncle said. "He had no choice."

I pushed open the door to the greenhouse, and the conversation stopped while I set down the tray.

"Did you go to the opera?" Sanmu asked. In front of Fourth Uncle, he refrained from gestures of affection.

"Yes, to Cheng Yanqiu's afternoon performance."

Fourth Uncle snorted. "His style is overwrought, his singing mediocre."

Cheng Yanqiu went up in my esteem.

Sanmu grinned at me and I went upstairs, hoping they would

both leave to go out for supper, that Sanmu wouldn't stay the night so that I wouldn't have to hide the turmoil of my feelings. But the front door opened and shut, and when I looked out the window, there was only Fourth Uncle crunching his way down the gravel path. Old Tan saluted as he opened the gate, his stance straight and respectful.

As Sanmu's footsteps came up the stairs, I willed myself to be more vigilant, even more controlled in front of him. Fox's influence wouldn't last much longer. Whatever intrigues Sanmu and his uncle were concocting, I wouldn't let them ensnare Wan Taiyong. I just wanted him out of Shanghai, safely back in Harbin.

"Your uncle doesn't like me," I said, looking out the window so that I wouldn't have to face Sanmu. "I worry that you'll give me up. Tell him I was the one who killed Wan Baoyuan."

He pressed his lips to my neck. "Never. And it hardly matters now. We're all implicated in his death because we disposed of the body. Besides, I think any conspirator would laugh if I told them a schoolgirl was responsible for Wan Baoyuan's death." His voice turned teasing, his hands more lingering.

"Fourth Uncle has a lot on his mind," he murmured. He pressed his lips to my neck, ran his hands down my hips. "He's worried that Shea might turn up something about Wan Baoyuan's murder."

"If Shea turns up anything, he'll never tell either of us."

Sanmu sighed. "It's essential that Wan's death remain unsolved. If General Zhang retaliates against us, if there's another assasination . . . it's a delicate time for the Nationalist Party. We need every man of influence behind us, every resource to rebuild the party."

Then his kisses grew urgent and he didn't say anything more for a long while.

IT WASN'T UNTIL the next morning that he told me what Fourth Uncle wanted.

Fourth Uncle was willing to believe Wan Taiyong was not involved in any sort of conspiracy. His main worry now was what Shea might discover. Fourth Uncle didn't want to bring anyone else in to the situation until he knew more. He wanted us to remain close to Wan Taiyong, to take him out on the town, to the races, to parks. To win his friendship and his confidence. To lend a sympathetic ear and learn whatever Shea had shared with his client.

"If I took too much time away from the newspaper or family business," Sanmu said, "it would make me seem more interested in him than I should be. Fourth Uncle says it's up to you, Jialing. I wasn't so sure yesterday, but now I think he's right. It has to be you."

"What sort of reason would I have to follow him everywhere, all day?" I asked, brushing my hair in front of the dressing table. "Why can't Fourth Uncle's people cosy up to Wan Taiyong?"

There was a pause. "Please, just do as I ask."

"All right," I said, getting back into the bed. "If you'll do something for me."

He smiled and kissed my fingers. "What is it? Do you want your own car and driver?"

"No, nothing for me. For Anjuin. Can you help find her a husband?"

Sanmu pulled me closer. "I know you've been unhappy since you argued with her. Would she accept your help?"

"No. But she doesn't have to know it's my idea. In fact, if the Yangs believed you had used your connections to help her find a husband, even Grandmother Yang wouldn't protest." I pressed my lips against his shoulder. "If you know of someone suitable, just bring it up with Dajuin. Please, Sanmu. Anjuin has always said she doesn't have to be a First Wife. She just wants children of her own."

He nodded. "I'll do what I can. And you'll do your best to win Wan Taiyong's trust."

It was not a request.

Mr. Wan:

Jialing mentioned how much she enjoyed her day out in your company. She also mentioned that you wanted to see more of Shanghai before you return to Harbin. May I ask a favor?

Between the newspaper and family business, I have not shown Jialing as much of Shanghai as I'd promised. If you take her along with you as you explore the city, I would be very grateful.

In exchange, I'd be happy to lend you a car and driver to make your sightseeing more enjoyable. I hope you will consider my request.

Liu Sanmu

The ploy reeked of desperation and of Fourth Uncle. Both car and driver were his. It would look as though Sanmu was throwing his mistress at Wan Taiyong. Two weeks ago, he would never have considered a scheme that put me in such close and constant company with another man. Fox's influence was definitely slipping, and I was getting a first taste of how much Sanmu truly valued me.

"I'll join you whenever I can," Sanmu said, "supper every few nights, an afternoon at the Race Club, an evening opera performance."

If I spent all my time with Wan Taiyong, how could I get to Dragon Springs Road?

Worse yet, how could I fend off my feelings for him?

THERE WAS THE Shanghai Race Club. Taiyong studied the horses with interest but didn't place any bets.

There was Nanking Road, burnished with prosperity, busy with all the new shops that had opened since the end of the war. Foreigners had regained confidence in Shanghai. The city was sprawling out to the west, outside the boundaries of the international concessions. The Liu family would do very well out of their investment in Dragon Springs Road.

There was Fuzhou Road, famed for books and writing supplies. Taiyong purchased at least a dozen books, scrolls of fine paper, brushes, and ink sticks. The shopkeepers gave me curious looks and bowed to me on our way out. I knew what they saw: the sleek, spoiled mistress of a wealthy man.

Fourth Uncle's driver, a grinning giant called Gu, followed us from shop to shop, toting Wan Taiyong's parcels. I was there to watch Wan Taiyong, and the driver was there to watch us both. I encouraged Wan Taiyong to buy an extremely large and heavy inkstone.

"Have you any former classmates or friends living in Shanghai?" I asked Taiyong. "Did your cousin have any friends you would like to visit?"

That was also one of Fourth Uncle's ideas, to learn who Taiyong might associate with, whether he was in touch with his cousin's contacts.

But Taiyong shook his head. "I don't have any classmates or friends here. As for Baoyuan, he only wrote me the one letter, to say he would be buying his ancestral home. He didn't mention any friends."

There was Bansong Gardens, a private garden now open to the public for a small admission fee. There we encountered only a few other visitors. It was still too early in the season. Any spring foliage trying to emerge added no more than a hint of green to the scenery. We strolled through shades of brown, relieved only by the deep green of pine trees and a clump of bamboo. I saw Taiyong's disappointment as he gazed around the park.

"Without the distraction of foliage and blossoms," I said, "you can appreciate a garden's structure. See how the sun shines through the branches of that elm. It throws a tracery of shadows on the wall behind, as though the wall were a canvas."

This was my first visit to a classical garden in the real world. With delight I recognized what Fox had shown me in dreams. All her lectures were made real to me that afternoon. I pointed out to Taiyong the art of concealing and then revealing scenes through the use of winding walkways and corridors of shrubbery. Walls with lattice openings strategically placed to beckon with a view of the garden beyond. Still pools of water enhanced by the contrast of rugged, vertical rocks.

"You're quite learned on the subject," Taiyong said, his voice teasing. "Were gardens part of the mission school's curriculum?"

"I had a teacher who was fond of gardens," I said, thinking of Fox. "She made me see how skillful division of spaces makes a small garden appear larger. The unexpected touches. The unreal within the real."

I pointed at a small pavilion, its roof just barely visible behind a low hill. When I glanced over at Taiyong, he wasn't looking at the pavilion. He was looking at me. "I've never thought of gardens this way. I've only ever paid attention to open spaces."

"Oh, you've no idea how much I'd love to see those open spaces for myself." My words came out in a rush. "The grasslands you spoke of. Deserts where dunes rise in ridges like hills. Have you seen the Great Wall? Have you ever been to an oasis shaped like a crescent moon?"

"I've only been to the eastern end of the Great Wall," he said. "Someday I'd like to follow it west through Mongolia all the way to Jiayu Pass. I've heard of that oasis, yes, and I'd like to see it with my own eyes one day."

He smiled. "You're the first woman I've ever met who wanted to get away from courtyards and cities." He paused. "Well, perhaps the second. My mother loved the open plains and the grasslands."

"What are they like, the open plains?"

"One of the things I love about Harbin," he said, "is that it only takes a half hour on horseback to leave the city behind and enter the grasslands. So many people don't understand that landscapes of grass can be as beautiful as mountains or lakes. They're like an ocean when the wind blows, feathery tips of grass bending forward to the air, then falling back so that the entire plain ripples in waves of green and mauve."

His eyes shone with the memory, a look that filled me with an unfamiliar longing. When he spoke, I could picture the landscape he described. It was like being on a journey with Fox. I didn't want him to stop talking. His words painted pictures in my mind almost as vivid as Fox's dreams.

The grasslands fill the empty spaces between stands of deciduous forest where poplars and birches shelter at the foothills of mountain ranges. The grasslands follow river plains where tribesmen herd sheep and goats in shallow valleys of thorny shrubs and fescue. The grasslands stretch westward, to the edge of the Gobi Desert, where tall grasses give way to tufts of short dry tussock.

"Everyone thinks Manchuria is nothing but scrubby thornbushes and desert, hard-baked earth scattered with stones," he said. His eyes rested on some unseen horizon. "I've traveled for weeks in that landscape and I've never tired of its magnificence. The terrain transforms with each passing hour as the light changes. It's a hard-won beauty that reveals itself only to those who pay close attention. I miss it every day whenever I'm away."

I closed my eyes, imagining what it would be like to see such places.

His words were soft with yearning. His words made me want to see the landscapes he described. His words made me want to reach out with my hands and feel the stalks of tall grass waver with the wind. I had never wanted anything so much in my life.

Except for him to say my name out loud with that same yearning.

When I opened my eyes, he was looking at me, his eyes as soft as his words.

No. This could not be happening.

SANMU INVITED TAIYONG for dinner at a favorite restaurant, a modest dining spot at the edge of the Old City that specialized in *xiaolong bao*, "little dragon" soup dumplings. The owner greeted Sanmu with many bows and barked at a waiter to clean off a table. He seated us with a flourish of his dish towel, and although he stared at me a bit too long, his expression remained welcoming. The round table felt too small, too intimate. I felt too close to Wan Taiyong. I tucked my feet under the chair.

"May I ask whether Mr. Shea is making progress?" Sanmu asked.

"He's said it will be nearly impossible to locate Baoyuan's older brother." Wan Taiyong carefully conveyed another of the delicate dumplings into his bowl. "Too many years have gone by. As for clues to Baoyuan's death, it's difficult because of the workers' strike that was going on at the time. Shea hasn't learned much more than what the police know. Which is nothing."

My full attention was given to keeping my eyes away from Wan Taiyong. I signaled for more tea, asked the waiter to bring more steamed buns, told another to bring sweet vinegar with shredded ginger. My meal was tasteless. I couldn't let my composure slip. Couldn't give in to the urge to touch Taiyong's hand when I passed him the teacup. Couldn't let Sanmu realize the color in my cheeks had nothing to do with the warm, steamy air of the restaurant.

"There is someone else Shea wants to contact," Taiyong said, "even though he doesn't think anything will come of it. Yang Dajuin, the seller of the property."

Sanmu smiled. "A good man. His sister is a very sensible young woman."

"If Shea doesn't uncover anything soon, I will have him stop his investigation," Taiyong said. "It's one thing to find small clues, but he hasn't made any progress at all. Besides, I must get back to Harbin. My company is very busy."

I could almost see Sanmu sink back in relief, but he merely held out his cup for more tea.

A FEW DAYS later, I took Wan Taiyong to Zhang Yuan, a private park. Its grounds were famous for a magnificent rockery, four man-made lakes, and a grove of fountain bamboos. We didn't speak to each other during the drive. Wan Taiyong sat up front beside Gu and they chatted about automobiles.

I thought the park would be quiet and empty at this time of year, as Bansong Gardens had been. Instead, we walked through the moon gate entrance and were met with shrieks and giggles.

On the wide, hard earthen path circling a small lake, young women were riding bicycles. Some pedaled with confidence, some teetered along. Their friends stood beside the path calling out encouragement. There was a rack of bicycles and a sign, LEARN TO RIDE. BICYCLES AND LESSONS AVAILABLE.

A bicycle skimmed past, a man running behind the rider. "Look ahead of you, not down at the wheel," he shouted. The rider leaned dangerously to the right, but the man grasped the back fender and straightened the cycle, still running.

"Baoyuan taught me to ride a bicycle," Taiyong said. "Shooting, archery, horseback riding, ice skating. There didn't seem to be any sport he couldn't master in a day."

"Learn to ride, Young Miss," the attendant said, coming up to us. "Three times around the lake and you'll be pedaling on your own."

Taiyong looked at me, but I shook my head. "Not even if I teach you?" he asked, smiling. The wind had blown a wisp of hair across his forehead. I dug my hands deeper into the pockets of my coat.

"Especially not you," I replied, trying to return the banter.

The attendant shrugged, then watched intently as a pair of young women rode past, resplendent in brightly colored tunics, brows knitted in concentration. Bound feet pushed against the pedals.

"High-class prostitutes," the attendant said, grinning. "They're learning so they can ride around in public parks. Good advertising. Looks modern."

Taiyong and I continued deeper into the park, past the lake and the novice cyclists. Here the garden was empty of visitors. Its famous bamboo grove rose ahead, vibrantly green amid the dull browns of bare earth and wilted undergrowth. Taiyong headed for the grove, but I pointed to the other side of the garden.

"The pavilion," I said. "It will give us a perfect view of the bamboo grove. We should go there first."

It was a gentle climb, but frost still covered the shaded path and I slipped on a patch of frozen ground. Taiyong caught me by the arm. I steadied myself, but he didn't let go. He took my hand in his, and when I looked up at his face, I could barely breathe.

Silently we walked up the steps of the pavilion. The pavilion was octagonal, fitted with carved lattice screens on all sides. The screen that faced the bamboo grove was open. Taiyong pulled its hinged panels shut and then we stood in shadow, the interior of the pavilion pierced with light coming through the latticework, geometric patterns that fell on the floor, on our faces and bodies.

There was no Fox at work here, no one's will but mine and his. It was real.

He kissed me. I let him do as he pleased. His lips caressed my throat, his fingers explored the skin along the neckline of my blouse, and then his hands moved along my back.

I didn't care if he thought me no better than a prostitute. I didn't care if he believed I was habitually unfaithful to Sanmu. It didn't even matter if he thought Sanmu had thrown me at him. It was far, far better if he was only using me, because then he would leave Shanghai with no further thoughts of me, and he would never see me again. For at least then he would be safe from Fourth Uncle.

Despite myself, I began to cry.

"What is it, Jialing?" he whispered. "Don't you want this?"

"Yes," I sobbed, "but you're going back to Harbin. And I'm . . . I'm going to hiccup, which is what always happens when I cry."

He laughed and sat on the bench that circled the inside of the pavilion. He pulled me onto his lap and put one arm around me. I leaned against his shoulder, waiting for my hiccups to subside.

"Do you know when I began to think of you as more than just a rich man's mistress?" he said. "It was the day we walked through the lobby of the Astor Hotel."

The hiccups were quieting down. I sniffled.

"All those people turning their backs to you, all those sideways glances. I realized how difficult your life must have been, how difficult it still must be. Yet you straightened your shoulders and sailed through the crowd like a queen. I thought I'd never seen anyone more defiant or more beautiful."

"I'm just an orphan," I said. "*Zazhong*. My mother was a prostitute. I don't expect anything from you, Taiyong. Just these few days together."

"You're not very good at listening, are you?" he chided. "You're much more than that."

Every mote of dust hanging in the light was part of this moment. The faint scent of pine needles, the sound of wind shaking the trees outside, the taste of salt tears on my lips. These details were vivid and unforgettable. I understood what Leah meant. I had never felt life as intensely as I did in that moment. The pain was exquisite, a long sharp needle of comprehension that pierced my happiness, knowing that this could not last, that it would inevitably come to an end.

"Your hiccups have stopped," he whispered.

He kissed the palm of my hand, and it was as though I'd lost any will of my own. I didn't move as he kissed each of my fingers. I shuddered from the intimacy of his touch as he undid the pearl buttons on my cuff and kissed the inside of my wrist.

We slid down to the floor of the pavilion.

WHEN I ARRIVED home at Yuyang Lane, there was a note from Sanmu. He had to spend some time with his family. I almost sagged with relief. I couldn't face him. Not now. With the note were tickets to an opera performance.

Please take Mr. Wan to the opera tomorrow.

ANOTHER AFTERNOON PERFORMANCE, this time a troupe from Henan performing *The White Snake.* We sat in a private box, the one from which Sanmu's wife had been observing me just a week ago. There was no one else in the box. The lights went down and the orchestra began to play, a bamboo flute and the two-stringed *banhu,* the high plaintive notes of the *suona* horn.

Taiyong leaned over and spoke quietly, never looking away from the stage.

"I must leave tomorrow. The company has called me back," he said.

"Tomorrow?" I nearly dropped my fan in dismay.

"Forget about Liu Sanmu. Come back to Harbin with me, Jialing. He'll forget about you soon enough. Shanghai men change mistresses all the time."

For Taiyong, everything was so straightforward. His thoughts were as direct as an arrow released from the bow. But I couldn't afford such simplicity of thought and purpose. Sanmu and Fourth Uncle would fear the worst if I ran away with Taiyong. They'd worry that I might confide in Taiyong one day and tell him how his cousin really died. Even in faraway Harbin, I couldn't hide from Fourth Uncle's hounds if he decided to set them on my trail.

How could I explain to Taiyong that to follow him would be to put us both in danger? Even just revealing the danger put him at risk.

I shook my head, hiding my face behind my fan. "No, Taiyong, please. You must go back on your own. I can't leave and Sanmu can't know about us."

"Jialing, do you really think I would be asking you to come away with me if I didn't care about you?" The hurt in his voice pierced me with guilt, made me want to cry out that I loved him, that I would follow him anywhere. "I know you don't love Liu Sanmu."

I shook my head. "I can't go with you."

There was my mother and Fox. There was Anjuin.

"If I don't see you at the Shanghai North Railway Station tomorrow afternoon, I'll go without you." He reached into his jacket and pulled out an envelope. "If you decide to come later, wire me at the address in the note. I'll meet you at the train station in Harbin."

Onstage the White Snake transformed into a beautiful young woman. The actor sang in a lilting falsetto, one hand outstretched in a stylized gesture that signaled eternal love.

WHEN I RETURNED home and had shut the door to my room, I reached in my handbag for the envelope Taiyong had slipped me during the opera. It contained a folded sheet of notepaper with a short message and the telegram address for his office in Harbin.

> Your lineage doesn't matter to me, nor does your relationship with Liu Sanmu. Harbin is a city of refugees and émigrés. You would not be the first to go there to escape your past, and no one will ask, including me.

There was also a first-class ticket from Shanghai to Harbin.

MY LIFE IN Shanghai was going to change, I knew that. Soon, without Fox's influence, Liu Sanmu would tire of me, and I might have to leave the house on Yuyang Lane. In time, Sanmu might forget me, but Fourth Uncle would not. Fourth Uncle, with his cold un-blinking eyes, was not a trusting sort. To him I would be an aban-doned mistress, an unreliable woman who might be tempted to vengeance, someone with a secret worth money. Even if Sanmu discarded me, I couldn't go to Harbin. I wouldn't bring danger to Taiyong.

I locked myself in the bathroom so that Little Ko couldn't in-trude. Then I turned on the taps and sat in the tub, the sound of running water an accompaniment to my sobs, the water a pool for my tears.

A LETTER ARRIVED from Yun Na. They had moved into their new apartment and she was inviting me to visit. From her cloying words, I knew she was hoping to draw me closer into the Yang circle, but I didn't mind. It would be an opportunity to see Anjuin. It would also distract me from thinking about Taiyong, now three days gone.

From my dressing table drawer I pulled out a photograph in a simple wooden frame, a graduation gift from Miss Morris. Anjuin had come to the modest ceremony, my only family. The two of us stood beneath a banner that read UNITY MISSION SCHOOL CONGRAT-ULATES THE GRADUATING CLASS OF 1919. In her old-style tunic and trousers, she looked much older than I did in my school uniform. She smiled out from the photograph, her broad face with its flat features pleasant and serene. I looked at Anjuin, at our clasped hands. If only she were here with me now. How I missed her calm intelligence.

Beside her, I looked younger than my eighteen years although I recalled feeling very grown up that day. I studied my face in the photograph as though it were that of a stranger. Despite my proud smile, there was a guarded look about my eyes that hinted at a suspicious nature, of a reluctance to trust, of knowing that my destiny would always be uncertain. Would it be possible for Anjuin to forgive me after I had been so heedless with my words? I was prepared to say anything to regain her friendship. I would kneel to beg her forgiveness if that's what it took.

It's easier not to love, Fox had said.

Yet Fox had loved her human friends, of this I was certain. She loved my mother, loved me. How long could anyone live, even an immortal, without giving in to love?

WHEN I GOT to their door, I knocked cautiously. It was Yun Na who answered. Before I could say anything, she enfolded me in a hug. As if we were the best of friends. Taken aback, I handed her the gifts I had brought, a canister of fine tea and a box of pastries from an expensive French bakery.

"Come see my new little boy, dear Jialing," she said. "And Grandmother is here from Ningpo to spend some time with her latest grandson."

The new apartment had high ceilings and large bright windows. Grandmother Yang sat by one of those windows, cradling the infant and looking out at the street. Yun Na's two other children played quietly with a set of wooden blocks, a maidservant sitting beside them on the floor. Anjuin was nowhere to be seen.

"I hear we have you to thank for putting Dajuin in this apartment," Grandmother Yang said. I bowed to her.

"You have Mr. Liu to thank, Grandmother," I said.

"Look at you," she said, peering at me. "Now you're living in a fine, foreign house. And dressing like a foreigner."

Despite her peevish words, I couldn't help but feel sorry for the old woman. She looked older and more tired than I remembered.

"Where is Anjuin?" I asked.

"She's gone to Changchow," Grandmother Yang said. "She left early this morning. Her father has opened a dry goods store there. She will help him run the store. I just hope he listens to her."

It was as though ice water drenched my clothing. Anjuin had left Shanghai without telling me. Did this mean she no longer cared for our friendship? From her wide smile, I could tell Yun Na was eager to take Anjuin's place in my affections. I was the mistress of a wealthy man, a man who had been very helpful to Dajuin.

Yun Na exclaimed over the pastries and ordered the maidservant to bring tea. She chattered away, mistaking my silence for interest. She told me that Dajuin had been promoted and now she could afford a servant to keep the apartment clean and help in the kitchen. Grandmother Yang would stay only for another week.

"Oh, and Jialing, I must tell you something. A foreigner came by yesterday to speak with Dajuin and Anjuin. A detective!"

"Oh?" My fingers felt clumsy, the small teacup too slippery. Taiyong had said Shea would be speaking to the Yangs.

"He was looking into the death of Wan Baoyuan," she said. "The man who wanted to buy the property on Dragon Springs Road before your Mr. Liu bought it. Mr. Shea said Anjuin's information was very helpful."

"How's that?" My hands were trembling as I put down my teacup.

"Anjuin told him Wan Baoyuan had been driving Mr. Liu's car. The detective didn't know that. He said that little tidbit could change everything."

Downstream toward the rapids, a piece of wood thrown into the current.

WHEN I ARRIVED at Yuyang Lane, Sanmu's car was there. When I greeted him inside, there was no kiss, no smile.

"I've been here an hour," he said, after a pause.

"I'm sorry you had to wait. I wasn't expecting you, Sanmu," I said. "I went to see the Yangs. Listen, I must tell you what they told me."

"Let's have lunch first," he said, rather abruptly. "You can tell me after we eat."

A simple lunch was all Little Ko and I managed to pull together, some vegetables and tofu, a fish soup, steamed rice. After she put all the dishes on the table, I sent Little Ko home for the day. I didn't want her overhearing what I had to tell Sanmu.

Sanmu was taciturn, preoccupied, and I didn't interrupt his silence. Finally, after I made tea and brought it in, he spoke up.

"Jialing, I've been waiting all day to tell you something." He looked deeply unhappy.

His wife had attempted suicide.

Their marriage had been arranged when they were just children, but his wife had been sent to the McTyeire School for Girls. Her family wanted to be sure she had an education suitable for the wife of a man with modern, Western ideas. Through all their years of marriage, Sanmu had never been interested in concubines or mistresses. He considered himself happily married and there was much affection between them.

"I would even say there is love," he said, pacing alongside the table. "Yes, in fact, I do love my wife. And this, this arrangement with you, has hurt her deeply. She felt humiliated and pushed aside. It's as though my feelings for you were exorcised when I realized how desperately unhappy I had made her. You've been like a kind of madness, Jialing, a fever. And now you're a fever that has burned itself out."

So Fox's influence, already waning, was now depleted.

His remorse was not just over his wife. He had taken advantage of my youth and vulnerability. After giving me a comfortable life for these past several months, he wouldn't put me out on the street right away. But he had to end it.

I had been expecting an end to this arrangement, and now I felt only the relief of certainty. "Sanmu, I understand. Really, I do. But please, please, listen to me. Mr. Shea has been to visit Dajuin."

Perhaps if he hadn't just come from his wife's bedside, the news about the car would've been easier to take. His face sagged as he slumped back into his chair.

"The car. I forgot about the car." He put his head in his hands.

"If Shea asks, you could say Wan Baoyuan didn't take it that day," I said. "You were out in Chapei all day, covering the protests. If anyone saw a car, it wasn't yours."

"It's where the car went afterwards, Jialing. Whether anyone noticed me driving the car out of Dragon Springs Road." He ran a hand through his hair. "But you don't realize—the car isn't the worst part. Wan Taiyong sent a note to say he had to return to Harbin very suddenly. He said he's accepted that his cousin's death was a random murder, and he's told Shea to give up the investigation. It was dated three days ago."

I didn't understand. "Then why was Shea still talking to the Yangs yesterday, after Wan Taiyong had already gone?"

"Because even when a client has given up, Shea will carry on if the case catches his interest. That's how he's earned such a formidable reputation for tenacity."

My breath caught, tangled in fear. Then I realized that part of my distress was seeing Sanmu so unhappy. Despite everything, I still felt warmly toward him. I owed him a great deal, for myself, for the Yangs.

I reached over to take his hand.

"The first time I saw you, it was at *Xinwen Bao* the day the Royalist warlord Zhang Xun invaded the Forbidden City," I said.

"Everyone else was shouting and milling about and you just kept writing your article. The second time, you gave back the money that clerk cheated from me."

His smile said he was fond of me, even if he was no longer in love. "You were just a schoolgirl. I was so angry that one of my employees had defrauded you."

"Sanmu, you've been nothing but generous since then," I said. "I'll leave this house tomorrow if you want. But there's one thing I must beg of you."

He looked hesitant and unconsciously pulled his hand away.

"It's not for me, Sanmu," I said. "Remember I asked whether you could help find a husband for Anjuin? She's living in Changchow now. Her father has opened a shop there. Please, have you any connections in Changchow?"

He relaxed.

"I haven't forgotten, Jialing," he said. "Our kinsman Judge Liu is head of the clan in Changchow. I will write and ask whether he can recommend a matchmaker. He may even know a good family. I know how much you care about Anjuin. I promise."

His hand reached for mine. Trust and forgiveness trembled on the table between us, delicate as butterfly wings.

Then the front gate buzzer sounded. It was Old Tan signaling to the house he had just let someone in the front gate. I turned my head to see Mr. Shea walking up the path to the house. Sanmu's hand slid off mine.

CHAPTER 22

I won't take up too much of your time," Shea said. The wicker chair in the greenhouse seemed too fragile for his large frame. "It's about the day of the student protest, when we had the general strike back in June of last year. I'm investigating the death of Wan Baoyuan."

"How can I help?" Sanmu said.

"I've learned that Mr. Wan sometimes borrowed your car. Do you know whether he used it on the day of the strike?"

Sanmu shook his head. "It was a very chaotic day. I went to Chapei with Yang Dajuin to interview some of the workers and student leaders. Mr. Wan had a key for the car, so if he borrowed it that day, I wouldn't have known."

"Has a car come up in your investigations, Mr. Shea?" I asked.

"Not yet. I was hoping you could save me some time. Well, can you give me the make and description of the car?"

"It was a 1917 Pierce-Arrow."

"Color?"

"Dark green, very dark green." I hoped that Shea, jotting this down in his notebook, couldn't see how reluctantly Sanmu gave up this information.

As promised, Shea didn't take up much time. He refused tea and left.

"Now I wish we'd reported Wan's death to the police," I said, watching Old Tan open the gate for Shea. "Then it would've been a simple case, you defending me against rape and me defending you against Wan."

"Now I wish I'd listened to you," he said, his smile wry.

"Sanmu, don't tell your Fourth Uncle about this visit from Shea. Not yet," I begged.

"Jialing, I must. What else can we do?"

"Let me talk to Shea," I said. "He has a soft spot for me because his daughter and I were friends. I'll ask him not to look any further. I'll tell him what we should've told the police. I'll ask him to keep it confidential."

"You'll do nothing of the sort." He held me tightly by the shoulders and shook me. "Do you hear me? Nothing. Now I must get back to my wife, but you will not go near Shea."

I WAS NO longer Sanmu's mistress, but he would still support me. For now.

The house had been leased for a year and I could live in it for the remaining few months of the lease. After that, who knew what Sanmu would be willing to do for me? He had promised his wife he would never come to Yuyang Lane again. Instead Fourth Uncle would come to give me money each week.

Sanmu could just as well have had his driver drop off the money so I was certain Fourth Uncle was doing this to keep an eye on me. He came the very next day to make his conditions clear. He expected a reckoning of what I spent each week. His eyes, cold as a fish's, made it clear he resented every copper Sanmu gave me and was determined I wouldn't take advantage of his nephew's generosity.

"You've been a servant yourself," he said. "You don't need one to keep the house clean."

That was the end of Little Ko. As soon as Fourth Uncle left, I gave her two sets of dishes. I had never entertained, never used them. We both wept and she rode away on a handbarrow, taking with her a fortune in English porcelain.

I wondered how long it would take before Fourth Uncle made me leave Yuyang Lane. I gathered more of my expensive Western clothing and went to the pawnshop.

IT WAS EASIER to keep the kitchen warm, so Fox had moved the pallet bed there from the *erfang*. My mother dozed, unaware of my presence. I sat on a low stool beside her, my back against the stove's warm bricks. Spring was slow in coming and the days, though clear, were still cold. Arid winds from the north gusted through the city, scouring skin and stealing warmth. I cupped my hands around a bowl of hot water, taking the occasional sip.

She loves the jade bracelet you gave her, Fox said. Even when her mind is muddled, she always remembers it was your gift to her.

Fox padded around the kitchen, dressed in a long blue tunic

and black trousers. Had anyone happened to see her, she would've appeared like any servant in a middle-class family. Except for the glittering beaded scarf wrapped around her head like a turban.

The Central Residence was rubble now, workmen carrying away the broken bricks and tiles. In a few days they would begin demolishing the Western Residence and Fox would be powerless to stop so many. By then, perhaps my mother would be dead and it wouldn't matter. I watched her sleep and tried not to think of Taiyong, now four days gone, more than halfway to Harbin.

Use that train ticket, Fox said. Run away to Harbin before Fourth Uncle decides to take matters into his own hands. I'm sure he means you harm. Accidents happen.

I shook my head. "If I vanish, it won't be to Harbin. If Fourth Uncle hunts me down, I won't lead him to Taiyong's door. I'll think of something, some other way to survive. But while my mother lives, I'm staying."

All I wanted to do was curl up beside my mother, have her comfort me, somehow take away the agony as easily as she had once soothed the pain of a cut finger, a skinned elbow. Her sleeping form brought a fresh wave of sorrow. It was too late. I had taken too long to warm to her, to understand what she had sacrificed for me. She had been content to accept the miserly dregs of affection I offered her. And now she was dying.

Fox knelt beside the pallet bed and put a heated brick wrapped in cloth beside my mother's feet.

"I was thinking that after my mother has died, you could use your powers to help me find work, Fox," I said. "Something domestic. We could do it the way you managed Sanmu, just a visit every week or so to maintain your influence."

Ah. I was planning to go traveling again once your mother

and the Western Residence were gone. Try again to search for another Door.

I slumped back against the brick sides of the stove. Because of me, she had given up a chance to go through the Door. I couldn't ask her to stay in Shanghai just to look after me. Could I go with her somehow?

She cleared her throat. I've been thinking. There is something else. You could become a Fox.

If I'd been standing, my knees would have given way. Instead, I dropped the bowl of hot water, which shattered on the brick floor. My mother muttered and turned over in her sleep. Fox retrieved the broken pieces of porcelain and poured another bowl of hot water for me. She tucked the quilt more securely around my mother. I continued to gape at her, uncomprehending.

Ever since the day Anna vanished through the Door, Fox said, I've known you possessed the potential to move into the spirit world. Not all humans can see the Door.

"I thought Foxes were born into Fox families," I said. "I've never heard any stories of humans turning into Foxes."

Just because there aren't any stories doesn't mean it hasn't happened. She paused. Do you remember all those journeys we took together in your dreams? When you saw landscapes through the eyes of a Fox and felt the ground beneath your paws? I was teaching you what it could be like to live as a Fox.

"But, Fox, that began when I was only a girl. Why did you wait until now to tell me I could become a Fox?"

She sighed. Why did the mission school want its students to wait until you were older before converting to their foreign religion? You had to understand what such a choice meant.

The transformation itself wouldn't be difficult, she assured me. Only a small nip on the wrist, just enough to draw blood, followed by a moment of complete surrender to her powers. One night of sleep and in the morning I would wake up a Fox.

Fourth Uncle would never find you. And if you choose, you can make certain that Taiyong will always be in love with you.

I imagined changing my appearance, vanishing from Shanghai and from Fourth Uncle's suspicious eyes, free as the wind to drift through faraway landscapes. I remembered the swell of confidence that had surged through my limbs when Liu Sanmu first turned startled eyes on me and imagined what it would be like for Taiyong to feel such passion for me until the end of his days. The end of his days.

It's not a trivial decision, Jialing. Her words broke into my thoughts. Promise you'll take the time to think it through.

"Could I do the same to Taiyong?" I asked. "Make him a Fox?"

She shook her head. Only a natural-born Fox can turn humans into Foxes. And even then, if Taiyong doesn't have the potential, it would kill him.

"Tell me about other humans who became Foxes," I said. "Why no stories?"

She hesitated. For some reason, humans who become Foxes don't seem to enjoy their lives much after a hundred years or so. They stir up trouble and let themselves be captured and killed. Humans don't seem to understand how to be a Fox.

But it would be different for me. She had prepared me. I wasn't worried. I understood what it meant to be a Fox. So really, what was there to consider? When the time came, when Liu Sanmu no longer paid my keep, I would become a Fox.

"I'll think it through, Fox," I said, though I had already decided. "I promise."

WHEN I RETURNED that evening to Yuyang Lane, Gu was there.

I didn't have a house servant anymore, but Fourth Uncle had given me his car and driver. Gu would now park in front of the gate every day and insist on taking me wherever I needed to go.

I soon found he wasn't the helpful sort. When I went to the market, he didn't walk behind to carry my shopping while I browsed the stalls, but whenever I glanced toward the car, he would be watching. When I returned to the car carrying bags heavy with vegetables and fruit, Gu just grinned and opened the trunk of the car for me.

WHEN I MET Leah at her favorite French café, she was thoroughly delighted to learn I had the use of a car and driver.

"I'm going to invite you out every day just to have the use of your car," she exclaimed. "How generous of your Mr. Liu."

"It's not generosity," I said. My favorite pastries might as well have been balls of boiled dough. It had been several days since my last visit to Dragon Springs Road. How could I get away from Gu? I had to take food and money so that Fox could care for my mother. "The driver is there to watch me, Leah. How can I get away for an hour or two?"

"Are you having an affair?" she exclaimed.

Because of Gu, Leah was convinced Sanmu wanted to keep an eye on me because he still cared for me and was jealous I might find another patron.

I rolled my eyes. "I can't tell you about it just now, but it's not some man."

"Well, we can go to my mah-jongg club tomorrow afternoon," she said. "That's worth hours of time. Your driver can doze in his car and you can slip out the back to go meet your man."

I sighed. "I've said, there is no man. But the mah-jongg club is a good idea, thank you. Can I take you home now? Sanmu's

Fourth Uncle is coming to the house this afternoon. You'd think such an important man would have better things to do than ask me why soap costs so much."

Gu took his time bringing the car around and didn't bother opening the passenger door for us. Leah's expression was one of polite disinterest. When we reached her apartment, she insisted I come upstairs to see her newest evening dress.

"It will only take a few minutes," she said. "I must have your opinion."

But once we were inside the door, she turned to me with a worried frown. "I was joking before about your affair, but I'm not joking now. Are you stealing from the Lius? What have you done to make Liu Sanmu want you under surveillance?"

"Nothing of the sort," I said, shocked "How can you even think that of me?"

"Because that driver of yours is a gangster." She shrugged at my shocked expression. "Peng gets mixed up with all sorts of people. He took me to a party once and pointed out the big bosses to me. I recognize your driver. He was a bodyguard for one of the gang leaders."

I thought of Gu, his burly arms, his huge hands. Gu, hired by Fourth Uncle.

"Jialing, what have you done to have this man dogging your footsteps?" she asked. "He's dangerous."

But not as dangerous as Fourth Uncle's suspicious mind.

BACK AT YUYANG Lane, I changed into a tunic and trousers of dark gray, the plainest set I owned, and slipped on some cloth shoes. I braided my hair in a simple plait and scrubbed my face clean to present a modest and traditional appearance for Fourth Uncle.

The mirror showed a very ordinary young woman. Chinese, but not quite. Jawline too strong, nose too pronounced, complexion too pale. Fourth Uncle would see only a *zazhong* girl, someone who would never be allowed into the Liu family, not even if I gave them a son.

Fourth Uncle arrived by rickshaw. His stern looks demanded obedience, and for as long as I could collect money from Sanmu, I would not give Fourth Uncle any cause to complain. At least, not more than usual. I smoothed back my hair and opened the door to greet him, this man whose goodwill I had to retain. If I'd ever had it.

He settled down at the dining table and placed an abacus beside the notebook I handed him. Its first page listed my purchases from the past week. Inside the notebook, an envelope of receipts, each one numbered to match an item on the list. Fourth Uncle had set the rules, and I had entered the amounts carefully.

I stood across the table from Fourth Uncle, like a schoolgirl whose homework is being graded. Fourth Uncle said nothing; the only sound in the room was the disapproving click of abacus beads in their wooden frame. Fourth Uncle couldn't possibly want to be here any more than I enjoyed his company. Perhaps if all my expenses were in order every week, he would get bored and stop coming.

Leah had counseled spending all the money, or at least appearing to spend it all.

"Stores are happy to write you receipts for any amount," she said. "If that uncle of Sanmu's thinks you can get by with half the amount, he may only give you half next time."

"It's Sanmu's money and I won't cheat him," I said. "I don't believe Sanmu will go back on his word. He'll give me exactly what he promised. I can always write to let him know if his uncle becomes unreasonable."

Fourth Uncle shut the notebook. "You eat out too often."

I bowed my head and said nothing. There was the sound of coins being placed on the table and the chair being pushed back. I breathed a sigh of relief and willed myself not to look at the stack of silver coins. I would wait until Fourth Uncle had gone. I would not let him see me concerned about Sanmu's generosity.

Then the front gate buzzer sounded, and a minute later, Shea's tall figure appeared under the magnolia trees, striding up the path. Behind me, I felt, rather than saw, Fourth Uncle grow very still.

"I will open the door for Mr. Shea," he said. "You stay here."

Somehow it wasn't surprising that he knew Shea on sight. Why would Sanmu be the only person in the Liu family to use Mr. Shea's services? I sat down and counted the stack of coins. It was the same amount as the week before.

"Girl, Mr. Shea wants to speak with you," Fourth Uncle's voice from the drawing room.

Mr. Shea stood on the rug across from Fourth Uncle, who was seated. If Shea was surprised to see Fourth Uncle at the house, he didn't show it. Gossip must have reached him by now that Sanmu had put me aside.

"I won't take up much of your time, Miss Zhu," Mr. Shea said. "I understand that Master Liu here already knows about my investigation into Wan Baoyuan's death." There was a question in his voice.

Fourth Uncle disguised his anxiety as impatience. "My nephew and I have no secrets from each other, Shea. Ask the girl your questions now or not at all."

Shea cleared his throat. "I spoke to a rickshaw driver who

claims that he saw a dark-green car with black fenders pull out of Dragon Springs Road that day. This suggests Wan Baoyuan could've gone to visit the Yangs."

"The police questioned Dajuin already," I said. "He never saw Wan Baoyuan that day."

"That's true," Shea said. "But for now I'm just looking for confirmation that such a car was at Dragon Springs Road. It was raining heavily and the rickshaw driver could've been mistaken about the color. When I went to see the Yangs, Miss Yang told me she and her brother were at the market and waited out the rain there, but that you were home. Did you see or perhaps hear a car? A knock at the front gate?"

Fourth Uncle's silence was a dagger held against my throat.

"No," I said. "I didn't. As you say, it was raining heavily. And I was ill in bed that day, for quite a few days actually. I wouldn't have heard anything."

Shea cleared his throat again. "Miss Yang also said there was someone living in the Western Residence who might've seen an automobile. Or perhaps even seen Wan Baoyuan if he went to Dragon Springs Road. A former servant. A woman called Ping Mei."

Fourth Uncle's already upright posture stiffened. His head turned slowly, his cold unblinking eyes observed me, a serpent watching its prey.

"No," I repeated. "She wasn't there. She doesn't live there anymore."

"Miss Zhu, please," Mr. Shea said. "This is a murder investigation. All I want is to ask this woman a few questions. Miss Yang said it's very likely this woman is still there squatting in the Western Residence."

Again, I shook my head. Fourth Uncle stood up.

"Mr. Shea, are those all the questions you have?" he asked.

WHEN THE GATE shut on Shea, Fourth Uncle picked up his cane and walked to the front door without a word. Then he turned and pointed the cane at me.

"I told Sanmu you couldn't be trusted. You knew that servant woman was there but didn't tell us. Do not attempt to leave this property. I'm telling Old Tan you're not to go out the gate."

The door slammed.

How could I get out to Dragon Springs Road? I had to warn Fox. I had to get my mother out of there. Fourth Uncle would show no mercy to a servant woman. And now that Fourth Uncle had found reason to distrust me, not even Sanmu's goodwill would save me from Gu's big hands. Accidents happen.

I gathered up the stack of coins from the dining room table and ran upstairs. I put the money in my handbag. On second thought, I pulled my school satchel out of a bottom drawer and emptied the contents of my expensive handbag into its canvas compartments. Then I sat on the bed. How could I manage to get past Old Tan? And Gu?

The front gate buzzer sounded.

I ran to the window. Old Tan had let Shea in again.

"Why did you come back, Mr. Shea?" I cried, nearly sobbing with relief as I opened the door. "How did you get in?"

"I told the gatekeeper I'd left something behind," he said. "I came back because Master Liu seemed to make you nervous. I thought I'd see whether I could speak to you on your own. My dear child, what's the matter?"

"I need to go to Dragon Springs Road," I said "I must see my mother and get her out of there. She's in danger. From Fourth Uncle."

"Your mother?" He raised his eyebrows.

"Ping Mei, the woman with the burned face you found in the Old City, she's my mother," I said. "She didn't want me to know at first because she was so ashamed of herself."

"Why would she be in danger from Master Liu?"

I didn't care anymore what Shea learned. "Because she was there. She was there the day Wan Baoyuan died, and Fourth Uncle doesn't want you to talk to her. He'll kill her before that happens. He's told Old Tan not to let me out the gate, and even if he did, I'd have to get away from Gu, my driver. Oh, Mr. Shea, can you help me?"

"Is Gu the driver beside the black car? The car is gone."

Gu's huge hands, his burly arms. A bodyguard who worked for gangsters. Had Fourth Uncle gone with him to Dragon Springs Road or had Fourth Uncle sent him on his own to find my mother?

Would Fox be able to protect my mother? Fox, who despite all that she said about it being easier not to love, cared for me and my mother. Fox, who was not truly immortal. Fox, who couldn't starve or fall ill, but who could be killed.

Shea shook me gently by the shoulders. "Bring with you whatever is necessary. We can get past Old Tan. Somehow I don't think Master Liu has told him what's at stake."

OLD TAN'S STATION was a roofed-in niche built against the wall. There, perched on a high stool, he could look through open brickwork onto Yuyang Lane. When he heard the crunch of footsteps on the gravel path, he gave me a reproachful look.

"Miss Zhu, you know Master Liu doesn't want you to go out. I can't open that gate for you."

Shea pulled out a handful of silver. "A man needs to empty his bladder once in a while though, doesn't he?"

Old Tan's arm convulsed ever so slightly. Shea dropped silver coins into the outstretched palm. Eight, nine, ten. The gatekeeper shuffled away to the corner of the garden, where panels of ivy-covered trellis hid an outhouse.

I stepped out the gate. I climbed into Shea's automobile and we left Yuyang Lane. I doubted I'd ever see it again.

CHAPTER 23

It was clear that Shea was accomplished at steering around Shanghai's traffic, but he wasn't driving fast enough for me. While he drove, I told him everything. How I had recognized Wan Baoyuan as the same man who had been watching Master Shen's funeral. How Mr. Shih of Nanyang Shipping, who had remarked on seeing Wan Baoyuan in Shanghai three years ago, had been found murdered.

How Sanmu had put together the pieces and suspected Wan Baoyuan might be one of Mah Juhou's assassins. How Wan Baoyuan's attempt to kill me had confirmed that suspicion. How Sanmu had come to my defense. How Wan Baoyuan had nearly killed him.

"Until then, Sanmu only suspected," I said. "He had no proof, only information about Wan's political loyalties, his circle. But poor Mr. Shih and I were the only ones who knew Wan Baoyuan had been in

Shanghai the day Mah Juhou died. Sanmu said Wan would've seen us as loose ends he had to tie up."

Shea's eyes flickered at me then turned back to the road. "I remember Shih's murder," he said. "Very professional. The Shanghai Police thought he'd gotten on the wrong side of some gangsters."

"It was my mother who saved us," I said. "She beat Wan Baoyuan over the head with a chair leg and killed him. Sanmu said we shouldn't get the police involved because if information leaked out, we would be in danger from Wan Baoyuan's fellow conspirators. It would bring the Nationalists and General Zhang's Fengtian clique into open conflict, something the Nationalists don't need right now. Better to make it seem like a random murder."

The car swerved and dodged traffic. Rickshaws and handbarrows, automobiles and street vendors loaded down with shoulder poles weaved along the streets. On the sidewalk, a prostitute in a flowered tunic and trousers strolled into a store, followed by her amah. At the corner, a letter writer had set up shop with a stool and portable desk, ready to take dictation. It seemed impossible that such mundane events could continue on as though it were a day like any other.

It seemed as though every car and every rickshaw in Shanghai obstructed our route. I wanted to scream with frustration when the railway crossing ahead of us dropped its barricades, stopping traffic on both sides. The Shanghai to Hangchow train clattered past on its way out of Chapei Station. Finally the barricades lifted. Automobiles, carriages, and rickshaws advanced slowly across the railway tracks. I wanted to leap out and run the rest of the way.

"So Liu Sanmu is certain you won't tell anyone all this," Shea said, "but his Fourth Uncle isn't so trusting?"

"Fourth Uncle is mixed up in something to do with the Nationalists and gangsters," I said. "Neither of them knows it was my mother who killed Wan Baoyuan. Sanmu thinks I was the one who did it, but he told his uncle that he was Wan Baoyuan's killer to make sure Fourth Uncle would help get rid of the body."

Shea frowned. "How could Liu Sanmu not have known your mother was there? Not seen her attack Wan?"

"Sanmu forgot he saw my mother," I said, "because Fox made him forget."

"Fox?"

By the time the car swung onto Chung San Road, Shea had been silent for several minutes. His silence had begun with my explanation about Fox and had grown even heavier when I told him about the Door and Anna.

"I can't believe any of what you just told me, Jialing." Shea kept his eyes on the busy road. "I fear your mind is unbalanced if you believe a Fox spirit has been your guardian or that my Anna walked through a door into the land of immortals. It makes me wonder if anything else you've said is true."

"You don't need to believe me, Mr. Shea," I said. "Just help me save my mother."

We turned into Dragon Springs Road, the homes on each side now a collection of finished and half-finished houses, some of the construction still open to the street, others already hidden behind high brick walls. Dust and dirt were everywhere, workers carrying building materials on shoulder poles, others pushing handbarrows. At the far end, in front of the Western Residence's gates, we saw the black car.

Shea had to drive slowly to avoid the workers. I couldn't wait and jumped out. I ran to the Western Residence and pushed at the gate. It had always slid open for me, but today it stood ajar, the heavy lock smashed.

There was a faint smell of wood smoke, no more than I would expect from a fire in the kitchen stove, but I ran. I ran through the front courtyard and the bamboo garden, the pebbled path grinding under my cloth shoes with every step. I saw a small, still form on the paved courtyard and I ran faster.

There was blood on her muzzle, but Fox was still breathing. A length of wood lay on the ground beside her, a post salvaged from the ruined *erfang*, blood smeared on one end. As I stroked her fur, I could see her limbs twitch. Was Gu here with Fourth Uncle or was he on his own?

The smell of smoke was stronger now, and I realized it wasn't coming from the kitchen but from the main house. I heard a cough and looked up. Gu was coming out of the main house. He stepped over the threshold and stopped when he saw me. He grinned, the same look as when he watched me struggle with heavy bags of shopping.

I heard Shea call my name, but I didn't turn around. I was staring at the red flickering glow from the windows behind Gu. Suddenly I understood. I tried to run past Gu, but he caught the sleeve of my tunic.

"No, no, Young Mistress. Why did you have to come?" he chided. "Now I have to take you back to Yuyang Lane."

He struck me and I fell to the ground.

"Leave her alone." Shea's voice. The sounds of a struggle.

I didn't bother looking back at the two men. I got up and ran to the main house.

At the center of the bedroom, flames crackled. The wood Fox had stacked so carefully on the veranda was piled around the charcoal brazier. On the other side of the fire, my mother lay on the bed frame, curled up and facing the wall, her small form neatly arranged, her tiny feet peeping out from the hems of her trousers. I heard her cough. She was unconscious but still alive. The old wood, dry as tinder, burned higher each second that I delayed.

Trying not to breathe, I edged around the fire, holding my clothes against my body and away from the flames, thankful I wasn't wearing a dress. My mother's eyes were closed, and there was a slow trickle of blood from one nostril. I couldn't tell whether she had been hurt anywhere else, but there wasn't time to be gentle. I managed to drag her to an upright position, then realized I couldn't carry her safely past the flames. She lolled against me, heavier than I thought she would be in her unwieldy state.

A figure stepped through the smoke.

Together, Fox said. We lifted my mother between us and sidled past the blazing center of the room. When we got outside, I gasped gratefully at the fresh air. Gently, we laid my mother down on the paving stones of the courtyard. Fox sank down to the ground and so did I. Only then did I look around.

Gu lay motionless, sprawled by the bamboo garden. Shea was staggering to his feet. He stared at Fox, at her amber eyes shining through a soot-smudged face, at her tunic and trousers in autumn hues. She panted, pink tongue and white teeth showing, blood smeared across her nose and cheeks.

There was a crashing sound from the main house. The posts and beams holding up the roof had weakened from the heat. The air in the courtyard was choking me, as if the smoke was trapped within its walls. I began coughing again. From outside the walls I could hear shouts of "Fire!"

"We must get away from the smoke," Shea said, his voice

calm and authoritative, a voice trained to take control in emergencies.

He scooped up my mother as though she were no heavier than a bundle of rags. "Let's get out of here. I'll return for Gu when you and . . . when you're both safely out."

I knelt down beside Fox. "Are you all right?" I asked, my eyes watering from the smoke.

She sat up and nodded. Suddenly her body stiffened. Even though she was in human form, I could almost see her ears pricking forward. She was staring past me, at the rock garden.

The arch in front of the rock garden shimmered. The Door was opening, its glowing edges growing more and more distinct as the gap widened. It was larger than I remembered. Beyond the door was an orchard in full flower. I saw the fresh green of new leaves and a froth of pink and white. It was a vision of springtime so intense it seemed distilled from a thousand years' worth of springtimes, eternal and constant.

Behind me, a hoarse gasp from Shea.

The Door was now wide open and the entire courtyard radiant with sunlight pouring out from the portal. A breeze blew in from that other world, carrying with it the scent of peach blossom. It pushed the smoke away from us, back toward the burning building. Music floated through the courtyard. "Full of Joy."

The roar of flames, the crash of timbers falling down, the heat and noise—they all receded. We were mesmerized by the portal.

"What . . . what is it?" Shea croaked. His gaze was fixed on the scene beyond the door.

"It's the Door, an entrance to the land of immortals," I said. "Where Anna went."

Jialing. Fox was in her animal shape again, her body wriggling with excitement. It's wide, wide open. Who knows how many it will let through this time? Hurry! Let's bring your mother with us.

"You go first, Fox," I said. "You can't give up your chance again."

Then you must decide quickly, before I leave, Fox said. Just in case you don't get through. Do you stay as a human or as a Fox?

To slip through crowds unseen in the daytime, then run at night beneath moonlight and clouds. To be free of the fear of hunger, the encumbrance of illness. To shape my features so that I would never again hear the taunts of *zazhong*. To dazzle any man and make him love me. The conquest of the unreal over the real.

I could help Anjuin. I could find some way to give her a better life.

I could go to Manchuria and find Wan Taiyong. I remembered the rush of triumph that had surged through my veins when Liu Sanmu looked at me, his eyes widening in desire and confusion. It would be the same with Taiyong. He would love me. I would never worry about losing him. Except to death.

How many different kinds of pain can there be?

For Anjuin, when I knew I had lost her friendship, it had been a sharp sensation in my chest, like citrus squeezed onto a cut.

For my mother, since I had known she would die, a long, slow slicing pain through the center of my heart.

For Taiyong, it was a relentless throbbing ache that filled my entire being each morning, from the instant I woke up to when my swollen eyelids closed in the darkness of my bed, and all the murky restless hours in between.

If I lived for hundreds of years, how many more people would I love, how much pain would I endure when they died?

Slowly, I shook my head. The moment I made my decision, Fox

knew. She pressed herself against my ankles, her body trembling with eagerness. This time she didn't hesitate.

Good-bye, Jialing. She sprang through the door, a blur of autumn colors.

On the other side, a woman knelt on grass as bright as jade. Her back was to me. She stood up, her robes falling in silken folds, garments that been out of style for three hundred years. She glanced over her shoulder and I caught a flash of green in her eyes before she turned and walked away under the rows of peach trees, into eternal springtime.

The Door stayed invitingly open.

"I thought you were talking about a fairy tale." Shea stood beside me, his voice ragged, incredulous. He was still holding my mother in his arms. "But how can I believe Anna is over there when I saw her body?"

"The body is only a shell, Mr. Shea," I said. "She's there, safe on the other side. Anna went through, as Fox did just now."

"A Fox spirit. From a Chinese folktale." His voice shook. "What am I supposed to believe?"

"Believe that Anna isn't gone. Believe that she's there, on the other side of the portal. Believe that the gods are giving you a chance to go through and find her." The Door would let him in. Somehow I knew this.

"In our fairy tales, there's always a price to pay when mortals enter an enchanted land." He straightened his shoulders. "But if Anna's there, I'll go. If there's a price to pay, I'll be the one to pay it."

The outlines of the door began to shimmer.

"Go then," I said. "Quickly, Mr. Shea. And take my mother with you."

He nodded and took a deep breath. He marched through the door, his steps firm, a soldier on his way to battle.

As soon as he crossed the threshold, all the soot and dirt on his clothing vanished. He put my mother down on the grass. He gazed around and without turning to look behind, he strode out of sight.

The door was now more than halfway shut but it had become translucent and I could see my mother in the shimmering light of the orchard. She sat up and turned around and I saw that she was young again, her features free of pain, as lovely as in my memories. Her smile was unrestrained and joyful. Her smile invited me to cross the threshold.

I shook my head. The Door wouldn't let any more people through. I could feel it.

"You've suffered enough for three lifetimes, Mama," I said. "You deserve to go through. But I want to live at least one lifetime in this world. I'll be all right."

There was nothing to forgive, nothing to explain. Her love washed over me to erase all the years that had come between us.

Then the Door closed and light drained from the courtyard.

THE KITCHEN WAS starting to catch fire as I ran behind its back wall. I veered to the right and dashed through the narrow strip of garden at the very back of the property. Sparks were falling, but I ducked beneath the spindly fruit trees. Their branches caught the red-hot specks before they could singe me, but their bare brown twigs would soon succumb to the falling embers. Cries from the courtyard told me rescuers had entered the courtyard and found Gu's unconscious body.

Pushing open the secret door, I emerged at the back of the

Central Residence. The shed on the other side had been torn down and the door was clearly visible, a secret no longer. But my escape went unnoticed because there were no workers at the construction site. They'd all gone to watch the fire.

Dragon Springs Road was filled with curious bystanders. I walked out, head down, face streaked with soot. I could tell from excited comments that the fire had spread and workers had given up their haphazard attempts to save a place that was supposed to be torn down anyway.

There was nothing of my life there now.

I would never return to Dragon Springs Road.

CHAPTER 24

When I boarded the train at the Shanghai North Railway Station that day, my only thought was to escape from Sanmu and Fourth Uncle, to put some distance between us. Surely, in a country the size of China, with all its upheavals and territorial disputes, I could manage to disappear. With or without Wan Taiyong's help.

My thoughts gained clarity as the miles unfurled. Nanking, my first destination, was only two hundred miles away from Shanghai. Then Peking, more than nine hundred miles away from Shanghai. Harbin, another eight hundred miles from Peking.

I traveled third-class. With my grimy face and dirt-streaked clothing, a scarf tied over my hair, I was just another poor passenger. My fellow travelers stared out the windows, played games of dice, and fed their children. Those new to the landscape expressed their dismay as the train took them farther and farther from the homes they knew, covering distances greater than they had ever traveled. The immensity of the terrain before them was unfathomable. I could see it in their eyes.

Those who had made the trip before turned their backs, no longer interested in the scenery, looking for ways to pass the long hours. I pretended to sleep on the hard bench seats, head thrown back like the other travelers, a scarf over my face to indicate I didn't want to be disturbed. The satchel tucked firmly behind my back held all my possessions.

Before I left Shanghai, I had bought a sheet of paper and an envelope from a letter writer near the train station.

Dear Sanmu:

I am reminding you of your promise to find a husband for Anjuin.

Master Yang now runs a dry goods store in Changchow. You can ask Dajuin where it is. You've said you have relatives in Changchow and would use your connections there.

Sanmu, I beg of you this one last kindness. If you have even the faintest memory of affection for me, please help Anjuin. It is the only favor I will ever ask of you, for as long as I live.

Jialing

It was a letter I could've penned and posted any time before my last day at Yuyang Lane. I addressed it to his office. I had to believe that Sanmu could be trusted to keep his word. I did believe. Perhaps one day Anjuin would find it in her heart to forgive me, to recognize how young we had been when we quarreled. It was too much to hope that I might meet her again and rekindle our friendship. I couldn't imagine how that would be possible now that I had fled Shanghai. It was enough to imagine her smiling and content, surrounded by her own children.

AT STATIONS ALONG the way, I bought food from vendors, using my coins as sparingly as possible. I bought only steamed bread and fruit, a paper twist of tea. I always bought a newspaper though, anything from Shanghai. They were inevitably a few days old.

Finally, I saw the news I'd been waiting to read.

TWO DEAD IN EXTERNAL ROADS AREA FIRE

Two bodies have been recovered from the burned wreckage of an abandoned home at 21 Dragon Springs Road, in the External Roads area. The house belonged to the Liu Family Real Estate Company. Rescuers also found a man unconscious and injured on the property. He has been identified as Gu Hong, a professional bodyguard.

One of the bodies has been identified as that of Robert Shea, a private investigator. His car was found outside the property and witnesses saw him enter the gates.

The other body, of a woman, is yet to be positively identified, but from the jewelry found on the body there is good reason to believe it is that of Zhu Jialing, missing since the day of the fire. Witnesses saw both Zhu and Shea get out of Shea's car and enter the gates.

The body is only a shell, Fox had said when Anna's body was found. Why the gods chose to discard her body at Yung An Cemetery is not for me to guess.

Why the gods chose to place my mother's body and Shea's inside the burning building was not for me to guess either. But I was grateful for the deception it offered. My jade bracelet had deceived Sanmu into believing it was my body they'd found.

With Shea gone, Fourth Uncle had nothing left to fear. There was no one to carry on the investigation, no one who cared enough to look into Wan Baoyuan's death, Mr. Shih's murder, or the woman known as Ping Mei.

Before I fled the Western Residence, I had crouched beside the hydrangea shrubs and reached inside Fox's den to retrieve the small cache of money hidden there. Groping for the cloth bag, my fingers had brushed against a lifeless form, the fur still warm. I stroked it gently between the ears before withdrawing my hand. The gods had chosen to place the husk of Fox's body in her den.

Had I made a different decision, Fox would've conferred her powers on me, a final gift before she crossed to a land where they were unnecessary. If I'd taken Fox's powers, I wouldn't be worried about my welcome in Harbin. Even if Wan Taiyong had read my telegram with indifference, I would've searched for him, made him love me.

But it would've been a meaningless love, as artificial as a pine tree cultivated in a shallow basin, any wayward emotion, any deviation from passion pruned and wired, shaped to create an imitation of love. The unreal in the real.

If I'd taken Fox's powers, I could've wandered anywhere in China, altered my features, prodded minds to give me unquestioning acceptance. This was the most tempting of all. As a Fox I could've denied my true appearance. But I would've always felt ashamed, ashamed to think of Leah and Grace battling the humiliation of being treated as *zazhong* through all the years of their lives, Leah fierce and Grace accepting.

If I'd taken Fox's powers, I could've lived for hundreds of years, known and loved many people. But then I would've had to watch them die of illness or old age. How many different kinds of pain can there be? How much loss can the human heart endure?

I knew why those other Foxes, once human, had wanted to die. Their hearts had remained human even though they wielded the powers of a Fox. They were ready to die because they had lost too many loved ones over the centuries, because they had suffered such an accumulation of blows to the heart that all love had been beaten out of them, all joy turned to ash.

It was better to tread my own path in life as a human.

CHAPTER 25

At the train station in Peking, I found my way to the station's telegraph office.

Then I boarded the South Manchuria Railway, a Japanese-owned line that ran between Peking and Harbin. I finally felt safe enough to take advantage of my first-class ticket and enjoyed a compartment to myself. The attendant brought a kettle of hot water, and I gave him some coins for a few packets of tea leaves. In solitary luxury for the first time in five days, I locked the door of the compartment and washed myself in the tiny bathroom. I slept soundly for hours.

Then the morning sun warmed its way through the thin curtains, and I awoke to the splendor of a lonely landscape.

The train traveled northeast through the great central plains, where fields newly tilled for millet and sorghum spread across endless flats of yellow soil. The plains were shaded here and there by thickets of deciduous trees. These gave way to landscapes barren of crops, rolling and rocky hills. Small streams cut through the terrain, their steep banks revealing hard, pale earth beneath a deceptively lush layer of grass.

I saw the terrain as Fox would've seen it, as she had taught me to see it, noticing the things that mattered to her. I saw stands of birches and pines, oaks and poplars, recognized trees by the shape of their canopies and the flutter of their leaves in the wind.

I caught glimpses of deer, nervous herds tucked into notches between hills. I sensed smaller creatures—marmots, hares, and rodents—hidden in their burrows waiting for the safety of night. When the wind parted meadows of feathergrass, I spied families of brown-eared pheasants gleaning for seeds and insects.

Almost always the hard blue sky yielded sightings of a lone hawk circling overhead, power and patience in the slow tilt of its wings. At twilight, a sudden flutter of movement disturbed the sunset as starlings settled on branches.

While everyone else slept at night, lulled by the steady, swaying motion of the train, I stood by the window to watch the moon keep pace with the train. What would it be like to set out toward that horizon with Wan Taiyong, to wade through that windblown landscape together? What did it feel like for a bird the first time it stepped off the nest, trusting in updrafts and hollow bones to keep it aloft?

Your lineage doesn't matter to me, Taiyong had written. *Harbin is a city of refugees and émigrés. You would not be the first to go there to escape your past, and no one will ask, including me.*

My heart outraced the rhythmic grinding of the train's wheels as Harbin drew closer. The outskirts of the city loomed, and then they filled my window, the derelict buildings and run-down houses I'd come to expect at the fringes of every town.

Then the train slowed, and the streets of Harbin came into view, busy with automobiles and coaches, the sidewalks as crowded as any in Shanghai. I fought the urge to jump off the train before it reached the station, to walk away and vanish into the throng. What would I find in this new city?

Dozens of flags decorated the roof of the train station, the multicolored stripes of the republic and the yellow banner of the Fengtian clique. On the platform, I saw as many foreign faces as Chinese ones, perhaps more. From carriage windows, passengers leaned out to wave and shout, but I merely pushed down my window to look out. The chilling wind that blew in drove all warmth from the little compartment.

All along the platform, beggars and touts assaulted travelers in a babble of languages, cries for charity, offers to carry luggage, promises of comfortable lodgings. I looked for a tall, slim figure, but no one raised a hand to wave at me, no one hurried across the platform to my window. He wasn't there.

I kept looking, even though the cold bit through my thin coat. The other passengers withdrew from their windows and I watched them descend from the train. I fought down disappointment, tried to ignore the terror tracing its way down my spine. Beyond Harbin, where could I go? Korea? Japan? I turned my back on the platform.

Then a voice called. "Jialing?"

Wan Taiyong stood there on the platform, just below my window. He carried a large box and wore a huge coat with a shearling collar turned up against the cold. A fur hat covered his head. I almost collapsed onto the seat in relief, but then I saw the strained expression on his face. Was it regret?

"I almost didn't come," he said, his voice hesitant. "I couldn't believe the telegram because I read the article in *Xinwen Bao* about the fire. I thought the telegram might've been delayed by some mishap, that you'd sent it before you left Shanghai. Before you died. Then I realized it had been sent from Peking."

"I wasn't in the fire. It was another woman," I said, searching his face for some clue to his feelings. "But it means Liu Sanmu thinks I'm dead. And he can continue believing that."

"Why didn't you get off the train?" he said. "Are you having second thoughts?"

"No. Not at all," I said, suddenly shy. "Taiyong, I didn't get off because I didn't see you on the platform."

"Please. Get off now," he said. "I'm here."

Pulling my satchel over my shoulder, I ran along the carriage to the door and down the few steps to the platform. Only then did we smile at each other, at the misunderstandings that might have prevented our reunion.

I pointed at the box he was holding, thick cardboard tied with string. "Is that for me?"

He put the box in my hands. It was heavy. "Ice skates," he said. "The lakes are still frozen."

The box dropped to the ground, and I threw my arms around him, laughing.

"Jialing," he said, his lips against my cheek. And this time, when he said my name, the grasslands were in his voice.

ACKNOWLEDGMENTS

My gratitude to Antonia Levi for suggesting that I check into the memoirs of women missionaries who lived in China before the First World War; this avenue of research filled in so many gaps. Big thanks also to Patricia Webb and Amanda Vinoly, who read an early version of the novel when it was just one big bundle of woe, for their kind but firm advice to pare things down so that the novel contained one story instead of several. If Jennifer Pooley hadn't insisted that I give Fox a bigger role, this novel wouldn't have taken shape the way it did. Jen, many thanks from me and also from Fox.

To my editors at HarperCollins Canada and William Morrow: Iris Tupholme, Lorissa Sengara, and Jennifer Brehl—thank you for providing the insights and suggestions that sharpened the story. And extra thanks to Iris and Jennifer for believing in *Dragon Springs Road* back when it was nothing but a skimpy outline. To Jill Marr, who has been my literary agent, career coach, voice of reason and friend, all contained in one dynamic package: thank you, Jill, for being all that.

About the author

About the book

Insights,
Interviews
& More . . .

Read on . . .

Meet Janie Chang

Ayelet Tsabari

JANIE CHANG is a Canadian novelist who draws upon family history for her writing. She grew up listening to stories about ancestors who encountered dragons, ghosts, and immortals and about family life in a small Chinese town in the years before the Second World War. She is a graduate of the Writer's Studio at Simon Fraser University.

Born in Taiwan, Janie has lived in the Philippines, Iran, Thailand, and New Zealand. She now lives in beautiful Vancouver, Canada, with her husband and Mischa, a rescue cat who thinks the staff could be doing a better job. She is the author of *Three Souls*. ❧

Reading Group Guide

1. What was the longest time you were ever left alone as a child?

2. One of the central themes in *Dragon Springs Road* is that of identity and belonging. Which story elements echo this theme?

3. *Dragon Springs Road* is set during a time of great social and political upheaval. Discuss how Grandmother Yang's reactions to change differ from those of her eldest grandson, Dajuin.

4. Fox spirits are popular in Chinese folklore. What culture(s) are represented in your family's background and what folktales do you know about supernatural creatures?

5. Missionaries in nineteenth-century and early-twentieth-century China faced many challenges. Have you ever met or known anyone who was a missionary in a foreign country?

6. From the tidbits of information Fox shares with Jialing, it's clear that Fox has her own agenda. If you were to tell the story from Fox's point of view, how would you describe the motivating factors behind her decisions?

7. Jialing is disadvantaged because of her mixed race, but other characters also suffer because of the customs and values of that era. Discuss these characters and how their situations contrast with our twenty-first-century expectations.

8. What would you do if you were given the opportunity to become a Fox? ⌒◞

Behind the Book

My original intention was to write a novel based on the rags-to-riches story of Luo Jialing (1864–1941), an orphaned half-French Shanghai girl who sold flowers and sexual favours to survive. She found her way into a corner of Chinese history when she married Silas Hardoon, a Sephardic Jew who became the "wealthiest man east of the Suez Canal."

In the nineteenth and early twentieth centuries, Westerners settled in Chinese cities such as Shanghai, Hong Kong, and Harbin. Inevitably there was intermarriage and mingling of the races. It was fairly easy to find accounts of Eurasians who belonged to the upper classes; literate and successful, their lives were documented in private and public records. But when it came to the Eurasian underclass, I found very little. Only in missionary journals and memoirs could I find references to orphaned Eurasians, and even then only brief snippets. They sketched a grim picture.

This inspired me to abandon the Cinderella story of Luo Jialing (but I kept her given name for my protagonist) and write about a harsher reality. With her mixed race, Jialing offers a window on a time and place that another character could not. At the same time, I hope the novel also conveys the complexities that defined the status of Eurasians in China; their places in society varied according ▶

to wealth, geography, gender, and prevailing attitudes toward Westerners (which changed with each era and not always for the better). Jialing's story is only one version of what it meant to be biracial in China a hundred years ago and she is luckier than most.

As for Fox, of the many supernatural beings in Chinese folklore I could've borrowed, she seemed a natural choice. At first glance, Fox would appear to have nothing in common with an orphaned Eurasian girl. Jialing will struggle all her life because of her appearance while Fox can change her appearance and influence how people think. Yet Fox, who shifts between human and animal, also struggles. She wants to transcend her earthly existence but lacks the qualities needed to become *xian*, a fully spiritual being. They are both on a journey for identity and self-acceptance (although with the benefit of time, Fox is further along in her quest).

In ancient times, legends spoke of Foxes as attendants to the heavenly Queen Mother of the West. Fox spirits were also sages, counselors to rulers. In contemporary Chinese pop culture, however, Foxes have been reduced to mischievous seductresses. I wanted to reclaim some dignity for Fox by giving her more purpose than mere mischief. I have also taken the liberty of adding to her talents. Why shouldn't a Fox transmit her abilities to humans via a small bite? Surely werewolves and vampires have set a precedent!

I will confess to taking liberties with "Full of Joy" by saying it's an ancient melody. Actually it was composed in the 1950s but it's such a lively and cheerful tune that I'm sure Chinese audiences from a thousand years ago would've loved it as much as I do.

Many other details in the novel, however, have been inspired by true events: the reference in Miss Morris's letter about the fate of Eurasian girls who learned English comes from an 1889 letter to the British Colonial Secretary. The double suicide of the young Englishman and his fiancée is based on the account of a Shanghai shipping magnate who wouldn't allow his nephew to marry a Eurasian. In the scene at the racecourse, the young McBains are how I imagined the children of multimillionaire George McBain, who married a Chinese girl and was banned from Shanghai's British Country Club as a result. His vast wealth made him and his Eurasian family otherwise impervious to social censure.

It is more profitable to raise geese than daughters, goes an old Chinese proverb.

Certainly there were families who cherished their daughters, but those who ill-treated their womenfolk could do so without fear of legal reprimand. Just being poor and female was a tragedy. Mary's tale of how her auntie smothered a newborn comes from an account of a woman who "did what was necessary" when her family was starving. ▶

Infanticide and selling daughters to brothels or into bondage as servants (under conditions that qualified as slavery) were accepted practice when families faced dire poverty. And while new industries provided opportunities for females to earn a living outside the home, too often it was under cruel conditions. In fact one only has to do an Internet search on "child labor silk factories" to get an idea of what it was like, and what still takes place today in some countries.

When Grandmother Yang insisted that Anjuin remain unmarried, she was advocating the beliefs of the Faithful Maiden cult, which flourished during the Ming and Qing Dynasties. It carried Confucian notions about chastity for women to ridiculous excess. Some Confucian scholars claimed that "after a girl is promised in marriage, she belongs to her husband." Thus by extension, if the fiancé dies before the wedding, the girl becomes a widow who must remain chaste and faithful. For the sake of remaining incontestably chaste, some women even committed suicide. The practice had already died out by the time Anjuin was "widowed," so given time and the right family connections, Grandmother Yang might've allowed Anjuin to marry or become a concubine (which is what happens—Anjuin goes on to become Stepmother in the novel *Three Souls*).

Family stories inevitably found their way into *Dragon Springs Road*. The Door comes from one of those stories. According to Chang family legend, during the eighteenth-century reign of the Qianlong Emperor, my six-times-great-grandfather vanished through a doorway and became an immortal. The beautiful dancing ghost who foretold death made an appearance to one of my ancestors when he was a little boy, too young to fear what he saw. First Wife's descent into madness is the tale of a many-times-great-aunt who could not conceive. You can read these family stories on http://www.janiechang.com/the_family_stories.

As far as I know none of my ancestors encountered Fox spirits, although as Fox would say, "Just because there aren't any stories doesn't mean it hasn't happened." ❧

Janie Chang
Recommends . . .

For many historical novelists, research can turn into a fascinating rabbit hole because, well, we love history. Here are some of books I read with great interest and pleasure:

- *Bound Feet and Western Dress: A Memoir,* by Pang-Mei Natasha Chang. Doubleday (1996)
- *Chinese Dress from the Qing Dynasty to the Present,* by Valery Garrett. Tuttle Publishing, an imprint of Periplus Editions (Hong Kong) Ltd. (2007)
- *The Cult of the Fox: Power, Gender, and Popular Religion in Late Imperial and Modern China,* by Xiaofei Kang. Columbia University Press (2006)
- *Eurasian: Mixed Identities in the United States, China, and Hong Kong, 1842–1943,* by Emma Jinhua Teng. University of California Press (2013)
- *Four Sisters of Hofei: A History,* by Annping Chin. Scribner, (2002)
- *The Gospel of Gentility: American Women Missionaries in Turn-of-the-Century China,* by Jane Hunter. Yale University Press (1984)

- *On Chinese Gardens,* by Chen Congzhou. Tongji University Press (1984)
- *Shanghai,* by Harriet Sergeant. Jonathan Cape Ltd. (1991)
- *Shanghai Policeman,* by E. W. Peters, Earnshaw Books Limited (2014)
- *Shanghai: The Rise and Fall of a Decadent City,* by Stella Dong. HarperCollins (2000)
- *Things That Must Not Be Forgotten: A Childhood in Wartime China,* by Michael David Kwan. Macfarlane Walter & Ross (2000)

An Excerpt from *Three Souls* by Janie Chang

Pinghu, China, January 1935

We have three souls, or so I'd been told.

But only in death could I confirm this.

The moment the priest spoke the last prayer and sealed my coffin, I awoke and floated upward in a slow drift of incense smoke, until I could travel no farther. I settled in the rafters of the small temple, a sleepy wraith perched in the roof beams. I had knowledge, but no memory. My first thoughts were confused, for clearly this was the real world. But surely I no longer belonged here. When would I take my journey to the afterlife?

Below me, pale winter sunlight from an open doorway illuminated the temple's dark slate floors. Men and women in white robes crouched in front of an altar stained by decades of burning incense sticks. Noise assailed me from all directions. The tapping of wood-block instruments, the wailing of paid mourners, the chanting of acolytes. On the altar, a wooden tablet gleamed, gold-painted characters carved into its newly varnished surface. An ancestral name tablet, carved for a family shrine.

Song Leiyin. Beloved Wife. Dutiful Daughter.

I recognized that name. My name.

It was when the priests had finished their chanting that I saw my souls for the first time, three bright sparks circling in the air beside me. They were small, shining, and red as embers, but I knew that to the living they were as invisible as motes of dust.

One of the sparks floated in a lazy arc to rest atop the varnished tablet. A delicate rustling at the back of my mind said this was my *yang* soul. I could feel its presence, stern and uncompromising. My *yin* soul wafted down to settle on the coffin, a careless, almost impudent movement. My *hun* soul stayed beside me, watchful as a cat in a strange neighborhood.

I turned to my *hun* soul, a question forming in my still-sleepy mind, when a small, pale face in the crowd below caught my eye. A little girl in mourning robes of white, white ribbons woven through her braids. She knelt behind a man bent so low with weeping his forehead touched the slate floor. The girl shuffled on her knees and the elderly woman beside her put a warning hand on her back. Obediently the little girl stooped down again, her expression blank but for the slightest quiver of her lips. Her dark eyes were dull and rimmed with red. They should have been bright, alive with curiosity.

How did I know that about her eyes?

Memory flickered and I recognized the little girl. My daughter. Weilan. She was so still, so silent. I snapped into wakefulness and in the next moment, I was beside her on the slate, my arms around her thin shoulders. ▶

Mama is here, my precious girl. I'm still with you. But I couldn't feel her. I drew back, suddenly cautious. I didn't want to frighten her. I was dead.

She took no notice of me and that made me weep, my relief struggling with disappointment, for although I longed to hold her, I didn't want to give her nightmares about her mother's ghost. I stayed kneeling beside her, whispering all the pet names I used to call her: *Small Bird, Sesame Seed, My Only Heart.*

I hoped for a tiny gap between our worlds, a crack that would allow my comforting thoughts to reach her even if words could not. She was only seven, so young to be motherless. Who would listen to her chant her times tables now and rub her cold hands on winter days? Who would arrange a marriage for her and teach her how to embroider cloth slippers as gifts for her husband's family?

A restless, elusive tugging sensation told me I didn't belong in this world, but I vowed to resist for as long as possible. If there was any way I could take care of my child, even if I couldn't be seen or felt or heard, I wouldn't abandon her until it became impossible for me to stay.

Borne aloft on the sturdy shoulders of hired mourners, my coffin left the courtyard. I followed, drifting beside my daughter as the funeral procession traveled through the streets of the town, my *yin* soul riding on top of the coffin. Beside my final resting place, I watched the ceremonies. The man who had been weeping arranged food offerings in front of the grave. Weilan lit a bundle of incense sticks, her small hands nearly blue with cold.

Tense and anxious, I watched as the coffin was placed in its grave. Surely once my body was buried, I would be snatched away to the afterlife.

But nothing happened. I was still here.

I returned to town with the funeral cortège, but my *yin* soul remained behind at the grave, and in my mind's eye it shared with me what it saw. Workers were piling earth into a smooth mound on top of my burial spot.

When they finished, however, I didn't drift upward, nor did my consciousness fade into oblivion. When was I supposed to begin my journey to the afterlife?

At the front gates of the estate, fewer than a dozen people entered, all that remained once the mourners had been paid off.

"Come, Granddaughter," said the old woman. Her voice sounded tired, strained but kind. This was, had been, my mother-in-law. She would be the one to bring up my daughter now. "I told Old Kwan to have some sweet-date soup waiting for us. Let's go and warm up in the dining room." She led Weilan away.

I stood waiting by the temple, my mind full of questions. Finally my *yin* soul returned, sliding along a thin shaft of winter sunlight. It joined the two other sparks in a slow circling above the altar. ▶

I'm dead and buried, I said to them. *Am I not supposed to leave this earth now? Or will the gods let me stay to watch over my child?*

But they ignored me and I drifted among the rafters of the temple, silent and perplexed.

My souls spiral down and come to rest on the altar.

We are ready now, says a stern voice, and there is a taste of mustard at the back of my tongue. My *yang* soul. Although his red spark remains balanced on the wooden tablet, an elderly man wearing a round scholar's cap appears beside the altar. He resembles my grandfather as I've seen him in photographs, with steel-rimmed glasses and a goatee. He is dressed in a high-necked *changshan* gown of deep blue silk over loose black trousers.

Yes, let's begin. A new voice tinkles like wind chimes, accompanied by the scent of camellia. The bright ember of my *yin* soul dances in midair, circling the confines of the courtyard. She comes to rest beside the old scholar, a schoolgirl of fifteen with deep brown eyes below wispy bangs, a long pigtail thrown over one shoulder. Her ankle socks and navy uniform blazer match perfectly, her white blouse is spotless.

Leiyin needs to remember, says a third voice. My *hun* soul flies down from the beams overhead and I feel my hair being pulled, a light, playful tug. Its image joins the other souls. It manifests as a silhouette of light, shaped like a human, as brilliant as the morning sun and as featureless. *Before she can ascend to the afterlife, she needs to understand the reason for her detention in this world.*

This is punishment? This doesn't look like hell, I say, feeling a wave of panic. *Where is the underground maze? What about the fanged demons, the chambers of torture? What is this twilight existence if not the afterlife?*

This isn't hell, nor is it the true afterlife. My *yang* soul turns to me, a slight scowl on his seamed face. *You could say it's the afterdeath. And you're still here because in life you were responsible for a great wrong.*

I don't remember anything about a great wrong. Bewildered as much as indignant, I want to remember my life. Surely I was not, had not been, a criminal.

Soon you'll remember everything and so will we. My *yin* soul pulls the ribbon off her pigtail and shakes out her hair. She begins braiding it again. *Relive your memories. Only then will you understand what you must do to ascend to the afterlife.*

And why do I need to ascend anyway? I know I sound sulky, rebellious.

As soon as I ask this question, an eager swirl of emotions radiates from my souls. In my mind's eye I see them, three red sparks lifting into the air toward a portal that spills golden light over the horizon. Beyond the portal flicker ▶

tantalizing glimpses of grassy landscapes, mountain lakes, and eternally blossoming orchards. This vision makes me yearn to rise up toward that portal and join my souls. Now I understand the restlessness that invades my being, an upward pull I can't follow so long as the manacles of my sins weigh me down to this world.

We must ascend. Reincarnation awaits us in the afterlife. My *yin* soul spins so that her pleated skirt twirls up around her, a circle of navy blue. *There, we will have a chance for new lives, new hope. But if we stay too long in this existence . . .* As her voice trails off, I hear in it a small tremor.

First, she must remember, my *hun* soul interjects. It reaches out a shining limb and pulls my hair again, this time a firm and peremptory tug. *You must understand the damage you did. Then you must make amends to balance the ledger. Only then can we ascend together to the true afterlife.*

So we will go together? You won't go now and leave me here? Relief.

We are your souls, we're part of you, my *yang* soul snaps. *We can't leave until you do.* He glares at me through moon-shaped lenses.

Don't mind yang, says my *yin* soul, who has finished braiding her hair. *He's not happy unless he's berating someone.*

Where should we begin? my *hun* soul asks. *On the day of the party?* ▶

Yes, the day of the party, the other souls agree.

The day you first stepped off the path that had been paved for you, my *hun* soul says.

I have no choice. How else can I reclaim my memories, discover what to do next? At this moment I can't even remember what Weilan looked like as a baby.

My *yin* soul sinks to the floor and tucks her knees under her skirt, a child waiting to hear a story. My *yang* soul settles on a stool near the door and brushes a cobweb from his black trousers. My *hun* soul drifts to the altar, and with a single bright fingertip gently strokes my name tablet.

Suddenly I'm standing on a street lined with sycamore trees and high, whitewashed walls. I'm watching a schoolgirl climb down from a rickshaw. But in that same moment, I'm also that girl, my foot about to touch the curb.

I know everything about my life before that moment.

I know nothing of what is to come. ❧